THE BLACK TULIP

THE BLACK TULIP

A NOVEL

MILT BEARDEN

RANDOM HOUSE

NEW YORK

Copyright © 1998 by Milt Bearden

All rights reserved under International and Pan-American Copyright Conventions. Published in the United States by Random House, Inc., New York, and simultaneously in Canada by Random House of Canada Limited, Toronto.

Library of Congress Cataloging-in-Publication Data
Bearden, Milt.
The black tulip: a novel / Milt Bearden.
p.   cm.
ISBN 0-679-44791-1 (acid-free paper)
I. Title.
PS3552.E172B58   1998   813'.54—dc21   97-37224

Random House website address: www.randomhouse.com

Printed in the United States of America on acid-free paper
2   4   6   8   9   7   5   3
First Edition

For Marie-Catherine

ACKNOWLEDGMENTS

I would like to thank the Publications Review Board of the Central Intelligence Agency—in particular Molly Tasker and John Hedley—for reviewing the manuscript to ensure that it contained no information that was still classified. The CIA's review was eminently fair and reflected sound judgment as to what was actually secret, and needed to be protected, and what was not. I am thankful for their prompt action and thoughtful assistance in telling a story that is based on my thirty years in the CIA's Clandestine Services.

Milt Bearden
September 1997

Nobody seems to know just when and where the black tulip story originated. One credible theory traces its origins to the early spring of 1980, and the death of a Lieutenant Semyon Popov in a field near Mazār-e Sharif. He died clutching a rare black tulip, native to northern Afghanistan. It was an exquisite flower. He had picked it himself just seconds before and was admiring it when a sniper's bullet found his heart and ended his life. For some reason, the story goes, one of his comrades threaded the tulip into the buttonhole of the fallen soldier's tunic, and he went home with it stuck on his chest.

Sometime later in the war, the large transports flying dead soldiers home for burial took the name of the Black Tulip, and the rare flower of Afghanistan became established in the Soviet Union as a symbol of death.

ONE

ONE

CIA HEADQUARTERS, LANGLEY, VIRGINIA, MAY 28, 1985

Alexander Fannin pushed through the yellow door marked 7D70—DIRECTOR OF CENTRAL INTELLIGENCE, in neat block letters. The bright color always struck him as quaintly festive, out of place with the more subtly shaded universe that lay behind it, but he doubted Bill Casey even thought of it at all.

Alexander smiled at his self-indulgent distraction. He had come to turn in his badge to Casey, shake the old man's hand, and end his decade-long employment with the agency.

He nodded to the DCI's protective-security detail behind a glass-walled cubicle, two blank-faced, close-cropped young men in identical discount-house blazers, who exchanged stern, knowing glances. Their eyes never left the tall, dark-haired man casually dressed in a buff sport jacket, charcoal slacks, and blue turtleneck as he crossed to the open door of Casey's office where his executive assistant, Dottie Manson, stood waiting.

"Hi, Alexander," she said, ushering him into the large, birch-paneled suite perched seven floors above the Virginia countryside. The lush foliage of late spring already shielded the Potomac River from view as it wound its way past the CIA's Langley headquarters. "You're looking relaxed for a man about to quit in a huff."

"Is that what he thinks?" Alexander asked, glancing around the empty office.

"He's in there." Dottie pointed to the director's conference room. "And that's what I think, not what he thinks. He said you're to wait here until he's finished. He said you should read a book or something."

Casey's office was comfortable, tastefully appointed, but rumpled like the man who occupied it. Alexander eyed the stack of new books on the corner of the desk—they ranged from American history to economics to oil politics—and knew that at the end of the week Dottie would send them with Casey when he flew up to Long Island for the weekend. On Monday he would probably recommend at least one with great animation. Casey was always telling people what books to read, even how to read them.

Alexander took a seat on the overstuffed sofa and closed his eyes. He had no regrets. It was time to go.

Alexander had been a natural for the CIA's clandestine operations directorate. Born to a Russian father and a Ukrainian mother, both wartime refugees from Stalin's U.S.S.R., he spoke each language without accent, along with near-native Polish and good German. He was recruited by the agency after a stint in the army flying helicopters in Vietnam, part of the time for CIA paramilitary operations. His first few years in the agency had been nonstop excitement, and even when a confused aimlessness set in and the agency's mission blurred at the end of the turbulent seventies, he felt certain about who he was and the value of what he was doing.

As soon as Casey was sworn in as DCI in 1981, Alexander felt renewed energy at Langley. From the start, he got on well with the flamboyant New York lawyer who brought the political clout of a close association with the new president.

By the end of Casey's fourth year, he and Alexander had developed an easy friendship. They charted the widening fissures in the Evil Empire from Warsaw to Moscow, and both agreed the time had come for more "creative efforts," as the old man called them. They began making intricate, ambitious plans for what Casey called the endgame. Then Alexander's troubles intervened.

It started as a purely personal matter. While traveling in Asia a year earlier he happened to meet Katerina Martynova, a stunning Ukrainian woman, and fall in love.

Katerina's parents, refugees from wartime Ukraine, had met in the tight-knit Russian expatriate community in China during the turmoil of 1945. Lara Chumakova and Michael Martynov married in Shanghai and settled down to build their lives. But war and revolution forced them to flee with their infant daughter just ahead of Mao's armies in the last days of 1949. They resettled again, this time among a growing population of Russians and Europeans who had fled China's chaos for the safety of the British Crown Colony of Hong Kong.

Katerina's father scraped together his Shanghai savings, borrowed a little money, and taking what seemed to some a foolhardy risk, imported a small stable of racehorses from Australia. Catching the wave of a post-war gambling boom, his modest initial investment at the high-rolling Happy Valley Race Course grew into one of the dozen largest trading houses in Hong Kong, Martynov Trading Corporation, later anglicized to Martin House. Katerina was schooled in Switzerland and France, and by the time she met Alexander, she was a rising star in East Asian political journalism. A year later when they decided to marry, the fallout was immediate.

Alexander's formal notification of his intent to marry a foreign national tripped the CIA's computers, and cryptic references to Katerina and her family's suspected ties to underground Ukrainian opposition networks inside the U.S.S.R. scrolled out. Alexander knew about the contacts with the Ukrainian opposition but saw no incompatibility with his work for the agency. He had made his own discreet query of the databases and thought the raw data on Katerina and her family noncontroversial; he dismissed it as the usual émigré gossip. It was manageable, he thought.

But the CIA's chief of counterintelligence, Graham Middleton, seized on the tantalizing tidbits, seeing an opportunity to knock an adversary out of play. Middleton viewed Alexander's quick rise as an obstacle to his own career, but most of all, Alexander's unconventional origins offended his squeamish Ivy League sensibilities. He resented him even more after Casey arrived at Langley. Alexander, in turn, saw Middleton as a plodder, an agency "royalist" who hesitated to exploit the nascent weaknesses in the U.S.S.R.

Now Middleton had exposed the one flaw that no one at the CIA, not even the DCI, could overlook, "a personal counterintelligence question."

Katerina had asked Alexander not to divulge to the CIA that her mother had a twin sister still living in Kiev and that the two women had for the last fifteen years carried on an elaborate secret correspondence. Their communication was disguised in the style of an ancient Russian fairy tale, "The Tale of the Maidens of Kiev," and through this veiled exchange, the twins filled in the gaps in their lives since their separation in wartime Ukraine four decades before. As the fairy tale unfolded over the years, Katerina's mother deduced that her sister's son was an officer in the KGB, though she also believed that he despised the Soviet regime.

Alexander knew that if he reported this information to the CIA, the agency would not hesitate to exploit it, and in the process put Katerina's family at risk. He detailed his misgivings to Casey, acknowledging that he was prepared to resign quietly if the DCI thought it best. Casey instructed him to use the phrase "possibly/details lacking" to answer the portion of the CIA questionnaire covering family members of the prospective spouse who might reside in a Soviet-bloc country. And then he should sit tight and see what happened.

What happened was a maelstrom in the counterintelligence staff. Middleton interpreted the statement as an outright obfuscation. He planted suggestions that Katerina Martynova was tethered to a KGB leash and was being run against Alexander. Counterintelligence specialists analyzed every sentence she had written in the *Far Eastern Focus,* drawing the ponderous conclusion that she had "sometimes been critical of U.S. foreign policy," and that her criticisms of U.S. policy played to known KGB themes.

As the scent of scandal in Casey's inner circle spread, conspiracy theories multiplied. Middleton fed the speculation, shrewdly shifting the focus from Katerina to Alexander, weaving his origins into a pattern of deceit and betrayal. The fact that he was born to Russian-Ukrainian parents in a displaced persons camp in postwar Germany had been a strength Alexander brought to the CIA. But now increasingly convoluted scenarios were fed into the CIA's notorious rumor mill, each new version more baroque than the last, and all bringing into question Alexander's loyalties and raising the possibility that he had been under KGB control from the day he joined the agency. In an organization where truth was always fiercely guarded, rumor and fantasy made the rounds unshackled. Explanations of a recent string of "counterintelligence anomalies," as they were solemnly called in the trade, were recast to coincide with Alexander's association with Katerina. By then Alexander had had enough.

On the advice of Lee Tanner, chief of the Soviet Division and a sensible, unflappable political hand, Alexander volunteered for a polygraph. After a grueling three-hour session he was given an unambiguous clean-pass by the Office of Security—"no deception indicated." Undeterred, Middleton put out the line that the results might be "just a little too good." Soon, competing theories on what was behind the results swirled through the corridors—self-hypnosis, drugs, special KGB training.

Alexander saw it was too late to walk the story back; he told Casey he was resigning. Casey told him he wasn't, and in a compromise Alexander had agreed to take a couple of weeks off. That was ten days ago.

Bill Casey was already talking when he entered the office. "Thought I'd let you have two whole weeks off, did you?" he said, settling awkwardly into a chair.

Alexander studied the white-haired old man, his blue chalk stripe, shoulders dusted with dandruff, the soup-stained regimental tie askew around a collar one size too large. The effect was a careless, gawky appearance that

Alexander thought part of Casey's charm. That and his gruff, unyielding loyalty.

"I thought you'd decided to fire me before the two weeks were up. And if you don't, I'll quit. Which way do you want it?"

Casey didn't return Alexander's smile. "I'm not going to fire you, and you're not going to quit. Not until you get back from Moscow."

"Moscow?"

"Tanner wants you to call out Tokarev. He's missed his last three scheduled meetings, and Moscow Station is locked up too tight to try an emergency contact. Can't make a move without dragging around thirty KGB guys. You've got to go in and find him. Tanner tells me he'll come out for you, but only for you."

"Why didn't Tanner ask me himself?"

"Because he knew I would make the decision. That's what I do around here."

"Okay, Bill. But why go in? Tokarev's always been jittery; he's a flaky guy. It's what made him come to us in the first place. We've let him put himself on ice before. Why take a huge risk now, before we know if there's really a problem?"

"You've been cut out of this operation since . . ."

'Since my loyalties were called into question by your counterintelligence chief," Alexander snapped.

"All right. What you don't know is that Tokarev was scheduled to make a delivery a month ago—the mother lode on the radar and weapons systems for their next generation of interceptors. It's the last batch for the project, the culmination of years of work."

Alexander weighed the old man's request carefully, but his anger was clear. "Bill, this isn't some half-baked test to prove my loyalty, is it? You know, send Fannin in to ferret out Tokarev. If it works, Fannin's clean; if it fails, and Tokarev's rolled up, then we'll know Fannin's dirty. I might expect something like that from Middleton. You're not pulling some crap like that on me, are you?"

"You know I'm not. We need this stuff from Tokarev. Christ, this guy's literally been our secret hand designing the avionics of every fighter the Soviet Union will be flying into the next century. Nobody's going to play around with this operation."

There was another long pause. "I'll do it because it needs to be done. And because you've asked me to do it. But it changes nothing. I'm still finished here."

"Alexander, I want you to know that I understand what you're going through. When everything else has been stripped away, all we really have is our honor and our loyalties. I know what Middleton's doing to you, but that's his job, ferreting out the moles. It's a brutal job, but it's got to be done. You know that."

"That's bullshit, Bill! Middleton's settling a score and you know it."

"Yes, I do. But I also believe the KGB's gotten to us somewhere. That's why I can't, don't even want, to rein him in."

"I'm not arguing that. It's clear either somebody in here is working for the other side, or the other side is reading our communications. All I'm saying is that I'm not the problem and that Middleton's crossed over the line in the way he's come after me."

"Go to Moscow and find Tokarev. Then come back here and we can talk this over. And remember what I always say."

"What's that?"

"It only hurts for a day." Casey rolled his eyes and shook his head, giving Alexander a rare glimpse of the pain he had been enduring under constant attacks from the media and Congress.

"I'll go to Moscow, Bill. But when I get back there won't be any need to talk this through again. I think you know that." Alexander rose. "I'll go see Tanner now."

Casey smiled. "Don't bother. He'll meet you in Berlin. He's already on his way with your Polish documents and stuff, and he'll take you through Checkpoint Charlie for your drop-off in East Berlin. Then you're on your own, as usual."

"You never have doubts, do you, Bill?"

"You can't have doubts about the important things. You leave tonight. And, Alexander." The old man smiled broadly. "Don't get caught. Middleton tells me there's not enough good trading material in the whole free world to get you back if they get you."

MOSCOW, 2336 HOURS, MAY 31, 1985

Adolf Tokarev felt his heart stop when the harsh ring of the telephone shattered the quiet of his drab Moscow apartment. He had turned off his television set over an hour before, just as the evening news finished, and was sitting in the darkness trying to deal with his fear. He had been on the roller coaster for almost ten years. There had been highs and lows ever since he decided to betray the Soviet state, but mostly highs from the delicious, exaggerated sense of well-being and power his ability to damage the system generated in him. He was immune, he'd told himself. Now, he was frozen in terror. He was even more terrified than the time two years ago when word began to filter out that the Committee was hunting down a CIA spy in one of the aviation-design bureaus.

That night he had removed the cyanide pill from its embedded concealment in the thick frames of his glasses. It had been implanted there by CIA technicians, and he had been instructed that if he bit down hard on the pill, death would be almost instantaneous. He became so certain of his compromise that he had gone to a hastily called meeting with the pill tucked in his cheek, convinced he was walking into a KGB ambush. Later, when he told his CIA contact, Janos, the man lost his temper. Get rid of the pill! he demanded. He hated them; there were better ways to deal with your own compromise. Besides, Janos cheerily told him, the Committee would take care of him just as fast—with a bullet in the head.

Now as he sat in his apartment listening to the telephone scream, he wished he had the pill back. After the fifth ring, he answered.

"Hallo."

"Adolf? Is that you, Adolf?"

His throat tightened, making it difficult to form the words. "Who is calling?"

"Adolf, it's Misha. I have news from colleagues in Kiev for you."

Misha with news from Kiev—it was the parole he had long ago memorized. It was the open code for an emergency meeting. And the voice. It was Janos, his contact. He felt queasy, disoriented, but hopeful.

"Misha, how are you?" His voice cracked.

"Adolf, why don't you ask me in person? I can walk to you in moments. Why not meet me on the street and we'll sit and have a drink like we always do? No need to wake your family with our noise."

"Ah, Misha. I have been ill. It's my circulation, you know."

"Of course, Adolf. All the more reason to step out the door right this minute and meet me. Perhaps you'll even improve your circulation—a little walk in the fresh air and a little drink for the heart and stomach. I've brought a bottle. We can share it in the park."

Tokarev understood what Janos was trying to do. Move quickly enough, and even if the telephone is tapped, one could be out and back before the KGB's thugs could react. He looked at the clock on the table. Fifteen seconds had passed.

"All right, Misha. I'll have that drink with you."

"Wonderful. But could I ask you a favor? Could you bring the small bag I left at your apartment the last time I stayed with you? I keep forgetting to get it from you. And when you come out, Adolf, just walk toward the station. I'll meet you along the way."

"I'll bring it with me. I'll see you in a few minutes."

There was no bag. But Tokarev knew what Janos wanted. He quickly got his briefcase from his closet and twisted the thick handle for a moment, maintaining a steady pressure with both thumbs in just the manner he had been shown long ago. After several seconds a pressure-sensitive catch released, the handle separated, and two small cylinders spilled out. He stuck them in his pocket and hurried from his apartment. Though the night was cool, perspiration beaded his forehead.

One minute later he was walking toward Kiev Station. Passing an alley, he was startled when the tall man stepped out of the shadows.

"Hello, Adolf."

Tokarev quickly looked up and down the street. It was deserted. "We don't have much time. There is trouble."

"What trouble?" the man asked, drawing him back into the shadows.

"They know there's someone in my bureau. Two other engineers have disappeared, but they're still looking. That's why I don't come to the meetings now."

"Adolf, we've been through this before. Are you sure this time?"

"I'm absolutely certain. This time there is no mistake!"

Alexander could hear the fear in Tokarev's voice. "Do you have anything in your office or in your apartment that will incriminate you?"

"Only these. These are what you really want, what you came for. I'm happy to get rid of them. They're the end of it, anyway. The project is done. These have everything you need." Tokarev handed over the two cylinders, both subminiature cameras with exposed microfilm sealed inside.

Alexander took the cylinders. "Listen carefully. You can survive this scare just like you did the last one. They have no way of knowing it's you they're looking for. Try to relax."

"They know it's in my bureau. The director told me in confidence they have some solid information on the traitor; 'the description of the man they're looking for sounds almost like you, but that's impossible, isn't it, Adolf?' He said that to me! They're looking for me! Someone has betrayed me!"

Tokarev was terrified. Alexander knew the story made sense. Tokarev probably had been betrayed by some narrow description of a CIA spy in an aviation-design bureau. A small group in Langley knew about the superspy in aircraft design, but only a tiny group knew Tokarev's name.

"Go home. And tomorrow go to work as usual. There's nothing else you can do now. You've never asked us to get you out of here, so it's too late to think of that now."

"I couldn't live anywhere else." Tokarev paused, inhaled deeply, and then forced a smile. "And when things calm down, I'll put up a signal to meet your people. Maybe the pretty young woman will meet me for a few minutes sometime. I liked her. She has courage, like all of them. Yes, it will be fine. Thank you for coming, Janos. Now you must go."

This is a man who knows he's about to die, Alexander thought. He squeezed Tokarev's hand.

Alexander had timed the meeting perfectly. He reached Kiev Station minutes before boarding time for the night train to Warsaw.

As the train pulled out he waited in his compartment for the conductor to bring his bed tea and collect his Polish passport and identity papers. He couldn't have known that three white Volga sedans, each with four men inside, had just converged on the apartment block where the aviation-design engineer lived.

TWO

—————

Graham Middleton had studiously cultivated his image as the CIA's counterintelligence conscience, down to the affected tweedy, owlish appearance he thought befitting the solemnity of his work. Some thought he tried to capture the peculiar physical mystique of the CIA's discredited counterintelligence legend, James Jesus Angleton, but he never pulled it off. Most who understood Angleton's destructive legacy wondered why he'd even try.

Middleton was quietly listening to Soviet Division Chief Lee Tanner brief the DCI on Fannin's contact with Adolf Tokarev in Moscow four nights before. He was alert for any nuance or vagary Tanner might offer that would satisfy his own agenda for Fannin.

"What about the microfilm?" Casey asked.

Tanner spread out a sampling of the more than one hundred exposed frames. "These show you the quality of the photography. There was one hundred percent recovery. These documents seem to have the final data on the avionics systems they'll be using in their fighters for at least the next generation."

Casey flipped through the photographs of wire diagrams, blueprints, and tight Cyrillic text, all sharp and readable, and shoved them across the conference table to Middleton.

"Is there anything in these photographs that makes you wonder whether Tokarev mightn't be under their control, Lee?" Middleton asked.

Tanner shook his head. "The preliminary analysis is that these new documents are genuine, like all the rest. It's just too complex, even for the

KGB, to have brought him under control and then manipulated the information he's passed us. I say no. He wasn't under hostile control when he took these photos."

"But can we be sure, Lee?" Middleton's question was more a statement.

Casey groaned in exasperation. "Graham, we can't ever be sure. But sometimes we just have to prepare ourselves for that most elusive prey—success." Casey impatiently pressed his intercom. "Is he here yet? Good, send him in."

Moments later Alexander was flipping through the photographs himself. "Adolf's quality is always the same—distance, framing, lighting—everything just right. I think I could pick his work out of a foot-high stack of document photography."

"Maybe he had help with these," Middleton added.

Tanner jumped in. "Of course we need to be skeptical, but it's reasonably certain that these photographs are genuine. What do you think, Alexander?"

Alexander decided that his last hour as a CIA employee would not collapse into a futile shoot-out with Middleton. "I think they're fine, Lee. What is certain is that Adolf Tokarev handed them over to me personally in Moscow, that the cameras themselves had not been tampered with, at least Technical Services swears the special seals weren't broken, and that the information on the film is too complex to have been manipulated. If he was under KGB control when he took these, we'd probably see everything a little out of focus, or some key frames totally unreadable. It's easier for the KGB to botch the photos than to try to create an entirely false set of documents."

"Unless the photography has been manipulated for all the years we've been dealing with Tokarev. You were with him at the beginning, weren't you, Alexander?"

"That's right, Graham," Alexander said evenly. "Almost ten years ago." He turned toward Casey. "There's another thing for certain, Bill—Tokarev is convinced he's about to be caught and that he's been betrayed. After precisely four minutes with the man he was about to buckle with terror, the kind of deep, pit-of-the-stomach terror peculiar to the collective Russian psyche. If they are closing in on him, he was betrayed by someone who knows where he worked, but apparently not his name. His bureau director—"

Dottie Manson walked in with a cable. "They said to break in with this."

Casey read it and slid it across the table to Tanner. "What's it mean, Lee?"

"Moscow Station has just spotted a signal that Tokarev is ready to receive a resupply of equipment."

"Then what?" Casey asked, his face a mask.

"We put up a signal which tells him we have read his signal and are going to meet him on such and such a night, usually about five days later, and at such and such a place."

Casey was already impatient with Middleton's carping; now he was starting to find Tanner's didactic explanations tedious. He rolled his eyes and shifted his gaze to Alexander. "What do you think?"

"He's under their control now."

"How can you be so sure?" Middleton insisted, now reading the cable.

"Adolf Tokarev could not have recovered from his terror and asked for a new supply of cameras in four days. They've got him and now they're playing with us."

"I agree," Tanner said. "They've got him and now they want us to help them tidy up. They want one of our Moscow officers."

"And they've picked the one they want. Look at the last paragraph on the surveillance status report," Alexander said.

Middleton read aloud, "Total, prohibitive surveillance coverage continues for all station officers with sole exception of Paul Wombaugh, whose coverage abruptly ceased the morning of 2 June."

"I'd say that they picked Tokarev up a day after I met him," Alexander said.

"Or maybe the same night."

"Yes, Graham, that, too, is possible." Alexander was beginning to wonder if he'd get through this without going for Middleton's throat.

Casey emitted a groan that the three men understood. "Then they want Wombaugh to come out for Tokarev?"

"Yes. They probably think he's our best Moscow officer—and they'd be right—and they've decided to get rid of him as part of the bargain. They believe we'll send him out to meet Tokarev, regardless of the danger. They'll use Tokarev as bait."

"What are your recommendations? You first, Alexander, since you were there."

"It's easy, Bill. Send Wombaugh in."

"Into a certain ambush!?" Middleton was incredulous.

"Yes. There's nothing to lose except Wombaugh gets a little roughed up and spends a few hours cooling his heels in the Lubyanka."

"And to gain?" Casey asked.

"I see nothing to gain," Middleton interjected.

Alexander shifted in his seat, exasperated. "There are two important things to gain, Bill. First, on the remote chance that Lee and I are wrong and Tokarev is not under KGB control, we'll be back in contact with him. But the second reason, the one you'll appreciate more than Graham might, is that you have the means to get a personal message to Tokarev before he dies. It's something you should want to do. You can ask Wombaugh to say on your behalf anything you think important to a man who's about to die because he worked for you. Something like, 'Thank you, Adolf, and God bless you for what you've done for us.' "

Casey didn't ask Middleton for an opinion, and the counterintelligence chief, sensing Casey's growing impatience, didn't offer one.

Casey turned abruptly to Tanner. "Lee, draft a cable to Moscow for my release. Tell Moscow we know it's an ambush, but tell them to go ahead anyway. Instruct Wombaugh to tell Tokarev exactly what Alexander just said before the world caves in on him. And tell Wombaugh I have the utmost confidence in his courage. Thank you all. Alexander, would you stay behind for a moment?"

Casey led Alexander to a sitting area. "I admired your self-control back there. Middleton was more of a sonofabitch today than usual, but you didn't let him get to you."

"I didn't want my last hour on duty with the CIA to degenerate into a petty fight, particularly one I've already lost. If anything, I'm more hopelessly tainted now than before I went to Moscow. When Wombaugh walks into the ambush in five days, and he will, Tanner and some of my friends might believe we just had bad luck, but Middleton will make sure the others are convinced I was behind it."

"They'll go with whatever Middleton feeds them. I know that. So this is it? You're out of here?"

Alexander wondered why Casey was putting up no resistance. "Yes, Bill, I'm going home to start packing up for Hong Kong. Want to come to a Ukrainian wedding?"

Casey flashed a broad smile. "Wouldn't that just choke up that jerk Middleton? Yeah. Why not?"

"Bill, you should know I'm not walking away from what we planned to do about the Soviet Union. I'll be working as hard against the Soviet system on the outside, with Katerina's people and the networks inside the U.S.S.R., as I was prepared to do here with you. Your people might run into me where our lines cross, and when they do, please help them remember we're on the same side."

There was a faint, puzzling smile on the old man's lips. "Alexander, you go out there and do whatever you think might make a difference. You might even be in a position to do some things for me that damn few people here can even dream of. I'll be in touch from time to time. This is going to be just fine, but I want your promise on one thing. Never turn me down when I call you."

There it is, Alexander thought, Bill Casey turning a setback into a victory.

Alexander rose and extended his hand. Casey took it, and with his other hand unclipped Alexander's badge from his jacket. "I'll keep this. It might come in handy sometime," he said, leading Alexander to the door. "Dottie, take our friend here down to the basement and put him in my car. He's quit in a huff. Just like you said he would."

Alexander did not call Casey when Wombaugh was arrested with Adolf Tokarev in Moscow on the night of June 9. It was a made-for-television production, a starburst of violence, beautifully choreographed, filmed and described in the Soviet media as "exemplary service by the competent organs." Casey had not called him either; the arrest was too predictable, too anticlimactic for both men. Too sorrowful. But Wombaugh called him the day after he arrived in Washington after being released from Lubyanka Prison and expelled from the U.S.S.R. He told Alexander he'd had twenty seconds with Tokarev before the KGB took them down, but that had been enough. He'd told Tokarev thank you and Godspeed from Bill Casey and from Janos and from all of his friends. He said Tokarev looked calm, almost serene, in the seconds before his world came to an end. Wombaugh thought Alexander would want to know that.

WASHINGTON, D.C., AUGUST 5, 1985

It was midmorning when Alexander's phone rang. "Whatcha been doin' for the last two months?" It was Casey.

"I'm leaving tonight, Bill. Dottie has my forwarding address in Hong Kong."

"I know you're leaving tonight. I'll be there in one minute. You'll be gone for the rest of the day, but you'll make your plane."

"Gone where?"

"I'll tell you when I see you."

The blue sedan, bristling with antennae and heavy with armor, eased to the curb in front of Alexander's Georgetown town house just as he stepped outside. Casey's follow car blocked the narrow shaded street while Alexander slid into the seat beside the DCI.

"This is really discreet, Bill. About all you could add would be flashing lights and a siren."

"You want me to turn 'em on?" Casey grinned and tapped the seat of the security officer in front. "Gimme that file."

Moments later Alexander was reading a cable sent the day before from Rome Station. It said that one senior colonel in the KGB, Directorate K—Counterintelligence, First Chief Directorate, U.S.A. and Canada—by the name of Vitaly Sergeyevich Yurchenko had defected to Rome Station while traveling in Italy. Plans were under way for the immediate transport of Yurchenko to the United States, with an estimated arrival at Andrews Air Force Base, Maryland, in the early hours of August 5, 1985.

"Are they here yet?" Alexander asked Casey.

"An hour ago. Keep reading."

Alexander flipped to the second page. And there it was in the spare language of a CIA cable.

YURCHENKO ADVISES THAT FORMER CIA OFFICER TERMI- NATED BY AGENCY TWO YEARS AGO FOR PERSONAL UNSUIT- ABILITY WHILE IN PIPELINE TRAINING STATUS FOR MOSCOW STATION VOLUNTEERED HIS SERVICES TO KGB. THAT OFFICER— KGB CODE NAME "MR. ROBERT"—HAS COMPROMISED A NUM- BER OF CIA HUMAN SOURCES IN MOSCOW AND ABROAD AS WELL AS TECHNICAL OPERATIONS IN USSR. MOST RECENT ARREST OF AVIATION-DESIGN ENGINEER ADOLF TOKAREV WAS BASED ON INFORMATION PROVIDED BY "MR. ROBERT" TO KGB. YURCHENKO ADVISES THAT HE KNOWS OF NO OTHER KGB PENETRATIONS OF CIA AT THIS TIME. ADDITIONAL COUNTERINTELLIGENCE INFOR- MATION WIL BE SUBJECT SEPARATE MESSAGES.

Alexander leaned back and exhaled. "So that's what it was. That's what's been happening to us."

"You know who it is, don't you?"

"It's Ed Howard. He was a disaster waiting to happen."

"He's happened," Casey said without emotion.

"Where is he now?"

"Santa Fe. The FBI's watching him."

"What do you want me to do?"

"I want you to go out to the safe house now and spend some time with this guy and then call me tonight and tell me what you think."

Alexander's eyes narrowed. "You don't need my take on him. You're just letting me in on this so I can close the circle on Middleton."

"There's that. But I do want your opinion."

"Wait, don't tell me. Middleton's already putting out the sick-think story? Yurchenko's part of the James Jesus Angleton monster plot?"

"That's right. He's just 'wondering' whether Yurchenko's been sent over to protect someone else. He wanted to polygraph Yurchenko as soon as he got off the plane. The others want to wait until he settles down. Middleton knows that all these KGB guys blow the polygraph, but it plays to his hand. He wants to cast early doubts on Yurchenko."

"You said it yourself, Bill. That's what the sonofabitch gets paid for."

As the motorcade pulled into the basement of the headquarters building, Casey handed Alexander his CIA badge. "Here, you might need it."

Alexander smiled. "You still interested in a Ukrainian wedding?"

"You bet I am," the old man said as he struggled out of the car. "Call me when you're finished."

Minutes later Alexander was being driven to the safe house in Oakton, Virginia, where Yurchenko was being held under protective guard.

OAKTON, VIRGINIA, 2100 HOURS, AUGUST 5, 1985

Vitaly Yurchenko was running on nervous energy; the lean, sandy-haired six-footer paced the dining room of the safe house, digging with strained animation into the recesses of his memory to come up with yet another nugget, another justification for the monstrous crime he had committed against the Soviet Union. After a burst of mental energy he would sit back down at the dining room table, finger his long, scraggly mustache, and slip into moody thought. Yurchenko hadn't slept in two days; he needed to get it all out. He turned to Alexander. "I want to speak to you alone for a few minutes."

"Why don't you guys take a break," Alexander said to the three debriefers at the table, two from the CIA and one from the FBI.

The FBI agent and the senior CIA officer rose and stretched, welcoming the break. The second CIA debriefer hesitated. "Alexander, you might need me here to take notes. I'll stay."

"No, Rick. He wants to speak with me alone."

"I'll be quiet, Alexander. It'll be as good as alone." Aldrich Ames smiled, revealing uneven teeth, badly discolored by tobacco and neglect. Before Alexander could answer, the other CIA officer broke in. "You heard the man, Rick. Let's break for a while."

Christ, Alexander thought, Ames must be taking notes for Middleton.

When they were alone, Alexander asked Yurchenko, "Vitaly Sergeyevich, is there something you are holding back that you only want to tell the DCI, William Casey?"

Yurchenko shook his head. "That's the usual question, Alexander. That is your name isn't it? I heard the other one call you Alexander."

"Yes, Vitaly Sergeyevich, Alexander is my name. And yes, we always ask that standard question of officers from your service who come to us, just in case you know there is a mole in the CIA and fear that he might be in your reception committee. Then you get to talk directly to the DCI. That assumes, of course, that the DCI isn't the mole." Alexander broke into a smile, which Yurchenko returned.

"I have given his name already, this mole, your Mr. Robert. He betrayed Adolf Tokarev, and another the KGB is searching for in Hungary. Mr. Robert called him 'the angry colonel.' And there were others. Perhaps he betrayed the Acting Rezident in London, Gordievsky; I told your boys in Rome the KGB had him back in Moscow under interrogation. They're using drugs on him." Yurchenko took a deep breath. "I wanted to speak to you alone for a moment because I have been here almost a full day and Mr. Casey has not yet telephoned. Doesn't he know I have come to work with him?"

So that's it, Alexander thought. Recognition. We're all alike. "Vitaly Sergeyevich, Mr. Casey had not phoned yet because he has spent much of the day with our president and his cabinet, briefing them on your courage and convictions and explaining to the president how indebted we are to you for joining us in the struggle." Alexander checked his watch. "Mr. Casey asked me to call him on his private line just about now so he could thank you personally."

Alexander stepped to the door and spoke to the chief of the security detail. "Set up a call to the DCI for me on the portable phone. Then bring it in here."

Seconds later Ames was at the door to the dining room. "Is something up? Do you need me to sort anything out for you?"

"For God's sake, Rick, give yourself a break. I do not need any help. Are you doing this for Middleton, or are you just nosy?"

Ames smiled again. "Just trying to be helpful, Alexander."

Moments later Alexander had Casey on the line. "Yes, Mr. Director," Alexander said with exaggerated formality. "I am sitting with Vitaly Sergeyevich now, and we are alone." He handed the telephone to Yurchenko.

The KGB colonel sat up a little straighter in his chair as he listened to the DCI for almost a minute. Then he spoke very deliberately in strained English. "Mr. Director, I wish to thank you for allowing me to join the struggle. And I am certain, like you, that we will win. Thank you, Mr. Director Casey." Yurchenko handed the phone to Alexander, his face filled with relief.

On his way to Dulles Alexander got through to Casey.

"Whaddya think?" the old man barked.

"I think he's real because I can't believe they'd send him to us on a deception mission."

"You think he's real. So do I. But others besides Middleton won't think so."

"Screw the others. And screw Middleton. But Yurchenko's fragile and he'll need some tender care. By the way, he was deeply touched by whatever you said to him. I think you should see him personally in a few days, after he settles down."

"Yeah, I'll do that. Maybe dinner. Well look, Alexander, you go out to Hong Kong, and don't forget to answer your phone."

THREE

Over lunch at a discreet restaurant the CIA station chief in Hong Kong told Alexander he had received an urgent request. "The director wants to meet with you in Washington. He asked that I book you a flight to-morrow. There was no paper and he told me not to put anything in writing. His instructions were brief. Stay at the Hay-Adams, a room will be reserved, contact no one else at the agency, and he'll have you picked up at nine Friday morning."

"That's all?"

"That's all, except that he didn't seem to consider the possibility you might not come."

CIA HEADQUARTERS, LANGLEY, VIRGINIA, DECEMBER 1985

Friday morning Dottie Manson was waiting when the elevator opened into the DCI suite. "Hi, Alexander," she said, raising her cheek for a kiss.

"Hullo, Alexander. How've you been?" Casey called from behind his cluttered desk. "You never did invite me to that Ukrainian wedding."

"Just protecting you from yourself. I figured you'd come if we asked you."

Casey grinned. "You're right about that."

Alexander took a seat. "Yeah, for both our reputations. But I think you've been too busy since I left. It looks to me like you've got your second wind."

"Whaddya mean?"

"I've been following you in Eastern Europe, Bill. You're doing the things we talked about before I got run out of here."

"Like what?" Casey looked warily over the top of his steel-rimmed glasses.

"Like Poland. The printing presses and sudden, unlimited supplies of newsprint to start with, and now the mobile radio broadcast stations. Solidarity is alive and almost well after being on the ropes. There are ripples, strong ones in western Ukraine and even some in Lithuania."

Casey studied Alexander's face. "Ripples? Graham Middleton tells me that in the four months you've been gone, you're already piggybacking our operations in Poland. He whines to me that you're stealing us blind, using our printing presses and newsprint to get your Ukrainian independence message out on the street in Kiev. Same thing in Vilnius. He screams about conflict of interest—taking what you knew here and using it out there. And Lee Tanner tells me that you and whoever you're working with are good enough that Middleton can't actually pin you down. He's hearing things, but can't prove it. It makes him even bitchier."

"I'm careful. Solidarity's not even sure where the help comes from, but nobody in Gdańsk wants to look too hard for an answer. Some of them might suspect you're behind it, but they're not pressing for truth."

"People are doing good work around here now that they understand where we're headed. Everybody went crazy for a while when your buddy Yurchenko walked out on us and Howard escaped. And we've still got some kind of a problem in Moscow. Something we can't pin on Ed Howard."

"You didn't call me back here to talk about Yurchenko or about Middleton's whining complaints or a new problem in Moscow, did you?"

"No. You following what's going on in Afghanistan?"

"As well as I can. It looks like the Soviets are bogged down, but it looks worse for the Afghans."

"It's plenty bad, but it's not over yet," Casey grumbled. "The Soviet Air Force is murdering them. We're finally going to quit fooling around and give the Mujaheddin whatever they need to turn this war around. To win it. That's where you fit in."

"What could make that kind of difference?"

"Real weapons. Stinger missiles, for openers," Casey said. "We're going to stop pulling our punches. We're going to ignore George Shultz and the Foggy Bottom crowd fretting about pissing the Soviets off, and get serious. The president has agreed and so have the Pakistanis, President Zia himself. But Zia has placed tough conditions on putting in the new weapons. He wants us to move inside Afghanistan for this new phase. He probably has a point. He thinks that if we do the Stinger training and deployment inside Afghanistan, the Soviet Air Force won't strike into Pakistan."

"Sounds pretty simplistic to me," Alexander said.

"Zia hasn't done a simplistic thing since he hanged old Ali Bhutto."

"Where do I fit in?" Alexander asked.

"You're going to manage everything for me inside Afghanistan. Zia said that the new equipment like the Stingers, maybe some antitank missiles later, and some British and Spanish weapons after that, all has to be handled outside the known CIA arms pipeline into Pakistan. You can think like a Russian and you know more about special operations than anybody I've got around here now. We leave tomorrow night for Pakistan. I'll send a car for you at eight."

"Just a minute. First, don't you think Middleton will try to torpedo this? I know you're the DCI, but the barons in the operations directorate have to be on board, or things won't work."

"They'll be on board. Middleton still has you in his crosshairs, even more since the troubles didn't end with Ed Howard. Yes, we've lost some more people in Moscow, but the new problems point to someone here with us today, not to you. We lost an operation that started after you left, which makes Middleton's case against you only look like a grudge. He's got no support. Are you in or out?"

"I'm in, Bill, but I have some conditions. I'll do this as *your* man, Bill, not as a CIA employee. I won't accept any controls from your bureaucrats or interference from your lawyers. And you'll have to accept that I'll continue to be involved in other matters on my own that would drive Middleton crazy. And finally, I want reassurances from you that I'll always have a direct, secure line to you, one that bypasses any other chain of command. If that's all okay with you, then I'll be ready tomorrow at eight."

"I knew all of that when I asked you to come see me. We'll talk on the plane."

The next evening Alexander arrived at Casey's black C-141 Starlifter on the VIP ramp at Andrews Air Force Base. The chief of Casey's security detail helped Alexander aboard and led him to the entrance of Casey's VIP compartment, a box about half the length of a railcar lashed into the cargo bay. Inside the soundproof module he met the DCI's personal physician, Jim Hodges, who always traveled with the old man.

"Hi, Doc. Working already?" Alexander noted the stethoscope hanging from Hodges's neck and the blood pressure cuff in his hand.

"I just put him down in the front," Hodges said, nodding toward the closed door to the forward compartment. "He wants you to join him when we're airborne."

Alexander settled into one of the seats, glancing around at the other two passengers, a communicator seated at an equipment rack tying into a crypto link with CIA Headquarters, and an air force steward who would manage the galley for the long flight. The DCI's three-man security detail would travel in the cavernous cargo bay. Within minutes the huge aircraft began its roll.

Alexander entered the DCI's quarters and found the old man in robe and pajamas finishing a call, his white hair mussed. He was seated before a map table cluttered with books and cabled messages.

"Talking to your stockbroker?" Alexander slid into a seat across from the DCI, taking in how frail Casey looked in his night clothes.

Casey grinned. "You know, Alexander, this is still the best part of the job. Getting into this mean-looking, unmarked black bird and flying off to do something that I believe will make a difference. This is when I'm convinced I've got the best job in Washington."

"You've got the worst job in Washington, Bill. You just make it look like the best. Washington eats its DCIs."

"You want one of these?" Casey pointed to a glass.

"What is it?"

"Tonic water. But you know how bad that stuff tastes, so I put a little rum in it."

Alexander laughed. "Yeah. Let's have one."

Casey pushed a button on the bulkhead and ordered another tonic. When the steward appeared with it a moment later, Casey poured in a shot of rum.

Casey sipped his drink. "Do you remember when I came to Langley and you told me you thought we'd lost sight of our central mission, that the CIA's effectiveness had been destroyed. You were pretty blunt. And you know what?"

"I was right?" Alexander asked.

Casey nodded. "By the end of the seventies the CIA was a wreck. All those darling liberal intellectuals like Arthur Schlesinger and John Galbraith were telling the world that the U.S.S.R. was a permanent reality and to think otherwise was nothing more than wishful thinking. Carter scolded America for its 'inordinate fear of communism' before Brezhnev diddled him in Afghanistan when he wasn't looking."

Alexander nodded. "Carter took the Soviet invasion of Afghanistan as a personal insult. His motivation for doing the right thing isn't important from the historical perspective. The fact that he reacted is. But on his earlier orders we'd dismantled most of the programs we had for working against the Soviet Union. We had to start over again from scratch, and for the first couple of years that you were at Langley, you didn't show much interest in doing anything about the Soviet Union."

"Sure I was interested, but I saw what a disaster I had inherited. I had to spend the first four years getting my assets in place, building an organization, watching history. Now I'm ready."

"Ready for what? Do you really believe you can bring down the Evil Empire?"

"I believe we can, Alexander. And the timing will never be better than now."

"Why?"

Casey leaned back. "The Soviet Union has lost its continuity. For almost sixty years, the place was run by only three guys, Stalin, Khrushchev, and Brezhnev. After Brezhnev died, Andropov and Chernenko came and went in quick succession before the Soviet establishment could get its bearings. They can't handle loss of continuity like that, not the government and not the Russian people. They've forgotten things that used to be axioms, like how you have to use central control, coercive force, and old-fashioned managed fear. Then on top of all that this new guy, Gorbachev, comes along with his fuzzy notions of reform."

"So what are you going to do about it?"

"We press them across the board. It has to be now, and it has to be a total effort. We squeeze them in Afghanistan, in Poland and the Ukraine and the Baltics. And we throw up economic roadblocks everywhere at the same time."

"Gorbachev may think Afghanistan's a losing game, but walking away from it will put at risk the central proposition that has held the empire together for the last forty years. No Soviet leader can ditch the Brezhnev Doctrine without suffering the consequences."

Casey nodded. "We have a source in Moscow telling us that Gorbachev has given the army a deadline to get Afghanistan under control or he'll pull the plug on them."

"Is the army telling Gorbachev it can win?"

"It is, and some of his generals may even believe it. Every army has generals like that, even ours. That's why we're on this plane right now. We can't let it even look like they're winning."

"Keeping the other guy from winning a clear-cut victory is not always hard."

Casey nodded. "For a resistance movement, just not losing *is* winning."

"Is that where I come in?"

"Yes. You go to Afghanistan and keep the resistance fighting until the Soviets give up and pull out. That's the key—make everybody in the Soviet empire believe that Brezhnev really is dead, along with his doctrine of stepping in to stop antisocialist . . . whatever—"

"Antisocialist degeneration is their phrase," Alexander said.

Casey nodded. "That's right. Red Army intervention in Budapest,

Prague, and Kabul, and pulling the strings behind Polish martial law. If the people in the Bloc can be convinced that the Red Army won't intervene, it will all fall down. This can be done. But it has to be done now and all at once—Afghanistan, Poland, the downward pressures on oil prices. I'm working with the Saudis on that. The Russians have been living off the OPEC windfall for too long. The Saudi oil minister and the king know that. We're going to break the Soviets' bank."

Casey took off his glasses and rubbed his red and watery eyes. He looked more like someone's grandfather than the consummate Washington power broker. "Hodges gave me a potion. Makes me sleep like a baby, but it also makes me talk too much when I mix it with a little rum. See you when we land."

Alexander shuffled through a flight bag that had been tagged with his initials and placed under the seat in front of him. Inside were a stack of briefing books on the situation in Afghanistan, biographies on the key Afghan and Pakistani players, and a sealed envelope with his name on it. Inside he found a personal note from an old friend, now director of the CIA's Technical Services, advising him that the DCI had asked him to provide any and all support Alexander might need. At the bottom of the list he had written that Technical Services still held a pristine Polish identity packet for Alexander, with passport, identity papers, and all the elements of a convincing alias legend for one Polish Communist Party official by the name of Gromek Jasik. The second Polish identity, Janos Luks, had been retired because of a known compromise. Alexander reflected on the "retirement" of Janos Luks and the frightened Adolf Tokarev. And then he thought of how much time it had taken him to build the Gromek Jasik identity, the painstaking backstopping that had been built into the nonexistent person. And he had never used it; it was still completely clean. He leaned back and willed himself to rest.

FOUR

ISLAMABAD, PAKISTAN, DECEMBER 1985

As the C-141 began its approach to Islamabad, Alexander felt the confining disadvantage of the Casey module—he couldn't see out. There were fake windows, complete with diffused light coming through drawn curtains, but the light was only a thoughtful deception to comfort the claustrophobic. Closing his eyes, he leaned back in his seat and waited for the touchdown. He felt the flaps extend and the landing gear lower into place, followed by the yawing motion as the pilot lined up with the runway.

The aircraft was still taxiing down the runway when Casey, looking refreshed and all business, walked into the back of the module and handed Alexander a cable. "The schedule for the next fifteen hours. What's the local time?"

"Seven in the evening."

"We've got dinner with Zia at Army House at nine-thirty."

As the C-141 groaned to a brake-squealing halt, two black Mercedes sedans pulled up to it. The air force crew chief lowered the ladder to the tarmac and stepped aside as the DCI's security chief got off to survey the situation. He nodded to Casey to exit the aircraft, followed by Alexander. The welcoming committee whisked them to a car and within a minute the party was speeding to the Pakistan Army guest house.

Exactly two and a half hours later Casey and Alexander and their Pakistan Army escorts rolled into the circular drive lined with burning torches at Army House, where they were saluted by an honor guard. General

Mohammed Zia Ul-Haq stood waiting under the portico of his sprawling colonial residence. Beside him was General Akhtar Abdur Rahman Khan, Zia's intelligence chief responsible for coordinating all aid to the Afghan Resistance.

Dressed elegantly but simply in a well-fitting long black tunic and wide white trousers, Zia greeted Casey as the rangy old man moved awkwardly up the steps. After a brief exchange, Alexander heard his name and saw the general turn to him with smiling black eyes. "Welcome to Army House, Mr. Fannin. Bill has told me all about you. I am pleased to meet you."

"I am deeply honored, Mr. President, both to be your guest and to be a small part of what you are doing," Alexander said.

"Let's all move inside where we can relax and have a little talk before dinner." Zia's graciousness was disarming.

In the sitting room, Zia took a seat on a large, overstuffed couch upholstered in white-on-white patterned silk, motioned Casey to a matching chair next to him, and allowed Alexander and General Akhtar to choose their seats across an ornate, glass-topped coffee table. The small room was full of the symbols of General Zia's statesmanship: photographs of him with every leader of China since Mao, and a signed photograph of King Hussein of Jordan, where Zia had served as a military adviser in the King's Palace during the tense days of Black September.

"How was the flight, Bill?" the president asked with genuine interest.

"They take pretty good care of me these days, Mr. President," Casey answered. "But how I am is not as important as how you are and how the people of Afghanistan are right now." Casey showed no self-consciousness about skipping the amenities and moving the conversation directly into the reason he had come to Pakistan.

"We've become bogged down, Bill. The Mujaheddin can't seem to dig themselves out of the rut they're in. Nothing seems to be going for them, including their bickering leadership in Peshawar. General Akhtar and his people are doing all they can, but I think that whatever it takes to move the resistance to take up the battle, rather than waiting to die as martyrs, will have to come from within them. Right now the Russians have the upper hand. It will take something dramatic to bring the resistance out of their depression."

"The decision has been made to pull out the stops," Casey responded. "We're ready to send Stingers in numbers to make the difference."

Alexander watched Casey and Zia size each other up. Zia senses that Casey isn't going to become bored with Afghanistan in another six months and leave Pakistan in the lurch. He knows there are three more years before the next U.S. election, the earliest Washington could jerk the rug out from under him, that sooner or later the relationship with the United States will sour, but for now their interests have converged.

"That's where Alexander comes in."

"Ah yes, Mr. Fannin, please tell me what you think of the state of play in the Great Game next door." Zia turned to Alexander with those flashing black eyes and the honest smile that seemed so at odds with the preconceptions of the dictator who had controlled Pakistan for a dozen years.

"Mr. President, I would use your words to make my points. You refer to the invaders as the Russians, not the Soviet Union as the governments and media in the West do. That, in my opinion, is important. This struggle could be a war between Imperial Russia and a bordering country, a continuation of the expansion the Russians left unfinished at the end of the last century when they moved up to the Oxus River and ran out of steam. In 1979, it seems, they thought they had the might to finish the job, and that the rest of us were too distracted to stand in their way." Alexander paused, but saw in Zia's eyes an invitation to continue.

"Your second characterization was to put the war in the context of the Great Game, the historical backdrop to three Afghan wars in the last hundred and fifty years. That it is, but this struggle goes beyond squabbling over the territory between the Indus and the Oxus. It will determine how the greatest drama of the second half of the century plays out."

Casey glanced at Alexander as if to suggest he leave the speechmaking to him, and brusquely entered the conversation. "For the last five years, Mr. President, the United States has provided assistance to the Afghan Resistance. Some people on our side thought it was in American interests to provide just enough assistance to the Afghan Resistance to bog the Russians down—they call it fighting to the last Afghan. I am now proud to say that my president has decided to join fully in the battle. He believes that giving the Afghans only enough to fight a little longer cannot make us proud as a nation."

"Bill, Mr. Fannin," Zia said, "we are agreed on the magnitude of the battle, and the far-reaching effects it may have. But in the end there is no real choice. We have on Pakistani soil more refugees than the rest of the world's refugee population combined, some three million people. Imagine settling ten million Mexican refugees in Texas and California. We can't do this forever. Nor can we lose sight of the cost of this war to the Afghan people. There are another one or two million Afghan refugees in Iran, perhaps a million already killed by the Russians, another million or two wounded, and at least two million in internal exile, driven from their homes by the war's brutality." Zia glanced up at an aide in the hall, and turned to his guests. "I have just gotten my subtle signal that dinner is served."

Zia led the small party through a set of lace curtains into his small dining room, furnished with the charm of the Kipling days when Army House was the social hub in Rawalpindi. On the dark, hand-rubbed rosewood table, Zia's army stewards had laid out the food for the guests to serve themselves. There was chicken tikka, the tangy skinless chicken roasted over fan-blown trays of charcoal; lamb qorma, a mixture of stewed lamb pieces in creamed spinach; rice pilau with chunks of roasted lamb, raisins, and onions; and separate skewers of lamb kebab. Round loaves of heavily leavened roghi nan, hot from the tandoori oven, and thin chapati breads baked on a flatiron skillet were placed in stacks around the table. For drinks there was the choice of lhasi, the thick sour dairy drink reminiscent of buttermilk, and a variety of soft drinks. No alcohol was served at Army House. The stewards also served water, poured conspicuously from Evian bottles, presumably to reassure the travelers that it was safe to drink. A nice touch, Alexander thought.

Casey, as always, ate like he was hungry. After the dinner conversation moved through the obligatory subjects of Zia's short-iron game and the current state of play with neighboring India, the Pakistani president turned to Alexander. "Why do you suppose, Mr. Fannin, that Bill Casey chose you for this job he and I have worked out for you in Afghanistan?"

Alexander hesitated for a moment. "Mr. President, I hold no claim to being an expert on Afghanistan or its people. I do, however, know the Russians. I spoke Russian before I spoke English, and I can think like them and feel like them. And I know what we can do to beat them. The Russians will try to make you believe they will carry the war to Pakistan, but they will not. The Soviets do not attack strong and resolute countries on their borders. They only invade their friends. They never attacked Turkey and haven't threatened Finland since their failed Winter War in 1939. In attacking Afghanistan they thought they were invading a weak and submissive country. They have quite possibly made a fatal error."

The Pakistani president turned to Casey, who was beginning to show the strains of a day whose length he could no longer calculate. "Bill, you and our new Alexander and General Akhtar can work out the details on all this tomorrow. Now I know you must be exhausted."

Casey and his friend Zia exchanged a few more pleasantries on the way to the cars. "Bill, I think you have made the right choice for our experiment in Paktia. Even the name Alexander has a romantic ring for this region. I will wager that in no time our Afghan brothers are calling Mr. Fannin Sikander, the first Alexander to come to the Khyber over two thousand years ago."

HONG KONG, JANUARY 6, 1986

Katerina stood alone on the verandah of the villa that had been her parents' wedding gift to her and Alexander four months earlier. Wrapped in a shawl against the January chill she felt Alexander's presence behind her before he spoke. "I'm packed. Ling's loading the last of it now. The rest of it, mainly the books I've set aside, will be picked up next week. Someone will call."

She put her arm around her husband's waist. "One of your spooky friends with an impossibly cryptic message?"

"Something like that." Alexander kissed the back of his wife's neck.

"Do you know what today is?" Katerina's question was pensive.

"Christmas? At least my father's Christmas. But somehow I doubt that's what you mean."

Katerina pulled her shawl more tightly around her shoulders. "Partly, yes, but it's more than that. My mother believes today is the most hopeful time of the year, a moment of endless possibilities. She thinks of this day the way some people think of the coming of spring. When I was only five she taught me how ancient pagan celebrations of the winter solstice and the Orthodox celebration of Christmas eventually came together in a great gathering of faiths, a symbolic joining of historical forces, a merging of lives and fates. A true Epiphany. She believes all of that without equivocation."

"Do you?" Alexander asked.

"I do, and so do you, I think. Not, perhaps, to the extent my mother does, but only because we're not as old and certainly not as wise as she is."

"Is this what's making you so reflective?"

"Come, let's go in now." Katerina took her husband's hand and led him through the villa to the dining room, stopping before a priceless sixteenth-century reproduction of the icon of Our Lady of Vladimir that in the Orthodox practice was mounted high in the far right corner. On the wall below it were three candles in a wrought iron holder. They solemnly lit the tapers, then silently crossed themselves, Katerina in the Roman custom and Alexander in the Orthodox, and turned to kiss each other gently on both cheeks.

The table was set with the dishes traditional to the Russian Christmas feast—potato salads, herring in sour cream, pickles, three kinds of sausage, small bowls of horseradish, aspic, and marinated mushrooms and olives. Alexander and Katerina toasted each other with small glasses of chilled vodka. They ate sparingly from the main course of roasted pork and cabbage and spoke little. When they were finished, Katerina prepared tea from a samovar, pouring a small amount of the deep orange essence into two Russian porcelain cups. She carried them into the library where a gift-wrapped package lay on the rosewood coffee table. She handed it to her husband without a word.

Unwrapping the package, Alexander found a thin volume, bound in leather and embossed in gold-leaf Cyrillic, THE TALE OF THE MAIDENS OF KIEV. He thumbed through the parchment pages, admiring the beautiful calligraphy Katerina's mother had used to painstakingly write out her private correspondence with her twin sister. Alexander kissed his wife gently, touching her face with his hand. "Thank you, Kat. This is a treasure."

"Mother wanted you to have it with you in Afghanistan. She only finished it this morning. You'll have time to read it on some lonely night in your mountains, but right now I want you to read the chapter that just arrived, the one I haven't told you about. It's a special surprise for you." Katerina opened to a page near the end. "Start here."

Alexander read aloud, " 'And the evil Tsar sent the only son of Catherine of Kiev far abroad beyond Bukhara to spy out the land of the warring khans. A clever and most able young man, who spoke the tongue of the Persians as would a native, he saw immediately the futility of carrying out a war against the khans in the tangled valleys where even the Macedonian had suffered serious wounds and near defeat in a great battle so long ago. But he shared not his doubts with the Tsar or with the Tsar's *oprichniks,* who were ready to give their lives and souls for their leader, for he concluded most wisely that the war with the khans would be the undoing of the Tsar, a moment for which the lad was ready to give his own life and soul.' "

Alexander put the book down, his bemused smile gone. "When did she receive this?"

"While you were off wandering around the Khyber Pass with Casey, getting ready to join forces with the khans."

"So this is what's behind tonight's somber lesson of the Epiphany and merging fates. What is it that your mother says about coincidence?"

"She says there are no coincidences. There is only fate."

"And is it fate that she has learned that her sister's only son, the clever young lad who has been sent off by the evil Tsar to spy against the khans, is now in Afghanistan where he has concluded that the war there will be the undoing of the Evil Empire?"

"Of course. And mother is even more convinced that you'll cross stars with Anatoly, the son of her twin and my namesake, Katerina."

"Well, the odds are about a hundred and twenty thousand to one against it. But at least I'll have the advantage of knowing who and where he is. He doesn't know about me yet."

Katerina touched Alexander's arm. "Mother is writing you into the next chapter of the tale. He will hear all about you soon enough."

Alexander drew her closer to him and kissed her gently.

TWO

FIVE

"They're lost!" Salahuddin whispered with a rasping urgency to the two men lying beside him in the rocky brush. The Soviet Army jeep had passed their hidden position near the road twice within the last five minutes. On the second pass the men had seen four occupants in the open vehicle, their white faces and khaki uniforms set off by the moonlight.

"If they double back one more time we'll know for sure they're lost. Then we'll kill them." The Afghan with the full black beard and the loosely wrapped white turban, the one they called Fat Engineer Latif, spoke softly to his two fighters. He looked over at the short, wiry Salahuddin and saw a familiar look of something close to sexual arousal in the small man's hawkish face. "Mohammed!" he whispered to the third man lying beside him. "Get set up."

Mohammed Ishaq slipped the rocket element of a grenade round into the muzzle of his RPG-7 grenade launcher, the flared warhead protruding from the end of the weapon. Working by feel alone, he removed the metal nose cap and pulled the safety pin attached to a short cloth streamer out of the warhead tip to arm it. Then shifting into a crouch, he raised the stubby weapon onto his right shoulder, brought the distant jeep into the optical sight, and began tracking it.

Down the road about five hundred yards, the scout car had pulled to a stop again, and the three Afghan guerrillas could see a faint light snap on in its interior.

Latif tapped Mohammed Ishaq on the shoulder. "They *are* lost. If they double back and pass by here again, make your shot when they're abreast of that empty oil drum about fifty yards up the road. They'll have to slow down for that big hole in the road."

Mohammed Ishaq nodded. "A clear shot. It should be easy, *Insh'allah.*"

The jeep quickly reversed its course. The driver maneuvered in jerks and starts, fear pushing him beyond the fragile limits of self-control. The engine stalled. The driver shifted roughly and slowly retraced his route for the third time.

The four occupants of the jeep heard the loud, exhaling swoosh of the five-pound rocket as it left its launcher at 375 feet per second, but there was no time to interpret the sound before the projectile detonated on impact with the left front axle. The explosion knocked the engine off its mounts and sent the jeep careening crazily to the left toward the ditch, where it flipped over on its back.

Latif and his two companions each poured half a clip of 7.62 mm sub-machine gun rounds into the rolling wreck and were moving toward it before the tracer rounds had burned themselves out.

The driver was dead. He was still wedged in his seat, the capsized jeep crushing his skull against the road. The other three soldiers had been thrown clear. Two lay motionless in the ditch, the third lay sprawled on the road about ten feet away. As the three Afghans came abreast of the hissing wreck, he rose unsteadily to his knees, raised his submachine gun, and pulled the trigger. A single round kicked up a puff of dust five feet in front of him. Its flat report was punctuated by the loud metallic clang of the breach of the submachine gun locking open. Then silence. Empty! The ammunition clip must have been knocked out of the Kalashnikov when he was thrown from the jeep. The young man frantically slapped the earth searching for the missing clip.

As Salahuddin stepped quietly up to the soldier, he slowly raised his hands above his head in a primordial sign of submission and settled into a sitting position on his knees, desperate, disbelieving terror in his clear gray eyes.

Salahuddin moved his face close to the young soldier's trembling lips, and smiled reassuringly, even gently. He brushed his lips against the young man's forehead, and tenderly slipped the V formed by the outstretched thumb and index finger of his left hand under the soldier's jaw. He tilted the soldier's blond head slightly upward and squeezed his neck firmly. When he was satisfied with the tension in the soldier's neck muscles, Salahuddin drew his long-bladed knife from its scabbard, and in a single fluid motion cut the young man's throat and pushed his head down to his knees to direct the pulsing lines of blood away from his own feet and legs. He closed his eyes and sang out softly, "*Allah hu akhbar.* God is great."

Mohammed Ishaq came upon the second soldier lying on his back with his chest laid open, exposing white bone. Pink bubbles rose and fell from the gaping wound as he strained for breath. His eyes were glazed as he slipped into shock. The Afghan looked the wounded soldier closely in the face, then stood up and shook his head in Latif's direction, speaking softly. "This one will die."

Latif nodded. Mohammed rolled the soldier over on his stomach and squeezed off a single round of the Kalashnikov into the nape of his neck. The soldier's body straightened out in a rigid, convulsive bounce as the bullet severed his spinal cord.

Knife still drawn, Salahuddin moved quickly to the third soldier, but Latif gripped his shoulder. "Not too quick with your knife on this one, Little Brother. He's an officer."

The man wore the insignia of a senior lieutenant. Latif glanced back at the unit designator on the overturned jeep and saw that the men belonged to the 105th Guards Airborne Division, the same unit that had fired the first shots of the war in Kabul in the winter of 1979.

Latif rolled him over to see if he had any other injuries. Except for a superficial wound on his forehead, he seemed unhurt. "We'll take this one with us. He might be worth something. Get their weapons and maps and any papers you can find. Let's get out of here!"

With his headlights off, Latif moved out onto the moonlit Gardēz road and turned toward Logar province. After several minutes, a Russian voice crackled on the captured field radio.

"Gorky Five. Gorky Five. Please respond with your location. Do you need assistance? Gorky Five. Gorky Five. Do you copy? Please respond. Over."

Latif fumbled with the knobs until he switched it off.

KABUL, 40TH ARMY HEADQUARTERS, 2000 HOURS, AUGUST 25

Colonel Anatoly Viktorovich Klimenko had been at his desk at the sprawling headquarters of the Soviet Union's 40th Army for more than fourteen hours. His routine day had been transformed two hours ago when he received an incident report on an action from the night before. With military understatement the first sketchy details had been outlined: a skirmish had occurred during the late evening of August 24 on the Kabul-Gardēz Road just south of the outskirts of Kabul. A senior lieutenant of the 105th Guards Airborne Division, one noncommissioned officer, and two conscripts had apparently strayed too far south and run into a rebel ambush. A scouting patrol from the 105th had come upon the wreck of the jeep and the bodies of the NCO and two conscripts a few hours after they had broken off radio contact and had been reported missing. The

NCO had apparently been executed, a single bullet in the back of his neck, though the report observed with sterile detachment that he had also suffered several other wounds, any of which would probably have proved fatal.

That's for sure, thought Klimenko. Almost any wound could prove fatal with the spotty medical care available to the Soviet Expeditionary Forces. He read on. One of the two conscripts was killed by a knife slash to the throat, apparently after having put up a brief but ineffective struggle. The other conscript was apparently killed outright in the ambush.

Apparently . . . apparently . . . apparently! Klimenko thought the word the most overused in 40th Army reporting.

The report stated further that the bodies of the three soldiers were not otherwise mutilated, something the writer thought unusual enough to note. There was no sign of the lieutenant who had been in command of the outing, and who, Klimenko thought, had been stupid or inexperienced enough to wander into the ambush in the first place.

Klimenko skipped a few lines of details, looking for a clue to why this routine incident report had been sent out of channels to his KGB Special Action unit for information. He scanned down to the names of the dead soldiers and the missing lieutenant. Staring hard at the officer's name, he began to wonder just how long it would take before hysteria set in. There could only be one Senior Lieutenant Mikhail Sergeyevich Orlov of the 105th Guards Airborne Division. He was the son of General Sergei Ivanovich Orlov, Commander of the Soviet Western Group of Forces in the German Democratic Republic, one of the most powerful officers in the Red Army. It was an open secret in Moscow that he was measuring the carpets in the cozy office of the chief of the general staff, and that would only be a holding pattern until he could move up to defense minister.

Klimenko flipped back to the cover sheet of the incident report to see if an information copy had been sent to WGF Headquarters in Wünsdorf in East Germany. It had. It would only be a matter of time before the reactions started coming in.

At precisely 2005 hours Klimenko's telephone began its tinny, nerve-rattling jangle that only the Red Army Signal Corps could adopt as a standard. "Klimenko."

"Anatoly Viktorovich. My dear Tolya. This is your cherished, and probably only real friend, Sasha. What a mess! Polyakov just got off the phone with Wünsdorf. To put it bluntly, Polyakov, with only minor inspiration from General Orlov, has decided that more than anything in the world he wants Orlov's beloved boy back right now, and in one piece."

"I have the report in front of me," Klimenko said to his friend, Major

Alexander Petrovich Krasin, personal aide to the First Deputy Commander of the Soviet 40th Army, Lieutenant General Boris Semyonovich Polyakov. "I was wondering how long it would take the old boy network to kick into action."

"Not long. Polyakov wants Orlov found before he gets his precious little ass buggered by half the crazy Dushman in Kabul province. Stay there. I'm on my way." Sasha dropped the receiver into its cradle without signing off, just as he always did.

Klimenko heard Krasin's heavy footsteps in his outer office a few seconds before his friend burst in and collapsed unceremoniously into a chair.

"It must have been like this when Napoleon was advancing on Moscow, all panic and everybody trying to cover his ass," Krasin exclaimed, propping his dusty boots on Klimenko's desk. "Polyakov is in a temper tantrum. He's convinced that Orlov's boy is going home to daddy in a zinc box along with all the other boy heroes stacked up at the airport morgue. And he's convinced he'll take the fall. There's always a plot against Polyakov."

"Is he going to try to fix things by ordering some Dushman village flattened in retaliation?" Klimenko asked with a weary irony that he shared with few officers in Kabul. "If these guys in charge think that we're ever going to have our way with these people, they haven't been paying attention to history for the last five hundred years."

Krasin looked at the only officer in Kabul he thought of as a friend. "Tolya, these people haven't been paying attention to anything but themselves for the last seventy years. All history begins with Red October, or haven't you heard."

"Is that when history begins for you, Sasha?"

"Tolya, I'm a soldier. Soldiers in this army don't have histories, pasts, or futures. Not anymore. But if I did have a history, or better yet, if I had a future, it wouldn't have a damn thing to do with Red October. Does that shock you, my friend?"

Klimenko smiled. "I wouldn't be shocked by anything you did. It wouldn't even surprise me if I heard that you'd taken off to join some bandit warlord on the other side of the Khyber."

Sasha cocked an eye at Klimenko but let the remark pass. "What about you, Tolya? Where does your future lie? Or do you boys in the Committee for State Security have it so good that you can put up with all the silliness of building socialism?"

"Sasha, sometimes I wish it were that easy. I wish I could just tell myself to just be happy, that I've got it made. But I can't. And you can't either."

"That's why I keep coming back to this miserable pile of rocks. Awful as it is, I feel closer to being alive here than I've ever felt back home."

Sasha had been in at the beginning, Klimenko thought, in the same division as young Orlov. He was a young captain in the 105th Guards Airborne Division that spearheaded the Soviet invasion of Afghanistan on the snowy night of December 24, 1979, Christmas Eve in the non-Orthodox world. The 105th did most of the quick work that night, smothering the weak resistance put up by the palace guard, and within a few days it was all over. Afghanistan was under fraternal Soviet control.

"Why is that, Sasha? I ask you because I feel the same thing."

Krasin was serious. "Because we're going to find something, maybe even our souls, here in these mountains. Does that make sense?"

"Yes, I think so. But tell me, Sasha, you didn't come all the way over to the office of your only friend in the world to talk about the relentless search for destiny, did you?"

Sasha smiled broadly. "As a matter of fact I did. My destiny for today is to tell you that you're screwed. You, dear colonel, have been selected by my beloved and respected commander, the exalted Field Marshal von Polyakov, to resolve the problem of General Orlov's missing paratrooper."

"Does this mean he's holding off on the scorched-earth bullshit?"

"The only thing that might make him hold off on his idea of massive retaliation is the thought that Orlov's boy is alive, and that you, dear Anatoly Viktorovich, being the KGB colonel with the biggest and brassiest set of balls in 40th Army, are going to get the precious boy back before he needs an asshole transplant." Then Sasha dropped his feet back to the floor and leaned over Klimenko's desk. "Yes, Tolya, you are going to fix this little thing for Polyakov, and in doing so make my life easier. But in the process I'm sure you'll move us closer to our destinies, which might be death and dismemberment."

Klimenko looked across his desk at his friend. "Sasha, did I ever tell you that you are one crazy son of a bitch? I don't think that even you know what you're saying half the time. But yes, my dear friend, I'll be happy for the distraction of looking for the missing paratrooper. But don't get too far from me. I want you by my side."

Sasha stopped at the door on his way out. "I wouldn't miss it, Tolya."

Klimenko considered his new task. The operational side of the problem might be interesting, but the politics made him wonder if any of it was worth it. Whenever he was alone his thoughts came back to the politics of the war, the fraud of the whole system. Increasingly he found himself puzzling out the years that had led him to where he was now.

Klimenko had been the very model of the mythical New Soviet Man. He graduated from Moscow State University with a coveted red diploma for exemplary achievement in Asian studies. It seemed only natural when KGB recruiters materialized to woo him aboard. He moved straight into training for the KGB's elite First Chief Directorate, whose responsibility was foreign intelligence. He continued to excel during three additional years of study, first at the Committee's own language institute, where he learned English and Arabic and perfected his Persian, and later at the Andropov Red Banner Institute for trainee operations officers. He was marked as a comer even before his first assignment to Tehran in 1976.

Engaged in the collection of political and military intelligence under Line PR–Political of the KGB's large Tehran Rezidentura, Klimenko had developed a good network of informants within the opposition movements in the Shah's crumbling Iran. By 1978 his raw intelligence provided a confident prediction of the turbulent course the Iranian Revolution was about to take.

Klimenko accepted philosophically the embroidery that his boss, the KGB Rezident, began to stitch into his intelligence reports and assessments in 1978 that made it look as if developments in the country were the result of the tireless work of the KGB Rezidentura. A clever, ambitious man who followed the foibles of the American "Main Enemy" closely, the Rezident was aware that CIA assessments of the Iran situation in the last days of the Shah placed overdrawn emphasis on a dramatic, if not imaginary, increase in Soviet influence in the Persian Gulf, particularly in Iran.

It was a heady period for Klimenko. The Americans were on the run in Iran and elsewhere. The Soviet Union had moved into Afghanistan, and would have that little affair tied up shortly. Then they would be poised for a final push to the Persian Gulf itself. The Americans' client, the Shah, was about to crash and burn, and Anatoly Klimenko, ace of KGB spies in Central Asia, had only to chronicle it. The Rezident could do as he liked. If he wanted to turn the story into the Order of Lenin for himself, what was the harm? If the Americans were pushing the theme of the Soviet threat in Iran so hard, why not let the Rezident get a little credit for an imaginary victory? Both sides got what they wanted. Even better, they got what they deserved.

Matters got far more complicated when Americans were taken hostage and the Rezident had to do some fancy backtracking to avoid being credited with directing the takeover of the U.S. Embassy. Moscow Center was touchy about outright acts of war against the Americans. After all, some rules and conventions applied in the struggle against the Main Enemy. Klimenko had helped dig him out of that hole.

Klimenko finished up his five-year tour one week after the hostages were released. His intelligence on the timing of their release—on Inauguration Day—was so good that the shameless old Rezident again found ways to take credit for it. He had precious little time at home in Moscow before he was assigned to the KGB Special Action Group attached to the Soviet 40th Army in Kabul. He spent six months training with the paramilitary operations group, Group Alfa, and had soon earned a reputation for daring. Some of Klimenko's missions had taken him deep into Pakistan, where he and his men conducted successful sabotage operations and a handful of assassinations.

He had thought about going home for a while, perhaps even of finding a wife, but that had been more than five years ago, and now he was back in Kabul doing very much the same things he had done in 1981. This time no one talked about getting home anytime soon. A couple of weeks ago, in a speech in Vladivostok, the new general secretary, this Mikhail Sergeyevich Gorbachev, had actually called the war a "bleeding wound." But Klimenko had already concluded that there was no future for the state he had served so long.

Two events had pushed him over the edge. His father's death eight months before had been senseless, caused by a corrupt system in terminal failure. A victim of chronic lung disease, his father would have such difficulty breathing that Klimenko's mother, a gynecologist at the Kiev University Clinic, would take him to the clinic and administer oxygen until his symptoms eased. During his last attack she again put him on oxygen, and half an hour later he was dead.

Klimenko's mother had the oxygen analyzed and discovered it was a combination of room air and carbon monoxide—car exhaust. She called for an investigation, and learned that the state corporation producing the oxygen had illegally diverted its entire production to the defense sector. Unable to satisfy demands for medical oxygen, they substituted plain room air for oxygen in the tanks they sent to most of the hospitals—the exceptions being hospitals and clinics reserved for the nomenklatura. During winter they moved their gasoline-driven compressors into a closed area to keep warm and ended up filling the oxygen bottles with a mixture of room air and carbon monoxide.

As the investigation began to uncover more details, including a growing number of deaths resulting from the contaminated oxygen, the protective system kicked in. Two officials from the "competent corporation" paid a visit to the clinic and told the director and Klimenkova that they would be wise to drop the investigation. They said they had information that workers at the clinic had actually contaminated the oxygen bottles themselves, and that arrests were possible. The investigation was dropped.

The second irreconcilable event was the nuclear catastrophe at Chernobyl in Klimenko's native Ukraine four months later. Such a deliberate, cynical sacrifice of tens of thousands exposed corruption on a scale that overshadowed even the death of his father. After an incredible five days of denial the Soviet authorities finally declared an emergency. They had known the magnitude of the radiation leak in the first hours following the meltdown of Chernobyl's reactor, and had they acted decisively then, the harm to the population, particularly to the children, might have been greatly reduced. A little iodine, declared the outraged Klimenkova, readily available and easily administered, could have saved tens of thousands of Ukrainian children from going to early graves with thyroid cancer.

Klimenko shook his head wearily and picked up his secure telephone to make a direct call to the KGB liaison office at KHAD, the Afghan Secret Service Headquarters across Kabul city.

Major Shadrin answered after the second ring. "Shadrin."

"Major, I want you to personally handle something very important. I want you to check on the current holdings of important Dushman prisoners in Pul-I-Charki prison and any other detention areas in the country and give me the names of all prisoners of significance. If you can do so, I want them broken down by affiliation to the rebel parties in Peshawar. I am looking for good solid trading material, and I need it today. Do you understand?"

"I think so, Colonel," Shadrin answered.

"By the way, see if you can do this without half of Kabul knowing about it. I know that's not easy, but I don't want the bandits in Peshawar to get hold of this until the time is right. Do you understand?"

"Yes, sir. I'll try, but just checking the lists will probably alert the KHAD, and you know how riddled with Dushman penetrations the Afghan special service is. I'll do my best."

"Do so, Major," Klimenko ordered and broke the connection.

SIX

It was after dark when the caravan of twenty mules and thirty men reached the caravansary at the edge of a village southwest of Kabul. Alexander and the caravan leader, Al-Musawwir, the Fashioner, had set off eight days earlier, just before the cooling relief of sunset in Pakistan's North West Frontier Province. They crossed over zero line, as the border with Afghanistan was called, in the dark, making their way through the blood- and history-drenched Khyber Pass, the tortured slice through the secondary ridges of the Hindu Kush, called, with a verbal economy uncharacteristic of the Afghans, the Eastern Mountains.

Later they broke away from what had once been a romantic stretch of the Grand Trunk Road, an ancient thoroughfare built to ease the commerce of the Mogul Empire. The ruins of Mogul signal towers that once relayed complex torchlight signals over the fifteen hundred miles from Kabul to Calcutta in a few hours were still discernible. This same route through the Khyber to the Indus and beyond had been traversed over the millennia by the supply trains of Alexander of Macedonia, by the conquering hordes of Genghis Khan, and by Kipling and Lady Sale on journeys of great conquest and shattering despair and defeat.

Their destination was known simply as Twenty-five Kilometer Village, its precise distance from Kabul. The central gathering place was a small teahouse that was ready to serve any passing wayfarer so long as he was on the right side of the war. There Alexander and the Fashioner waited for Al-Hadi, the man Alexander called Rambo. They were about to set out on their next operation—a rocket attack against the puppet Afghan Army ammunition dump in Kabul.

After eight months in Afghanistan, Alexander blended almost perfectly into the setting. Deeply tanned and with a full black beard and longer hair, he was indistinguishable from the Afghan fighters trekking with him into the heart of the Soviet occupation. He and the Fashioner and a young fighter they just called the Boy took food and tea from the grizzled old owner of the teahouse, a man of indeterminate age known only as Mullah Arif, a part-time mullah and supporter of the jihad and full-time business-man whose smile displayed a single front tooth. Dressed in his oily shalwar chamise and a soiled turban and smelling of wood smoke he poured strong sweet tea into the small handleless cups, adding two car-damom seeds to each as a small concession to extravagance and out of genuine respect for the Fashioner and his comrades.

Later, when Alexander and the Fashioner were resting on straw mats under the starlight, Mullah Arif approached them out of the darkness. "They're coming!" he announced in a hushed whisper. Seconds later they could hear the straining engine of the Bedford as it pulled up the last half mile of the old road.

The truck was running without lights, and so had probably not been spotted by the orbiting AN-26 airborne warning platforms in the area around Kabul. Alexander could see the driver and two other men in the cab and counted half a dozen heads above the high walls of the truck's bed. One of these leaped to the ground and came toward the Fashioner. He was several inches shorter and slightly built. At first glance his grimy, roughspun shalwar chamise marked him as a likely urban Shia, to be avoided for any number of reasons, most of all because the urban Shia were thought unclean. His filthy beard was matted and tufts of hair stuck out from under the frayed edges of his grimy Afghan Army hat.

Alexander greeted Rambo in Russian. "Commander Hadi, what is that stink coming from your truck?"

"Sikander Sahib should know that the stink of my Bedford is shit. It hauls honey barrels from the cesspools of the infidel Russian Army." He spoke like a mullah at Friday prayers. "It is a powerful deterrent to those who would search me, for it is written that the true believer cannot handle the shit of the infidel."

Alexander laughed and embraced the Kabul guerrilla he had come to respect as much as any commander in the war. He wondered what the reaction might be if the Soviets knew that the man causing them so much grief in Kabul was the funny creature who hauled shit out of their camps.

Rambo turned to the Fashioner. "Fat Engineer Latif and some fighters are bringing in a Russian prisoner, a lieutenant. Latif wants to bargain."

"What does the old bandit want?"

"Probably everything you've got. But if you want the lieutenant, offer him a handful of radios and call it a deal."

Soon, a small Suzuki van groaned into the village and its occupants led a Russian officer into a low building. A few minutes later Latif expansively greeted the Fashioner.

"My brother commander, we heard you were coming to Twenty-five Kilometer Village and made a special effort to welcome you to Logar province." Turning to Alexander, the hulking man switched to English. "And the added honor of meeting with the Friend has made the effort most rewarding."

Alexander took Latif's outstretched hand. "My compliments and those of all the Friends to Engineer Latif. The stories of your exploits have reached my leaders who sing your praises. You are well known as a mighty warrior."

"I am honored that we are joined in a great struggle against a common enemy, Sikander. Together we will defeat him, *Insh'allah.* But first, there is a matter we should discuss. Perhaps over tea?" Latif ambled toward the teahouse with his arm around Alexander's shoulder.

Inside old Arif's smoke-blackened back room Latif set a cloth-wrapped package before Alexander.

"Sikander has often spoken of the need to deal with Russian prisoners, shall we say, more thoughtfully than we have in the past. I agree, and have traveled here at great risk to discuss with my brother commander possible means for dealing with the freshly captured lieutenant. I have his papers."

Alexander picked up a wallet and an officer's red identity booklet. He thumbed it open to the photograph page. Staring back at him was the face of a handsome young man looking defiantly into the camera.

"Senior Lieutenant Mikhail Sergeyevich Orlov," Alexander read aloud from the document. "He looks like he's ready to take on the world. We've seen that look before, haven't we?" He handed the identity card to the Fashioner, who saw what Alexander meant: the young man's arrogant confidence.

Alexander shuffled through a few pieces of pocket litter. In the lieutenant's wallet he found a photograph almost hidden under a leather flap. In it Orlov stood stiffly in a new dress uniform between a striking woman of about fifty and a taller, older version of himself, a man wearing the uniform of a Red Army general. Seeing that Engineer Latif was engrossed in conversation with the Fashioner, he slipped the photo back under the leather flap. His face betrayed nothing as he wrapped the documents back in the cloth. "What plans do you have for this lieutenant?"

"He is of little use to me, Sikander. More of a burden. But I am mindful that you may have an interest. Perhaps there would be some political value in a young lieutenant, as you have often said."

"A colonel might bring political returns, but a young lieutenant is barely better than a conscript. Nevertheless, you were right to bring him to us. Is he fit to travel?"

"He is only slightly wounded. But, come, see for yourself, my friend."

As Latif led the men across the village, Alexander dropped back with the Fashioner. "Musawwir, hidden in the lieutenant's wallet is a photograph of a general in the Red Army who looks like Orlov with about thirty years more mileage on him. I'm almost sure it's his father, General Sergei Ivanovich Orlov, who commands the Red Army forces in East Germany. We may have within our grasp the precious son of General S. I. Orlov."

"We must move carefully. If Latif begins to smell our interest, his price will skyrocket."

Alexander and the Fashioner stopped at the door of the low building. Sitting against a wall inside was Latif's prize, his hands still bound with rope and a blood-caked gash on his forehead.

Alexander took Latif aside. "You're right. The lieutenant looks in good enough shape to travel, but he'll probably be more trouble for us to haul to Paktia than he's likely to be worth."

Latif flashed a smile in the moonlight. "My brother Salahuddin, who now sits with the Russian, first thought that this lieutenant should be killed outright. Perhaps he was right. If this lieutenant is of no value to you, what difference does it make if there is one more Russian martyr? Or do they have martyrs?"

"Yes, Engineer, they have their martyrs. But I will take this lieutenant off your hands, if only because of what I have said about captured officers."

"That would help me greatly, Sikander."

Alexander placed his hand on Latif's shoulder. "Please do not be insulted by what I am about to say, Engineer Latif, but though I would never offer you anything in trade for this humble lieutenant, I have always admired you greatly as a commander and would like to help your fighters in any way I can."

Latif shifted his heavy weight. "I could accept nothing from the Friends in return for this prisoner. You may have him if it is your desire." He paused. "But my fighters are always in need in their struggle against the Russians, Sikander."

Alexander knew the price was about to be announced. "I know that Engineer Latif would not trade this vile human refuse for any personal advantage, but I could not rest well if I had not helped, somehow, to make my brother commander and his *mujāhids* more effective in the jihad."

Latif gave Alexander a sidelong glance. "There is one thing you might do to help."

"Please tell me, Engineer."

"I am in need of ten handheld frequency-hopper radios and two base stations."

"Engineer Latif knows well that I can only supply each commander with five handheld sets and one base station, but even then delivery can take weeks or even months."

"If Sikander can deliver five handheld sets and one base station in one week I will be forever indebted. But I will be even more indebted to Sikander for relieving me of the burden of this troublesome lieutenant."

"Done. If you remain here until Musawwir and I return tomorrow, we will take the lieutenant off your hands then. The radios can be picked up in one week at special operations in Paktia."

Latif gravely took Alexander's hand. "It is agreed, Sikander."

Alexander spoke to the Boy. "Think you can set up the burst radio for a message to the Friends over there?" He pointed at the southeastern horizon.

The Boy nodded. From a small pouch in his satchel, he carefully removed an object tightly wrapped in rubberized cloth and secured by Velcro straps. Unfolding the cloth, he revealed what appeared to be a black electronic system with three separate metal sections, each about the size of a paperback book. Using cables stored in the pouch, he joined all three pieces. "Moodge proof," Alexander had once described the deceptively simple design that prevents easy misuse. There were Moodge-proof cameras, Moodge-proof timing devices, everything but a Moodge-proof war. The Boy oriented the assembled radio to the southeast and a radio repeater in direct line of sight from Twenty-five Kilometer Village.

"It's ready," the Boy said.

Alexander took a short, pointed plastic stylus from a storage slot in the radio and began punching it gently into what appeared to be a miniature keyboard. Several minutes later, his clear message scrolled across a rectangular liquid-crystal display window:

1MJ FRM 2MJ RPT 1MJ FRM 2MJ:

PLS RELAY TO TFX KHARGA OP PLANNED FOR 1700HRS LOCAL TOMOR-ROWX NOW SENDING 25KMVILX PLS TRACE IMM LT MIKHAIL SERGEYEVICH ORLOV 105 GRDS ABN DIV BORN 17JUL60 MOSCOWX PROBABLY SON OF RED ARMY GENERAL S I ORLOV OF WESTERN GROUPX ORLOV IN FRIENDLY HANDSX BUT HAVE MADE ARRANGEMENTS TO TAKE CONTROL TOMOR-ROWX TRUST IN GODX ENDX ENDX ENDX

"Go ahead and send it," Alexander said to the Boy. A small light in the first section of the assembled radio set burned red for a split second; then a second small green light ignited and stayed lit. The message had been enciphered in an electronic one-time pad and then transmitted in an on-air burst that lasted for less than a second. The red light indicated a successful transmission; the green light was the electronic handshake from the receiver in the Eastern Mountains telling them that their message had been received and decoded. Without this handshake they might have had to transmit again, and more time on the air meant another opportunity for the Soviet radio direction–finding sites to take another look at the strange signal.

Rambo joined Alexander and the Fashioner to brief them on the rocket attack. "We're going to use Site Bravo to launch our attack," Rambo announced to the others. "The other two sites the satellites found for us are probably as good, but we can get to Bravo safely tonight. The mulberry grove there belonged to a man named Abdul Karim. The father of one of my fighters, Mullah Suleiman, will lead us. You will ride with him. I'll bring the Bedford by a different route."

Karim's Grove, 0330 Hours, August 26

Suleiman was an intensely devout Muslim who invoked whichever of the ninety-nine names of Allah fitted the desperate task at hand. The name of Ya-Qahhar, the Destroyer, had rolled over his lips more than seven hundred times when the Suzuki wheezed into Karim's abandoned grove just three miles west of the massive ammunition dump at Kharga. The main farmhouse no longer had a roof and three of the four walls had partially collapsed. The few outbuildings, except for one, were in almost as bad shape, and everything had suffered from the two years of drought brought about by the destruction of the irrigation system. The Fashioner and Alexander were surveying the damage when they heard the thrashing complaint of Rambo's Bedford as it pulled into the courtyard. Within less than two minutes his men had unscrewed the bolts that secured the planks above the long I beams of the chassis supporting the bed. Nestled in the concealment compartments of the specially engineered I beams were eighteen green wooden boxes, each containing a 107 mm free-flight rocket.

Two additional boxes, one a metal ammunition box of the kind formerly used by the U.S. Army for .50-caliber machine gun ammunition, and another exactly like those carrying the rockets, but filled with coils of light, dun-colored electrical wire and a dozen E-cell batteries, were secreted in the cavities. There was also a Silva compass, some duct tape, a coil of brown string, three coils of brown one-inch-wide metal measuring tape, six brown sectional stakes, a bayonet for a Kalashnikov that also served as a wire cutter, and two large cans of spray paint in two shades of brown.

"Let's get down to work," the Fashioner urged. He turned toward the Boy. "Uncoil the electrical wire and lay it out in parallel lengths directly in front of the farmhouse."

The Fashioner then spread a computer-generated map of Site Bravo on the planking covering an old well in the courtyard and snapped on a flashlight. The men gathered around it and began to orient themselves. Everything was represented: the house, the well, even the stone at the side of the well, worn concave by Karim's forebears. Annotations in Dari marked every object that had been identified.

Checking the legend carefully, the Fashioner located the azimuth from Site Bravo to Kharga as eighty-six degrees, almost due east. Setting the compass and sighting along it, he scanned the imaginary elevated flight path the rockets would take. "It's perfect," he said to Rambo. "A clear shot—at least if these drawings are right."

"The drawings are always right," Alexander said matter-of-factly.

Moving quickly, all three men began laying the twelve-yard lengths of tape on the clay courtyard, taking pains to lay them on an eighty-six-degree bearing pointing directly at Kharga. They secured each tape with long nails.

They cut three-yard lengths of string, and secured them perpendicular to the tapes at the zero-, two-, four-, six-, eight-, and ten-yard points on the tapes until they had created a latticework of tape and string. The time was 0438 hours.

Within minutes the first helicopter crews from Kabul airfield would mount up for their morning patrols. By precisely 0515 hours they would begin their low-altitude sweeps of the areas around Kabul likely to have served as staging areas for the Dushman bandits the night before.

Stepping up the pace, the men set the boxes containing the rockets at each of the intersecting points of the strings and the tapes until all eighteen boxes were in place. The two Afghans carefully rested each rocket in a rounded cradle machined out of the side of each box. A circle around the body of the rocket calibrated the distance from Site Bravo to Kharga and created the exact angle of elevation for the rocket to fly true to its target. Additional lines were marked on each rocket for Alpha and for Charlie, the other two options for the operation. The men worked their way down the grid attaching the wires to the firing rings circling the base of each rocket.

The Boy quickly retrieved the mysterious new blackout box the Friends had just brought to the war to help detect enemy helicopters. The contraption was about half the size of a cigar box, its top fitted with shielded lightbulbs, red and green, and two adjustment knobs. He had heard Alexander tell the Fashioner it was a disguised Fuzzbuster, asking him not to tell the others for fear the Soviets would learn the secret. The

Boy didn't know what a Fuzzbuster was, but he knew the blackout was magic. He switched it on, waited a few seconds and announced, "It's burning green and steady, the all-clear signal."

The Fashioner opened the metal ammunition box. The circuitry of the timing device had been developed in the laboratories of the Office of Technical Services in CIA Headquarters at Langley. He pressed the red button of each connector, inserted the ends of the wires in the holes, and released the buttons completing the electrical contact. Then he snapped into place eight of the twelve E-cell batteries.

Alexander handed his friend a twelve-hour time pencil, a six-inch-long brass tube. After attaching it to the wire leading from the board with the connectors, the Fashioner gave it a quick twist. Bringing together two red dots at the end, he released the corrosive acid. Then he set it back in its pressure clip inside the box and attached the wire leading from it to the power pack with the batteries.

It would take exactly twelve hours for the acid to eat its way through a thin wire holding a spring-loaded metal pin. The wire would break and the firing pin would slam home, completing the electrical circuit. The fireworks would begin at 1700 hours.

Now ready for the last element, Alexander retrieved from his vest pocket a glassine envelope. He unfolded the sheet of paper inside and handed a felt-tip pen to the Fashioner. "Sign one of the ninety-nine names. Be creative, Musawwir, old friend."

The Fashioner gave it a moment's consideration, then scribbled a signature. Alexander refolded the paper inside the ammunition box with the timing equipment and just before he closed and sealed the lid, slipped in an object ten inches long wrapped in tissue paper.

"They're in the air," the Boy called out. The red light in the box was burning brightly, blinking in cadence with a tone that was growing in strength.

The Fashioner quickly tossed one of the two cans of camouflage spray paint to Rambo, who motioned his *mujāhids* to move into the one remaining outbuilding with a roof. He and the Fashioner quickly backed down the lines of rockets, spraying the whole configuration until all of the sharp lines and edges blurred. A helicopter gunship at one thousand feet and traveling seventy-five miles an hour wouldn't see a thing.

TWENTY-FIVE KILOMETER VILLAGE, 1500 HOURS, AUGUST 26

Alexander, the Fashioner, and the Boy were tired and hungry when they reached Mullah Arif's at midafternoon. They had caught a ride with a group of *mujāhids,* stopping only once for noonday prayers. Mullah Arif welcomed his returning guests, and offered them hot green tea with sugar and cardamom seeds and a yellow Afghan melon that had been cooled by scraping away a patch of its hard skin and leaving it out in the sun for over an hour. The evaporation through the scraped skin left the flesh of the sweet melon deep inside as refreshing as winter.

After a few minutes of wordless rest Mullah Arif broke the silence. "Fat Latif left this morning. He left two fighters behind to guard the Russian and asked me to give you this." He handed the Fashioner a folded piece of cotton cloth about the size of a sheet of letter paper. On it, in tightly controlled Dari script, Latif had written:

> In the name of God the Merciful, the Benevolent, I send you greetings. I have left for you this 26th day of August the Russian lieutenant that the Provider delivered into my hands. I have asked Harun, brother of Humayun, to stay and guard him and to accompany you to Paktia to take charge of the radios the Beneficent has seen fit in His goodness to deliver to the jihad through the good offices of the Friends. Trust in God. Latif. 26-VIII-86.

Alexander turned to the Boy. "Set up the burst radio on receive. We should have a message waiting for us." Within a minute the radio emitted a sharp tone and the green light began blinking. The Fashioner joined Alexander as he read the scrolling display:

IMJ FOR 2MJ RPT IMJ FOR 2MJX FOLL IS RELAY FROM TASK FORCE QUOTEX IT ESSENTIAL THAT YOU TAKE CONTROL OF ORLOVX WE CONFIRM THAT CAPTIVE ORLOV IS SON OF WGF COMMANDER ORLOV WHO IS KNOWN TO HAVE SON IN 105TH GUARDSX FURTHER COLLATERAL INFO CONFIRMS ORLOV SON HAS DISAPPEARED AND THERE MUCH EXCITEMENTX END QUOTEX TRUST IN GODX ENDX ENDX ENDX

Alexander turned to the Fashioner. "I'll leave tonight, ahead of you. About the last thing I need to do is help you drag the son of the commanding general of the Western Group of Forces around Afghanistan. Sooner or later Moscow will hear about it—at least after we get a swap arranged—but there's no need advertising my involvement until it can't be avoided. You bring Orlov in yourself. Keep him at the Ponderosa and call me when you've arrived."

SEVEN

KARIM'S GROVE, 1700 HOURS, AUGUST 26

The air at Karim's grove was dead still. At 1703 hours the corrosive acid in the time pencil ate through the last few microns of wire holding back the firing plunger. All but one of the eighteen 107 mm rockets ignited properly. Within three-and-seven-tenths seconds seventeen rockets were on their way toward Kharga, three miles to the east.

In what would later be described variously as the vengeance of God, superb planning and execution, or just plain dumb luck, what followed was a signal event in a war that had been going badly for the Afghan Resistance. Eight rockets inflicted varying degrees of damage, most of it minor. Eight more missed Kharga altogether, but did some damage to civilian targets. One white phosphorous rocket, however, flew as if guided by the hand of the Destroyer and pierced the sheet metal door of the half-buried storage warehouse containing the entire supply of surface-to-air missiles delivered by the Russians to the Afghan Army for protection against air attacks from Pakistan.

The exploding white phosphorous ignited the fuel tanks of the SAMs, setting off a chain of secondary explosions that spread through the giant Kharga facility, which was loaded with 40,000 tons of ammunition.

40TH ARMY HEADQUARTERS, 2230 HOURS, AUGUST 26

Sasha had been in Klimenko's office for almost an hour. Both officers sipped vodka and quietly watched the pyrotechnics from the window.

Sasha was first convinced that Kharga had been an inside job or another one of the impossibly stupid accidents that the Afghan Army seemed to perpetrate regularly. "Looks like our donkey-dick brothers have blown themselves up again, dear Colonel," he announced as he burst into Klimenko's office.

"Not this time," Klimenko said, pointing to the metal ammunition box on the table, a spray of clipped wires still protruding from its closed lid. "Take a look. We found this ten minutes after the first blast at Kharga. It was part of a setup the Dushman must have put in place last night. Our counterbattery radar had a lock on the launch location while the rockets were still in the air."

Sasha shook his head. "Look at the way this thing is engineered. Looks simple, but it's not. Probably works every time."

"This was inside the box when they found it." Klimenko handed him a folded sheet of white paper.

Shasha read aloud in literary Russian:

My Dear Colonel,

May I congratulate you and your comrades for at least being able to find out after the fact what we have chosen to do to you, and how we have done it. Please do not make the mistake of thinking that this attack that has so seriously damaged your puppets' capability to wage your genocidal war was a stroke of luck or an isolated setback for you and your murderous clients. I can assure that this is just the beginning, and that you will be hearing and seeing more of the same as the weeks roll on. I will not waste my time telling you to get out of Afghanistan, Colonel, for I know that you personally decided long ago that this is the proper choice. You will all ultimately leave our country, but until such time as you are finally across the Oxus, we will continue to help you dig your graves.

Ya-Muntaqim

"What's this at the end?" Sasha asked, pointing to the Fashioner's Arabic signature.

"It says the Avenger. It's one of the ninety-nine names of Allah," Klimenko said quietly.

"What about this My Dear Colonel stuff? What about this personal decision stuff? Do these Dukhis know you?" Sasha asked with a raised eyebrow.

"It's a game, but a very sophisticated one. When I first saw the letter I actually felt afraid for the first time since I've been here, but when I thought it over I understood that something like this would keep being handed up the line here at 40th Headquarters until it eventually got to a colonel. Any colonel would do. Think about it. There isn't a major or a lieutenant colonel at 40th Headquarters who would accept responsibility for this. These guys know us that well. I really did feel that the Dukhi bastards were talking to me personally when I read that note the first time. I think I know who might be behind this little love note, the Kharga attack, and all the other things that add up to a major shift in the war. I'm convinced that our American friends have decided to raise the stakes. I think they're actually going to try to win this war, not just bleed us or fight to the last Dukhi. I've been getting reports about some strange construction and foreign visitors to Parachinar and Paktia. I've seen the satellite photos of the area and something is definitely up. Sigint is also picking up new encrypted communications links from Paktia that we can't break out. I believe my new problem is a man the Dukhis call Sikander, their ancient name for Alexander of Macedonia, a CIA man who speaks native Russian, according to some reports. They have people like that. I think he wrote that letter, and sent along this too." He tossed Sasha an object about ten inches long wrapped in tissue paper. "Go ahead. Open it. It won't blow up."

Sasha warily unrolled the tissue paper and held up a silk black tulip.

"Yes, Sasha. He has a sophisticated calling card. The black tulip."

"If I were you, my dear Colonel," Sasha said mockingly, "I would watch my ass before the clever bastard who sent you this little flower sneaks into your bed and sews your balls into your mouth. It doesn't make a bit of difference whether he's got a nice homespun name like Alexander or if he's another red-eyed Abdullah. These crazy bastards are beginning to get to me. Too many boys have taken a ride in a Black Tulip. I would also worry about a lot of people around this building who will believe those Dhukis were addressing you in that note. You'd better watch yourself."

Klimenko considered himself Ukrainian first and a Soviet citizen and KGB colonel second, but he was careful to conceal those feelings. Any sign that might be taken for Ukrainian nationalism could become dangerously complicating in a society that didn't allow for deviation. His earliest, and most dangerous, deceptions had begun during his vetting by the Investigations Department of the KGB. His immediate family background looked impeccable. His parents were members of the Communist Party. Klimenko himself had belonged to all the proper youth wings from the Young Pioneers to Komsomol, and finally to the Party itself. He and his parents had frankly discussed the sham of their Party membership, but rationalized it as one of life's crude necessities.

Their family secret, one that would not only have kept him from being accepted by the KGB, but would have landed his parents in the Gulag, appeared intact. Eighteen years before, when he had been in his third year at Moscow State University and had been approached by KGB recruiters with a career offer in foreign intelligence, his parents finally told their son that his mother's sister had escaped from the Soviet Union and was now living in Hong Kong. Katerina described the chaos surrounding the death of their parents in Nazi-occupied Kiev in 1943, and how her twin, Lara, then seventeen, had disappeared into the Maritime Provinces of the Soviet Far East and was last heard of somewhere around the port city of Nakhodka, near Vladivostok.

Katerina survived the war believing that she was probably the sole living member of her family. But she never gave up hope that Lara was alive somewhere, and made some uninformed and unassisted efforts to find out what had become of her. The trail led nowhere; in a country where the war dead numbered more than twenty million, all but the most resourceful and determined eventually gave up, their heartbreaking Sign of Life notices with their terse instructions yellowing on the bulletin boards of post offices and train stations across the Soviet Union's eleven time zones: "Katerina Chumakova of Kiev seeks any information on the fate of her beloved twin sister Lara, born in Kiev on 4 April 1926. . . ."

But though Katerina was no more superstitious than the Slavic norm, she sensed that her sister was not dead. At times she felt she knew what Lara was doing at a given moment. She told Viktor she was convinced that Lara had had a child, a beautiful girl who could be their own son's twin.

Viktor had been patient with his wife, and even accepted the possibility of some distant communication between identical twins that could not be explained rationally. That was within the grasp of his intellect, but he could never really share her belief that her sister still lived until the lacquer box appeared in 1967, when their son Anatoly was nineteen years old.

It was a perfect copy of the hand-painted and richly lacquered papier-mâché boxes from the Russian village of Palekh, down to the minute detail of the ancient fairy tale elaborately painted onto the lid. It was accompanied by the story of the fairy tale itself, relating in grand Slavic style the heroic struggle of two young maidens of Kiev, handwritten in an elegant Cyrillic script on four sheets of yellowed parchment.

The box and the envelope containing its story had been delivered to Katerina at the Kiev University Medical School by old Artyom Bhotsan-Khartschenko of the Russian Language Faculty, known for his extensive knowledge of linguistic folk history, and among a small group for his links with the Ukrainian diaspora from Mukden to Michigan. Khartschenko handed the small package to Katerina one day, saying only that it had come from the Far East.

That night she told Viktor that she'd received word from Lara. She had memorized the story, coming again and again to the two lines that were the central theme:

> *For the maidens were marked by the love of their God who had laid His hand on their shoulders, and leaving His mark He fused their hearts, and promised them never to part.*

Viktor knew well the strawberry birthmark on his wife's shoulder where she had been touched by God, and knew the story she and her sister had made up as little girls to explain this small imperfection that they both carried. Looking closely at the box, he could see faint markings on the shoulders of the two maidens, who, in a stylized way, looked hauntingly like his own Katerina. Then she said that Lara was the only living soul who could have written such a fairy tale. Everyone else who knew about the birthmarks had long since died.

Even after the old professor died, Katerina made use of Khartschenko's network to secretly correspond with her twin sister. "The Tale" eventually grew to more than one hundred pages containing every detail of their lives since they had been separated more than twenty years before.

The family decided together that Anatoly take the offer from the KGB since turning it down might attract even more prying. Once he had been cleared, he and his parents decided that the family secret had survived. They stored it along with all their other secrets in the locked mental compartment every citizen of the Soviet Union carefully maintained.

Another great fireball lit up the blue-black sky over Kharga. As Klimenko watched the flames, he thought of Sasha's parting words. He agreed: he'd better watch himself.

EIGHT

The sun shimmered on the snowcapped peaks of the Eastern Mountains that strained toward their distant rendezvous with the Karakorams, the Himalayas, and the Hindu Kush on the ancient Silk Route. They enveloped Alexander and ultimately protected him. He lived in almost perfect harmony with them, and had chosen this site as his base for the latest round of war between the Afghans and their invaders. *Bolshaya Igra.* The Great Game.

He had chosen the base with a little help from the computer mainframe at the National Reconnaissance Office in Washington, D.C. The computer analyzed the imagery of the area fifteen miles inside Afghanistan, just north of Parachinar, the Parrot's Beak of Pakistan's North West Frontier, looking for a protected valley that was virtually impossible to hit using either conventional gravity bombs or even the smartest guided bombs in the Soviet arsenal. Likewise for surface-to-surface missiles launched from a northerly or westerly direction. Eventually the mainframe selected a site within the tortured labyrinth of the Eastern Mountains that satisfied these requirements; only a nuclear attack could take it out, Alexander was cheerily assured by a straight-faced analyst.

After Alexander moved into the site six months earlier he agreed with the analyst immediately. The sheer walls of the narrow valley rose over six thousand feet and the switchback roads never yielded more than a few hundred yards of straight line for a bomb run that would have to start at a point already too far above his hideout to be effective.

A functional living and work space had been blasted out of the rock wall and expanded by building a two-story structure onto the entrance of the main cave. It blended perfectly with the mountain face, shielded from above by natural outcroppings, and by the heavy pine forest that crept above the valley floor. Among the network of man-made caves, two served as storage areas and the third as quarters for Alexander's handful of American officers who either worked full-time or visited part-time at Paktia. Another housed a diesel-powered generator that made ingenious use of a natural chimney to release the exhaust fumes high above the base camp, enabling the entrance to be sealed by a soundproof door. As a result the generator was nearly silent, lighting the cave network, running the pumps for the water system and the extensive equipment Alexander had installed in the climate-controlled communications center in the main cave.

A fifth cave served as a briefing and training center for what had become known in the resistance as Special Operations. After the main facilities were completed, at the Fashioner's suggestion Alexander had built a mosque for the use of the *mujāhids* who came to receive training. Beside it was a building that served as an eating and sleeping facility.

Ground-level security was provided by two troops of *mujāhids* carefully selected and commanded by Pakistani officers. The valley itself was further secured by virtue of its being within a region controlled by over fifty thousand Mujaheddin, all well-armed and dug in. It would take a Soviet division to penetrate the defenses.

On a high ridge was a well-camouflaged camp for fifty Mujaheddin and a handful of Pakistani officers. Their job was to control the ridgeline and the air above it, and to man the central communications bunker dug into the cliff face and camouflaged into practical invisibility. In the bunker was Alexander's communications relay center that maintained twenty-four-hour contact with key Mujaheddin commanders throughout Afghanistan. There was also a signals-intercept site. The Pakistani and Afghan radio operators continuously monitored most of the important enemy communications nets in Afghanistan.

For a helicopter-borne infantry attack to be successful, the aircraft would have to fly right into the 14.5 mm antiaircraft emplacements on the only area suitable for a landing zone. An infantry attack moving up the western face of the mountain would have to make its way up in single file on ledges less than a yard wide. Such a climb would be difficult for an experienced alpinist under peaceful conditions; trying it under enemy gunfire would be close to impossible. About the only viable route was a difficult path on the eastern face of the mountain, the side controlled by the Mujaheddin.

It had been a challenge to get established in Paktia, made even more difficult by Alexander's initial doubts about moving more than ten miles inside Afghanistan in the first place. Casey had beaten back his skepticism, saying he could make it work, and he'd been right. When the construction of his camp had been completed, Alexander named it the Hermitage, after Peter the Great's magnificent Winter Palace in St. Petersburg.

The radio call from the Fashioner came at midmorning, alerting Alexander that he and his guest had arrived under escort at the Ponderosa, his base camp about five miles from the Hermitage.

"How is your visitor?" Alexander queried into the handheld frequency-hopper radio.

"Still in one piece," the Fashioner answered.

"Let's get off the air. I'll be at your location within the hour." Alexander walked down to Special Operations and found J. D. Sawyer waiting for him.

J.D. had been his first choice as a chief of operations. In addition to his five years' experience in Special Forces, he spoke excellent Dari, one of the two main languages of Afghanistan, and had a solid academic and practical understanding of what the Afghans and their war were about. At thirty-five, and after eight years with the agency, he was destined to become a real expert on Central Asia.

"Let's take a bike ride," he said to the former Green Beret. "Musawwir just called in. He's at the Ponderosa with our lieutenant."

Twenty minutes later at a sentry post one thousand yards outside the main camp, they waited briefly until a radio exchange produced the expected wave-through. Along the last winding half mile to the Ponderosa, Alexander noted the increasing evidence of a well-planned security perimeter. There were several emplacements of ZU-23 double and quad antiaircraft cannon, and even more emplacements of 14.5 mm AA guns, all manned by serious and attentive crews. As they drove through the main camp they heard the telltale blast of radios as they passed gun emplacements, evidence that their approach was being dutifully signaled ahead.

Pushing up the final ridge and down into a broad pine-filled hollow, the Americans were struck by the natural order of the Fashioner's camp. Low-slung, mud-walled buildings built onto the side of the mountain extended into dugout caves. A widely dispersed network of ammunition bunkers had been carved into the mountainsides, each separated and insulated from the next. Stone-lined paths had been laid between the buildings. Everything appeared in natural harmony with the beauty of the forest and the snowcapped mountain peaks.

The Fashioner was waiting for them at the foot of the steps of the main camp building.

"Looks like we knocked their bolshevik butts in the dirt at Kharga, Musawwir," Alexander said as he embraced his friend. "My people are sending some satellite pictures."

The Fashioner grinned broadly.

"How is your prize holding up?"

"He's in the lockup down the valley. He's in good enough shape for a trade."

Alexander nodded. "We've got a confirmation from some intercepts of frantic open telephone talk between Kabul 40th Army, Moscow, and Wünsdorf that Orlov's son has gone missing. When Latif hears what he gave up for a handful of radios, we'd better all sleep with a Makarov under our pillows."

"Let's call on our guest." The Fashioner led them through a stand of pines into an area of deeply buried ammunition bunkers. Stopping at one of them, he pulled open the door and motioned to the occupant inside. Seconds later a Red Army lieutenant stepped into the sun. He saw only tall silhouettes ringed by bright halos until his eyes adjusted fully to the light.

Alexander spoke first in Russian. "Your father thinks the Dukhis have already cut off your balls and sent them to him in Wünsdorf in a caviar jar. He's going to be relieved to hear that you're in such good shape, Lieutenant."

"My name is Mikhail Sergeyevich Orlov." The lieutenant squinted and drew himself into a near military brace. "I am a senior lieutenant in the Army of the Soviet Un—"

"Why don't you cut out the crap, Lieutenant Orlov," interrupted Alexander. "This kind of thing never works out the way they taught you at the Frunze Academy. Don't worry about your father approving or not approving; all he wants is to get you back home and out of the hands of our friends here. I can make that happen, but if you keep behaving like a little tin soldier, I'll turn around here and leave you to the Dukhis."

"Who the hell are you and what is your authority here?" Orlov showed no sign of intimidation.

"Fair question. I am a private citizen who has volunteered to take part in the great patriotic cause of handing you and every other son of a bitch born north of the Amu Dar'ya his ass until you stop murdering these people and leave this country. Some of you understand this, beginning with your illustrious general secretary. I know who you are, and I know who your very important father is. He is terrorizing everybody below the rank of general between Wünsdorf and Kabul to get his precious boy back in one piece. What about it, Lieutenant?"

"You're an American," Orlov declared. "I've heard that eastern Afghanistan was crawling with CIA, but you don't quite fit the picture and neither does your Russian. I thought you were a Dukhi when I first saw you at the village."

"Lieutenant, let me tell you something. You've received kid-glove treatment for the last ten days because my big Afghan friend here and I heard about your capture, figured out who you were, and made an arrangement to get you out of the normal prisoner-of-war channels. I'm not asking you for gratitude; we did this because it was in our interest. Personally I don't give a shit what happens to you, but stop acting like you're in charge here. If you don't want to cooperate, my big friend here will hand you over to his countrymen."

Orlov reflected for a moment. "Where do we go from here?"

"I arrange to get a bunch of our people out of your prisons, and then I hand you over to your people. But until then, you will be the obedient guest of the mightiest warrior of the Fourth Afghan War, Al-Musawwir. All you have to do is keep your mouth shut and do as you're told until you get traded back to your army. Then maybe I'll have the good fortune to meet you again somewhere in these mountains and shoot you dead. It would be senseless to try to make a break for it. If you do, Lieutenant Orlov, you can be sure that your daddy will receive that jar of caviar."

Back at the base camp communications center Alexander and J.D. found Tim Rand, a thirty-year-old CIA man who handled a wide variety of tasks.

Alexander entered the crisp air-conditioning that kept the equipment from overheating. "Do you have the Alpha package set up for a broadcast?"

"It's all set. I can have you on the air in a few minutes."

Alexander drafted a message and handed it to Rand, who typed it into a keyboard unit. Moments later Alexander gave him a second clear text message.

Rand turned to Alexander. "Everything's set," he said.

The first message had been sent to the CIA Station in Islamabad where it was received within a couple of minutes after satellite relays broke all linkage between Alexander's Paktia base and the station a hundred and fifty miles away. There was little chance that the Soviet signals intelligence units even copied this method of transmission from their intercept sites around Kabul, but the extra precautions were prudent.

The second message used the communications set employed by clandestine agents to signal their CIA controllers, and was being transmitted on a system that had been deliberately delivered into the hands of the KGB's 16th Chief Directorate, Signals Intelligence and Cryptography. The CIA Station in Kabul ran an elaborate ruse allowing the KGB to capture a clandestine radio intended for an ostensible Afghan agent of the CIA in Kabul. Included in the "captured" cache were the cryptographic materials enabling the KGB to decipher any messages sent on the same system. The KGB were led to believe that the Americans were not aware of the loss. The operation allowed Alexander to send spurious encrypted message traffic to be intercepted and broken by the KGB whenever it fitted his needs, as it did now.

Moments later Rand reported to Alexander. "Both gone. Both worked."

"Let's see how well."

NINE

A week after the ambush, Polyakov thundered to Sasha, "Worthless fucking KGB. If I don't get some action I will personally send that incompetent Ukrainian asshole of a KGB colonel to Wünsdorf to explain to General Orlov why we can't find his son." Sasha passed the message along to his friend, enjoying the KGB officer's growing discomfort.

Klimenko had put out lines to the various resistance parties, and had come up with seventy-two positive sightings, putting Lieutenant Orlov in every corner of Afghanistan from Herāt in the far west, where he was supposedly the guest of warlord Ismail Khan, to the crowded corners of Peshawar in Pakistan, from Mazār-e Sharif in the north to Qandahār down south. Every resistance group in Afghanistan seemed to have information on Orlov, almost all of it for sale. One rebel commander was even willing to send a hand and ear from the lieutenant to establish the authenticity of his claim, but prepayment would be required.

None of these reports passed Klimenko's logic checks or even piqued his interest. By the end of the tenth day he began to worry that if he didn't get a solid lead soon, the politics of the problem would take over. Polyakov and the army crowd would shift their priorities from getting Orlov back to just getting Klimenko, their real sights lining up on KGB Chairman Viktor Chebrikov.

On the afternoon of the tenth day he got his break. He was studying it when the telephone jangled. "Klimenko," he said wearily.

"Tolya, this time I am not shitting you. Polyakov has decided that ten days is enough, and he's going to have your ass. He said he would have that fat-assed, vodka-soaked defense minister tell Chebrikov that you have botched the Orlov case so thoroughly that you will be responsible for the boy's death by buggery and dismemberment. I shit you not, unless something breaks on Orlov in the next few hours, you will be history, Tolya!"

Looking at the intercept before him, Klimenko smiled. "Sasha, please go into your boss's office and tell him that Anatoly Viktorovich says hello and that the general should go fuck himself."

"Great! Now he wants to commit suicide!"

"Sasha! I've found Orlov!" Klimenko blurted into the phone, concerned now that Krasin would burst into Polyakov's office with his message.

"You really found him?"

"Yes, and now all I've got to do is get him back."

"Shall I tell Polyakov that you have something on Orlov?"

"Tell him precisely the following: As of this afternoon Orlov was in the hands of Dushman who are clearly aware of his value alive. He is in good shape and is probably in southern Nangarhar or in Paktia. Then you can tell him to go fuck himself."

Ten minutes later Krasin burst into Klimenko's office. "Polyakov's already on the telephone to Wünsdorf telling Orlov's daddy that he has managed to find his precious missing son while the Kabul KGB was jacking off in the ashes of Kharga. If you're shitting me about this we will both have to head for the Khyber."

"Take a look at this." Klimenko handed the intercept to Krasin.

TOP SECRET/SPECIAL CONTROLS AND ACCESS. NOT TO BE REPRODUCED OR DISSEMINATED WITHOUT ORIGINATOR CLEARANCE. The date-time group of the transmission was shortly after noon on September 4, 1986. Origin of the transmitter was probably Paktia province, or southern Nangarhar province. Message addressee was probably the American CIA base in Peshawar.

The second sheet gave the Russian translation. Krasin studied it word by word:

> From Alpha Four to Alpha Onex Msg onex rpt msg onex Pls advise pertinent info and interest in Lt Mikhail Sergeyevich Orlov DOB 17Jul60 Moscowx Orlov captured ten nights ago south of Kabulx Wounded but in no dangerx Photographs on his person and other evidence indicate Orlov may be son of general officer in Red Armyx Will alternate holding area for Orlov daily until further guidance receivedx Believe Orlov can bring about release of significant numbers of our brothersx Pls advisex Trust in Godx End msg onex Endx

"How does it look to you?" Sasha asked his KGB friend, deferring to Klimenko's professional judgment.

"It's genuine. The information on Orlov is accurate. Even the photograph with his father is in our follow-up report on him. The transmitter for this message, as well as the crypto system, are known CIA systems. The only reason the 16th was able to break out this message was because we got lucky a couple of weeks ago and picked up a radio cache laid down by the CIA station here in Kabul. There's no doubt about this. Orlov is in safe hands, so to speak." But Klimenko's voice betrayed doubt. It looked too easy.

ISLAMABAD, PAKISTAN, SEPTEMBER 4

Jim Houston, the CIA's station chief in Islamabad, read the message from Paktia, then carefully drafted a response. It would be sent from a transmitter in Peshawar later that same day, using the same Alpha radio and cipher system that Alexander had used for the KGB intercept operators.

> Alpha One to Alpha Fourx Msg onex Rpt msg onex Acknowledge receipt your msg onex Friends advise that Mikhail Sergeyevich Orlov is son of Soviet commander of western group of forcesx They stress it imperative that he be treated in accordance with all accepted international protocols on handling of prisoners of warx The friends accept no responsibility for the capture or subsequent treatment of Orlov but strongly advise that you act in accordance with international law and arrange for prisoner trade with Soviet occupation forcesx We agree with friends' assessmentx There is nothing to be gained from harming Orlov, despite his complicity in murderx There is much to be gained from using him to free our brothersx You are authorized to conduct all negotiations for prisoner exchange but first clear lists with Alpha Onex Pls acknowledge concurrence with this guidancex Trust in Godx End msg onex End endx

Houston rechecked the message from Paktia to assure himself that he had all the points right. He thought it a little overdone, but understood that the legalistic excess would be a source of comfort in both Moscow and Washington.

TEN

Klimenko looked at the new Alpha intercept. The language was straightforward:

> Alpha Four for Alpha Onex Msg twox Have transmitted by courier letter with photo of Orlov and copy of identity card to Russian adviser at Ali Khelx Have requested a meeting with no more than two Russians from Kabul with authority to discuss exchange of Orlov for all brother commanders known to be held by Kabul regimex Meeting place is two days hence at tank with soldiers site nine miles from Ali Khelx Have assured Russians that there will be no rpt no effort to attack maximum two unarmed helicopters from Kabul arriving Ali Khel for negotiations in two daysx We can guarantee the safety of Russians coming this meetingx Pls forward soonest names of all brother commanders known to be in hands of Kabul regimex Will need this list before initial meeting with Russiansx Envision initial meeting will establish negotiating positions onlyx Do not expect much otherwisex Would hope that this negotiation will not be overly drawn out but am prepared to take as long as needed to ensure release of our brothersx Pls respond soonestx Trust in Godx End msg twox EndxEndxEndx

It all fitted with the message that came in from Ali Khel four hours later:

From Major Andrey Belov/Ali Khel Detachment One for Commander 40th, Kabul.

Sir!

We have received from an unidentified rebel commander a letter in perfect Russian explaining that one Senior Lieutenant M. S. Orlov (probably identical to Subject of 40th/Kabul Circular Message/Secret 0456/86) is safe and well and in the hands of unnamed rebels. Letter requests a meeting between (presume) rebel commander holding Orlov and no more than two Soviet Army officers from Kabul 40th who are authorized to commence negotiations on the exchange of Orlov for unnamed Dushman prisoners held by the government of the Democratic Republic of Afghanistan. Date for the meeting suggested as two days from now at a site about nine miles from my position. The rebel commander has provided guarantees that there will be no attack against helicopters without rocket pods arriving Ali Khel from Kabul for negotiations.

Included in the letter was a photograph of Lieutenant Orlov dressed in Afghan attire and an apparently legitimate copy of his officer's identity card. I am acquainted personally with Orlov and can verify that the photograph is of Lieutenant Orlov of the 105th Guards Airborne.

I am sending your office the letter and photograph with the supply helicopter scheduled to arrive at Kabul about one hour after sunset tonight. I have a secure means to get an answer back swiftly via courier to the author of the letter. I will await your early instructions.

Respectfully,
Major Andrey Belov

Klimenko immediately sent a reply to the major asking him to prepare for the arrival of two officers from Kabul 40th with two helicopters without rocket pods at one hour after sunrise two days hence, and to send word to the rebel commander that a meeting was agreeable. He ordered Belov to arrange for transport and security for the meeting at the site known as Tank With Soldiers. He signed the radio messages with Krasin's name because the order was tactical and beyond his own authority.

Then he called Sasha. "Krasin, get your worthless ass over here," he said, and hung up.

Ten minutes later Sasha burst into Klimenko's office already shooting off his mouth. "You're beginning to sound like that idiot I work for."

"Sit down, Sasha, and read the two latest communiqués on Orlov."

Sasha read both the radio message from Major Belov and the Alpha intercept, the latter in both the English original and the Russian translation. After he finished he said, "I know this major in Ali Khel. He was with me the first time around in the 105th when we came for Christmas about a hundred years ago. He's back for his third go-around. He told me once that as much as he hates it here, he can't go home without literally going crazy within a week. Lost his wife to some Kremlin warrior, and feels hopelessly lonely back there. There are a lot of boys like that. He's a pretty good officer."

"Can we rely on him to set up a meeting with the Dukhis for us?"

"What do you mean us?" Sasha shot back.

"You and I are going to Ali Khel the day after tomorrow to meet these Dukhis who have carried off General Orlov's precious son. You will organize the MI-8s. I want two helicopters, both without rocket pods, and you will have to keep that jerk boss of yours from trying to send one of his worthless colonels down to Ali Khel to grab all the glory."

"Don't worry about Polyakov or anybody else in 40th trying to steal your glory on this caper—at least not yet. If there's half a chance that the Dukhis will cut off the lieutenant's balls before they hand him over to you, he will want the operation to be one hundred percent KGB. But if you get Orlov back for him in one piece, he might have you thrown out of the next helicopter and take all the credit himself."

"Good. Then it's all settled. Arrange the helicopters for day after tomorrow, arriving at Ali Khel at precisely one hour after sunrise."

Sasha studied his good friend for a long moment and then said quietly, "Okay, I'll do it. I'll also brief Polyakov so that you don't set him off in a rage. I'll explain that by going along myself I'm giving him the option to step away from this if it goes bad, or to steal it from you if it starts to look good. He'll like that."

That evening, Klimenko received via helicopter Belov's envelope containing the photographs and the letter from the rebels holding Orlov. The lieutenant was dressed in Afghan garb, and Klimenko noted his awkward self-consciousness after almost two weeks in captivity.

Klimenko read the letter carefully, then retrieved the one found in the timing device at Karim's grove. The paper grade and weight of both matched exactly. There were no watermarks. There never were. The CIA always used sterile bond. Both letters were typed by American electrics with Cyrillic fonts, he was certain. No Soviet-made machines looked this good.

But it was the literary style that clinched it: perfect Russian, if somewhat stilted. Klimenko knew the letters had been written by the same person, but he also knew that he should keep what he had deduced to himself.

He picked up the telephone again and dialed slowly because the archaic switching system couldn't handle speed.

"Shadrin."

"Major, I want that final list of Dushman prisoners in my hands by 0900 hours tomorrow morning. I will be traveling to the border area the day after tomorrow to start some discussions on this matter. Can you have it to me by then, and reasonably complete?"

"This list is as complete as I can get it, barring some new captures in the next day or so. It's over forty names, and you'll have it tomorrow," the major answered.

A few minutes later Major Shadrin dialed a number he had committed to memory almost a year ago.

It was answered on the second ring. "Nikitenko."

"Sir, this is Lieutenant Dmitrov at the dispensary. I know it's late, but you asked me to let you know the minute the results of your blood work were back from Tashkent. I just received it and your liver functions look fine. This is the third normal report in the last three months, and it probably means that you're fully recovered from your bout with hepatitis, at least for now. But you should still exercise care."

"Thank you, Lieutenant. Good news is welcome, late or early. Could you send the written results over tomorrow morning by 1100 hours?"

"Yes sir, no problem at all. Eleven hundred tomorrow it will be."

Shadrin hung up and ran his finger down a list of coded phrases written into his notebook until he found "late or early." Next to it was the notation "minus twelve." That set the time for the meeting with Nikitenko twelve hours earlier than the hour mentioned on the telephone. He had just over an hour and a half to get to the usual quiet place. Shadrin felt proud. Sometimes he actually liked the snitch game he was playing, particularly if it brought him closer to bringing down the arrogant Colonel Klimenko. Nikitenko would believe him now that Klimenko was a dangerous defeatist, Shadrin thought. He'd have to pay attention to him with the speculation spreading around 40th Army Headquarters that the "Dear Colonel" letter was intended for Klimenko, speculation that Shadrin had carefully fueled.

Nikitenko sat in his office at 40th Army Headquarters for several minutes musing over Shadrin's call. I hope Shadrin has something more on Klimenko than his little Chekist notebook full of the colonel's irreverent, defeatist quotes. Maybe Shadrin finally has the means to get even with Klimenko for revealing him as the coward he is. It didn't matter that Klimenko had been right, that Shadrin really was a coward. Nikitenko knew about such desires to get even.

THE PONDEROSA, 0830 HOURS, SEPTEMBER 5

Alexander rode his camouflaged dirt bike up to the Fashioner's camp early the next morning, then walked to the ammunition bunker area where Orlov was being held.

Orlov had seen Alexander when he rounded the bend in the path, but kept his eyes closed. Only when Alexander's shadow crossed his face did he sullenly acknowledge that his privacy had been invaded.

"Don't bother to stand to attention," Alexander greeted him.

"I only stand at attention for real officers in real armies, not for free-booters like you," Orlov said with half a smile.

"Don't kid yourself about the trappings of real armies, Lieutenant. These people are doing a better job of soldiering than your army has since it invaded this country."

Once again Orlov was taken aback by this man's slightly old-fashioned Russian. At first he hadn't been able to figure out what made it so distinctive, but he now realized that it was the absence of socialist argot that set him apart from contemporary Soviets.

Orlov spoke clearly and with dignity. "Surely you haven't come here to tell me how pathetic my army is, how rotten my society is, and how much better off I might be in California, or wherever the CIA puts the U.S.S.R.'s misfits and rejects these days."

"No, Lieutenant. I'm not going to try to talk you into having doubts about your army, or about the fraud in your system, or the rottenness of your ruling class. From the look and sound of you, you're probably doing all that yourself. Most of you are, and you don't need my help. And I'm certainly not going to try to talk you into going to California, or any place else we're resettling your growing number of misfits, as you put it, because you haven't earned it."

"Then I'm not going to get the standard CIA pitch they warn us about before we come out here? You know how it goes: you offer me the ticket to Hollywood, the Chevy pickup truck, and the blonde with long legs and big tits, and I go on TV and say 'Fuck Communism.' All my friends back in Kabul are going to be disappointed when I tell them that thc CIA had me in its clutches and didn't even try to tempt me with all the usual decadent bullshit."

"We don't need any more spoiled brats."

"What happens next? When can I get back to my people?"

"I'm working on it now. By now they know that you're safe and in the hands of someone, how shall I put it, responsible. I'll be meeting with your representatives shortly. It may not be as fast as you'd like, since I'm going to ask the thugs in Kabul to empty their prisons before I hand you over. It hasn't always been so easy for Russian soldiers to return to the great Red Army after being taken prisoner." There was a slight shift in Alexander's tone, signaling an about-to-be-shared confidence.

"What would you know about that?" Orlov asked warily.

"I know what my father told me. He knew all about what happened to Russians who got themselves captured in the Great Patriotic War."

"And I suppose you're going to tell me about it?"

"Yes, because you should know about what happened to my father and a lot of other fine Russian officers."

Alexander sat down on the rough bench next to Orlov. "My father was a senior lieutenant in the Red Army when he was captured by the Germans in 1941, at age twenty-six, almost exactly your age. He spent more than three years in German labor camps, first in Poland and later in Germany. In early 1945 he was liberated by the U.S. Army after it crossed the Rhine, and like a lot of young Soviet Army officers he took up the fight alongside the Americans as they moved toward Berlin. He was seriously wounded outside of Dresden in April 1945. It turned out that his wounds saved his life. After the Germans surrendered, tens of thousands of Russians who, like my father, had been in labor camps, were handed over to the Soviet Army. I don't know which threatened Stalin more, their captivity by the Germans or their exposure to the Allies after they were liberated, but his solution for these now suspect officers was a bullet in the neck or disappearance into the Gulag.

"The American armored commander gave my father a choice: go east and take his chances with the Red Army, which was almost no chance at all, or stay put and eventually return to America with him. He went to America by way of a displaced persons camp in Germany, where he spent two years and where he met and married my mother, a Ukrainian girl who had seen her share of horrors. I was born in that DP camp, one of the original stateless urchins in General Marshall's Europe. We went to the United States when I was a few months old."

Orlov believed every word of it, and it shook him. "That's all part of history now."

"You're probably right," Alexander said thoughtfully. "Certainly not for someone like you, with your pedigree. But there's a side of the Red Army—the side they still don't mention at Frunze Academy, the side even your father won't talk about—that is sheer terror. Tell me what they taught you about the Red Army officer corps being cut down between 1937 and 1939."

"A few disloyal officers were removed for plotting the overthrow of established authority, and . . ." Orlov paused in the middle of his textbook answer.

"Forty thousand officers were taken out behind the shed and shot in the back of the neck!"

"I've never heard such a number before! Nobody talks about it—not my instructors at the Frunze, not my father, nobody!"

"All of these secrets will come out, Mikhail Sergeyevich. You can't keep them dammed up much longer." As Alexander left, he handed him a Russian-language edition of Solzhenitsyn's *Gulag Archipelago.* "You don't have to read this, Mikhail Sergeyevich, and please don't think I'm using it to get you to defect. But you might find it illuminating considering what we've just been talking about."

Alexander returned wearily to his office, where Rand had two messages waiting for him. The first was a cable from Houston in Islamabad, transmitted over a secure CIA cipher system, giving him a list of Muja-heddin commanders believed to be in the hands of the Kabul regime and worthy of being traded with the Soviets for the turnover of Orlov. The forty-seven names had been provided by the leaders of the seven resistance groups in Peshawar. Houston also noted that he was sending a second list over the compromised Alpha system that had over ninety names on it, but that about fifty of these were believed dead, and that this could be ascertained during the course of negotiations with the Soviets.

KABUL, 1530 HOURS, SEPTEMBER 6

Klimenko studied the latest intercept from Alpha One, presumably from the CIA operation in Peshawar, to Alpha Four, the man in Paktia he was certain he would meet up with the next morning. The message contained a list of ninety-four "Brother Commanders," and invoked the name of God in asking Alpha Four to secure their releases. Klimenko looked at his own list of Dushman commanders held in Pul-I-Charki and other prisons in Afghanistan. It had only thirty-three names. He hadn't expected the opening round to start off with such a wide gap, but if Alpha One was giving away its opening position he was sure that the CIA knew that the Russians could read their radio traffic. He was not sure why they were giving away their position, but knew he would figure it out as he moved into the negotiations. He was increasingly satisfied that he had kept secret the fact that the capture of the cipher system had been a setup.

ELEVEN

Major Andrey Belov was at the helicopter landing pad just after sunrise. He took out his collapsible telescope and began to scan the horizon in a slow three hundred sixty degrees. Bleached earth was broken only by the harsh, jagged features of the terrain as it dropped vertically around him. The entire basin appeared deforested; only a few sturdy scrub pines had survived the destruction of battle or the foraging for fuel.

Belov swung his scope back to his own fortress compound. In the last century it controlled commerce and tribal mischief from what had been an ideal vantage point, but it had hardly been improved since then. The low building he used for his own quarters was protected from most up-range Dukhi firing positions, but the rest of the fort looked hopelessly primitive perched atop the plateau, and Belov knew he could do little to improve its defenses. It represented the futility of everything he had seen in the four-plus years he had spent doing his "socialist internationalist duty" since the invasion of 1979. What a crock of shit, he thought. His reflections were broken by a squelch blast from the radio hanging from his belt.

"Volga, this is Aurora One. Do you read me, over?"

"Aurora One, this is Volga. I read you loud and clear. What is your ETA?"

"Volga, we will be above your position in twelve minutes, approaching from the northwest. Do you copy, over?"

"I copy you, Aurora One. All is clear at the landing zone. I will release green smoke when I hear your engines. Do you copy, over?"

"Roger, Volga. Green smoke. Aurora One out."

THE HERMITAGE, 0445 HOURS, SEPTEMBER 7

The Fashioner and Alexander drove out of the narrow valley alongside a creek swollen with runoff. The water level would rise during the day as the increasing heat accelerated the snowmelt, but at this time of year the trail would not come under water.

They had sent Engineer Musa and ten *mujāhids* ahead to a preselected site near the meeting place last evening. Alexander had instructed Engineer Musa to have an open tent erected, and the ground laid with Afghan carpets. It had been agreed that the representatives of the resistance would arrive at the site first, followed by the Russians an hour later.

TANK WITH SOLDIERS, PAKTIA, 0550 HOURS, SEPTEMBER 7

The sun had cleared the crest of the hills. The ornate tent had been set up in a small stand of pines beside a briskly running stream and the carpets laid out carefully beneath its cooling cover. Camp furniture was in place, bottles of mineral water and a variety of soft drinks had been set in the creek to chill. A large brass samovar was perched on a low wooden table, a charcoal fire glowing in its belly as it heated water for strong black tea. It was a scene from a century or more ago, when other foreign armies had ranged up and down these valleys playing a game that involved parlaying more often than fighting.

Two hundred yards from the tent was a dismembered Soviet T-64 tank, white numbers 232 visible on its battered turret, its treads and bogey rollers long ago removed by scrap dealers, leaving only the tank body, turret, and cannon barrel. Atop the tank, which had been disabled by a land mine and bore the marks of target practice by youthful Afghan gunners, were two crudely fashioned straw dummies carefully wired into place. Wearing Russian summer battle uniforms, their crude, clownlike faces had been drawn on heavy white cloth, and topped with Russian hats. This macabre spectacle had become the perfect photo opportunity for *mujāhids* and journalists alike, and each side knew exactly where this unique landmark was.

The Landcruiser pulled into the meeting site at a few minutes before six, and Alexander and the Fashioner dismounted. "Let's see if we have company in the area," Alexander said as he pulled out a blackout and switched it on. Instantly the red light blinked in sync with the audio.

The Fashioner was cheerful. "We should have company in about an hour."

ALI KHEL, 0600 HOURS, SEPTEMBER 7

The first MI-8 set down at Ali Khel at almost exactly 0600 hours. The three Soviet officers and four soldiers instinctively bent down and away from the chopper blades as they hurried to where Major Belov was standing at attention. "Welcome to Ali Khel, Colonel," he said as he greeted Klimenko.

Klimenko looked around at the old fort and said wryly, "This must be the best kept secret of Afghanistan, Major. I can see why you volunteered for this garden spot."

Turning to Krasin, Belov slapped his old comrade hard on the shoulder. "I heard you were back, but I thought you'd given up soldiering for a headquarters job. It's good to see you, Sasha!"

"And you, Andrey. I heard that you'd gone native down here."

Belov led the officers to a Soviet Army scout car. Smoothing out a map on the hood, Belov briefed his visitors. "We will leave here in a few minutes and proceed along this creek for ten miles to the site called Tank With Soldiers. Our four patrols report that everything seems quiet. My lieutenant is already at the meeting site."

"Volga! This is Volga One. Do you copy? Over."

"I copy, Volga One. What do you have for me, over?" replied Belov.

"Dushman team arrived at my location about five minutes ago. Security situation unchanged. You are cleared to depart for my location, with arrival at 0700 hours. Do you copy, over?"

"Copy, Volga One, and out." Turning back to Klimenko, he said, "We will proceed from here with my Afghan captain and four of his troops following us to a point two miles from the site, where he will drop off with his men and wait. We'll make the last couple of miles alone and link up with Lieutenant Panov, who will be with us at the meeting. Each side is allowed two principals and two armed combatants along for security. It looks pretty straightforward to me, but of course it could all turn to shit, in which case you two can kiss your asses good-bye."

"Always cheerful, Belov. That explains the brilliant career you've had as the oldest major in the Red Army," Sasha said.

"We ought to move out now," Belov said, "but one last word, gentlemen. As long as you're here at Ali Khel don't wander away from the main compound for any reason whatsoever. I have mined all the approaches to the old fort. There are two exit channels, but only I know them with any certainty. Not even my Afghan comrades know how to get out through the minefields. They might take off when the shells start coming in if they think they can get through the mines. I have to make this same speech to all of my visitors, because one of your fat-assed desk jockeys from Kabul, a thoroughly worthless major, took off souvenir hunting by the crashed helicopter a month back, and got his dick blown off, along with just about everything else. We had to send him back in three bags."

"I heard about that," Sasha said. "When the graves people got his body back in Kabul they found most of the big pieces but not his dick. It really bothered them, particularly that fat bitch in the morgue at the airport. She really got worked up over that."

TANK WITH SOLDIERS

Waiting comfortably in the tent, Alexander and the Fashioner heard the growl of the Soviet scout car straining in low gear. As it came into view a hundred yards away, a Soviet officer left his position of cover where the Afghan Army patrol was reported to have been holed up and climbed in. A minute later the vehicle pulled up fifteen yards from the tent, and two of the Soviets, both unarmed, but one of them carrying a shoulder bag, got out and walked briskly toward the tent. The other two officers remained with the car.

As he looked at the Fashioner Klimenko thought, that's one of the biggest Afghans I've ever seen. The Dukhi behind him looked a little older, but was probably no more than about forty. Each of them looked confident and intelligent, and he wondered which one was his pen pal.

"I am Colonel Ivan Vasilliyevich Belenko, and I am authorized to speak for the Commander of the Soviet Expeditionary Forces in Afghanistan in the matter of Senior Lieutenant M. S. Orlov." In fluent Dari, Klimenko opened the negotiations by giving himself an alias. He did not bother to introduce Sasha. "My comrade does not speak Dari, but he understands English well, as do I. Which language would you prefer?"

The Fashioner answered, "For the convenience of your major we can conduct your discussions in English. Shall we take our seats?"

Klimenko began. "Shall we dispense with formalities and get straight to the business which has brought us together? I assume you are authorized to deal with us?" He did not wait for an answer. "My statement is intended to be straightforward and reflects the position of the First Deputy Commander of the Soviet Expeditionary Forces in Afghanistan, General Boris Polyakov. It is as follows: You are to bring about the immediate release of Senior Lieutenant M. S. Orlov whom you have illegally detained since August twenty-fifth, when bandit elements of your population murdered three of Lieutenant Orlov's comrades, all Soviet citizens, near Kabul on the road to Gardēz, and took Lieutenant Orlov captive. I am not offering concessions for the release of Lieutenant Orlov, but am prepared to advise you of the consequences if you fail to release him."

The Fashioner responded without hesitation. "I agree that we dispense with the usual formalities, Colonel, but I take your opening statement as a useless threat. Were I to take it seriously, I would simply tell you to fly back to Kabul and tell General Boris Polyakov to go fuck himself, but I believe that will not be necessary. You know what we have come here to accomplish, so let us get on with it."

Klimenko also knew that his opening threat was necessary theater for the audience back in Kabul. He wasn't certain which of the two men was in charge, but he sensed that the Fashioner was not his pen pal. Either way, these two were no primitives. "I'm listening." He leaned back in his chair.

Alexander was watching Belenko with a mix of professional interest and unease. Something about the way the man spoke and carried himself seemed familiar, but he couldn't place it. Belenko wore the insignia of an infantry colonel, but his bearing and demeanor were not those of a combat-line officer in the Red Army, and his Dari was just too good. He handled himself more like a staff officer. Belenko was probably not even his name.

On the other hand, the major with him looked every bit the combat veteran. His battle dress uniform was faded and he wore the telltale blue-and-white striped paratrooper's T-shirt. The major and the colonel seemed to have little in common, but they showed signs of an easy friendship.

The Fashioner pulled out a neatly typed three-page document, and pushed it across to Klimenko. "This is a list of our brother commanders known to be held prisoner by the Kabul puppets. There are ninety-four names on the list, and you will note that they have been arranged in alphabetical order in Dari. Here is a second list of the same commanders with the names transliterated into Russian so that you can work swiftly to locate these men and bring about their early release," the Fashioner said as he handed over the second list. "Our position is simple. We will release Senior Lieutenant M. S. Orlov when all of our brothers on this list have been handed over to us at a location of our choosing. We will not waste your time or ours in futile searches for compromises."

Klimenko examined the list, then spoke to his companion in Russian. Sasha handed him the Soviet list, and he studied both, scowling in concentration.

Alexander's unease grew.

Klimenko set the documents in two neat stacks, leaned back and took off his hat to wipe his brow. "It appears to me that you have chosen to put the excesses of your opening position in these documents, gentlemen. Some of the names on the list you have provided are of men who were captured more than two years ago. Many of them died shortly after they were taken prisoner by our forces or by those of the legitimate government of the Democratic Republic of Afghanistan. In most cases they died from wounds received in battle before their capture. Others died during indiscriminate rocket attacks by your side against Kabul. What expression do your American friends use? Friendly fire, isn't it?"

The Fashioner looked at Klimenko evenly. "We accept that some of the brothers on our list have been martyred since their capture by the Russian invaders and their Kabul puppets. We all know about the conditions at Pul-I-Charki, Colonel. But in those cases where our brothers have died, we will expect you to give a convincing accounting. Only then will you get your precious Lieutenant Orlov. I would add, Colonel, that Orlov's identity is well known to us. He is no ordinary lieutenant."

Klimenko studied the Fashioner for a long moment. "Let us assume for the sake of argument that our interest in Lieutenant Orlov would be the same regardless of his identity. Let us assume for the sake of argument that we are prepared to address any discrepancies on our separate lists. Here are the names of thirty-three detainees now in the hands of the Kabul government who are in reasonably good health and can serve as the basis for our discussion. As with your list, the names are in both Dari and in Russian."

The Fashioner took Klimenko's lists, glanced at the one in Dari, and handed them both to Alexander, who kept up the pretense that he was Afghan. He looked more closely at the Russian list.

The Fashioner spoke carefully. "I will accept for the sake of argument that your side can resolve any discrepancies between the lists."

Klimenko leaned forward in his chair. "Might I suggest, then, that this opening session be concluded. I will communicate the essence of our discussions to Kabul and ask that the competent authorities resolve the discrepancies in your list. I ask that you do the same with the materials we have given you, and that we meet here again tomorrow to discuss any new information that we may have discovered overnight. I would greatly appreciate it if you would refrain from firing at our helicopters flying in or out of Ali Khel, as this would only impede our progress."

"Agreed," said the Fashioner. He then rose and said, "May I offer the colonel and his fellow officers a chilled drink before you return to Ali Khel?"

"Yes," said Klimenko as he and Sasha stood up.

The Fashioner motioned to the two nearby *mujāhids* to bring the drinks from the creek. When Klimenko looked at the trove, he didn't know whether to laugh or simply stare in disbelief. Symbols of the great Western foes—Perrier, Coke, 7UP—were arranged before him. These guys have chilled Perrier, Klimenko thought, and we can't even get our hands on enough water-purification tablets to keep our troops healthy. He picked up three Cokes and handed them to Sasha, motioning with a nod to the nearby jeep, then took a Perrier. Turning to the Fashioner and Alexander, he raised his drink. "Gentlemen, to your health and the successful conclusion of our business."

Alexander drank to the toast and in perfect Russian added, "To the completion of our task, and to the service of the Motherland."

Klimenko raised his can again. "To the service of the Motherland." *So this is my pen pal,* he thought.

• • •

An hour later in his office Alexander and the Fashioner studied Klimenko's list. The Russians had done an earnest job. The difference between the lists was only fourteen names. "It's in the ballpark," Alexander said. "They must want Orlov badly enough to forgo the usual dickering."

"I think we can narrow the difference some more tomorrow. We need to get the list of the fourteen unaccounted for to our friend Rambo. With his lines into Pul-I-Charki prison, he may be able to tell us if any of the fourteen have died or are too ill to use as trading material. Can we get an answer from him within a day?"

"It's worth a try. I'll get something off to him as soon as we finish here."

"It seems to me it's up to Belenko to account for the others, the fifty-odd we figured were dead, and he should be able to do that within a week or so. It will probably take another week to arrange for the swap. Our brothers could simply step through the border at Torkham Gate into Pakistan. We can hand Orlov over at Tank With Soldiers at the same time."

Alexander looked at a calendar on his desk. "That would probably be the first week of October."

The Fashioner nodded. *"Insh'allah.* I'll be here tomorrow morning at seven. By the way, what did you think of our two Soviet friends today?"

"I think we're dealing with the right guys. But Belenko really has me racking my brain. That's probably not his name. He must be a ringer for some Soviet I've met in my murky past, but I can't pin it down. I haven't got a make on the major, but my guess is that he's a repeater, one of those war lovers who keeps coming back looking for something, but never finding it."

"It's going to take us a few years to see what this war has done to a generation of Afghan boys. It's going to be hard for them to go back to their old society after the war ends—if it ever does," the Fashioner said wearily.

"It will end," Alexander said.

"Yes it will, and we'll win it," the Fashioner said.

ALI KHEL, 1530 HOURS, SEPTEMBER 7

Klimenko and Sasha sat in the only building in Ali Khel big enough to serve as a headquarters orderly room for the Soviet advisers to the DRA battalion.

"I think their first list is about twice what they eventually expect us to hand over to them. I'm convinced they're simply trying to smoke out the fate of their commanders who have died along the way," Klimenko said as he studied the lists of prisoners.

"Maybe we should have held back a few names so that we could sweeten the pot tomorrow."

"I don't think so. If it were a carpet-bazaar deal, they'd have given us a list of every known dirtball who's gone missing since Alexander of Macedonia came through. They could have asked us to empty Pul-I-Charki prison, but they didn't." Turning to Belov, he said, "Major, I've got to send a signal to Kabul."

On the way to the signals van Klimenko thought about his encounter with the Russian-speaking Dushman. He had no intention of telling Sasha about the exchange of toasts to the Motherland quite yet.

Late that night Alexander went through the hidden door in his bookcase to his private quarters, a windowless cave with amenities. He took a long, hot shower, and feeling almost drugged, settled into bed. He glanced at the silver-framed picture of Katerina on the nightstand, and then stared hard at the features he now realized he'd seen in a Russian colonel's face that morning. Reaching under his nightstand he took out a slim volume bound in leather and read again the story of the heroic struggle of two fairy-tale maidens from Kiev. When he finished two hours later, he knew why he had been so bothered that morning by the Russian colonel. But could it really be true? And what could it mean?

TWELVE

Klimenko and Sasha were drinking tea and eating stale ration biscuits with Belov when a haggard Shadrin entered the room.

"The watch officer at the special center had this envelope for you, Colonel. He acted as if he were handing over the Romanov diamonds." Shadrin proffered the top secret intercept of the Alpha message that Alexander had transmitted the night before.

After carefully reading the intercept, Klimenko folded it into his breast pocket.

"Last night we received sensitive and reliable intelligence from our agents in Peshawar reporting that the Dushman have inflated their original list of prisoners significantly, and that they are actually seeking the release of only about forty-seven Dukhis. The thirty-three that were on our original list were all on theirs as well, which leaves a difference of only fourteen. How did you do with the prison records last night, Major?"

"I worked all night with the worthless KHAD prison wardens and came up with some, but not all, of what you asked for. We can probably squeeze out a few more, but it may take longer than you'd like, possibly a month," Shadrin responded.

"Let's see what you have. We need to show some progress at our meeting with these bastards in a couple of hours."

"We located three in Pul-I-Charki and one in a holding area near Baghram. These four weren't on our original lists because they were so badly wounded or ill they had been listed as dead two months ago. The only trouble is the hardheaded bastards didn't die. You're going to have to make the choice of ordering them killed off or handing them over to the Dukhis ninety percent dead."

Klimenko thought for a moment. "I'll play it straight and tell the Dushman that we've located another four who are just about dead, and that it's their choice whether we hand them over, possibly killing them in the process. Are there any medical reports on them?"

"Prison medical records are pretty thin, as you can see: chest wounds, moribund; gangrenous leg, moribund—that kind of diagnosis." Shadrin handed the colonel a thin file.

"What are the chances of finding any more on the list alive?"

"Not good. We can confirm that of the fifty-seven remaining names on the list, about forty died after capture."

"You did well, Major. We're getting closer to the position we need to be in to negotiate the timing of the swap, certainly close enough for the second day of discussions."

"Thank you, Colonel." In spite of his deep hatred of Klimenko, Shadrin was pleased that his work had been recognized.

Klimenko checked his watch. "We have about two hours. Shadrin, you can come along to meet the Dukhis. You might learn something."

When they were alone, Klimenko said to Sasha, "I want you to help me split up our two Dukhis this morning. I think our silent friend, the smaller of the two, may be willing to talk a little more openly if I can get him away from his big brother commander."

THE HERMITAGE, 0630 HOURS, SEPTEMBER 8

Alexander joined Tim Rand in the communications center to review the overnight message traffic. When he came through the steel hatch on the floor, Rand had laid out the messages on a small table along with a mug of strong black coffee. Houston in Islamabad acknowledged receipt of his message of the night before, but offered no guidance or recommendations in the Orlov affair. A second message, an ostensible Alpha answer from Peshawar, had been prepared by Houston, and was thus readable by the KGB in Kabul, acknowledging receipt of the Russian list of thirty-three names, praising Allah for the progress so far, and urging him to continue to pressure the Russians for accountability on all ninety-four brothers, alive or dead. Finally, Rambo confirmed that six of the fourteen commanders whose names were transmitted to him the previous night had died in prison during the last year. He added that the six martyrs had used different camp names when they were captured and there might not be any record of their capture or deaths under the names on the Peshawar list.

When the Fashioner joined him in his office for tea at seven-thirty, Alexander brought him up to date. "Rambo reduced the list of fourteen by six last night."

"It looks like the bargaining's about over."

"So it seems." Alexander paused, distracted. "Musawwir, I need a favor. I think I can squeeze a little more out of that Russian colonel if I can get him alone. See if you can get that major to wander off with you for ten minutes or so."

TANK WITH SOLDIERS, 1000 HOURS, SEPTEMBER 8

Klimenko opened the meeting with a brief statement recounting the progress of their efforts. "We have learned from Kabul that in addition to the thirty-three names we provided, another four prisoners on your list have been located. Three are in Pul-I-Charki prison, one in Baghram. All four are in the last stages of terminal illness; none is expected to live long enough to be exchanged for Lieutenant Orlov. Moreover, we have located records of the deaths of forty of the remaining fifty-five names on your list. These two files contain that information." Klimenko pushed the two files toward the Fashioner.

"This is progress, Colonel." He began to study the files.

"In our searches of the prison records, we have found that the use of more than one nom de guerre—camp names, I believe you call them— makes it difficult to keep track of the real identities of our prisoners. Some of the discrepancies between our two lists can be explained by the fact that we are holding them under different names. The same applies to the dead rebels."

The Fashioner snapped, "Colonel, for the sake of civility, let's refer to the missing as simply 'men.' Agreed?"

"Agreed," Klimenko said with a tight smile.

After studying the documents for almost an hour, which was interspersed with the Fashioner's requests for clarification, he stood up and said, "Gentlemen, I suggest a short break for tea or a cool drink. Major, would you like to offer these to your men in the jeep? I'll fill a small pot with tea from the samovar and you can carry the drinks."

Sasha readily agreed, seeing the chance to split the Fashioner off from the other Dukhi.

In the tent Klimenko spoke in Russian. "You're no Afghan. Who are you?"

Alexander stared at Klimenko for what seemed a painfully long time, then spoke in Ukrainian. "Colonel, I'm a lot like you. I had a Ukrainian mother, as you do. My father was Russian, while yours is Ukrainian."

Klimenko felt strangely disconcerted. "Of course my parents are Ukrainian, but we are all citizens of the Soviet Union."

Alexander was convinced that he had solved the riddle about this man last night, but instinct told him to move forward one careful step at a time. "Belenko isn't your name, but it's not far from your real Ukrainian name—at least the sound of the last two syllables. Am I right?" he asked, his voice devoid of menace.

"You seem to have all the answers. Why don't you tell me more about myself?"

"Do you like Russian fairy tales, Colonel? I do, particularly the old Ukrainian stories."

"I learned some as a boy. Everybody did." Klimenko was struck by a faint sense of imminent discovery.

"My favorite is 'The Tale of the Maidens of Kiev,' a story about identical twins and their struggle to be reunited over the years after being separated by war. Do you know that one?"

Waves of heat went through Klimenko. He removed his hat and wiped the perspiration from his brow, revealing a smaller version of the famous Gorbachev birthmark peeking out from under his hairline. His mouth was dry. "I know the story."

Alexander continued softly, almost afraid that his voice would crack, " 'For the maidens were marked by the love of their God . . .' "

Klimenko completed the lines from memory, " '. . . who had laid his hand on their shoulders, and leaving His mark He fused their hearts, and promised them never to part . . .'

"Can this be possible? Who are you? You wrote the letter in the timing device used in the attack on Kharga, and you sent the black tulip. You're the Alexander in Paktia."

"Yes, those are incidental to what we know right now, wouldn't you agree, Anatoly Viktorovich?" Alexander threw the name at Klimenko.

Back at the jeep, Major Shadrin and his bored comrade, Belov, were watching Sasha and the Fashioner work their way up the hill. Belov had them in his telescope as they made their way near the top of the hill. He handed over the glass. "Here, take a look. That big Dukhi seems to be leading our fearless major to the place where all those Spetsnaz guys bought it about a year ago. What a mess that was! It took us days just to haul their bodies back to Ali Khel and fly them back to Kabul."

Shadrin trained the glass on Sasha and the Fashioner, then swung it down the hill where Klimenko and Alexander were talking under the shade of the tent. Alexander's face filled the field of view. Shit! That guy's speaking Ukrainian. I can almost make out what he's saying. Shadrin reached into his breast pocket for his notebook as he held the telescope on the men under the tent.

• • •

"As you have now discovered, Anatoly Viktorovich, your mother Katerina is the twin sister of my wife's mother, Lara." Alexander reached into his shoulder bag and drew out a silver-framed photograph. "Recognize her?"

Klimenko looked at the photo and inhaled sharply. "It could be a picture of my mother as a girl. This is Lara's daughter."

"Yes, it's Katerina, your mother's namesake. But look closer. It could be your twin sister. Do you see yourself in the photograph?"

Shadrin strained his eye through the telescope. Klimenko's back was turned, but he was convinced that he read the words "your mother" in Ukrainian on the lips of the Dukhi. He had even handed Klimenko something from his bag. What the hell is going on?

"This makes us relatives, doesn't it, Anatoly Viktorovich?" Alexander said softly, still feeling the disbelief he knew Klimenko shared.

Klimenko didn't have a chance to answer. Sasha and the Fashioner approached just as Alexander slipped the photograph back into his bag.

"We can cover more of this tomorrow, Colonel," Alexander said in English, adversarial formality once again marking his tone.

Klimenko rose as his comrade and the Fashioner came in. "I think we have accomplished about all we can for today. I now have a request—no, a demand—that must be fulfilled before we can proceed. I must speak with Lieutenant Orlov personally. Only after I have seen him can we begin making plans for the exchange. This is on the personal order of General Polyakov."

Sasha studied his friend's face. He knew Klimenko was lying about Polyakov giving such an order.

"Your request is sudden but not unexpected," the Fashioner responded. "I'll agree on the condition that only one of you travel to the meeting with Orlov. I assume that will be you, Colonel Belenko," said the Fashioner.

"Agreed."

THIRTEEN

Major Belov forced the wheezing jeep up the last steep hundred yards onto the plateau of Ali Khel. By the time he pulled to a halt the radiator was blowing steam. The four officers dismounted with relief and walked toward the orderly room, Belov complaining as they went.

"I sent a requisition order for a new jeep to Transportation at 40th Army Headquarters two months ago," he said. "I told them that this jeep was six years old and had almost one hundred thousand rough miles on it. I pointed out that according to Soviet Army field regulations, a jeep is eligible for replacement after it has been driven fifty thousand miles under field conditions, or after it is five years old. Two weeks ago I got a snotty answer from the idiots in Transportation saying that the regulations had been reviewed, and that it had been determined that this particular model was now rated for seven years of field use or a hundred thousand miles, whichever occurs first, so I should shut my mouth and be happy. Did you see the Landcruisers these Dukhis drive around in? Air-conditioned, with tinted windows, for Christ's sake. We're not likely to see anything like that for another war or two."

"That's what you get when you work for the CIA," Sasha said.

Shadrin abruptly shifted the conversation to the two Afghans. "How good is the English of those two bandits? Or were you only speaking Dari with them?"

Klimenko answered in a distracted tone. "The big Dukhi speaks excellent English. The second one speaks passable English, but he hasn't had much to pass along in two days."

In a pig's ass! thought Shadrin. You were up to your lying ass in a conversation with that Dukhi!

Klimenko turned to Belov. "Major, I need you to crank up your transmitter for me again. I want to send Kabul a short update on the progress we made today."

After the two men left for the radio van, Shadrin asked Sasha, with a touch of conspiracy, to take a walk with him around the compound. Sasha, still puzzled by Klimenko's improvised lie about needing to see Orlov, sensed that the KGB major was probing with a purpose, and wondered why his friend was lying yet again to mask his interest in the second Dukhi. When they were out of earshot, Shadrin said, "Major, I need your help on a sensitive matter, but I must first have your word that you will keep what I am about to tell you absolutely secret. I am, in effect, deputizing you to assist me in an investigation ordered by the authorities of the Committee for State Security. Do I have your word, and do you understand the gravity of what I have said?"

"Yes to both questions," Sasha said, all the while thinking that these KGB shits took themselves more seriously than God.

Shadrin continued, "Our comrade Colonel Klimenko, I am convinced, is involved in a traitorous relationship with the enemy." He spun out the tale of his lip-reading exercise that morning, and added his original suspicions that were reinforced in late August by the chummy letter to "My Dear Colonel" from the Dukhis who had destroyed the Kharga arsenal.

When Shadrin finished, Sasha said, "Major, what you have just told me makes a lot of sense. As you may know, General Polyakov has also harbored deep mistrust and suspicions of the dedication, if not the loyalties, of your Colonel Klimenko, and has personally instructed me to insinuate myself next to him. You have brought those undefined suspicions into sharp focus, particularly now that Klimenko has created the conditions to take off alone tomorrow with the Dukhis. I agree that he is up to some treachery, and am certain that General Polyakov will personally reward you for this brilliant bit of investigative work. Of course you have my full support and commitment. Does anyone else in Kabul have this idea of Klimenko's treachery?"

"Not yet. That plodding colonel in the Counterintelligence Directorate, Karm Sergeyevich Nikitenko, knows that I distrust Klimenko, but I think he believes I'm imagining things, that I have a personal desire to destroy Klimenko. When I do nail him, he'll certainly try to jump on the bandwagon. I'll show you and General Polyakov all my evidence when we return to Kabul. It's all right here." Shadrin patted his breast pocket and Sasha saw the outlines of the KGB officer's notebook.

"I know Nikitenko is a dull-witted idiot who couldn't catch a real traitor if one were standing on his foot. When this is over, you can be sure that General Polyakov will know the precise truth about how this case was brought to a conclusion. You'll get the recognition that you deserve, and if Nikitenko tries to move in, we'll take quick care of him. How can I help you get the evidence you need? I assume you desire some positive proof?"

"Precisely, Major. I need you to carry a miniature tape recorder with you to tomorrow's meeting. You must then engineer a situation that leaves Klimenko alone with the Dukhi again, so that we record them discussing their treachery." Shadrin was nearly breathless and struggled not to show his excitement.

Across the compound Klimenko and Belov stepped down the ladder from the rear door of the communications van. The colonel called out, "Krasin, come over here. I need you."

Quickly Sasha said to Shadrin, "Meet me tonight at the bend in the wadi about one hundred yards behind the orderly room at 2100 hours sharp. Give me the recorder then, and any other instructions I need. We can talk quietly there. If you wander over to the edge of the compound now, you'll be able to see the place I mean. It's about halfway between the orderly room and the crashed MI-24D. Don't rush. Just walk easy."

"I know how to handle myself, Major," he reassured Sasha, momentarily annoyed that he, the brilliant counterspy, was being instructed on how to conduct himself.

Sasha strode toward Klimenko. Shadrin lingered, confident of his new allies. Personal recognition from Polyakov wouldn't hurt him at all.

ALI KHEL, 2100 HOURS, SEPTEMBER 8

Dinner at the old fort had been special. Major Belov had pulled out all stops and opened up his special reserves of Sevruga caviar, Kamchatka canned crab, and had his Afghans prepare for them hot bolani nan with scallions. There were even a few tins of American corned beef, sweet Afghan melons, and several bottles of Stolichnaya. He explained to his dinner guests that everything on the table, including the caviar, crab, and vodka, had come from Pakistan, the only place such supplies existed. Anything worth anything that survived the perilous journey to Kabul from the U.S.S.R. usually ended up smuggled into Pakistan, where it earned hard currency. He had acquired the makings of this evening's feast through the sale of scrap brass from the cannon rounds scavenged from the constant shelling around Ali Khel. The scrap dealer, a wily old Pathan, had thrown in the vodka, caviar, and crab to sweeten the deal, for which he paid about 10 percent of the daily fix on the London metals market.

Belov was describing with animated detail the barter system in Paktia province when the evening stillness was broken by the muffled thud of an explosion, followed by the rattle of stones and dirt showering the flat roof. All four officers dropped to the floor.

Belov crawled quickly across the room and hit the light switch. "Stay down!" he ordered sharply. "It was probably a dog or a goat. Every so often they wander into the minefields. But if we hear another one go off it may mean trouble. Sometimes the Dukhis drive sheep into the minefields to set them off so they can attack."

Klimenko slowly raised his head above the window, but saw nothing in the darkness. "It wouldn't make sense for them to play games with us now."

There was a knock at the door, and Belov's DRA captain rushed in.

"Major Belov, there's been an accident!" He quickly took inventory of the Soviet officers present, then added, "One of your officers has been injured by a mine down the wadi about halfway to the wrecked helicopter. It must have been the major who came in on the helicopter this morning. We can't get to him in the dark. We can't do anything until morning unless you bring out the minefield maps."

"Oh, shit!" Belov said angrily. "I didn't give Shadrin the briefing about the minefields. Where do you guys find these people?"

"I warned Shadrin about the mines this afternoon," said Sasha. "I gave him the same briefing you gave us. Maybe it was the vodka."

Belov turned toward the DRA captain, "Get some floodlights on the area where the major went down."

The officer left the orderly room, savoring the evidence that there was some justice in the world after all. These Russian shits mine us in, but it's their man who gets blown up. Allah must have a hand in this.

"What maps of the minefields?" Sasha asked. "There aren't any, are there?"

"No," Belov said resignedly. "We're going to have to probe our way. There's no exit channel back here."

At the rear of the building the DRA captain threw the floodlight switches, and the wadi took on a ghostly glow. The men saw what appeared to be a pile of rags down the wadi. The pile moved.

Klimenko started down the path. "Shadrin's not dead."

"Stay where you are, Colonel. If both of you KGB jerks are blown away, every creep in Dzerzhinsky Square will be gunning for me. I'm going down there myself."

Klimenko stopped in his tracks. "The first thing I need to know," he demanded of Belov, "is what kind of mines you have out there."

"Mostly toe poppers, but there are some of the heavier antipersonnel mines, too. Most of them are planted six to ten centimeters below the surface. You ought to be able to locate them with this, and by using glancing light." Belov handed Sasha a bayonet.

"Get me a rope about forty yards long. Do you have any chemical lights? I'll need two colors." He turned to Klimenko. "I'm going to crawl along the wadi, marking the mines with one color chemical light and the safe channel with the other. I'll give Shadrin whatever first aid I can, then tie the rope around him so that you and Belov can pull him back. I'll crawl along behind him guiding the two of you as you pull him."

Klimenko nodded as Belov returned with the rope and chemical lights. "I have sixteen green and ten red chemlights. They're American. I traded a hundred brass shell casings for them. You activate them by bending them. And here's a flashlight."

Sasha coiled the rope over one shoulder, and handed one end of it to Belov to tie to the iron grating on one of the windows of the orderly room. "Andrey, how far out do the mines begin?"

"Not less than ten yards from the bottom of the incline."

Klimenko, Belov, and Lieutenant Panov watched as Sasha reached the bottom of the slope and got down on all fours. Allowing his eyes to adjust to the lighting conditions at ground level, he used the flashlight to check for the telltale depressions in the earth where the loosened dirt had begun to sink down around the mines after a few rains. Then he probed carefully with the bayonet to locate the mines exactly. He could clearly hear Shadrin moaning.

Sasha marked his progress every few yards by laying two activated green chemlights about three feet apart.

"Less than ten yards to go," announced Belov. "Sasha's already laid down six sets of green lights. He's also put down seven red lights, but the spacing doesn't seem right to me; there ought to be one or two more. Well, with any luck he's found a safe channel."

Sasha carefully probed the last five yards to Shadrin, who was lying on his back. About two yards beyond him was a crater a yard across. He had been blown upward and backward when he stepped on the mine, and his left leg jutted off at a crazy angle from the knee. The right leg appeared to be doubled up under him until Sasha crawled beside him and saw that it had been blown off just below the knee. When Sasha looked into his face, he saw unalterable, irreconcilable death.

Shadrin's eyes were glazed, but he still hung on stubbornly to consciousness. He looked at Sasha. "You knew," he said weakly.

"What's that, Major?" Sasha asked as he moved closer to the major's lips.

"You knew . . . the mines . . . you did this to me . . . why?"

"Look, Major, save your strength. I'm going to get you back and get you fixed up." Sasha cut two lengths of the excess rope, tied them around

Shadrin's legs, and then slipped two chemlights into the tourniquets, twisting them until the bleeding began to subside. As he tied the rope around Shadrin's chest, he located the major's small, hardback notebook in his breast pocket. He put it in his own pocket while running his hands over Shadrin's mangled body looking for other pockets or papers. Nothing.

"You knew . . . the mines were here . . . why . . . why . . . did you kill me?" Shadrin was barely audible.

"Gonna be fine, Major, gonna be fine." Sasha carefully stood up, shining the flashlight on and off to get the attention of the officers forty yards away, and shouted his instructions, his voice carrying easily in the still night. "When I blink the flashlight once, you will begin pulling until I tell you to stop by blinking the light twice. After you've stopped I'll give you a signal to either move to the right or the left along the rim of the plateau to pull in a different direction to get the major around the mines I've located. Do you understand?"

"We understand," Belov shouted.

Less than a minute later came the light signal and the verbal command to pull. Belov and Klimenko began to do so at a slow but steady rate of about five yards a minute. Sasha had taken up a position five yards behind Shadrin, and they all listened to his cries of pain as he bumped along the rough ground.

The operation went smoothly for about half the distance. There were four separate direction changes as Shadrin was dragged around the red chemical lights. At the last change of direction Sasha signaled the pullers above him to move to the left before pulling again.

"You can't get the angle I need for this stretch from where you are. Tolya, slide down the slope to the floor of the wadi and move the rope farther to the left. Stay close to the wall of the slope. There should be no mines there. Belov, stay where you are. Do you understand?"

"We understand."

At the bottom of the slope, Klimenko moved carefully to the left until the angle of the rope appeared right for the next maneuver. Sasha signaled with one blink of his light and shouted to Klimenko to begin pulling, but this time he did not crawl behind Shadrin as the colonel strained to pull the wounded man; instead, he waited.

The distance between the two men grew to seven yards. Then Sasha pressed his face to the ground and covered his ears as Klimenko pulled Shadrin directly over the eighth mine he had located but not marked, just in case the major needed any help dying.

The mine exploded just as Shadrin's back was pulled over the pressure plate. The blast took off his head and much of his upper torso, and knocked Klimenko off his feet at the edge of the minefield. Belov was blown back against the grilled window of the orderly room.

After the shower of debris settled, Sasha took a look at what was left of Shadrin and worked his way through the green channel to the slope, where he found Klimenko dazed and bleeding from a gash over his right eye. He helped him up to the plateau where Belov stood, still holding the rope.

"Go ahead, pull him the rest of the way. It doesn't make any difference what happens now," Sasha said as he buried his face in his hands.

"It wasn't your fault, Sasha. You did your best," Belov said.

Behind them Belov and Lieutenant Panov pulled up the remains of the major, now a headless torso with one leg flopping obscenely in the dirt.

Belov looked at the mutilated bundle. "There's not enough of this guy left to send home in his own rucksack. If Kabul got pissed when we lost the other major's dick, there's no telling how hysterical they'll get when they see how much of this one we've lost!"

Later that night Sasha went to Klimenko's room and handed him Shadrin's notebook. "You might want to read this carefully and then get rid of it. Shadrin has been tracking you for a long time, ever since you sent him into exile with the Afghan KHAD. He was convinced you branded him a coward, and has carried an enormous grudge ever since. He told me today he hadn't convinced anyone in Kabul that you're as bad as he thinks you are, at least not yet. But he also told me Nikitenko's got his eye on you. It's all there in his little book. I'm ready to talk when you are, my friend." Sasha turned to leave. "Tolya, if you don't return from your visit to Orlov tomorrow, and just keep on heading east, I'll understand. I'll tell Kabul the Dukhis killed you, and probably Orlov. Polyakov will bomb some villages, blame everything on the Committee, and then life will go on."

FOURTEEN

At the meeting the next morning, Klimenko and Sasha looked weary, and Klimenko had a small bandage over his right eye. Neither Alexander nor the Fashioner asked the obvious question, nor did they note with particular interest that Shadrin was absent.

The Fashioner handed Klimenko a folded shalwar chamise, a Chitrali hat, and a vest. "Please change into these. It will take us about two hours to reach our destination. We'll allow you half an hour with Orlov, then bring you back here. While you're traveling to and from the meeting site, you'll be blindfolded. Is that understood?"

"Understood," Klimenko said, stripping off his shirt and trousers. "My comrades will expect me back here in six hours. That gives you some extra time. If I have not returned by then, they will assume you have broken faith, at which point the army will institute appropriate measures."

"Colonel, please spare us the threats. This is your idea," the Fashioner said with more than a hint of exasperation.

Klimenko tied the drawstring of the baggy Afghan trousers, pulled on the long-tailed shirt, slipped into the vest, and put on the rolled wool hat. Sasha looked at him and said in Russian, "Tolya, you look like one of our Spetsnaz boys out on operations."

"You can be certain, Major, that I will be happy to be back in the proper uniform as soon as I return. If I am not back by 1430 hours you are to return immediately to Kabul and report to General Polyakov. Is that understood?"

Sasha thought his friend was overdoing the authority angle, but went along with it. "Yes, sir! We will do as ordered!"

He and Belov watched Alexander steer the Landcruiser around a bend with Klimenko in the front seat beside him. "Let's hope he stays lucky," Sasha said. He walked over to the creek, took out three cool cans of Sprite, tossed one to Belov and said, "Get Panov over here with that vodka, we deserve a little holiday." With that he flopped down in one of the camp chairs, put his feet up on the table and settled in for the six-hour wait.

After the Landcruiser was well out of sight of the tent, Alexander spoke to Klimenko in Ukrainian. "You can take off the blindfold now."

"What about your friend in the back? What does he know?"

"He knows nothing. He knows I'm interested in talking to you, nothing more."

"This little conspiracy of ours has turned ugly," Klimenko said angrily.

"I didn't know you were a whiner. You haven't done anything dangerous or risky, at least up until now. Nothing's ever going to change in Russia unless people like you start to take some risks."

"Don't lecture me! And you can cut out all that patronizing crap you parlor counterrevolutionaries preach about how all us good folks in the U.S.S.R. ought to have some balls and stand up to the most repressive force in modern history. They must give all you CIA guys the same line. Every one of you people sooner or later gets around to telling us that we should all storm the Lubyanka with our pitchforks. That may eventually happen, but when we get around to throwing them out it won't be because a bunch of philosophers like you told us to do it."

His outburst over, Klimenko calmly related the events of the night before. After he described Shadrin's last quarter hour in the minefield, Alexander let out a low whistle. "What now? What do you do about Krasin?"

"Sasha is a strange one. He's not driven by loyalty to something as abstract to him and hopelessly corrupt as the Soviet state. Whatever loyalties he has now are strictly personal. He won't ask me anything more about this business as long as Kabul doesn't get onto the same scent that Shadrin picked up. If it hadn't been for Sasha, the major would have gotten what he needed to turn me in and get himself the Order of the Red Banner. I'd have ended up in the basement at the Lubyanka. As it turns out, all Shadrin got was a ride back to Moscow in a zinc box."

"And what about you? Do you agree with your friend Sasha about the hopelessly corrupt Soviet state?"

Klimenko eased back in the seat. "I'm like the young son of the Maiden of Kiev who joined the palace guard of the evil prince, only to betray the prince."

"But the son's betrayal ultimately frees the people, doesn't it?"

"Don't forget it's make-believe, and it's not finished yet. Nobody lives happily ever after in this life—at least not in my part of the world," Klimenko said.

"At the risk of pissing you off again, it's up to us to decide whether it has a good or a bad ending."

"I went over 'The Tale of the Maidens of Kiev' in my mind after the excitement with Shadrin last night and put it all together. My mother received a cryptic installment from Lara about three months ago, and we puzzled over it the last time I went to Kiev to see her."

"I never saw that chapter. I left before Lara wrote it."

Klimenko shifted easily into the language of the fairy tale. "It told of Lara, who betrothed her only daughter, the namesake of Catherine of Kiev, to a young man whose family had been driven from Russia during another great war years before. The young man, named as the Macedonian, was a brave and resourceful warrior, who brought the forces of good from a great shining city to the aid of the army of the Khan in its desperate battle with the forces of the evil Tsar."

"What did you make of it at the time?" Alexander still found it difficult to accept the twist of fate that had brought him together with Klimenko.

"Mother and I had different ideas about what it meant," Klimenko said. "In the end we never brought it together with contemporary events, beyond the apparent fact that Lara's daughter had married and that her husband was also fighting the evil Tsar, maybe even here in Afghanistan. But I certainly can't say that I was somehow prepared when you dropped the bomb yesterday. But what about you? Where is your part of the fairy tale headed? Or do you believe it all breaks down into a battle of purity against evil?"

"Yes, I do. But even being on the right side, somewhere along the line the agency began to lose faith in its mission. If anything, the CIA was too comfortable with the setup, too easygoing to believe in a real endgame, to go for a real victory. Your generation of KGB officers knows that the U.S.S.R.'s main enemy has always been its own system, but you've never believed there was anything you could do about it. The problem is, neither did the CIA. Both sides ended up going along with the status quo. You worked your way into the corrupt system and got your piece of the action. We had the righteous cause and endless resources to support it. It was a pretty good deal for both of us. Am I right?"

"I reached that basic conclusion fifteen years ago, but I wasn't going to storm the ramparts on my own. I was even able to persuade myself that things weren't all that bad once you carved out your own little piece of the action. And don't forget, to my generation you didn't look much better. You had just been run out of Southeast Asia with your tail between your legs, and the next eight years made you look powerless. You were a perfect enemy. You were on the run, and you gave us job security. We even began to develop a camaraderie with you, particularly in the mid-seventies. Then Chernobyl and my father's death convinced me I couldn't play the game anymore, even though I was winning at it."

"We knew your father had died, but we couldn't figure out from your mother's chapter in the tale just what happened."

"My father was murdered by the same corruption that has murdered tens of thousands of children in the Ukraine, even if they haven't died yet."

After a long pause Klimenko asked, "Your name really is Alexander, isn't it? I'd heard about the Alexander in Paktia, but I thought it was an alias. Most of the Dhukis call you Sikander."

"Yes, it's Alexander. Alexander Fannin. My family name was Falin. A good Russian name, but you won't find it in your central registry at the Lubyanka—my father changed it when he arrived in America in 1948."

"What about the years since 1948? What happened to you? What brought you here?"

"The first twenty-odd years were pretty standard stuff. I grew up in a first-generation Russian immigrant family in the Texas hill country. We spoke only Russian and Ukrainian at home, although both my parents learned English well enough."

"You've been a military man."

"I ended up studying Russian history, and had become something of an authority on the Red Army when the Vietnam War caught me up. I landed in Saigon for the last year of our part of the war, and got out of the army in 1974, but I did special-operations work with the CIA and Air America in Southeast Asia. I became obsessed with changing things in Russia. I've never hidden my personal agenda, and the CIA seemed the only game that had a chance at making a difference."

"Well, you've got the 40th Army tied up in knots. I agree with you about the war, though maybe not on the issues of good versus evil. These Dukhi friends of yours won't always look like the heroic freedom fighters of your propaganda posters. Someday you might even regret you had anything to do with them."

"Working with the Afghans to get the Soviet Army out of Afghanistan is an unqualified necessity today. The problems afterward won't be much different from the problems that were always there. They're Afghan problems and they'll have to work them out."

Klimenko chuckled. "Or not work them out. But I agree, we're not going to win this war for about a hundred reasons. Some in the Kremlin may think that they can win in another year with an all-out push, but they're wrong. You and your Dukhi brothers can still tie us down for years—forever, in fact. I know this part of the world better than the people in Moscow and Kabul who are calling the shots."

"I have no doubts about being able to tie the 40th Army down indefinitely, but that would only raise the number of dead Afghans."

"And dead Russians," Klimenko interjected. "You and your Dukhi friends are killing a lot of Russian boys who have no quarrel here but still end up going home to their mothers wrapped in aluminum foil. They aren't part of your war."

"It's the same for the Afghans. Mothers may get the body bags, but the politicians and generals take the casualties. This won't end until the losses get too high for your generals and their political masters. We kill the kids, pray for the mothers, and shove the losses down throats in the Kremlin. All of that's part of *my* war. I don't think anyone in Washington really understands how sensitive the generals in your army are about taking casualties. Americans always believe that everybody else values life somehow less than they do. But you can see how cautious your generals are about casualties through their tactics in these valleys."

Alexander hit an axle-jolting hole and redirected his attention to the road. When the trail had smoothed out again, Klimenko spoke first. "What about the women in our lives?"

Alexander nodded. "Katerina, your cousin and my wife, is the reason behind my formal break with the CIA. After we decided to marry it became obvious that sooner or later someone from the agency would take an interest in the twins, and eventually pick up your trail. Imagine the temptation of a CIA officer having a KGB colonel as an in-law. We decided to walk away from potentially a very large problem."

"I can imagine me walking in on Chebrikov and telling him, 'By the way, I think I've got a CIA officer as an in-law.' " Klimenko chuckled.

Alexander strong-armed the Landcruiser around a boulder-strewn curve. Thirty yards away a pickup truck stood in their path loaded with armed men who bore no resemblance to any local *mujāhids*.

FIFTEEN

From the backseat, the Fashioner studied the men. "I think we've got trouble. These aren't *mujāhid* fighters. They're Gulf Arabs or Algerian Muslim Brothers who've come looking for an Islamic adventure. Algerian fighters have been shooting up caravans and robbing supply trains all over Paktia. We may not have any trouble, but if I signal you, get out armed and be ready for anything." He slipped his AK-47 into the front seat between Alexander and Klimenko, and stepped out of the Land-cruiser, his Makarov tucked under his left arm.

The Algerians, led by a bald, clean-shaven Arab with a drum-fed Kalashnikov, gathered around the Fashioner menacingly. "You are crossing an area controlled by us without our permission. Who are you and why are you here?" he asked in almost indecipherable Dari.

"I am Al-Musawwir, a brother commander who is well known in all the provinces of the east. My own camp is just beyond the territory of Professor Sayyaf's camp, the territory where we are now standing, a fact you should know."

The bald Arab swung the Kalashnikov in an arc across the Fashioner's chest. "We will take your jeep for the jihad."

The Fashioner turned toward the jeep and signaled with his arm for Alexander and Klimenko to join him, while speaking in loud and exaggerated Dari to the Algerians. "My brothers welcome you to the jihad. It gives us all great courage to see such brave men as yourselves come from so far to fight the Russians. But I need my jeep to carry out the jihad. I will tell Professor Sayyaf that he must see to it that all of our brothers who have come to help us in the struggle are given the means to fight."

Klimenko slung the Kalashnikov casually over his shoulder, muzzle down and its pistol grip brushing his hand, and spoke softly to Alexander as they approached. "There's a problem. The bald guy said something in half-Dari, half-Arabic about taking your jeep."

"Be ready to follow either my lead or Musawwir's if this turns bad," Alexander said.

"I'll follow my own lead if this turns bad," Klimenko said under his breath.

"We must welcome our brothers from the Gulf to the jihad. They are seeking to find additional means of transportation, and we have the duty to educate them to the ways of the Pathan fighter," the Fashioner said in such rapid Dari that the bald Arab could not follow him. A look of confused distrust crossed his face, and once again he swung his Kalashnikov across the midsection of his three adversaries. Klimenko noticed that the safety on the rifle was on. The other Algerians were alert, but they couldn't understand what was being said either. Two had weapons slung over their backs, but the remaining three held their weapons at the ready. Klimenko calculated that there were six AKs against their one AK and two handguns, which seemed like odds they could beat. He moved forward slightly, standing even with the Fashioner. Alexander stood half a step back, his arms folded across his chest, his left arm still squeezed down against the Browning, his right hand gripping its butt.

Klimenko surprised the Algerians with his fluent Arabic. "We welcome you to the jihad and wish you all success in destroying the invaders. How is it that we can help you as all brothers should?"

"Who are you? You are not Arab; you are not an Afghan. How can you call yourself a brother? To do so is to blaspheme," declared the clean-shaven Arab.

"I am Al-Mu'izz, the Honorer. I have traveled a great distance from a place called Baku on the Caspian Sea to join my Muslim brothers in the holy war. This brother has traveled with me, but he does not speak your language except to read from the Holy Koran," Klimenko motioned toward Alexander.

"You will give us your jeep and your weapons for the jihad," the clean-shaven Arab said, returning to his original theme.

"But we cannot do this without bringing disgrace on our brothers who depend upon us. This you will surely understand."

"Your jeep is in the area we now control. All property on this territory is ours to possess." Furtively the Arab flipped off the safety on his AK, and brought it up. As it swung toward Klimenko's chest, the KGB colonel fired a long burst that stitched the Arab straight up the center of his body.

The last of the 7.62 mm rounds ripped into the man's stunned face as he dropped in his tracks.

As Klimenko's AK burst began, Alexander had pulled out his Browning and fired a 9 mm round into the nearest Arab's open mouth. Before the dead Arab hit the ground, Klimenko caught three of the remaining four Algerians full in the chest, throwing them violently backward, dark stains spreading in the sand under them. The last Arab fell to the ground, putting his hands on the Fashioner's feet, begging to be spared.

The Fashioner jerked him up and turned to Klimenko. "Translate this for me so there's no mistake," he said in English.

Klimenko stepped forward to face the terrified Arab, and as the Fashioner spoke he translated. "You have disgraced all *mujāhids* and you have blasphemed the jihad. For this you shall surely die, but not as a martyr. You are to leave the jihad. Go to Peshawar or go to hell, I do not care which, but if you are ever found anywhere in the jihad your eyes will be pierced by needles, all the bones of your legs and arms will be broken, and you will be turned into a sightless, crippled beggar."

The Fashioner slammed the man against the hood of the pickup truck and rifled though his pockets. He had an Algerian passport and a document identifying him as a fighter of the Sayyaf Party. "Get their passports, too," he said in English, motioning toward the dead Algerians, and Alexander and Klimenko picked over the five bodies. "I will deliver these passports to Professor Sayyaf and tell him that you have dishonored the jihad. I will also give these names and your photographs to our committees in Peshawar so that all will know of the disgrace you have brought upon our struggle. None of you will be among the many *Shaheed* of the holy war. Only the true believers are to be among the martyrs," the Fashioner said, while Klimenko added threats of his own. Then came the final insult. "Take off all your clothing and your shoes," the Fashioner shouted, bringing his Makarov up under the man's chin. The Arab stripped quickly, and stood naked, humiliated and trembling.

Klimenko shouted at him, "You came to kill us, not to rob us, didn't you?"

"I know nothing of this," the Arab whimpered.

Klimenko picked up one of the Algerian AKs, threw the bolt and shouted, "You will not go from here to Peshawar. You will die here now! You know who sent you to do this foul deed. Tell me or you will die now!"

"He knew who sent us," the man whined and pointed to the clean-shaven Arab. "He said that we were to kill Al-Musawwir and the American from the valley near Parachinar. I swear on the Holy Koran that I know no more."

After Klimenko's translation, the Fashioner said, "We'll let him live. He'll get the message back to whoever sent him and his friends."

Klimenko turned to the man. "You will not take the clothes of these dead infidels, for as you know it is written in the Holy Koran that if a man wears the bloodied clothes of a dishonored, he too will be dishonored and will die with the dogs." He took the man's clothes and walked briskly toward the Landcruiser.

The Fashioner picked up the drum-fed Kalashnikov and emptied it into the motor, dashboard, and wheels of the pickup truck, collected the remaining weapons from the dead Algerians, and walked away. Alexander removed the weapons from the truck and followed, leaving behind the stunned and naked Arab.

Back in the Landcruiser, Klimenko couldn't resist commenting, "It looks like your jihad is having some solidarity problems."

As they cleared the crest of the pine-covered ridge, the three men looked down into a little valley cut into the side of a natural bend in the mountain by a narrow, fast-running stream. The trail widened into a grassy pine-ringed clearing a hundred yards down the slope. The Fashioner downshifted, and the Landcruiser strained against the braking power of the engine.

Klimenko took in the beauty of the scene and the half-dozen armed Afghan fighters lounging at the far side of the clearing. And standing by himself near the stream was Senior Lieutenant M. S. Orlov, looking crisp and self-conscious in clean battle dress. A dozen *mujāhids* stood across the clearing.

Klimenko walked up to Orlov, who stood at attention. "I am Colonel Ivan Belenko, and I have been directed by General Polyakov to secure your release from the Dushman. I regret that it has taken me this long to locate you."

Alexander interrupted him in Russian. "Colonel Belenko, before you begin pursuing your own interests with the lieutenant, I must ask you to accommodate me in making a videotaped record of part of this meeting." He motioned to J.D. among the cluster of *mujāhids* to join him with his video camera and directed him into position.

As the cameras rolled, Alexander said, "This is a meeting between Colonel I. V. Belenko of Headquarters, Soviet 40th Army, Kabul, Afghanistan, and Senior Lieutenant M. S. Orlov of the 105th Guards Airborne Division. Today is September thirteenth, 1986, and this meeting is taking place in Paktia province, Afghanistan. Will you both please state your name and confirm that the information I have just provided is accurate?"

"My name is Colonel I. V. Belenko. What you have said is correct," Klimenko said with even more rigid formality.

"I am Senior Lieutenant M. S. Orlov. You have stated the true facts," Orlov said, audibly nervous.

"Lieutenant Orlov, have you been mistreated while you have been the guest of the people of Afghanistan?" Alexander asked.

"I have not been mistreated, but I have been held illegally by Dushman in violation of international law and of the laws of the government of Afghanistan."

"Please take off your tunic, Lieutenant Orlov."

Orlov looked at Klimenko, who shrugged and nodded, then slowly unbuttoned his shirt and pulled it off. Deeply tanned and fit, he looked like he'd been on a three-week holiday on the Black Sea.

"Please turn around slowly, Lieutenant Orlov. I wish to establish that you have not been physically mistreated during your stay with us. Are there any injuries to your legs, Lieutenant Orlov? Or must I ask you to remove your trousers?"

"I have no injuries whatsoever. There is no need to proceed with this indignity." He began to put his shirt back on.

"Colonel Belenko, will you state that Lieutenant Orlov is in good physical condition and free from injury?" Alexander asked.

"Lieutenant Orlov shows no signs of physical abuse or injury," Klimenko stated.

"Thank you both for your cooperation. That will be all that is required for the record." Alexander motioned for J.D. to cease filming, then turned back to Klimenko and Orlov. "I would suggest that you conduct your business within one half hour. You may talk in private, although we will keep you under observation from an appropriate distance."

Klimenko and Orlov walked slowly toward a small stand of pines. "You appear to have done well in captivity, Lieutenant. As you know, one of the essential duties of our soldiers who become captured is to maintain the highest possible level of fitness in order to deal with the physical and mental hardships of captivity. You have done well."

"I am aware of all of my duties while in captivity, and you may be assured that I have fulfilled all of them," Orlov said stiffly, not yet certain whether Klimenko was friend or foe.

"It's okay, Lieutenant, you can loosen up. All I'm saying is that you look fine, and it's to your credit that you do."

"It was clear from the second day that I was taken prisoner that they knew what they had and what I might be worth to them. Besides, I've gotten myself into the hands of the CIA."

"We'll have the exchange wrapped up soon, but it may take a couple more weeks. Do you have any personal messages for your parents? I'll probably speak to your father by telephone when I get back to Kabul."

"Tell him that I have never lost sight of my duties as an officer."

"Your father will be proud, and has every right to be. I want you to write him a letter and have it ready for our next meeting. It will help your father, and it might even take a little pressure off a certain Chekist colonel."

Orlov smiled. "I understand, Colonel. I'll have the letter when we meet next. There's not much left for us to talk about, and there's not much left for me to do except wait. Thank you for what you have done for me."

Alexander stopped on a ridgeline overlooking the rocky wadi where they had met the Algerian fighters. The Fashioner swept the area with glasses, then instructed Alexander to take a switchback trail down to the pickup.

"It looks like the five we killed haven't been moved, and the one we left alive seems to be lying propped up against a tree about twenty yards from the truck. Looks like he's dead." The Fashioner handed the glasses up to Klimenko, who focused them with difficulty on the naked form under the pines.

"Stop here!" the Fashioner ordered, as Alexander reached the edge of the wadi. "I'll go ahead on foot. Keep these handy." The two men got out and stood with their AKs at the ready.

The Fashioner heard the sound of death before he saw it. The steady buzzing of flies working on the man's wounds was loud even at a distance. He quickly pieced together what must have happened after they left the man stranded, and motioned to his two companions to join him.

Standing silently beside him Klimenko was moved to dredge up the Kipling verse in an exaggerated Cockney accent:

> *"When you're wounded and left on Afghanistan's plains*
> *And the women come out to cut up what remains*
> *Just roll to your rifle and blow out your brains*
> *An' go to your Gawd like a soldier."*

The man had had a bad time of it. His hands and feet had been cut off, as had his ears, nose, and lips. From the signs of the sweeping bloodstains caked on the earth, this had been done while he was still alive. His body was covered with small, carefully inflicted incisions that tinted the corpse reddish brown. The man had been blinded Afghan fashion by two surgical cuts straight through both pupils. Finally, his tongue had been cut out of his mouth, which was open in a mute scream.

"This wasn't torture in the process of getting information, you understand; it was simply torture for entertainment," the Fashioner said. "It probably won't make any sense to either of you."

The three men kept an eye on the ridgelines as they returned to the

Landcruiser. When they reached the trail that would take them all the way to Tank With Soldiers, Alexander switched back to Ukrainian and said to Klimenko, "This is the end of this phase of the Orlov negotiations. I assume you will clear up the final issue of the commanders unaccounted for on our list. I can guarantee that we won't have any new demands up our sleeves."

"I intend to get on with the roundup of your people. You have my word that whatever number of commanders we ultimately come up with will be all that we were able to find. Finding your people is hard work, and I think it will take about two weeks to round up everyone. I think it's realistic to assume that we'll have all of them, even the dying ones, in Jalālābād in about three weeks and can hand your men over to your representatives at Torkham Gate. We'll have to coordinate the turnover of Orlov in Paktia to occur at the same moment, which shouldn't be difficult."

Alexander said, "I think we should build in one more visit by you alone to see Orlov sometime before the swap actually takes place."

Klimenko nodded. Alexander's motives for extending their days in Paktia were the same as his.

THE PONDEROSA, 1500 HOURS, SEPTEMBER 10

The Fashioner poured green tea into the small cup and delicately set it before his guest. He watched as the man carefully measured out three heaping measures of sugar, dropped in two cardamom seeds, and slowly stirred the thick concoction. Mullah Salang was the unquestioned king of the mountain in the Khost area of Paktia province, a self-styled holy man and the leader of the largest and best-organized group of fighters in Paktia. In seven years his legendary courage and daring had prompted a great deal of suspicion. Those who knew him well thought that he was off his rocker, but this did not give the Fashioner or most fighters on the right side of the jihad any cause for concern. Mullah Salang's type of craziness fitted the war.

Both men were seated among piled cushions on the richly carpeted floor of the Fashioner's reception room. Salang was almost as tall as the Fashioner, more heavily built, with a wild head of pitch-black hair and an equally uncontrollable beard. His eyes were the burning coals of the true believer. The war gave meaning and a certain usefulness to Salang's mix of leadership and zealotry. He knew that the Fashioner was calling in a debt. During a heated battle in the Setow Kandow Pass, Salang had been wounded in the left knee by shrapnel. The wound became so infected that he would have lost his leg, a prospect more chilling to him than dying, if "Doc" Halliday, the Hermitage's resourceful former Special Forces medic, had not been called. Doc came into the Khost area with a portable industrial X-ray machine normally used to X-ray captured Soviet missiles to ensure that they had not been booby-trapped and to X-ray booby traps to disarm them. Doc jury-rigged the machine to locate the piece of shrapnel in Mullah Salang's leg, then operated immediately.

It was during Ramadan, the Muslim period of fasting, and Mullah Salang refused to allow Doc to inject him with a local anesthetic before the daily fast was broken at sunset. Medications were also forbidden under the rules of fasting, but Doc said that his patient could not wait the six hours before darkness fell. Islam might have bent most rules during a holy war, but this holy man asked for no quarter. So Doc cut out the shrapnel deep in the knee without anesthetic. As he later described it, Mullah Salang flinched, but just barely. Doc packed the wound with antibiotics and gave the wounded man additional injections after the sun set. Doc and Alexander's new friend was indebted to them.

"Maulvi Salang," the Fashioner addressed his guest using the slightly exaggerated religious title. "I need your help."

"You have only to ask."

"You know that the jihad has brought many fighters to help us drive out the Russians. But it has also brought some who have blasphemed the jihad, who have sown the seeds of distrust among the fighters of Afghanistan. Have you heard of the encounter I had with the Algerians in the wadi between here and Tank With Soldiers?"

"I know what happens in this province," Mullah Salang replied tersely.

"Then you know that they ambushed our brother Alexander and me, and that they were acting on secret instructions to kill us. We killed all but one of them, but were unable to learn who had sent them."

"I think your American friend is too impatient for these mountains," Mullah Salang said. "My men and I had more time to talk to your Algerian friend when we came upon him sitting under a tree. First he told us a story about bandits, and then another blasphemous story about being unable to wear the clothes of the dead because it violated the teachings of the Prophet, may he rest in peace. We instructed the wretch on the truth of the Koran, and he told us many things we wanted to know, as well as many that no longer interested us. In the end we decided he should talk no more."

"Was he sent by the men of Engineer Imam?"

"The Algerians were admirers of Engineer Imam, but I do not believe that they were ordered by the Party of God to commit this murder. I think that these men were aware that Engineer Imam is no friend of Al-Musawwir or of our brother Sikander, and I suspect that they were led to believe that Engineer Imam would be pleased with them and give them heavy weapons and an area of their own if they could show him their worth. Killing you and Alexander was their idea, but they were not without encouragement from someone who must be dealt with in Peshawar."

"What do you advise me to do about these men, Maulvi Salang?" the Fashioner asked.

"Nothing."

"Nothing?"

"Yes, nothing. I have already decided that these Algerians will die, and in a special way. It will entertain you when you learn of it."

"I am in your debt, Maulvi Salang."

"We will be equally in each other's debt when the Algerians have been killed," Mullah Salang said, and took his turn pouring green tea into the Fashioner's cup. "Tell Alexander I will keep my promise to him on car and truck bombs." He smiled mysteriously.

"Tell Alexander as well that once the Algerians are dispatched, I will turn to him for some of the new missiles on which he has been training your fighters and those of Engineer Imam."

"Alexander has already sent a schedule for you to send a team of five of your most intelligent and resourceful fighters to the Hermitage for training on the first day of October. He said that it will be good for the jihad when Maulvi Salang's fighters have the new weapon because they can kill the planes that fly supplies into the Khost garrison each day."

"They will be there on the first day of October. But now, my brother commander, I must leave you and be about the business of our Algerian friends." The large man rose with some difficulty. "My knee still refuses to perform sometimes."

The Fashioner walked him to his waiting bodyguard of five fighters. As he watched the jeep disappear, he thought, will these people ever be able to go back to what they were before this war? The question disturbed him, because he, too, was one of these people.

SIXTEEN

Klimenko had worked past midnight again. He knew he was alone in his access-controlled work area, but took a look outside his office anyway to be sure. The slow-witted security guard was half asleep at his post, so Klimenko retrieved from his safe Shadrin's small hardcover notebook.

In theory, the notebooks contained everything a KGB operations officer needed: summaries of operational case histories, brief descriptions of message traffic to and from Center, agent contact plans and instructions were all recorded there. Pages could not be removed, and if additional ones were required, they were to be sewn in by the officer himself. This was all standard operating procedure hammered home to all the would-be guardians of the revolution during their training at the Andropov Red Banner Institute, and it followed them through their careers, often to the pleasure and amusement of the CIA. When a KGB officer defected with his little bible, he was often able to reconstruct in intricate detail many years' worth of antidemocratic deeds.

At the end of each day an officer was required to turn his notebook over to the KGB Referentura, the top secret records registry. Klimenko had given Shadrin the appropriate written approval to bring classified documents with him to Ali Khel, which would later explain to investigators why the notebook was missing from the Referentura. But no one could easily link the missing notebook to Klimenko—no one, except perhaps Karm Sergeyevich Nikitenko.

Now, reading the tight, tortured scrawl Klimenko saw clearly that

Nikitenko had been investigating him for months. Here, in Shadrin's clipped notes, was proof that from the beginning Colonel KSN had an interest in Colonel AVK. Shadrin had written "why?" and circled it. Shadrin knew why *he* wanted to destroy Klimenko, but didn't know why Nikitenko did.

Klimenko knew why. It was the incident in Beirut. Nikitenko, the Acting Rezident in Beirut in early 1985, had been disgraced when three officers under his command were taken hostage by Hizbollah terrorists. Following six weeks of attempts to locate and free them, Nikitenko had drawn a blank. After one of the three died in captivity, Moscow Center dispatched a Group Alfa team lead by Klimenko to Beirut to take command of the rescue operation. Within ten days Klimenko freed the two surviving KGB officers in a violent and dramatic action that left all of the Hizbollah captors dead and earned him the Order of the Red Banner. Adding stinging insult to Nikitenko's humiliation, one of two rescued hostages, having been a longtime secret agent of the CIA, defected six weeks later. The system reacted promptly and vigorously; it focused all of its censure on Nikitenko, scapegoating the counterintelligence careerist for the string of sensational failures and packing him off to an exile job in Kabul. After the Beirut debacle, Nikitenko linked his collapsed career inseparably with Klimenko's rising reputation for heroism and resourcefulness. He set out to even the score, but with patience.

Most officers who knew him considered Nikitenko an unwavering believer, the latest entry in a family line of committed revolutionaries running back to the St. Petersburg revolution. He was a hard-core believer in a system of few true believers. Indeed, his name was one of those oddities in revolutionary vogue a couple of generations ago. Karm, drawn from *Krasnaya Armiya*—Red Army—identified Nikitenko's parentage as one of unswerving loyalty to the Soviet dream. He was proud of his name and all that it stood for, and he had been proud of his father for giving it to him and for later earning the Order of Lenin in Marshal Zhukov's army.

Nikitenko was perceived by a few of his KGB colleagues as a brilliant counterintelligence specialist with unlimited patience, a man who cultivated the image of an unimaginative plodder to shield his own secrets. But none could say with certainty what his secrets might be, or even that he had any secrets. There were rumors early in his career that he had family ties to Volga Germans, always held in great distrust by successive regimes. It was a suggestion Nikitenko carefully dismissed, but not vigorously to avoid attracting additional attention. He casually attributed his native command of German to having been sheltered by a German-speaking family in the Volga region after his mother and sister were killed in a German air attack when he was a child. With his father away at war, he explained, he adapted to the Volga German family that sheltered him. Those in the KGB Investigations Department who bored into his background confirmed his claims to purist Great Russian origins, and noted with due respect his father's impeccable pedigree as a communist and a war hero. With time the speculation subsided and few in the KGB bothered to look for his secrets, which was fine with Nikitenko. If people thought you had a secret, they would do anything to unearth it, and he didn't need anyone peering into his soul, looking for the dark truth, the tragedy that was his own family's piece of the awful history of the U.S.S.R.

Nikitenko's duties in Kabul were far beneath his abilities, but that was the intended humiliation of the assignment to 40th Army Headquarters. He was to keep a watchful eye on anything that smelled like a counter-intelligence problem. This involved running a network of spies and snitches within virtually every entity in the Soviet official presence in Kabul, except for the Red Army. That was the responsibility of the Third Chief Directorate, at least officially. Nikitenko's job was to find people, some of them colleagues and brothers in the KGB, of questionable loyalty, officers with defeatist attitudes, or those suspected of committing crimes against the socialist state. This included just about everybody in the U.S.S.R., but you did your job, never mind if it meant sabotaging someone else. Nikitenko didn't care if he was avoided, if not actually despised, by his fellow officers. He didn't need friends; they could only complicate matters, particularly if they wanted to dig for his secrets.

Klimenko thumbed through the notebook one more time, committed the details of Shadrin's investigation to memory, and then methodically tore out the pages and dropped them into a large paper burn bag reserved for papers requiring personal, confirmed destruction by the responsible officer. It was marked TOP SECRET—SIGNALS with Klimenko's personal identification number written clearly below the classification. He would take the bag down to the incinerator room later that night, toss it into the flames, and get a confirming signature from the incinerator watch officer.

Two days earlier they had loaded Shadrin's half-filled military casket aboard a Black Tulip IL-76 bound for Moscow. At the brief ceremony at Kabul Airport, Sasha gave a thoroughly convincing eulogy for his fallen comrade, including an inspiring description of Shadrin's last words among the mines at Ali Khel. "Even as Major Shadrin lay there dying," Sasha testified, "his blood soaking into the dust of the wadi, his last thoughts were only of the safety of his comrades. He implored me, 'Go back, Major, go back! There is another mine under my body. It will explode when you try to move me.' " Sasha's voice wavered, and then he went on. "There was no mine under his body. It was his own, nearly severed leg, but he couldn't have known that. Nevertheless, his last words and his last thoughts were of my safety, not his. That was the kind of man our fallen comrade was."

What a bullshitter, Klimenko had thought; Sasha really had the fallen-comrade business down pat. It was impossible to tell if any of the handful of officers present actually cared, except for the sad-faced, white-haired Nikitenko, who spent more time looking at him and Sasha than at Shadrin's zinc casket.

Lieutenant General Polyakov's briefing had been another charade. He had reviewed the videotaped session Klimenko had held with Orlov and had found it flashy enough to have it sent on the first available flight to General Orlov in Germany, who had already called Polyakov to express his gratitude. This reinforced Polyakov's decision to take active command of the Orlov rescue operation now that it looked like the lieutenant would turn up in one fit and tanned piece.

Klimenko knew that eventually Nikitenko would see his after-action reports, and wrote them with this in mind. Nikitenko would also see the debriefing reports covering Lieutenant Orlov's period of captivity, and Klimenko avoided creating any traps as he wrote his reports on his contacts with the Dushman and the Russian-speaking mercenary. He described Alexander as an unnamed foreigner, a Caucasian probably working for the CIA, who went to great lengths to appear as a Dukhi in both dress and manner, and stated without elaboration that the man spoke Russian. Omitting this fact could later cause him problems. His report was more exact about the Fashioner, whom he characterized as the primary Dushman negotiator. He provided more than enough information for the KGB file checkers to come up with the true identity of the man known as Al-Musawwir. As an insurance policy, Klimenko decided that he would take first access to Orlov once he was handed over at Tank With Soldiers. He would guide the debriefing and keep a lookout for trapdoors.

Now, almost as an afterthought, Klimenko retrieved the Alpha File from his open safe. Adjusting the lamp, he spread the latest intercept before him:

Alpha One from Alpha Fourx Alpha One from Alpha Fourx Following are Alpha Four conclusions and recommendations regarding negotiations of prisoner exchange as of 18Sepx Full details have already been sent by special courierx As stated in that report believe there is no advantage to holding out for additional names of brothers from Russian sidex Col Belenko probably truthful when he offered guarantees that his list would be full and completex Suggest we agree formally to proposal to take control of liberated brothers at Torkham at same time we hand over Orlov at Tank With Soldiersx Exchange

will take place before middle October if there are no further unfore-
seen complicationsx

New subjectx Regarding friends' inquiry if Lt Orlov willing to
come over to their side Alpha Two and Four respond that there are
no realistic expectations that Orlov would ever betray his army or
countryx Alpha Two and Four jointly assess Orlov as qte two hundred percenter qte who completely committed to Russian goals in
Afghanistanx Were it not for the release of our brothers it would
have been better had we killed Orlov outrightx

New subjectx Alpha Two and Four also unable provide any information of use to friends on negotiator Colonel Belenko (probably
alias) beyond physical description already forwarded by special
courier along with video recording of Belenko/Orlov official state-
mentx Only additional information is that Belenko can ironically be
qte credited qte with taking action which may have saved lives of
Alpha Two and Four during ambush by Arab bandits on road to
Orlov meetingx Belenko foiled ambush and killed three bandits (full
details to follow by special courier along with recommendations
for followup action)x Belenko obviously fully empowered by his
superiors to negotiate and with apparent good causex Belenko is
probably another qte two hundred percenter qtex Pls advise friends
that our goal in Belenko contacts remains liberating our brothers and
cousinsx Any thought of bringing Orlov or Belenko over to friends'
side is secondary and only wishful thinkingx Pls send agreement and
concurrence of all involved party leaders to exchange of Orlov for
brothers in writing by special courierx Trust in Godx Endx

Klimenko looked at the word "cousins" and decided that Alexander
knew he must be reading the Alpha messages and threw the word in
to alert him. Klimenko thought it was risky to get cute in the Alpha
deception messages, but few in Kabul would find any hidden meaning in
the word or sense that it was out of character in Dukhi correspondence.

Klimenko locked his working files into his office safe before he took
the burn bag and headed for the basement. At the vaulted door of the
incinerator room Klimenko was let in by the watch officer, a lieutenant,
stripped to his sooty undershirt. He felt the blast of heat on his face as he
stepped forward to sign the official visitors' log, listed the type of material
to be destroyed, and asked for a numbered hand receipt. He felt slightly
self-conscious about this charade, but he wanted the records to look
absolutely normal if Karm Sergeyevich poked around. He followed precisely the same procedure three or four times a month. At the lieutenant's
order one of his soldiers shut down the blower and opened the

incinerator's heavy iron door long enough for Klimenko to throw his burn bag into the flames.

Karm Sergeyevich Nikitenko had been sitting quietly in his darkened office across the interior quadrangle of 40th Army Headquarters watching the office two floors up from his and in the opposite corner of the building. For most of the last hour he had been sipping a large glass of vodka. He wrote in his notebook that the lights in Colonel Klimenko's working area were doused at a few minutes past midnight. He also noted that it was the third time in as many days that the Ukrainian colonel had kept such late hours, although he knew that there was nothing subversive about that. He waited another ten minutes, drained his glass, then walked directly to the basement. At the incinerator room he rang for admission. It was his third visit in as many nights. He usually came in quietly, always with his disarming smile, took a look at the destruction logs, and left after some small talk. Sometimes he brought along his own burn bags, but not tonight. Tonight he found what he was looking for in his first glance at the log: Klimenko's signed certification confirming his visit just a few minutes before. "Lieutenant, I'll want your men to sift the ashes after this burn is completed and cooled down. Don't add any more materials to this burn. Hold all contents from the sifted ashes for me until the end of your shift at 0800 hours."

"It might help if you'd tell me what you're looking for, Colonel," the young lieutenant offered courteously.

"I wish it were that easy, Lieutenant. I'm not even sure myself. But it's official Committee business, and it wouldn't be helpful for you to speculate with others about this. Do you understand me?"

"Very clearly, sir."

Nikitenko left the stifling heat of the burn vault with the same nagging thoughts he'd had two days earlier at the morgue at Kabul Airport when he inspected Shadrin's remains to see if they could provide any clues to what happened at Ali Khel. Krasin's report, countersigned by Klimenko, had suggested that alcohol had probably played a role in Shadrin's death, but that didn't fit what he knew of the major, so he asked that the cursory combat autopsy include blood-alcohol levels, something not usually done in combat-associated deaths, and decided to visit the morgue himself.

Nikitenko almost became physically ill when the 40th Army mortician, an obscenely fat and callous female major, gave him a look at Shadrin's remains. She clamored cheerfully over the stacks of frozen bodies in the freezer room until she located the plastic bag of what was left of Major Shadrin, wheezing and grinning as she dragged it across the floor to a table in the autopsy room. Turning her porcine face to Nikitenko, she gave him a flirtatious smile of gold-capped teeth. "Here's all we have of your major, Colonel. Pretty, eh?"

Nikitenko struggled with the bile rising in his throat as he looked down at the frozen wreck of humanity. "There's barely half a man here."

"Not to worry. When they get him home they'll throw some bags of sand in the zinc box to make it heavier. Otherwise the family will think we've shortchanged them. That was my idea. But it doesn't make sense to do it here and fly sand from Afghanistan to the Soyuz for burial, does it?" The woman showed obvious pride in the logic and economy of her suggestion.

"An excellent point," Karm said numbly.

"They'll weld your boy into his own box later, but the family will probably open it up on the other end. It's forbidden, you know, but everybody does it. They find the sand sometimes, but that seems not so bad if they're sure it's their boy. They think we don't care whether we mix their boys up. But we do, you know. I don't like sending 'em home with so many missing parts. Doesn't seem right to me. This one got killed in the same place another officer got his precious tiny thing blown off between his legs. I really put pressure on them to find me that boy's blessed little *khuy,* I did. Never got it back, but I did my duty."

"I'm sure you did, Major. You have a thankless job." Nikitenko held his handkerchief over his mouth and nose, still not certain he could get through this horror without vomiting. "By the way, did you do any blood work on this body? Any kind of an autopsy report?"

"Of course we did. All of them have autopsy reports attached to them. See for yourself." She gestured in the direction of the stacks of corpses, all with the proper paperwork in plastic envelopes attached to the bags.

"Besides, somebody from the Committee asked us to take a special look at this one. Wanted to know was he drunk when he died. Here's the report. We couldn't do that kind of blood work here, but I sent a sample off to Tashkent on the first flight. Had to go right to his heart to find enough blood."

She handed the autopsy report to Nikitenko. "Subject died of shock and loss of blood caused by multiple wounds to the upper, mid-, and lower torso. Traumatic amputations of lower extremities and explosive, blunt-force amputation of the head and part of the upper torso. The cause of the wounds was not known, and would have to be requested separately from the competent military authorities." Another entry indicated that the alcohol content of the blood was less than 0.04 percent.

"Tashkent did the test for blood alcohol, as the Committee asked, but found only a trace. Certainly nothing out of the ordinary. You can work backward from the amount of alcohol you find in the blood, you know, and give a good estimate of the levels at the time of death. Plus, they got him to me in less than a day and I had him in the cooler right away."

"Is Tashkent sure of these numbers?" Nikitenko asked. "Could the alcohol readings have changed because of the loss of so much blood or because you didn't take a sample until the remains were almost a day old?"

The mortician looked cranky. "I don't see what difference it makes whether he was drunk or not. It would have been better for him if he was, but he wasn't, and that's a fact."

As Nikitenko turned to leave the major caught his arm. "Wait! You don't wanna leave before you see the nice work I do when I have all the pieces."

Pulling the reluctant Nikitenko to an autopsy table in the corner she threw back a filthy, bloodstained sheet, revealing the naked corpse of a boy barely out of his teens, his eyes peacefully closed, cheeks artificially flushed with color, and a single round hole in the middle of his forehead.

"Pretty, eh? And I haven't even waxed over the hole yet!" The little pig eyes sparkled.

Nikitenko couldn't answer. He just stared at the dead boy, another young face grasping at his consciousness, the face of his mother standing in a field on the banks of the Volga River long ago, her cheeks flushed with outrage, her eyes flashing in confused defiance as an NKVD officer fired a single bullet into her forehead. Nikitenko saw his younger sister rubbing rouge into their mother's dead cheeks after they had carried her home and he had cleaned the blood from her face and hair. He heard his grandmother whispering softly in German as she held her daughter's eyes closed until they would no longer ease open on their own. *"Schlaf gut, Schätzli."* A muted sob forced its way from his throat.

The major tugged at his sleeve. "Pretty moving, eh? We don't even have to fix 'em up, but see what we can do when we're not so pressed?" Nikitenko jerked his head away from the boy's face, tears welling in his eyes. He tried to speak, but couldn't. Smiling weakly, he nodded and hurried from the awful place.

The visit to the morgue had compelled Nikitenko back to the Klimenko case. Shadrin never took more than an occasional drink. Nor could Karm imagine him wandering off into the dark to look around. Among Shadrin's personal effects, the major's notebook was missing. It was not at the Referentura, Nikitenko had checked. Shadrin had signed the book out on his own authority. And at the morgue the pocket was empty, so Krasin or Klimenko had taken the book.

THREE

SEVENTEEN

Engineer Ghaffar and his seven *mujāhids* had been on the move constantly since setting off with the first issue of Stingers a week ago. The Jalālābād airfield was three miles southeast of the city, and the Soviet garrison there was ideally situated near the point where the Kabul and Konar rivers began to wind their way north, skirting the Khyber Pass, into Pakistan.

Ghaffar checked the time. It was 1615 hours. If the intelligence is right, we will have some work in the next few hours. He and his men quietly fitted the three grip stocks with missiles, checked and rechecked their work, and turned on the blackout. The green lamp signaled friendly skies. Ghaffar took a small frequency-hopping radio from a rucksack and turned it on. As they settled down to wait hidden among the boulders, a few of the fighters quietly repeated the names of Allah, seeking help and guidance from the Creator of Death, the Avenger, and the Guide to the Right Path.

KABUL AIRFIELD, 1615 HOURS
Major Vladimir Maslov had been flying MI-24D attack helicopters in Afghanistan for more than three years. He had volunteered to return twice, not because he gave a shit about building socialism, he liked to say, but because he loved the incomparable feeling of invincibility that came with flying choppers against the Dushman. More than once he had heard

the staccato drumbeat of 12.7 mm machine gun rounds bouncing off the armor that protected him and his gas tanks. But as convinced as he was that he could control his fate, he was terrified that a tracer round hitting his fuel tanks could set him aflame. It was beyond his control, a lucky shot.

He believed the MI-24D was the meanest attack craft in service anywhere. His carried a full load of the latest antitank guided missiles, AT-5s, plus his rapid-firing 23 mm cannon and the 12.7 mm machine gun. He was not like most of the pilots in his squadron who drank themselves silly nearly every night on just about anything that was wet. By the time most of them were in the air at first light they couldn't be counted on for anything resembling sharpened reflexes, much less brilliant airmanship. Afternoon missions were almost as bad; some of the boys had probably already taken a few pulls from a bottle before the flight to Jalālābād. They'd better be good tomorrow, he thought, when the action starts down in Nangarhar. Maslov went precisely through his preflight check. His weapons operator was already squeezed into his separate cockpit below and in front, and his engineer was standing watch outside and would later join the two passengers in the main cabin in the back at the last minute for the flight down to Jalālābād.

He pulled on his headset and throat mike. "Kabul Tower, this is Thrasher Flight 22 leader. Request takeoff instructions, departure headings, and altitude."

"Flight 22, you may begin your roll to runway nine zero for takeoff with initial heading of nine zero degrees. Your altitude to Jalālābād is eleven thousand feet, flight path follows the Kabul River all the way. Do you copy?"

"Roger Kabul Tower. Runway nine zero. Initial heading nine zero degrees. Working altitude eleven thousand on the river route. Permission to roll?"

"Flight 22, you are cleared to roll."

"Thank you, Kabul Tower." The other six Hind-D attack helicopters fell into line behind Maslov. Within three minutes they were airborne and churning their way through the warm September air. Their route and assigned altitude would take them above the highest ground between Kabul and Jalālābād by at least a thousand feet.

As Flight 22 cleared Kabul, an Afghan voice on the Kabul Tower frequency crackled in Maslov's earphones just before he switched to the navigational frequency that Flight 22 would use for the rest of the flight. The transmission was in Dari, so he dismissed it and turned his full attention to flying.

THE HERMITAGE, 1630 HOURS

The Motorola MX-300 radio burst into life. Alexander made sure it was switched into the secure voice position and keyed the transmit button. "Go ahead."

"Seven at 1620 exactly on time." It was J.D.

Ten days earlier he had received an intelligence report that there would be a transfer of Soviet-piloted MI-24D Hind-D attack helicopters from Kabul to Jalālābād late on September 25. Attack operations against Mujaheddin supply lines were to follow for the next several days. One of the Afghan Air Force tower controllers at Kabul airfield, a man operating on orders from Rambo, had broadcast the apparently harmless open-code message in Dari on the control-tower frequency being monitored by J.D.'s team. ETA Jalālābād would be about one hour.

Alexander responded, "Broadcast to Apple Team," then slipped the MX-300 back into its charger, leaving the speaker on with the volume turned up, and waited for the squelch from the radio.

"Apple Team, Apple Team. Zero seven at 1620 for 1720. Do not answer. Do not answer. Repeat. Apple Team. Apple Team. Zero seven at 1620, 07 at 1620 for 1720 for 1720. Do not answer. Do not answer. Out."

Engineer Ghaffar stopped in mid-prayer. Seven enemy helicopters departing Kabul airfield at 1620 with an ETA at Jalālābād of 1720 hours. His men looked over at him as if waiting for some confirmation. Ghaffar nodded at their expectant faces, said in a low voice, "God is great! *Allah hu akhbar,*" checked his watch, and returned to his verse from the Koran. As he did so, he glanced at the blackout. It was still burning green.

"Jalālābād Tower, this is Thrasher Flight 22 leader. Do you copy? Over." Through his windshield Maslov saw the mountain peaks slipping beneath his aircraft. Everything looked good, but something nagged at him.

"Thrasher 22 leader, Jalālābād copies. We have you on radar with an ETA at 1720. Visibility unlimited. Wind ten knots from the northwest. Please use runway three zero. Do you copy? Over."

Maslov noted the time: 1712 hours. Eight minutes to touchdown. "Roger, Jalālābād Tower. Thrasher 22 will approach from southeast on runway three zero. ETA eight minutes. Thrasher 22 leader out." He flipped his radio to the intercom frequency, and said into his throat mike, "Drop in behind me and follow my lead into Jalālābād. We'll change course and fly in over the city. We'll approach from the north and swing around and come into the field from the southeast. I want to avoid a low approach from the east where the Dukhis might use us for target practice. Do you roger?"

Each of the other six pilots in Flight 22 acknowledged their flight leader's instructions. Maslov often changed course. He said it was his instincts, and they all believed in him. The six birds fell into line and began to drop altitude.

Later Ghaffar would say that he had uttered Ya-Rashid, the Guide to the Right Path, for exactly the one thousandth time when the blackout gave its first audible beep and the green light switched to red. All of his fighters fell silent and looked at Ghaffar expectantly, and he quietly ordered his other two gunners to their positions. "Wait until I give the order to begin the procedures," he said as he shouldered his weapon. "Abdul Hadi, start scanning to the north with your glasses."

Four minutes later Abdul Hadi cried out, "There they are, to the north. Seven MI-24Ds at about six-thousand-feet altitude, twelve-thousand-feet range. They'll probably fly over the city and approach from the southeast right into your sights!"

"*Insh'allah,*" Ghaffar muttered.

"*Insh'allah,*" every fighter answered.

"Jalālābād Tower. This is Thrasher Flight Leader. We have you on visual approach. We're flying downwind to come up on three zero. Is there any activity in the area? Over."

"Thrasher 22 Leader, this is Jalālābād Tower. You have the place to yourselves. The Dukhis haven't fired on us in almost a week. See you on the ground. Jalālābād Tower out."

"Altitude four thousand five hundred feet, range seventy-five hundred!" Abdul Hadi called.

"Engage BCUs!" Ghaffar called as he screwed his battery-cooling unit into the well.

"BCU engaged!"

"BCU engaged!"

"Begin tracking!" Ghaffar ordered, and all three gunners flipped the thumb switch starting the gyro motors. The sound of the warning from the blackout was joined immediately by the sound of the gyro motors gaining strength as the Stinger trackers acquired the heat from the approaching helicopters.

"Uncage!" Ghaffar ordered. The other two gunners hit the rubberized buttons, fully arming the Stinger missiles.

In less than two seconds the three gunners had fired. The first Stinger shot out of Ghaffar's missile tube and traveled the prescribed twenty feet on its launch charge, but its rocket motor failed to ignite, and it clattered among the rocks. But the second and third gunners had fired their missiles and the slender arrows moved toward their targets at twice the speed of sound. Ghaffar had already begun refitting his grip stock with another tube when the second missile launched by another gunner struck an MI-24D in the midsection. The helicopter exploded and fell off the southeast end of the runway just as the third missile found its target, blowing two rotor blades off the chopper and dropping it like a rock three hundred yards from the burning wreckage of the first kill. Ghaffar reloaded and locked on his second target among the remaining five choppers, now taking wild evasive action.

Major Vladimir Maslov had seen the two white trails racing across the sky from the ground below them. His weapons officer came over the intercom, "What the hell was that?" Maslov knew instantly. The two white lines disappeared behind him into his formation, followed immediately by two shuddering explosions that blew his helicopter forward as the missiles found their targets. The intercom frequency filled with a screaming babble of radio transmissions from the remaining five Hind pilots. Maslov heard his own voice ordering immediate evasive action to the surviving choppers as he pulled his aircraft hard to the left in a steep, frame-rattling dive. His only thought was to get inside the missile's arming distance, the three hundred yards the missile had to fly from the launch before its spinning tail fin would automatically arm the warhead. If he could close to less than three hundred yards the missile could still hit him, but it might not detonate. At least that was the theory Maslov clung to as he dived. He was two seconds short of his goal, flying straight at a cluster of boulders southeast of the runway when he caught the launch of the third missile in the corner of his eye.

"Oh, shit!" was all that Maslov had time to say as the white-tailed missile locked on to his helicopter. His last futile action was to fire fifty rounds of his 23 mm Gatling gun.

Ghaffar had picked his second target carefully. He wanted to kill the lead helicopter, and already had solid cheek-to-bone vibration from his grip stock signaling acquisition when his target came screaming at his position. The missile ignited its second-stage rocket motor instantly, and flew straight toward the lead MI-24D that had tipped over almost on its side and begun dropping toward him. As the gap closed to less than a thousand yards, Ghaffar saw bright flashes from the Gatling gun slung under the Hind. The cannon rounds flew wide of their target while the missile closed the remaining distance and hit the right engine. The debris fell only a hundred yards from his position.

"Gather up the equipment and be ready to move out in two minutes!" Ghaffar shouted to his fighters. "Hadi, destroy that Stinger that misfired.

Pound the center of it with a large rock. Don't strike the warhead!" The standing order had been clear: don't let functioning Stingers fall into enemy hands. Within three minutes his team was on its way to Pakistan to report its success.

Ghaffar took the frequency hopper from one of his fighter's packs and broke radio silence for the first time in a week. "Three confirmed kills at southeast end of the target airfield," he reported. "Four missiles fired. Apple Team returning to base."

The Soviet major and lieutenant in Jalālābād Tower stared dumbstruck at the oily black smoke billowing from the three burning wrecks. "What the hell is going on?" the major screamed. "Were those SA-7s?"

"No, sir, I don't think they could have been SA-7s."

"Why not?"

"Because those missiles worked, sir."

KABUL, 1730 HOURS

The telephone's tinny ring broke the silence in Klimenko's office.

"Tolya, the Dukhis have just bit off half of Polyakov's pecker. Have you heard about Jalālābād? Our Dukhi friends just took out three Bumble-bees with surface-to-air missiles. Jalālābād says there's shit burning all over the end of the runway. Everybody's going crazy, including Field Marshal von Polyakov."

"Were the missiles what I think they were?"

"You don't think it was SA-7s, do you? Those worthless pieces of shit can't hit anything. These had to be Stingers. Took out almost half a for-mation of Bumblebees, and made the pilots who didn't get their asses fried shit their pants. Major Bulletproof Maslov was the flight leader, and he bought it."

"After all these months of rumors and leaks in Washington about putting the Stingers into the war, it looks like it's finally happened. What's the fearless general going to do now, nuke somebody?"

"The first thing he's going to do is close down Jalālābād airfield until the investigation team looks over the mess tomorrow. Then he'll probably want to raise the stakes. People are already buzzing about launching air strikes into Pakistan, maybe take out some of the Dukhi training camps run by the CIA."

"A lot of good that'll do now," Klimenko said wearily. "By the way, let me guess which Red Army general will fly down to Jalālābād to lead the investigation tomorrow."

"You've got that right. None other than your favorite General Polyakov, who has already told me to get everything lined up for him in the morning, including your precious Sasha to carry his bags and take his notes for him. How'd you guess?"

"Can you imagine anyone more predictable than your general in a situation like this?" Klimenko asked. "Well, take good notes and tell me all about it when you get back tomorrow night. If you go into town, get me a couple of cans of caviar and four cans of Kamchatka crab. I'll pay you when I see you."

"Maybe I'll take the caviar and crab and head for the Khyber."

"Maybe you should, my friend," Klimenko said into a telephone that had already gone dead. He leaned back and smiled at Sasha's irreverence. He considered the frenzy at headquarters now that the Stinger had come into the war. He sometimes couldn't figure out his own people. Everybody knew that as long as the air force bombers and army helicopters in Afghanistan continued to blast everything that moved on the ground, sooner or later someone would give the rebels something that worked. There had been unruly debates in Washington, along with the usual deluge of leaks, for the last six months about using the Stinger here. The only halfway reasonable argument against it was that it would raise the temperature of the war a degree or two. The other argument, the one that warned of the dangers of the top secret Stinger technology falling into Soviet hands, rang hollow. The technology had been lost almost four years before when a GRU colonel in Europe bought the entire package from a NATO agent. The CIA knew all about that operation because the colonel was working for the agency when he stole the secret documentation. The CIA couldn't prevent the loss of the technology because their GRU man had a partner in the operation, another GRU officer. The CIA simply calculated the odds and then let the information go over in order to protect their man.

Now the GRU guy was living somewhere out on the West Coast. Probably got himself a pickup truck and a blonde with big tits. Crazy how things work out, Klimenko thought. Now the Dukhis can bring down a bunch of airplanes with Russian kids in them and that idiot Polyakov wants to up the stakes. Then he sat bolt upright in his chair and called Sasha back.

Sasha answered in the middle of the second ring. "Krasin."

"Sasha, can you come over here for a minute? I need to see you."

"What's the problem?" Sasha asked as he leaned against the door frame.

"You can't go to Jalālābād tomorrow." Klimenko closed the door of his office.

"And why can't I?"

"Whoever took out those MI-24s knows what we'll do next. They know that we'll fly the brass down to Jalālābād to look things over, and they'll be waiting for them. Don't ask me how I know this, because I can't tell you. If you don't get yourself off that flight, I think you'll die, my friend."

"Even if I believed you, it would take a pretty tall tale to convince the general it was a good idea for me not to go along."

"Tell him that worthless slug of a KGB colonel is making his move to pull together all of the Dukhi commanders for the Orlov trade, and that if you don't go along to keep him honest, the KGB might make a power play to get their boss, Viktor Chebrikov, all the credit for getting Orlov's little boy back in one piece instead of General Polyakov, who masterminded the whole search operation and trade. Will that fly with your general?"

"Probably, and I'll do it. But one of these days very soon you and I are going to have to get a little drunk and talk seriously about what's been happening. We're going to have to start admitting some things to ourselves and to each other."

"Fair enough," Klimenko said with a sense of relief he hoped didn't show. Sasha stared at him without saying another word, and then turned and left.

Klimenko dialed the number of the late Major Shadrin's replacement at KHAD Headquarters. When the new officer answered, he said, "Major Kuzmin, we have to move ahead one day the roundup of all the Dukhi commanders. Set it up for tomorrow."

"Yes, sir, but I wish I'd had a little more notice. Everything is set for two days from now."

"I wish you had more time too, Major. Orders from Polyakov." Klimenko hung up, aware that he was on thin ice if his hunch about tomorrow was wrong.

CIA HEADQUARTERS, 0800 HOURS, SEPTEMBER 25

Frank Andrews, the chief of the CIA's Afghan Task Force at Langley, was in Casey's outer office when the white-haired director stepped out of his elevator.

"Hi, Frank. What's up with you so early?" the director mumbled as he brushed by him into his office.

"This came in from Alexander an hour ago. It came through my channel, probably because he wanted the Task Force to see it first and get moving on it, but it's addressed to you personally." The director sat down at his desk and looked at the message.

For the director from the Hermitage:
"For though usurpers sway the rule
awhile,
yet heavens are just, and time suppresseth wrongs"

Shakespeare

Bill: You may wish to have one of your birds take a look at the junk piled up at the southeast end of Jalalabad Airfield runway during its next pass through the neighborhood. The burned stuff is what is left of three MI-24D helicopters brought down in the first Stinger ambush of the war. Shootdown at 1720 hours 25 September. Gunner's name is Ghaffar. (It means "the Forgiver," one of Allah's names.) How 'bout that for irony? Trust in God! Warmest regards,

Alexander

Casey looked at Andrews and smiled. "Can you believe that Shakespeare quote?"

"I think it's kind of neat. Nobody ever bothers to write like that anymore."

"Do we have pictures?"

"We're taking a look this evening. I'll probably have something for you before you head for home tonight."

The DCI reached for his phone. "Dottie, get me the president. I'll stay on the line."

Moments later Dottie's voice came over the intercom. "He's coming on."

"Ronnie, I've got some great news for you. I'm going to put you on the speaker. I've got Frank Andrews here with me." Casey pressed the speaker button on his console.

"Ronnie, it's Afghanistan. The Mujaheddin just took out three Soviet helicopters in the first attack using Stingers. This is going to be a day we'll remember. And just a month after our guys blew up that ammunition dump outside Kabul!"

"That's just great, Bill. I want you to send my personal appreciation to your people out there. Does the press have it yet?"

Casey looked over his glasses at Andrews as he answered, "Not yet. But you can be sure they will in another hour."

"Bill, maybe you should call the Hill, the 4H club, and give them a heads up. And the credit. They were a big help in pushing the Stinger thing through."

Andrews smiled at the president's reference to the four conservative senators most supportive of increasing the assistance to the Afghan Resistance—Helms, Hecht, Hatch, and Humphrey.

"I'll do that, Ronnie. It'll mean a lot to them. I'll also call Charlie Wilson. He's been a big help in the house."

"He's kept the Democrats with us on Afghanistan," the president mused. "Too bad Charlie's not interested in Central America. We could use some help there. Uh, I suppose George Shultz will hear from Dobrynin on this, don't you think, Bill?"

Casey cast a questioning glance at Frank, who shook his head and mouthed the words "not yet." "Yes, but not yet, Ronnie. We think they'll wait awhile before they send Dobrynin in to whine to Shultz." Casey grinned at Andrews. "I'll bring some photos down tomorrow for the morning briefing."

EIGHTEEN

TWENTY MILES WNW OF JALĀLĀBĀD, 0400 HOURS, SEPTEMBER 26

The three Mujaheddin were up before dawn. They prayed together, asking for divine intervention in the day's task. Deep inside the cave, the Boy heated a small pot of water above a can of Sterno. Along with green tea the men ate the dried fig and date bars they carried as lightweight rations. They whispered even though there was no possibility of being overheard, their furtiveness an instinctive response to the still hour and the nature of the work ahead.

KABUL AIRFIELD, 0530 HOURS, SEPTEMBER 26

At Kabul airfield the sun began to peek above the mountains and slowly flood the plateau with warmth and light. Security was tight. This morning's orders from the airfield commander had been straightforward: there were to be no random shots at departing aircraft. Many mechanized patrols were conducted inside the airfield perimeter. Beyond the fence, army patrols with their dogs could be seen casting back and forth in the distance. Their job, attended to more urgently than usual this morning, was to flush out would-be rebel gunners that might have infiltrated the long stretch of land below the glide path on the upwind end of the runway.

Sasha had told General Polyakov he would arrive at the flight line fifteen minutes early to supervise the preparations of the Antonov-26 command-post aircraft, but the real reason was to avoid riding in the general's staff car and risk having him change his mind and order Sasha to Jalālābād.

He moved about the cabin checking to make sure that the air charts and tactical maps were laid out, that there were two thermoses of hot, sickly sweet black tea, plus the third thermos of Georgian brandy the general liked to sip, even in the morning. A basket lashed against the far bulkhead was full of ripe mangoes from Pakistan, and several small paper bags contained dried apricots, almonds, and pine nuts to go with the brandy.

Klimenko had been right. The general hadn't argued with him when he told him that much as he'd like to go along with him to Nangarhar, he really thought he ought to keep an eye on that sorry-assed KGB colonel, especially since everything seemed to be going well on the Orlov trade. Polyakov had been quick to see the potential danger and decided that it was his own idea to have his aide stay behind to protect his interests.

As Sasha stepped down the ladder of the paratrooper door, the four-car motorcade came racing across the tarmac. Seconds later Polyakov emerged and walked briskly to the plane. Sasha was standing at loose attention as Polyakov approached, snapping orders to his staff scrambling at his heels. He paused for a moment and placed his hand on Sasha's shoulder.

"Krasin," he said with forced chumminess, "I'm sorry to leave you behind, but my decision is firm; you have to take care of our interests here. You know what I mean." He gave his major a conspiratorial wink and squeeze on the shoulder.

"Yes, sir, no problem. You can count on me."

0540 HOURS, SEPTEMBER 26

"Kabul Tower, Kabul Tower. This is Baghram Air Traffic Control. Please advise if there are any flight-activity restrictions in your area for the next hour." The Dari-speaking voice crackled over the speakers in the control tower at Kabul airfield.

"Baghram, this is Kabul Tower." The Afghan Air Force major on duty responded before the Soviet officer in charge had a chance to focus on the request.

"We have VIP traffic departing Kabul now," the major went on. "I repeat, we have VIP traffic outbound now—with continuing restricted flight activity between Kabul and azimuth 85-125 degrees, altitude 30 to 60. Do you copy, over?"

"Break, break! Kabul, this is Baghram. Break, break!" A new voice burst into the Kabul Control Tower with tinny urgency, this one speaking Russian with authority and irritation.

The Soviet officer in charge snatched the microphone from the Afghan major's hand, pushing him roughly out of the way. "Baghram, this is Kabul. Go ahead!"

"Kabul, this is Baghram. That last transmission requesting your report on flight activity in the Kabul area did not—I repeat, did not—originate from Baghram. Do you copy, over?"

"I copy you, Baghram Air Traffic Control. Please leave this frequency and go to landline with Kabul Tower immediately. This is Kabul Tower senior controller. Please contact me immediately on landline. Do you copy, over?"

"I copy, Kabul."

The Soviet officer in charge in Kabul Tower glanced down toward the end of the runway to see Polyakov's aircraft begin its banking climb. He immediately drew his Makarov and pointed it at his Afghan counterpart's head, issuing orders to two Soviet security guards.

"Place this major under arrest. Make sure he is held in isolation and talks to nobody!" The telephone at his console rang. "Kabul Tower. Colonel Filatov."

"Colonel, this is Major Dmitriev at Baghram. Some Dukhis broke into our traffic-control frequency and appear to have gotten an answer to their question. Do you guys have some VIP heading for Jalālābād?"

"How did you figure that out?" Filatov asked, his throat tightening.

"Your Afghan controller told the whole world that he had VIP traffic heading east from Kabul at about 0540 hours."

"I think you're right. I've had my DRA tower assistant locked up until we get a handle on this. Something like this happened yesterday when the flight of MI-24Ds took off and ran into that ambush in Jalālābād. I think this guy is in this up to his ears, both of which I'll personally carve off and make him eat until he tells me what I want to know. I'll get back to you when I have time. What's your name again?"

"Dmitriev. Major Ivan Viktorovich. Let me know how things turn out."

Filatov switched to the secure navigational frequency and pressed the transmit button, took a deep breath, and spoke deliberately to the radio operator on Polyakov's plane.

"Two zero seven, this is Kabul Tower. We have a possible security condition. Do you copy, over?"

"Copy, Kabul. I am handing you over to Iceberg security controller." He handed the mike to the security chief.

"This is Iceberg security, Kabul Tower. Please go ahead."

Filatov took another deep breath. "There has been a possible compromise of Iceberg's flight plan in radio traffic originating from Kabul Tower. We have arrested an Afghan Air Force major who broadcast Iceberg's departure time and flight-route information. It is possible that he did this in response to a coordinated rebel deception plan. We have no confirmation yet of the extent of the possible compromise, and this is to inform you as a precautionary measure only. Do you copy? Over." Filitov's brow began to sweat as he waited for the response.

"Kabul Tower, this is Iceberg security. I copy. Please stand by."

General Polyakov was enjoying the Georgian brandy and sifting through the bowl of pine nuts when his security chief and Major Karpov came into his cabin. The security officer made a straightforward report.

"Sir, we have just learned from Kabul Tower that there was an unauthorized broadcast giving your precise departure time and your general flight route to Jalālābād. The Soviet officer in charge has arrested the Afghan major who made the broadcast because he suspects that the man was working with the rebels, but knows nothing more at this time. My advice is to abort this mission, particularly since it is apparent that the Dukhis have a new surface-to-air missile capability."

General Polyakov flipped open the Soviet Air Force handbook on the Stinger missile lying on his map table, and found the passage he had read the night before. "Karpov, what is our altitude?"

"Our flight plan puts us at twelve thousand feet all the way to Jalālābād, and we reached that height about two minutes ago."

The general looked back down at the report. "If we're up against the Stinger, gentlemen, it starts running out of gas at about ten thousand feet and self-destructs at just over twelve thousand feet. Tell the pilot to take us up to eighteen thousand feet. Inform Kabul that I have decided to proceed to Jalālābād as planned. And tell them to send out armed recon aircraft. I want a combat air patrol with us for the entire flight. Understood?"

Major Karpov knew there would be no arguing. "Yes, sir, understood."

Alexander was in the communications center with Tim when J.D.'s voice broke in on the speaker of the Motorola. "Boss, we just got confirmation that a VIP aircraft departed Kabul airfield heading east, probably bound for J'bād at 0540 hours. This is what you figured. Over."

"Have you been watching the deception traffic we asked for on the frequency-hopper bands?"

"Roger. There's been a lot of chatter on all of the nets for over an hour. None of the Soviet intercept sites will be able to figure anything out from the pattern of radio traffic."

"Okay, I'll relay your message to Pear Team. The Soviets won't be able to connect our encrypted transmissions with the flight activity at Kabul, at least not with all the chatter on the radios right now. Alexander out."

Rand looked over at Alexander. "Shall I relay the message to Pear Team?"

"Yeah, tell Pear that he can expect something big and fat in the next quarter hour."

TWENTY MILES WNW OF JALĀLĀBĀD, 0555 HOURS, SEPTEMBER 26

The Fashioner, Malik, and the Boy reached their perch at over ten thousand feet as the message came in over the Fashioner's radio. They wasted no time setting up in a natural cleft in the rugged mountain just below the summit, with a three-hundred-sixty-degree view of the path from Kabul to Jalālābād.

The Fashioner placed the blackout on a rock ledge, then made sure he could see his two fighters well hidden in the rocks at five- and ten-yard intervals. He was about to utter a prayer when the blackout alarm sounded. He swept the rugged valley below him and to the west with his glasses, and as the blackout became more insistent, spotted two Hind-D attack helicopters racing through the valley below him at about three thousand yards. He called out to Malik and the Boy to stay in their concealed positions. Their plan was to allow any patrolling helicopter gunships to pass. Within seconds the Fashioner found what he was looking for, a black dot about four miles away and growing in size. When he called out to Malik and the Boy, both instantly brought their Stingers to their shoulders and waited for the command to fire.

Polyakov felt relaxed. Perhaps it was the second glass of brandy or the rugged landscape below him. He had never tired of the view of the Kabul River from the air as it forced its way eastward through the Tang-i-Gharu gorges. Afghanistan, he thought, is rough and unforgiving. It is right that it becomes part of Russia. It should have been long ago.

The lumbering Antonov passed over the Sorobi Dam, built by the Germans. By the time the plane flew over the Russian-built dams at Naghlu and the Dorunta gorge, the general knew that in a few minutes, his aircraft would clear the final stretch of the Eastern Mountains and make a corkscrew descent to the Jalālābād airfield. He took another sip of brandy and began to flip through his documents.

TWENTY MILES WNW OF JALĀLĀBĀD, 0558 HOURS, SEPTEMBER 26

The Fashioner held the Antonov in his glasses. It was now clearly identifiable as the multiengine Soviet transport aircraft.

"Malik, let the Boy take the first shot. You and I will hold our fire to see if he hits it and if they come after us. Young one! That transport is yours! It is just about in range, so start your firing sequence."

The Boy could feel his heart pounding in his throat as he set the

Antonov in his center sight and heard the command from the Fashioner, "Activate your BCU!"

The Boy screwed the BCU canister into the well and flipped the thumb switch out and down to turn on the tracker. Instantly the Stinger locked on the infrared emissions of the plane. He knew he had less than forty seconds to acquire his target and fire the missile before the firing sequence shut down.

"Uncage and fire when you're ready!" The Fashioner's command calmed the Boy. Concentrating on his target, he hit the Uncage button, elevated the weapon, and squeezed the trigger. They all stood motionless, watching the white tail of condensation, each uttering a prayer that the range was not too great.

The earphones of the pilot of the Antonov exploded with sound. "Iceberg! Iceberg! Two zero seven! Two zero seven! You have SAM lock-on! You have SAM lock-on! Bank left and dive! Bank left and dive!" But the pilot of the SU-24 flying combat air patrol five thousand feet above the Antonov knew that his warning was too late. Even as he shouted into his throat mike he was banking into a dive toward the source from which the white tail of the surface-to-air missile had seemed to rise. As he dropped the nose of his aircraft into its dive he radioed his wingman, "Three zero nine from 305. Three zero nine from 305. Maintain altitude while I make the first pass at the firing location. Do you copy? Over."

"Copy 305. Will keep an eye on you as you make your firing pass."

Polyakov was thrown against the bulkhead when his pilot made a futile attempt to evade the Stinger. He saw a blinding flash at the nacelle of the inboard port turbine engine as the left wing separated from the fuselage. There was no secondary explosion, no fire, only the sickening, spinning descent. The aircraft fell twelve thousand feet and burst into a fireball. For the last seconds of his life General Boris Semyonovich Polyakov felt betrayed; he thought only of how to take revenge on the idiot who wrote that the Stinger missile was ineffective at altitudes above ten thousand feet.

The Boy saw the left wing of the huge aircraft separate in slow motion before he heard the explosion. His quarry was still spinning toward the mountainside when the Fashioner launched a Stinger at a silver dart diving from about eight thousand feet above them. An instant later it made impact in the right air intake of the Sukhoi fighter, exploding in a giant red and black fireball. But before the wreckage struck the mountain, three air-to-ground rockets the pilot had launched in his last moments struck with a blinding flash above and to the side of the Boy. Looking at the ledge where Malik should have been standing, he saw only a smoking crater. The Fashioner was leaning against the rock face, a spreading red stain darkening the front of his shalwar chamise. The Boy hurried toward him as the second Sukhoi began its firing dive.

"Two zero seven, 207! Do you read me? This is Kabul Tower. Over." Filatov repeated his message for perhaps the tenth time since he had heard the voice with call sign 305 shout its warning to General Polyakov's pilot.

"Three zero five . . . 305. This is Kabul Tower. Please come in. Over." Filatov was near panic.

"Kabul Tower, Kabul Tower. This is 309. Iceberg aircraft and 305 have been hit by enemy missiles at grid coordinates Guavas 44-559 Mangoes 22-298. I repeat, Iceberg and 305 have been struck by SAMs at Guavas 44-559 Mangoes 22-298. Both aircraft impacted against mountainside with secondary explosions and fell into the river. There is no chance of survivors. I repeat, there is no chance of survivors. Do you copy? Over."

Filatov's answer was weak. "I copy, 309. Please stay on the target until Thrashers in your area have commenced search for survivors. Do you copy?"

"Roger. Three zero nine will stay on target and guide Thrasher search."

"Boss. You there? There's a shitstorm on the Kabul navigational frequency. Call sign 207, cover name 'Iceberg,' just got waxed thirty clicks out of J'bād, and call sign 305 caught the same trying to help out. Both aircraft were brought down by SAMs, according to call sign 309, who is still in the area. According to our books, 207 is the call sign for the Antonov used by the First Deputy Commander of the 40th Army, none other than your beloved Boris Semyonovich Polyakov. 'Iceberg' is his cover name. Kinda fits, doesn't it? Do you copy? Over."

"I copy loud and clear. Any word from Pear Team?"

"Negative. But call sign 309 has reported that the suspected missile team was sighted and destroyed by 305 before he caught the missile. Copy?"

"I copy. We'll stay on the Pear signal plan until we hear something. You'd better stay up there until this settles down."

"Boss, there's no need to start worrying about Pear until we know more. You copy?"

"Yeah, I copy. Keep me posted." Alexander felt pulled in two directions—a giddy elation and a sickening realization that he had just lost his friend the Fashioner.

KABUL, 0610 HOURS, SEPTEMBER 26

Klimenko's phone rang at exactly 0610 hours. He had been waiting for the call for an hour. "Klimenko," he answered quietly.

"Comrade Colonel, this is Colonel Krasin calling from Kabul airfield. There has been a serious incident involving the First Deputy Commander's aircraft. With the greatest regret and sadness I must report that it appears that the general's aircraft has been shot down by an enemy missile, killing all on board. I have no further details at this time. When I have further information I will telephone."

Sasha must think that all telephone calls into and out of the Kabul airfield tower were monitored. He was right. He would make several more calls to make sure that they all sounded normal to whoever read the transcripts.

NINETEEN

Alexander was back in the communications center at dawn waiting for J.D. to call in from the bunker burrowed into the mountain high above him. He didn't have to wait long.

"Boss, you there?" This was the only radio procedure J.D. ever used on the line reserved for the four Americans at the Hermitage.

"I'm here. How do things look the morning after?"

"More of the same. Fortieth Army really went crazy yesterday. There was nonstop air traffic on the Kabul–Jalālābād route well into the afternoon—Sukhois, MiGs, choppers all over the place. All of it Soviet planes, almost no DRA flight activity. An hour ago we got a radio message from the Fashioner's people across zero line telling us that the fighter the Fashioner left behind with his mules at the bottom of the mountain made it back to Pakistan alone. He said he had to leave because it got too hot. He saw the whole thing—the shoot down of the Antonov and the Sukhoi, the attack by the second Sukhoi, one of the Fashioner's guys getting blown off the mountain all the way down into the river. Might even have been the Fashioner, the guy thought. What it means is that one of the three guys on top for the attack got killed for sure, and the other two never made it back down the mountain, at least not before the guy watching the mules had to take off. You copy? Over."

"Yeah. What do you think? Over."

"Just what I told you, Boss. One of Pear Team killed and two missing."

"Okay, what else do you have?" It seemed likely that the Fashioner and the Boy were dead, but there was nothing Alexander could do until he had more to go on.

"On the positive side, they haven't stopped screaming since Apple Team took out that flight of choppers two days ago. The DRA Air Force guys are convinced that we've moved some of our first-line SAMs, the Nikes and Hawks, into the war. Since about noon yesterday DRA pilots have decided to call in sick. We aren't even picking up any of the usual early-morning Soviet flight activity out of Kabul today. Maybe the Soviet Air Force is taking a breather too. You copy? Over."

Alexander felt his spirits lifting. "I copy. How long will it take you to get down here? I want you to ride with me over to Parachinar airstrip to link up with the Beechcraft tonight."

"I'll see you at 1500 hours at the latest, okay?"

"Roger. We'll leave here just after sunset."

Alexander turned to Tim. "I want a short encrypted broadcast to Pear Team on the frequency-hopper net every two hours on the even hour beginning at 0600. Tell them they have struck a glorious blow for the jihad, that we know they are holed up somewhere waiting until they can move, and that we're sending help."

Tim Rand looked up at his boss intently. "You believe they'll hear us?"

"I don't know, but let's try."

NATIONAL PHOTOGRAPHIC INTERPRETATION CENTER, 0900 HOURS GMT, SEPTEMBER 27

The team of NPIC imagery analysts had been working for more than three hours on the data from one of the CIA's satellites. They quickly retrieved the imagery of Jalālābād airfield, calling up the digitized photography on their large screens. It was all there: three wrecked Hind-Ds lay scattered off the southeast end of the runway, the earth blackened around three piles of twisted metal from the kerosene-fed fires. A number of Soviet military vehicles were parked near the wrecks, probably the crash investigation teams trying to piece things together. Two Antonov transports and six Hind helicopters were also at the airfield, plus what appeared to be a freshly arrived squadron of five Sukhoi-24 ground-attack aircraft. It was a lot of activity for Jalālābād.

NPIC had transmitted the provisional photographs along with a narrative commentary to CIA for the DCI. The photo-interpretation team had already ordered the large imagery boards annotated with all the details of the first Stinger shootdowns in the war. These, they had been told, would be used for briefing kings and presidents of other countries. The CIA always used that kings and presidents line, but the team at NPIC actually believed it, since it was true.

The second task assigned to NPIC from the same imagery sweep was to look for anything that might fit the scenario that had been reported at 0603 hours at a location about twenty miles WNW of Jalālābād. This one was a long shot, one of those tasking requirements the CIA sent over occasionally. It was a clear case of not knowing what to look for or where to look for it, but please call us right away when you find it. NPIC had received such requests before, and every so often came up with the billion-dollar picture.

The team had screened some spectacular coverage of the Tang-i-Gharu gorge, but nothing caught their eye. Then the radio monitors in Paktia picked up repeated references to a location in Soviet radio traffic as "Guavas 44-559/Mangoes 22-298." Now the NPIC analyst called a colleague at NSA for help, and an analyst called back ten minutes later with a set of uncoded grid coordinates. Analysts at NPIC entered them into the system mainframe, as well as the exact time of the demise of the Antonov. Within two minutes the mainframe began delivering more refined digitized imagery. As the analysts began scanning the imagery, it became clear that their search had narrowed to a short stretch of the Kabul River. They began scrolling through the frames, looking for what might be the wreckage of a downed aircraft in or near the river, but staying alert for something more spectacular.

At just after 2200 hours they found what was to become the ultimate "Will you just look at that!" picture of the Afghan War. There, in crystal clarity, was a mortally wounded Antonov-26 airborne command aircraft in its last agonized seconds of free fall and positively identifiable as an airborne command post by its special communications antenna array visible on its underside. They could also read its five-digit tail number.

Studying more closely, they saw in the top right of the photo that the left wing of the plane was separated from the body by about fifty yards of blue sky. The photographic angle gave no clue that the plane had lost a wing because there was no fire or signs of the explosion that must have sheared the wing from the fuselage, just the body of the aircraft beginning a series of wingovers created by the sudden single-wing geometry.

"For Chrissakes, will you just look at that!" the group chief said with uncharacteristic awe. He caught the disapproving looks of his coworkers and quickly regained his composure. "Okay, let's quit staring at this like we've never seen a good picture before. Let's scroll through this entire segment to see what else we can piece together." He checked the time of the frame. It read 262303.45.65ZSEP86, a few minutes after eleven in the evening GMT on September 25, 1986, six hours behind local time in eastern Afghanistan. He turned to his chief interpreter.

"Let's get these printed for the kings and presidents crowd." Speaking to a young woman analyst, he said, "Mary, call your buddy over at CIA and let them know we might have a couple of interesting pictures for them in the morning. Also call the guy at NSA back and give him that tail number. They should be able to tell us something about the plane and who might have been on board. This might be the biggest shootdown since the navy got Yamamoto. Come on, let's move!"

As the group chief walked away the other analysts all rolled their eyes. "Will you listen to this guy? Yamamoto! We weren't even *born* then!"

THE HERMITAGE, 1900 HOURS, SEPTEMBER 27

Alexander threw his beat-up leather bag into the back of the Landcruiser, got in behind the wheel, and hit the horn to signal the Toyota pickup to move out. J.D. slid into the seat beside him. Since the run-in with the Algerians, Alexander had begun using an armed escort when he traveled far from the Hermitage. The Toyota had four armed *mujāhids* in the back, including one with a heavy machine gun mounted on a swivel above the cab, plus the driver and another fighter in the passenger seat.

It was a rough ride into Pakistan until they picked up a better trail to the little airstrip that served Pakistan's Parachinar region. Air service to Parachinar was irregular, with one, sometimes two twin-engine Fokker flights a week. One such flight was scheduled for today, but Alexander knew that his pilot, Fred Underman, would arrive at the Fokker's scheduled time in his Beechcraft B-300 King Air.

This scheduling ruse had been worked out with the provincial military-flight-control people as a means of keeping the profile of the B-300 flights low in the hope that they would attract as little attention as possible from the Soviet and DRA radar operators known to follow all flight activity in Pakistan's North West Frontier Province. Alexander was not convinced that the ruse did much good, but it didn't cost anything, and he followed the procedure because it made other people feel better.

A minute later he picked up the sleek lines of the B-300 as it dropped down for its landing. Before the plane had rolled to a stop, he joined the *mujāhids* gathered by their pickup, and took the one known as Engineer Youssuf aside.

"Engineer Youssuf, could you alert your Nangarhar brothers to move into the area of the Kabul River downriver from the Tang-i-Gharu gorge and about twenty miles upriver from Jalālābād to see if they can discover what happened to Musawwir and the Boy? I consider it important for the jihad."

Youssuf nodded. "I will send a message to Wali Khan. He is my cousin, but we are still friends, and I can trust him. He knows this area better than anyone and will do this for you."

Alexander smiled. He is my cousin, but we are still friends: Youssuf had summed up all of Afghanistan in that sentence.

KABUL, 1900 HOURS, SEPTEMBER 27

Karm Sergeyevich Nikitenko had been sitting in his office alone for the last three hours and had finally noticed that it had become so dark he could no longer clearly make out the objects on his desk. Across the courtyard of 40th Army Headquarters, he had seen Klimenko moving about his office twice during the last hour. He decided to wait him out as he had for the last three nights. He had nothing else to do, but then he hadn't really had anything else to do for twenty years, ever since his wife died and he gave up believing that he cared about his son or his daughter or that they cared about him. He was sinking into one of his self-analytical, self-pitying reflections when he saw Klimenko's light go off. He waited another five minutes before switching on his desk lamp and noting the time of Klimenko's departure in his notebook. Next to it on the desk were two blackened strips of metal, twisted and partially melted. They were nearly identical and both had identification tags attached to them in Karm's tight, handwritten script. One read: "Item One: 23 September— found in 40th Army incinerator after A. V. Klimenko personally placed his registered and personal burn bag in the incinerator at 0025 hours." The other tag read: "Item Two: Remnants of metal binder on unused standard-issue KGB officer's personal notebook placed in 40th Army incinerator by K. S. Nikitenko, Colonel, at 0025 hours 24 September."

Karm studied the twisted metal. He was convinced that Klimenko had thrown Shadrin's notebook into the incinerator five days earlier. He himself had thrown a similar notebook in at exactly the same time the next night under the same conditions. The watch officer had signed an affidavit attesting that he had witnessed Colonel K. S. Nikitenko retrieve both metallic items from the incinerator on successive mornings after the ashes had cooled. He had also obligingly initialed the identification tags. Nikitenko was satisfied that his experiment was scientifically controlled. The proof lay before him. He had no doubts that he was facing a brutal murder to cover up an even greater evil.

Nikitenko's mind slipped back to the scene at the Kabul airfield morgue and the bag containing what was left of Major Shadrin. He had to begin taking stock of the late Polyakov's own aide, Alexander Petrovich Krasin. If Klimenko had killed Shadrin, Krasin was certainly a willing accomplice. He again read through the transcripts of five telephone calls Krasin had made from the airfield to a variety of numbers, including Klimenko's.

Krasin's solemn recounting of Polyakov's death was clearly a sham. He would know that the telephones at Kabul Tower were tapped, but why didn't he just tell the story straight? Why all the theatrics? Nikitenko compared the airfield telephone transcripts with a second set from Krasin's phone in Polyakov's office, and noted the difference in tone. In a later phone call to Klimenko, Krasin bluntly revealed, "The only regret I have about not taking the flight to J'bād was that I missed seeing that idiot's face before he vaporized . . ." He also made a vague reference to the accuracy of Klimenko's hunches. Krasin had probably felt safe talking on Polyakov's own telephone, believing that the late general's stern dictum against anyone from the Committee touching any phones in 40th Army Headquarters was still in force. The general had said more than once at his staff meetings that if he ever caught someone from the Committee on his phones, he would cut off his dick.

I guess you can't do that now, my dear Field Marshal, Nikitenko thought. He placed the two melted metal binders in his safe along with the transcripts, flipped off his light, and left his office feeling very smug.

Across the courtyard Klimenko sat well back from his own darkened office window and watched the light in Nikitenko's office switch off exactly nine minutes after he had turned off his own light. It was the third night in a row that Nikitenko had called it a day within ten minutes of Klimenko staging a fake exit, and the second time he had caught Nikitenko sitting in the dark until he appeared to have left himself.

ZHAWAR, PAKTIA PROVINCE, 1900 HOURS, SEPTEMBER 27

Mullah Salang was doing what he did better than anyone, his imitation of the Islamic zealot. His audience was a ragtag band of eighteen Algerian fighters who had arrived in Paktia three months before looking for excitement and martyrdom. Until now they had done nothing for the jihad except disrupt the sense of order in Salang's area. Now he was holding court with his five fighters and the Algerians inside the mud-walled compound that they had commandeered for their headquarters. On the carpeted floor before them was a sumptuous meal that seemed out of place in the bleak setting. The centerpiece was a large goat that had been oiled and packed with aromatic spices and cumin seed and roasted in a clay oven. The glistening form lay on a bed of rice on an enormous serving tray. There were trays of pilaf with chunks of tender lamb neck and chicken, raita, a yogurt salad of cucumbers, tomatoes, and cilantro, and side dishes of spicy dhal and chickpeas. Bowls held the last mangoes of the Punjab season, and before each man was a long, flat loaf of Afghan nan, a sort of edible dinner plate.

The Algerians had been suspicious when they received word that

Brother Salang wanted to pay his respects to them with a feast of a roasted goat. They knew that the ambush of the CIA man and the Fashioner by fighters in their group had caused murmurs within the resistance, and the tales of the slow death of the lone survivor of the group who set the ambush heightened their anxiety. However, their fears were assuaged when he appeared with only five fighters in two jeeps bearing a mountain of food.

Salang sensed the Algerians' relief at seeing that he had brought so few men with him, and that they had left their arms at the entrance to the compound, as was the custom. But he also sensed their fear that perhaps the food had been poisoned, and he allayed it by sampling each of the dishes himself. Within an hour the goat looked as though it had been attacked by a small army, and the Algerians had lain back in relaxed contentment.

After two hours Salang announced that he and his men must return to their own camp for prayers. They would plan their strategy for a great battle in the near future against the puppet troops of Kabul in the garrison at Khowst. After repeated embraces and pledges of eternal comradeship, the Afghans drove out of the compound and pulled their jeeps to a halt on a rise one thousand yards away. Three of them began walking quickly back to the compound. Another, an electrical engineer, set up a radio transmitter, and put it down before Salang, who had spread out his small prayer rug.

The mullah prayed for three minutes, then took up the transmitter. Raising his face, he uttered softly, *"Allah hu akhbar,"* and pressed the red transmit button.

The Algerians were lounging on the food-laden carpet when the radio signal set off two claymore mines packed neatly inside the chest cavity of the goat. Each mine contained three hundred and sixty steel balls, all of which dispersed in an arc of sixty degrees, so that the field of coverage on either side was almost complete. The explosion sent roasted goat and mortally wounded Algerians flying against the walls. Three of the men sitting at the far ends of the carpet were not directly hit, but were stunned by the force of the blast and lay helpless, listening to the cries of their dying comrades until Salang's three fighters entered the room armed with Kalashnikovs. It took them half a minute to finish the job.

TWENTY

The Beechcraft's passenger door swung down on its hinges and Alexander looked up into the expressionless face of Jim Dangerfield, Underman's copilot. He acted as if it were completely natural to meet an old friend he hadn't seen in six years at some out-of-the-way strip in Pakistan. "Hi, Alexander. You look like a real dirtball with that beard."

"Don't knock it, Jim. Maybe going dirtball would change your luck."

"What for? I've got all the luck in the world!" He shoved Alexander's bags into the rear of the aircraft.

Looking at Dangerfield, Alexander saw the affectations from the late 1960s in Southeast Asia. Spare and trim at fifty-five, he still wore the uniform—black jeans, hand-tooled leather belt with silver buckle inlaid with gold, tailored white cotton bush shirt with gold-and-black first officer's epaulets, and a pair of cracked black flying boots. They had been handmade twenty-five years ago by an old Chinese cobbler in Hong Kong's Wanchai district who refurbished them every few years. Since he had died at his bench ten years ago, the cobbler's son had repaired them. Dangerfield refused to fly without them.

The final touch from the old days was the heavy gold Rolex with an oversize gold band. The Air America pilots used to sit around the infamous White Rose bar outside Vientiane and tell the girls and each other how they could buy themselves out of trouble up-country if they ever had to make a forced landing by selling off the solid gold links one by one. The gold bracelet had been placed on Dangerfield's wrist with a pledge of eternal brotherhood almost a quarter century before in a solemn Montagnard ceremony in the Laotian highlands. That was before he lost his left leg just below the knee to an antiaircraft round as he shuttled from CIA outpost to outpost in northern Laos. Dangerfield tied off the leg with his belt to stop the bleeding and made one more stop before flying back to the medics in Vientiane. He was back in the air in a little over three months. Twenty-five years later he could still drop any airplane onto any strip in the world.

Now he joined Alexander at the foot of the ladder. "You ready to get out of here? We've got a god-awful flight plan. First we pick up the Gulfstream in Karachi, then we gotta fly all the way down to Colombo, refuel, and head on over to Hong Kong. We've got a tailwind forecast from Colombo eastward and can probably make it all the way without having to refuel. Too bad you did whatever you did that got the Indians so pissed off that you can't even fly over their sorry-assed piece of real estate."

Alexander laughed.

When Underman finished topping off the tanks for the three-and-a-half-hour flight to Karachi, he said to Alexander, "Let's get out of here before another plane comes in and starts to crowd up the place."

Alexander climbed in behind Underman, and within minutes they were taxiing to the downwind end of the undulating runway. Dangerfield had already stretched out in back to catch some sleep before he took the controls for the next leg.

J.D. watched the aircraft lift off, then squeezed the button of his Motorola. "Wheels up at 1903. You copy that, Tim?"

"Copy wheels up at 1903. Message is on its way."

Half an hour out of Karachi, Alexander slipped into worsted wool trousers, an Egyptian cotton shirt, and a raw silk sport jacket. After exchanging his boots for a pair of loafers, he almost felt part of the Western world again until he caught his bearded reflection in the darkened window.

As the plane began its descent into Karachi, the sun had long since given way to a nearly full moon over the Gulf of Oman. The sprawling city lay around a natural deepwater port northwest of the great delta formed as the Indus River spilled the rich earth of Central Asia into the Arabian Sea.

After flying for several minutes over Karachi's densely lighted outskirts, Underman began to line up the aircraft on what appeared to be a sharp-edged, rectangular dark spot in the suburbs. As Alexander felt him maneuvering, he knew that the dark spot would soon reveal itself as the Pakistani military airfield. Seconds later the B-300 set down. Out the window, Alexander saw a truck with a FOLLOW ME sign above its cab pull in to lead the plane to a secluded parking area where a sleek silver-and-gray twin-jet Gulfstream stood parked in the shadows ready for departure.

"There's our ride for the next leg," Underman said as he pressed the groaning brakes and began to go through his checklist to shut the plane down.

Within a few minutes the three men had transferred their baggage to the Gulfstream and settled into their seats for the flight to Hong Kong. Dangerfield received clearance for immediate takeoff from the tower controller and taxied to the end of the runway. Alexander felt the power of the two jet engines press him into his seat as the throttles were pushed forward and the sleek bird began to lift off while half the runway lights still stretched in front of them.

Alexander settled back into the large reclining seat in the rear cabin and felt exhaustion wash over him. He had left behind Afghanistan and the war, and now was thinking about Katerina and Hong Kong. In nine months, there had been few letters between them and no phone calls. He felt a growing excitement at the thought of seeing her again and sharing with her his discovery of a new chapter in the fairy tale of the maidens of Kiev.

HONG KONG, 1100 HOURS, SEPTEMBER 28

Over the intercom Dangerfield announced, "We just got a hookup with Hong Kong Cable and Wireless. You can make some calls now if you want. We're about thirty minutes out."

Alexander pulled the cellular telephone from the console and dialed a number from memory. "Ling, this is Mr. Fannin. Yes, thank you very much. Right now I am about to land at Kaitak and would like you to bring some fresh clothes to me at the airport. No, please do not tell Missy that I am arriving. I want to surprise her. Thank you, Ling." He put the telephone down and smiled. The seventy-year-old houseboy had served Katerina's family for more than forty years. He had been with them in Shanghai before Mao's armies took the province and the Martynovs left China for Hong Kong, and he had run Alexander and Katerina's household since their marriage.

Alexander looked down on his favorite city. From a distance of ten miles he could see the sun reflecting off the windows of the skyscrapers crowded onto every available inch of Hong Kong Island and the Kowloon Peninsula on either side of Victoria Harbor. As the Gulfstream closed on the airport from the southeast, he began to make out the distinctive landmarks of the Central District. The towering Connaught Building stood in shaded green elegance in the distance. Once an architectural wonder with its countless round windows, it was now dwarfed by newer structures and diminished by the vulgar name the island's earthy Chinese population had given it: the building of ten thousand assholes.

Dangerfield headed straight at the whitewashed spot on Castle Peak to the northwest before banking right and dropping down toward Kaitak Airport's long main runway jutting out into the Fragrant Harbor. Laundry hung on the rooftops of the resettlement estates slipped beneath the lowered landing gear as Dangerfield brought the aircraft in on one of the most challenging landing approaches in the world.

After the Gulfstream shut down its engines, Alexander asked, "Where can I find you guys if I need you, the Ocean Bar or the Mandarin?"

"We've got rooms at the Mandarin, but you might find me at the Ocean if you need me. I hope we have a couple of days. I want to put some new soles on my boots over at Kow Hoo's," said Dangerfield.

"You'll get your two days, maybe even three, but we'd better be ready to head out of here by then."

Outside immigration, Alexander saw an expectant Ling anxiously studying the faces of passengers coming through the doors. He walked up to the old Chinese and said, "You are looking for a man who has changed much, Ling. Have you forgotten that a dead horse is still bigger than a live dog?"

Ling broke into a giggle when he heard Alexander fracture the Chinese proverb into nonsense. He took Alexander's bags.

"Ling, first let's go to the Peninsula. I want to clean up a little before we see Missy. Is she at the shop today?"

"Yes, Master, she will be there all day. She just come back from Jakarta yesterday."

Jakarta, Alexander thought. That's either porcelain or politics, or maybe both. Her porcelain collection was among the richest in the colony. As a political reporter, she worked at her own pace and picked her assignments at the *Far Eastern Focus,* the glossy weekly that consistently led Asian publications in reporting on the fast-changing scene from Adelaide to Vladivostok.

From the backseat of the Jaguar, Alexander watched Ling thread his way through Kowloon to the Peninsula Hotel. The streets were full of women looking busy, sunny, and happy, something he never saw in Afghanistan.

A few minutes later Ling pulled up to the portico of the Peninsula Hotel. The doorman swung the door open with a practiced flourish, and said tentatively, "Mr. Fannin?"

"Yes, Winston, it's me, and what I want most now is a hot shower in the Martin suite."

"Yes, Mr. Fannin. I'm sorry I didn't recognize you with the beard." The second-floor suite was permanently leased by Martin House. Somehow

Martin fit the Hong Kong ambiance more smoothly than Martynov, and Katerina slipped between the two names depending on the situation.

Ninety minutes later Alexander Fannin, in trimmed beard and a fresh linen suit, walked the quarter mile to Martin House on the Kowloon side of Victoria Harbor.

TWENTY-ONE

On the second-floor arcade of Martin House, Alexander wandered through the familiar maze of exclusive shops until he reached Dynasty Art. Through the shop window, he saw Katerina deep in conversation with an elegant Western woman.

He entered quietly and Katerina's head cocked slightly as she heard the doorbell jingle, but she didn't turn from her conversation. He walked to a glass case displaying an exquisite collection of snuff bottles and began to browse, with his eye on Katerina's reflection in the glass. He could not make out what was being said, but sensing that Katerina might look up at any moment, he turned toward her and spoke Ukrainian.

"Madame, if you will kindly ask the nice lady to get the hell out of the shop, and if you will lock the place up this instant and go off to a nice room in the Peninsula Hotel with me, I promise I will buy all of these fine snuff bottles at your outrageous asking price."

Katerina turned to face him and responded softly in Ukrainian and with a slightly bitchy elegance. "Oh, Alexander, my dear, how kind of you to drop in. I can hardly remember when I last had the pleasure of your company. May I have the honor of introducing Madame Galina Nosenkova. Surely you have heard me speak of the Nosenko family."

Alexander betrayed no evidence of the ambush. "Of course I am familiar with the noble Nosenko family! I am pleased to meet at long last the gracious Madame Nosenkova, whose reputation precedes her. I am sure, Madame Nosenkova, that Katerina has told you that my only known vice is my shameless indiscretion when it comes to snuff bottles and beautiful Ukrainian women. In this setting I am simply overwhelmed."

Nosenkova's smile was playful. "How charming. But I will leave you with Katerina to conclude your deal, or whatever else you have in mind." The color rose in her face as she kissed Katerina on both cheeks and smiled at Alexander as she walked out.

"Not very smooth, Alexander. I do hope that your cross-cultural relationships are less awkward with your Kipling people," Katerina said, as her husband pulled her gently to him.

"Hi, Kat." He looked into her hazel eyes.

"Hi, Alexander."

"You okay?"

"I'm okay. You okay?"

"Now I am." He kissed her again. "You knew I was coming today, didn't you?"

"Of course I did. I got a call from one of your spook buddies yesterday, a Frank No-Last-Name. He told me you were flying in sometime today. I think he referred to you as A. Yes, that's it. He said, 'A will be here tomorrow.' "

"I have Ling standing by with the car at the Peninsula."

"Not anymore, you don't. He called me. He even told me that you were spending too much time in the hot sun and that your skin was too brown. He thinks you'll start looking like a 'goddamn coolie from Fukien.' I've planned an outing."

"I'll defer to the lady from Shanghai. Whatever Martynova's got planned is fine with me."

"I have the *Hoping Jiang* at Queen's Pier. Ling will meet us there."

Alexander took her in his arms again. "I love you."

"Not as much as I love you. Now let's get out of here before someone comes in and makes me a better offer."

They were the last to board the *Morning Star,* one of a dozen ferries that plied Victoria Harbor from Hong Kong Island to the Kowloon Peninsula. As the ship began its five-minute trip across the harbor, they took seats in the bow cabin, conspicuously marked with a sign that read in both Chinese and English, SMOKING ROOM. PLEASE DO NOT SPIT.

Alexander had ridden the *Star* ferry hundreds of times, but each time he read that sign it suggested to him that there was a spitting room, possibly a secret one, somewhere else on board where people weren't allowed to smoke. He had shared this observation with Katerina soon after they had met, and she had told him that only some sort of a pervert would think that, but each time they rode the ferry together the sign made her smile.

As the ferry approached the Hong Kong side of the harbor, Alexander saw the *Hoping Jiang* lying alongside Queen's Pier. Ling was already on board. The fifty-foot junk had belonged to Katerina's father. The afternoon sun set off its classic lines with its yackel hull, teak deck, and three mahogany masts. It was outfitted with twin Volvo diesel engines, but Alexander and Katerina almost always raised the sails once they had cleared the tricky harbor traffic. They loved the sound of the groaning masts and the wind filling the sails as it heaved the heavy vessel though the water.

Ling and the crew cast off and the engines sent a shudder through her mahogany beams as she swung about into the busy harbor.

"Where to, Captain Martynova?" Alexander asked as he settled onto a cushioned bench behind the helm.

"First to Aberdeen Harbor for some tiger prawns, then we'll anchor off Wellington Island and let Ling and the crew go ashore after dinner so that we can have the boat to ourselves."

Forty minutes later he threaded the junk past the multistoried floating restaurants to where a decaying fleet of fishing junks was moored. He pulled up alongside a sixty-footer and Ling hopped aboard with astonishing grace, carrying a plastic bucket for the prawns. Chinese shadow-boxing and Chi, Alexander thought, convinced that Ling really did know something about the secrets of longevity.

Minutes later Ling returned with two dozen giant tiger prawns splashing in his bucket. He poured in half a bottle of white wine, stowed the bucket in the galley, and returned topside. "They get a little drunk and not mind so much goin' on the grill," he had once explained to Alexander.

Alexander eased out of the harbor and set a course for Wellington Island to the west. As the vessel cleared the shipping lanes, Alexander instructed the boatswain and crew to set her sails, and when they filled, he shut down the diesels. Moments later, Ling appeared with a silver tray holding two gin and tonics.

Katerina took a sip, then turned to her husband. "The wire services went crazy last month, first with the story about the rocket attack at Kharga near Kabul—the BBC had videotape footage—and then again a few days ago with stories about the Stinger missile being used for the first time. Today, a story is making the rounds that the Mujaheddin shot down a big-shot general within the last couple of days, and that the Americans were involved. The magazine's thinking about sending me to Kabul and Moscow to do the first of a series on a war turning bad for the Soviets. Is somebody getting lucky or are you guys that good?"

"Both." Alexander put his hand along the curve of her hip and let it glide down the silk of her dress to her leg.

"Is this war what you thought it was when you left nine months ago? Is it that big?"

"I think it will bring down the whole system. With Gorbachev deconstructing the Communist Party on the inside and the Red Army getting its ass handed to it on the outside, something big has to happen. Armies don't beat rebels like these. This war is going to turn out to be the greatest screwup the Communists have made in the seventy years of their miserable existence. Are you beginning to see any ripples in places where it counts, on the other side of the curtain?"

Katerina nodded. "I spent two weeks in Paris, Stockholm, and Vienna talking to our people in Solidarity and the Ukrainian and Baltic networks. Everybody's feeling the effects of what Casey's people are doing in Poland. The independence movement in western Ukraine has all the newsprint it needs. The Baltic organizations are getting new life. I've started quiet talks with Solidarity about using their radios in Poland to broadcast to the Ukrainian and Lithuanian audiences. They're just about on board, although they're concerned that they might be inviting a Soviet response if they get caught stirring up trouble inside the Soyuz."

"What do you think?" Alexander asked.

"I told them what you usually say in the face of Russian threats. No guts, no glory. But I used more elegant language."

Alexander laughed. "Have you been able to replay the news reports on Afghanistan?"

Katerina nodded. "From Warsaw to Kiev to Vilnius. I've put everybody on notice to pay attention to the fate of the Red Army in Afghanistan if they want to get a reading on how that same army might deal with the wave sweeping over East Central Europe."

"And?" Alexander raised an eyebrow.

"The idea has caught on. But that means that you, my brave heart, had better deliver a defeated Red Army."

"The Red Army is not getting out of Afghanistan with its honor intact. Now they lose if they stay or they lose if they go. If we do it right, we can actually win."

Later, after Ling and the crew had gone ashore for the night, Katerina and Alexander lay in the king-size bed in the captain's cabin on the raised afterdeck. The bright yellow South China moon drew a shimmering line of gold across Sandy Bay and filled the cabin as Alexander traced Katerina's spine with his finger.

"Are you ready for the weird part?" He kissed her back.

"What weird part?"

"I want to show you a little home video I directed."

Katerina sat up as Alexander stepped naked across the cabin to his bag, then went over to the VCR built into the bulkhead and slipped in a cassette. After a flickering start, the screen showed a Toyota Landcruiser driving on a jeep trail edged by tall pines. Katerina was struck by the beauty of the setting. Three men, one of them Alexander, got out of the Landcruiser.

The scene broke for an instant, and then restarted shakily from a different angle. The camera focused on two men, one of them wearing the uniform of a Soviet Army lieutenant. Alexander's voice could be heard narrating in English.

"This is a meeting between Colonel I. V. Belenko of Headquarters, Soviet 40th Army, Kabul, Afghanistan, and Senior Lieutenant M. S. Orlov of the 105th Guards Airborne Division. Today is September thirteenth, 1986, and this meeting is taking place in Paktia province, Afghanistan. Will you both please state your names and confirm that the information I have just provided is accurate?"

Alexander glanced across the bed at Katerina, who was studying the film intensely. As the camera zoomed in on the faces of the two Soviet officers, she sat up straighter.

"My name is Colonel I. V. Belenko. What you have said is correct."

"I am Senior Lieutenant M. S. Orlov. You have stated the true facts."

"Lieutenant Orlov, have you been mistreated while you have been the guest of the people of Afghanistan?"

"I have not been mistreated, but I have been held illegally by Dushman in violation of international law and of the laws of the government of Afghanistan."

Katerina watched the screen in agitation, goose bumps forming on her arms.

"Please turn around slowly, Lieutenant Orlov. I wish to establish that you have not been physically mistreated during your stay with us. Are there any injuries to your legs, Lieutenant Orlov? Or must I ask you to remove your trousers?"

"I have no injuries whatsoever. There is no need to proceed with this indignity."

"Colonel Belenko, will you state that Lieutenant Orlov is in good physical condition and free from injury?" Alexander asked in his off-camera, courtroom English.

"Lieutenant Orlov shows no signs of physical abuse or injury," Klimenko said.

"Thank you both for your cooperation. That will be all that is required for the record."

The video abruptly ended and the screen turned blue.

Without a word, Katerina pushed the rewind button on the remote and watched the footage again. As the camera zoomed in on the two Soviet officers, Katerina froze the frame and turned to Alexander. "We didn't think he was in the army. We were sure he was in the KGB."

"You were right. He's a colonel in the KGB."

She felt a chill. "I knew it from the first close-up. The eyes and the face. I thought I was looking at a brother I don't have. Then I saw the mark on his forehead just below the hairline. It seems that we all have that strawberry mark somewhere. But I can't believe that you and this colonel, my mother's nephew, my only cousin, are standing there in this incredible setting. Things don't happen that way."

"Yes, they do—at least sometimes. Want to hear the whole story?"

Katerina nodded.

Alexander lay down beside Katerina and began to describe the events of the last six months. When he finished more than an hour later, she touched his cheek. "I'm going back with you to meet Anatoly Viktorovich."

"I knew you'd want to," Alexander said, pulling his wife to him and kissing her gently. "I need your help with Cousin Tolya. We've got to convince him that he can do something that will make a difference."

Katerina narrowed her eyes, the moonlight amplifying the concern in her face. "You're not going to tell Langley about this, are you?"

"No. Langley can get its own KGB colonels. We'll keep ours a family affair."

TWENTY-TWO

HONG KONG, 0730 HOURS, SEPTEMBER 29

Frank Andrews answered his phone at the Mandarin on the second ring. He had been lying awake since four A.M., watching the CNN summary every half hour until he could lip-synch the news report.

"Frank. This is A. You know, A from Paktia." Alexander rolled his eyes and smiled at Katerina. "Where do we meet and when? I'm at least two hours away from Hong Kong Central."

"In the lobby at ten A.M. H has a suite where we can meet as long as we need."

"H? Wait a minute, don't tell me. I've got it." Alexander dropped his voice to a conspiratorial whisper. "You mean Houston from Islamabad?"

"Oh, for Crissakes. See you in the lobby."

"I'll be carrying a rolled copy of *Time* in my left hand," Alexander whispered.

At exactly ten A.M. Alexander looked up from his overstuffed chair in the Mandarin lobby and saw Frank Andrews walking toward him with the easy gait of a man who had been an NFL linebacker for two years before choosing a safer line of work in the CIA. "Let's go upstairs. Houston is baby-sitting the classified stuff and photo boards."

In the elevator Alexander looked at his friend closely. "You look pretty beat, my friend. How was the flight?"

"How can you make a twenty-hour flight and not look beat? Jesus, look at you. You've gone native with that beard, like somebody out of Kipling."

"Why don't you come back with me for a couple of weeks? It will do your soul good to fight a desperate battle against impossible odds."

Andrews shook his head. "I already am. All you have to do is deal with the 40th Army. The desperate battle against impossible odds is in Washington."

After the three men settled around a coffee table in Jim Houston's suite, Andrews began his briefing.

"I think we can cover most of the ground today. First, let's talk about what's happened in the last month. Take a look at these." Andrews handed Alexander a stack of lightweight plastic boards of black-and-white photographs taken by a number of CIA satellites.

The first set of three showed the 8th Army ammunition dump at Kharga five days before the August 26 attack, their storage bunkers and revetments full of stacked ammunition and equipment. He could actually distinguish individual stacked boxes of mortar rounds from the larger wooden boxes containing rockets. "The place was jam-packed, wasn't it?" Alexander said.

"And just waiting to blow. We've revised our estimates upward to about fifty thousand tons just before you hit them. Look at that one taken an hour or so before sundown on the twenty-sixth. Here's the morning-after shot."

Alexander held the photo next to the one of Kharga taken five days before the attack. The devastation was total. Every bunker and revetment in the earlier photo seemed to have been scooped out by a giant hand and torched into a blackened scar. Wispy smoke trails still drifted up in white corkscrews from some of the storage areas. "What effects are you seeing?"

"We're already seeing signs that the Soviets will have a hell of a time making up the losses. They won't be able to use Kharga for at least a couple of months. There'll be stuff cooking off there for weeks. This means that DRA and even 40th Army operations over the winter will have to be cut back for lack of ordnance, which ought to give your people a breather."

Andrews pulled the next imagery board from the stack. "This photograph has already been mounted for two presidents and one king—Reagan, Zia, and King Fahd in Saudi Arabia. This is *the* satellite photo of the war. We won't be able to top it."

Alexander looked at the dying AN-26. The resolution of the photograph had been enhanced by computer. It was all there: the missing wing, the tail number on the boom, the command and control antennae on the underside, the porthole windows of the right side as it heaved over.

"Look closely at the first window."

Alexander studied the photo. "Is there a guy's face in that window?"

Andrews nodded. "You're looking at what I have been assured is one very dismayed General Boris Semyonovich Polyakov just before he augured in."

"You know, a lot of folks in your town will say that this has gone too far, and that the Soviets might get pissed off now that we've popped one of their generals with one of our 'made-in-U.S.A.' weapons."

"They're already wringing their hands, but the president loved it, and so did enough key Democrats on the Hill to keep the whiners under control. What do you think the Soviets will do?" Andrews asked.

"Not much they can do. They'll scream at whoever might listen to them, but that will be about it. I don't expect them to bring the war across the border into Pakistan in the conventional sense. They might blow up a few bazaars, but they're already doing that."

"The Paks agree," Houston interjected. "Zia's still telling Casey that it's okay to turn up the heat, but not to let the pot boil over."

Alexander looked at Andrews. "Is Shultz ready to have Dobrynin scream at him?"

"I think so, but you can never tell. He and Casey don't even talk anymore. But it doesn't really matter now. There's nobody in Washington who'll do anything more than squirm unless something really bad happens. The debate on the Stingers is over. It's a different matter, though, when it comes to your operation in Paktia. The Soviets will do whatever it takes to get you."

Houston broke in. "The KGB Rezident in Islamabad, one of the great old-time hoods, has hit me up twice in the last two weeks on the diplomatic circuit, complaining that the American side is provoking the Soviets by becoming directly involved in the combat. He says it's no secret that the Americans have set up a base in Paktia and told me to draw my own conclusions."

Andrews interrupted. "Alexander, what the hell does it mean?"

Alexander shrugged. "It's in the culture. Russians don't like to provoke, and they like even less to *be* provoked. It's the same with threats. Telling you to draw your own conclusions is the closest thing you're going to get in the way of a warning from diplomatic thugs."

At six-thirty Alexander stepped out into the horseshoe driveway of the Mandarin where the Jaguar stood waiting.

"Hello, Princess."

"Take a close look, Sikander."

"My God! Look at the new girl!"

"You said that I was going to have to look like a boy if I was going back with you. How's this for a start?"

Katerina's long brown hair had been ruthlessly shorn to a tousled unisex cut that was more shocking than unattractive.

"Well, do I look like a guy?"

Alexander leaned over and gave his wife's left breast a gentle bounce. "Not quite, but close enough for the work I have in mind." He kissed her lightly. "Let's go home. I'm beat."

"Okay we go home, Master, but we no talkee that beat talk. You no come here long way make push-push one night then sleep all time to make Missy plenty sorry!"

"Where did you learn to talk that Wanchai trash, girl?"

"Where the hell do you think? I'm a media hack and have ears for everything in this colony. By the way, my parents are coming for drinks tonight. I didn't tell them about the video you showed me, but I did say that you had much to tell them."

"How do you think they'll react to this?"

"Mother will take it in stride. Don't forget, she sent you off to Afghanistan to find her sister's son. She has the romantic mind that invented the fairy tale in the first place. My father will have a more practical view. He'll be discreet, but sooner or later he'll get around to thinking how this connection might make a contribution, just like you."

Ten minutes later, Ling pulled into the narrow driveway of the old Martynov residence. They walked hand in hand through the large entry hall to the verandah overlooking the terraced gardens and the ocean beyond. Michael and Lara Martynov were watching the last of the sunset as their daughter and son-in-law stepped out to greet them.

Michael Martynov spoke first, as Alexander bent to kiss Lara on both cheeks. "Alexander, adventure agrees with you! You've lost ten pounds and I like the beard. Lara would never let me grow one. Said it made me look like a mad monk."

Lara stepped back. "Somehow I could never think of Alexander as a monk. Could you, Katerina?"

"A little mad sometimes, but never a monk. Ling, gin and tonics all around in the study, please."

After the four had settled comfortably in the book-lined study, Katerina said, "Alexander, why don't we all look at your video now?"

Her parents watched the segment in silence twice. Then Lara spoke. "Alexander, I do believe that you have found what you were looking for." She turned to her husband. "Michael, dear, the handsome young colonel in Alexander's film is Katerina's boy, Anatoly."

"Of course! I knew there was some powerful connection, but I couldn't figure it out."

"It took me two days to figure it out, Michael, and I had spent hours with him face to face."

"Is he really an army colonel?" Michael asked.

"He's a Special Services colonel—KGB—working with the 40th Army in Kabul. Would you like to see him again now that you know the riddle?"

"Please."

Alexander ended up running the tape four more times, and each time Klimenko's expression or mannerisms reminded Lara of her sister, Katerina.

After Lara and Michael left an hour later, Alexander and Katerina had a late dinner on the verandah, and talked about everything except Alexander's war, Anatoly Klimenko, and the immediate future. Ling brought them coffee and two large snifters of Armagnac, but two minutes later he reappeared bearing a cordless telephone on a tray.

"The man would not say who he was, only that it most urgent that he talk to Mastah."

Alexander took up the phone. "Let me guess. It's either F for Frank or H for Houston. Which?"

"It's F, you shit. You've got two choices. You can come back into town and we can go to the office, or I can come out to your place with a special telephone for a talk with your office in you-know-where."

"You come out here. Do you think you remember how to get here? Good. It will take only thirty minutes at this time of night."

Katerina's smile had disappeared. "Trouble?"

"I don't know," Alexander said. "We'll find out when Andrews gets here."

"It's trouble, and you know it."

TWENTY-THREE

Forty minutes later Andrews arrived in a car driven by a discreet, faceless man from the Hong Kong CIA Station. Andrews hauled a medium-size Samsonite suitcase up the steps, where Alexander took it off his hands.

Out on the verandah, he handed a few sheets of paper to Alexander. "Read this first, while I set up your toy." He laid the suitcase flat on the flagstones. Beneath a protective foam inner cover was a compact black satellite communications transceiver. Andrews lifted it carefully out of its rubber cocoon and placed it on the table. Then he took a small compass from its compartment, checked some written instructions and sought out a specific azimuth and elevation in the western sky. "I've got a straight shot at the bird we're going to use from right here. We won't have to move," he said, but Alexander was too engrossed in the cable to notice.

Typically straightforward, J.D. reported that Tim Rand had received a burst radio message from a transmitter using an out-of-date call sign that Alexander had used on the rocket-attack mission against Kharga back in August. From the use of the call sign and the gist of the broken English of the message J.D. concluded that the Boy was calling for help from somewhere near the point of attack against Polyakov's aircraft, that the Fashioner was alive but in bad shape, and the Boy was trying to get help on his own.

Alexander read the radio message again:

2MJ to 1MJ. Musavr hurt but not dyxx You must comxx He not
good walkxx I listen to youxx Help and trust in Godxxx

Not much, he thought, but enough to tell the story except for where they
were.

Andrews adjusted the antenna until a signal on the telephone-receiver
handset confirmed that he had found the satellite beam. "Okay, we're all
set. I've got a lock on the bird. Let me do a radio check with the Hermitage, and then you can take over." He pressed the transmit button.
"Hermitage, Hermitage. This is Hong Kong. Do you copy? Over." He listened to the reply and then turned to Alexander. "I've got your communicator. We're in our point-to-point mode, so there won't be anyone in
Washington taking notes. But I've put it on the speaker so I can follow the
conversation."

Alexander took the handset from Andrews and pushed the transmit
button. "Tim, this is Alexander. Do you copy? Over."

"Loud and clear. Please go ahead."

"Tim, how long ago did you receive the message from Pear Team?"

"Just over two hours. Actually we've received the same message two
more times since the first transmission two hours ago. The Boy must be
repeating the message to be sure we've got it. His location may not be
good enough to get our handshake signal, or maybe his antenna isn't set
right. Do you copy?"

"Copy. Give me your best estimate on how much more time he's got
on his batteries, assuming he's had his radio on receive since his first
transmission."

"Assuming he doesn't transmit any more and his batteries were fully
charged, he might have about three hours left, but if the time left on those
batteries is really important for what you're planning, cut it in half. Say an
hour and a half."

"That makes sense. Put J.D. on if he's there."

"Alexander, J.D. here. You copy?"

"I copy. Any ideas about this?"

"Just what I said in my cable. The only other thing I can add is that the
area around the shootdown is still being covered from the air. Mostly
choppers, but some ground-attack aircraft and a few Antonov reconnaissance platforms up there in orbit. We're following them closely up top in
the bunker. My people listening in on their radio chatter say it sounds like
the 40th Army is still out to get whoever took out their general."

"What's your recommendation?" Alexander asked his chief of operations.

"I say we go in and get them. It's just the two of them."

"If we can figure out exactly where they are. But I'm worried that they might be under control and that the SOS from the Boy is a setup to draw us in."

"I thought about that too, but there's not much we can do to verify that they're still free. Can NSA figure out anything from the radio traffic?"

"We'll check that out at this end. Even if they're not under control, we won't have time to hang out in that neighborhood, hot as it is. The Boy made it clear that Musawwir can't walk. We'd have to drop in right on top of them to make it work." He paused. "You and Tim stand by. I'll get back to you."

Alexander turned to Andrews. "I think we have to go in and pick those guys up."

"Can't you get the Paks to do it?"

"None of their choppers are equipped for this kind of job. We'll have to use our Puma in Peshawar."

"You think it's worth the risk? If they're under control, the Soviets will have a bunch of Americans dropped right into their laps. An act of war by the United States against the U.S.S.R. and all that. Half of Congress would go crazy."

Alexander considered this, but only for a moment. "It's worth the risk. First, I think we have a better than fair chance to pull it off; if I didn't, I wouldn't try. We can test the theory that they're under control, and we can buy some insurance before we actually drop on the ground."

Andrews chose his words carefully. "Alexander, these are just two guys in a war full of casualties. They knew the chances they were taking when they climbed up there to pop Polyakov."

"Look, Frank, the last five weeks have been a big turnaround for the resistance. But if Musawwir dies on that mountain after we had a chance to get him out, they'll never want to stick their necks out for us again. If we get him out, we'll be magic for the rest of this fight. If we try and fail, the effects will be almost the same. The people who count in this war will know that we're in it with them, and that we're willing to share their risks. I'm not saying we should charge in there just because Musawwir's my friend."

Andrews looked at Alexander hard and long. "All that sounds fine to me, but nobody in Washington will buy it, except maybe Casey. I assume there's no question about using what we like to call American assets— that is, Americans flying into Afghanistan in an American chopper."

"Of course I'm talking about using American assets. The Puma is registered to the Pakistani Air Force, but there's not much room for a plausible denial that it's ours."

Andrews reflected for a moment. "This is one of those situations where you choose not to burden Washington. If we do this, we do it 'uninstructed,' as the diplomatic phrase goes."

"For Crissakes, Frank. Let's just do it, and you can call home and tell them about it later. By the way, you're coming with me."

"As much as I'd love to, I won't. You'll need me more than ever in Washington when this goes down or goes south."

Andrews took the handset. "Hermitage, this is Andrews. Please provide me with the exact frequency on the transmitter used by Pear Team, then please stand by. We're leaving this channel, but will return as soon as we have new instructions for you. Do you copy?"

"Copy. The frequency is 425.773 MHz I repeat 425.773 MHz. Hermitage standing by."

"Washington Task Force, this is Hong Kong. Do you copy? Over."

The executive officer of the Afghan Task Force at CIA Headquarters in Washington replied, "Task Force copies." Bob Williamson's cheerful voice bounced back over the fifty-odd thousand miles. "What can I do for you this lovely morning on the Potomac? I thought you'd be out getting a second fitting on a cashmere sport jacket instead of working at this time of night."

"Bob, I need some help. First, turn off your speaker. I want this for your ears only, and no tape recording, please. Do you copy that?"

"Roger. Copy." Bob switched off the speaker and the tape recorder that copied radio exchanges with the field. "Okay, we're private. How can I help?"

"Bob, keep all of this theoretical and to yourself for the time being, and keep it informal and exploratory with the other agencies. Tell your NSA counterparts at the Fort and the people at NRO that we're simply going through a hypothetical exercise for the time being. Can you do that?"

"So far. What do you need?"

"I need two things within the next half hour. First, I want NSA to locate a transmitter sending burst transmissions from the area where Polyakov's plane was taken out two days ago. The frequency is 425.773 MHz. You have the exact coordinates from the satellite coverage of the shoot down. Second, I want you to ask the National Reconnaissance Office, still hypothetically, what kind of a visual signal a ragtag band of fighters in trouble would have to lay out on the ground for NRO to be able to pinpoint their location during the first reconnaissance pass after daylight tomorrow. You can tell them that they only have to look at the ridges above the left bank of the Kabul River in the same area where they got the shot of Polyakov's bird going in. Do you copy?"

"Roger, Frank. I think I can get this back to you in the next half hour, maybe less. Task Force out."

"Hong Kong standing by."

Andrews returned the handset to its cradle. "My friend, we will go ahead and do it as you suggest, but I do believe that one of these days you're going to get me fired or killed."

• • •

Williamson took less than half an hour to get back to Andrews. "NSA is still monitoring all activity in the area where Polyakov went down. My contact said they're still looking for the guys who fired the missiles day and night. There's ground-patrol activity down at the site of the crash. He also said that they picked up three short bursts at 425.773 MHz coming from the same area, but they couldn't read the message or locate the transmitter precisely. They could guarantee that the transmitter was within a one-thousand-yard circle of the coordinates of the shoot down. They'll continue to watch that frequency if we ask them to. You copy? Over."

"I copy. That's great, Bob. Try to make sure the Fort stays on top of the search efforts in the area for the next three days. Tell them we're expecting some significant activity in that location, but don't tell them what."

"How the hell could I tell them anything, Frank? I don't know what you're up to. Second issue. I just talked to my guy at NRO. He said that if your people could lay out something on the ground with good contrast and straight lines, at least one square meter in size, they'll find it if it's in that same area they imaged when Polyakov augered in. They said that some sort of a reflector would be great. Does that help? Over."

"Very much. Just what I needed. See if you can get your NRO contact back on the telephone and have him stand by."

Andrews turned to Alexander. "What do your guys carry on their missions that could be used as a signal on the ground for one of our birds to pick up? Has to be at least one meter square. Bob said a reflector of some sort would be ideal."

"A reflector. Christ, they travel light with only their weapons. Some rations, the little stove, and the medical survival kit that Doc designed. Wait a minute! Ask your guy if one of those aluminum-foil reflective thermal blankets that we use in cold weather survival kits would work. They're about six feet by four feet and fold into a package about the size of two packs of cigarettes."

Andrews raised Williamson and passed along the query. Moments later he was back on the radio.

"Frank, the NRO guy says that if that blanket is laid out and anchored firmly on the ground between 0700 and 0830 tomorrow morning they'll find it for you. It would be best if they could fold the blanket into a triangular shape. It's easier to spot something clearly man-made."

"Yeah, but it's easier for the Soviets to spot too," Andrews replied. "Okay, Bob, I'll be back to you within the hour. Thanks and out."

Andrews looked at Alexander. "Alexander, you know the rules. If we pull this off, nobody will even try to touch us. If we screw it up, they'll never let up on us."

Alexander raised the Hermitage on the radio handset. When they had finished giving their instructions to J.D., they packed up the satellite radio and moved inside to the study telephone. Fred Underman picked up on the second ring.

"Fred, get hold of Dangerfield and file a flight plan to get us back home tomorrow, the earlier the better."

"I can file the flight plan, but you might have to dig Dangerfield out of Wanchai yourself. He said something about getting his boots fixed and checking out some old friends at the 'O,' whatever the hell that is."

"You get everything ready for tomorrow. I'll find Dangerfield."

After Andrews left, Alexander found Katerina in bed watching the television. "Rise and shine. The fleet's in!"

They left the Jaguar in a parking garage on the edge of the Wanchai girlie-bar district and searched for Jim Dangerfield on foot. Alexander slipped his arm around Katerina as they walked into the garish glow of neon lights. Small groups of sailors and marines from the Seventh Fleet roamed self-consciously through the candy-store setting. Each bar along the strip had hand-lettered posters tacked at their entrances welcoming each of the three American fighting ships by name and number to the port of Hong Kong.

"There's our first stop, the venerable Ocean Bar." Alexander pointed at the blinking blue-and-red sign on the corner above the door of one of the oldest girlie bars in the Crown Colony. "Known the world over for its collection of the cleanest girls east of Suez. Old Pansy don't allow no girls with the clap to mess up her sailors, no ma'am." He pushed the door open and led Katerina into the strobe-lit interior.

It took a few moments for their eyes to adjust. Sailors and marines were grouped around the booths and tables with the little Chinese girls. Others were dancing to an unidentifiable sound coming from a stereo set in the corner. Alexander went over to the bar. "I need to talk to Pansy," he said when the bartender had leaned his head close enough to hear.

"Old Pansy or Young Pansy?"

"Old Pansy."

The bartender walked to the opposite end of the bar where three bar girls sat waiting to get lucky, and whispered to one of them. She wore a round name tag on her black silk cheongsam declaring that she was "Annie 54." She cast a surly glance at Alexander and Katerina and then disappeared.

A moment later the proprietress came through beaded curtains behind the bar and followed the bartender's nod to Alexander and Katerina. She was about seventy years old, but looked closer to fifty. Her hair was still jet-black, and her silver cheongsam was slit halfway up each leg. Aside from a couple of pounds pressing gently at the seams of her dress, she hadn't changed since the Japanese Chrysanthemum Division captured Hong Kong in December 1941. As she approached, Katerina caught a trace of suspicion behind her otherwise inscrutable face. But when she was a few feet away, she smiled, showing a mouth full of white false teeth.

"Alexander! Why that beard? You hurt your face? You too pretty to have hair all over your face. Shame." She looked at Katerina. "You watch this man. He tells plenty good stories. He stay away from Ocean for five years, and then come back like old friend who never go away. He belong you now?"

"He belong me now."

Alexander broke in. "Pansy, I need you to help me find Mister Jim. You know him from long ago. Jim with the wooden leg."

Pansy's face lit up. "That crazy sumbitch still coming in here. He messes with my young girls now. Only talks to Old Pansy. Never want to fool around." She spoke over her shoulder in rapid Cantonese to the girls collected at the far end of the bar. Annie 54 lifted herself off her stool and walked sullenly toward them. When Pansy spoke to her, the girl's eyes flashed recognition and she gave an animated response.

Katerina whispered in Alexander's ear, "They're saying the most obscene things about Mister Jim. It seems from Annie 54's appraisal that Mister Jim's leg isn't the only thing same-like hard wood all day long. At least that's my best Wanchai-bar-girl English for what she just said in Cantonese."

Pansy turned back to them. "Annie say that your friend buy Young Pansy out of here for two days for five hundred dollars Hong Kong this morning and take her out on wallah-wallah boat for ride to Lantao. Annie think maybe they back at Harbor View Hotel now where they do push-push. Annie say she can go see if you want."

Alexander said, "Annie 54, I would appreciate it very much if you'd bring my friend back here. Tell him that Alexander is looking for him and is in a plenty big hurry."

Twenty minutes later Jim Dangerfield walked in, his limp barely noticeable. He spotted Alexander in the corner. "Word is that you've got a search party out for me," he said as he squeezed into the booth.

"We're out of here tomorrow as soon as Fred can get clearance. You'll find him at Kaitak filing his flight plan and checking out the Gulfstream. You ready to go?"

"No. My boots are over at Kow Hoo's getting some new soles. I'll have to get them tonight. Just be at the airplane when Fred tells you to and I'll be there."

"Don't worry, Jim. I wouldn't fly with you if you couldn't find your boots. You probably can't get off the ground without them."

"Lotta guys would have told me if they were going to cut a trip short by a couple of days, Alexander. Lotta guys wouldn't be so capricious."

"Capricious. Christ, Dangerfield. Lotta guys wouldn't use words they don't even understand when they talk to the boss. See you at the airplane." As an afterthought Alexander wrote a name on a cocktail napkin and handed it to Dangerfield. "Put this name on the manifest."

"C. Martin. Who's this? Do I know him?"

Alexander gestured in Katerina's direction. "You do now."

Dangerfield smiled at Katerina. "You're the boss, Alexander. See you at the plane."

Ling dropped Katerina and Alexander at Kaitak Airport at six-thirty A.M. It took them less than five minutes to clear the perfunctory Hong Kong exit formalities and make their way to the small waiting room just off the ramp from where the Gulfstream was parked.

Fred Underman came in from the tarmac. "We're all gassed up, filed with the tower, and ready to go. Glad to see you're traveling light. I see you got C. Martin there with you. I'm Fred, I guess you know by now." He was more deferential than usual.

"Fred, please meet C. Martin, also known as Katerina. She'll be on the flight manifest we filed, but I don't want her name on any of your logs or reports."

"Whatever you say, boss. Keeping ladies' names out of logs is easy. I'm pleased to meet you, ma'am."

"And I'm delighted to meet you, Fred. Alexander has told me all about how you've flown him out of more trouble than you flew him into."

Underman was embarrassed. "Alexander can take care of himself. You probably know that," he said as they moved to the door.

As they boarded Alexander stuck his head into the cockpit and looked conspicuously at Dangerfield's feet. The spit-shined black boots were on the rudder pedals.

The Gulfstream had been airborne for an hour when Alexander opened the thick manila envelope Andrews had sent along. Katerina had been staring out the window, transfixed by the distant surface of the South China Sea, but now she turned to him.

"State secrets?"

Alexander nodded. "Secrets, yes, but I'm not sure they'll help us much." He pulled out a stack of documents. They were sorted into individual sets, each with a photograph stapled to a cover sheet. There were about forty sets in the stack.

"Langley did a detailed records check on the mysterious Colonel Belenko—an innovative analyst being helpful. I didn't ask for it," Alexander said. "They knew from my report that Belenko was probably a phony name, that he was thirty-five to forty years old, and that he spoke English and Dari. I didn't tell them he spoke Arabic. That might have led them to Tolya without any more help from me. The analysts fed the information into the database on Soviets, and told the machine to look for a three-syllable Ukrainian name as a first priority. This is the product of modern sleuthing."

"Why limit yourselves to Ukrainian names with the same number of syllables?" Katerina asked.

"Good question. It seems that our Soviet special services friends are often more predictable than either we or they think. It may seem old, but these guys usually pick aliases that have clues leading back to their true identities. They are usually throwaway aliases used once or twice by an intelligence officer when he thinks the people he is dealing with can't check up on him. Ethnic origin is the most reliable clue. It's subconscious. Most of them don't even know they do it, and the KGB hasn't gotten down to managing their throwaway aliases with computers. When they do, they won't like what they find."

"I'm not surprised," Katerina said. "Slavs are very predictable. Belenko, Klimenko. Your theory worked this time."

"Let's see what we've got." Alexander began flipping through the sets of documents, first looking only at the photographs. He had gone through about fifteen sets when he raised his eyebrows. "Bingo!" He pulled a four-page document from the stack and handed it to Katerina.

She looked at the photograph attached to the cover sheet of the report. It was a fuzzy copy of an old passport photo of Klimenko, probably when he was first posted to Iran. She began reading the report, handing pages over to Alexander as she finished them. The biographic data had everything one wanted to know about Anatoly Viktorovich Klimenko.

"What's 'According to Casket Source'? That's shown up three times already."

"Defectors, information from defectors is described with the code word 'Casket.' All it means is that some KGB defector has provided the information in that section of the report."

Katerina continued reading. "Here, read this page. Our cousin is one tough hombre according to one defector."

Alexander took the page from her. "I'll be damned. He was in on the KGB rescue operation in Beirut."

"Didn't I read something about that in the press?" Katerina asked.

"Only the public-relations part of it, something like, 'Soviet Hostages Freed in Beirut.' It's actually a KGB success story. Early last year, three

KGB officers from the Beirut Rezidentura were taken hostage by Hizbollah. During capture one of them was badly wounded in the knee by a ricocheting bullet. The Hizbollah didn't get him any medical treatment and he died, but it took almost ten days, and it really affected the other two KGB officers locked up in a closet with him."

"How do you know so much about this?" Katerina asked.

"It dovetailed with our own search for Bill Buckley. He was our station chief in Beirut who also had been captured by Hizbollah. We were talking quietly with the KGB about helping each other to get our people out alive, but they had better luck than we did."

"What do you know about what Klimenko did that isn't in the report here?"

"If I'm putting it all together right, Klimenko went into Beirut as an Aeroflot representative to negotiate for the release of the three KGB guys. He ended up handing over ten million dollars in ransom, but he loaded the bags with transponders, tiny homing beacons, and was wired with a transmitter all the time himself. As the two KGB officers and one corpse were traded for the dollars, a KGB Group Alfa team popped up in the middle of the deal. They captured six of the Hizbollah terrorists and executed them on the spot. The last two to die were brothers, and the Group Alfa boys thought it would be nice for each of them to carry something from the other brother into the next life, so they cut off their testicles, switched them, and sewed them into their mouths."

Katerina shuddered. "It says that Klimenko got the Order of the Red Banner for that operation, and that there was a lot of resentment and finger-pointing in the Beirut Rezidentura over the fact that an outside team had swept into town and got all the glory."

"That's right. The source of the report is one of the two officers Klimenko rescued, who showed his gratitude by defecting about six weeks later. Which made things ever tougher on the Acting Rezident in Beirut."

Alexander spelled Dangerfield for three hours on the Hong Kong–Colombo leg and then slept most of the way to Karachi. The twin-engine turboprop B-300 flew from Karachi to Parachinar in good time, and was beginning its descent when Alexander went up to the crowded cockpit. "After you drop us off, I want you to take this bird straight on to Peshawar and leave it parked on the ramp. Don't put it in the hangar. It's okay for it to be seen, and you can be sure it will. Then I want both of you to go to the Pearl Continental and check in. Shower up, and try to give the impression that you're taking a few days' rest time. After dark, take a cab from the hotel to the Peshawar Club, and at 2000 hours leave the club on foot and walk down the road about a hundred yards. There you'll be picked up and driven to the hangar. Okay so far?"

"Roger. What's the point?"

"Then check out the helicopter and make sure it's got extra night-vision sets. After that stand by and wait for a call. You may fly back down here tonight, or you may wait until tomorrow. If tomorrow, I'll let you know by 2200 hours."

Five minutes later the sleek Beechcraft touched down and Dangerfield let it roll to the end of the runway farthest from the parking apron. As the aircraft eased to a halt, a white Toyota Landcruiser with black-tinted windows pulled off the grass and up to the left rear door. In seconds two passengers had tossed their bags in the back and were inside before the Afghan escorts and ground-support personnel at the parking ramp could count them, much less make out who they were.

TWENTY-FOUR

It was cool and quiet in the cave. The soundproof environment was broken only by the low rustle of the air-exchange system filtering and recirculating the air in the living quarters chiseled out of the mountain. Alexander had showered and changed into a white cotton shalwar chamise while Katerina rested. Now he lay stretched out on his back on the carpeted floor, eyes closed, his abdomen and chest rising and falling in a controlled, rhythmic breathing. His feet were spread slightly, his arms outstretched, palms cupped upward, fingers curved and pointing toward the ceiling. Concentrating on his inner self, he felt himself sinking deeper into the hard floor beneath the carpet as the gravity forces drew the fatigue out of his body. His mind took control of his body, putting it into a comatose sleep for several minutes while he remained fully awake and alert, a detached observer. The fatigue of the last three days dissipated, radiating out through his fingertips.

Katerina sat on the edge of the bed watching his yogic sleep. Wrapped in a white terry-cloth towel, she dried her short hair with her fingers. After a few minutes the towel loosened and dropped around her hips. She ignored it and continued to watch Alexander.

Moments later he opened his eyes, completely alert and totally refreshed. He awakened his body more gradually, feeling new energy coursing through him as he tentatively flexed the muscles of his limbs. Katerina rose from the bed and stood over him, still naked and damp, one foot on either side of his waist.

Alexander looked up at her from the floor. "You know, at this moment I have the best view of your little strawberry mark I've ever had. I think it looks more like a rose with a short stem and leaves than the map of France." He pulled her down slowly until she straddled him, her knees tucked under his armpits. His hands moved up her smooth legs and hips to her breasts, his fingers tracing the dark lines of her tan.

"I'm going to have to stash you here, alone and out of the way for a little while, Martynova, okay?"

"You don't have to baby-sit me. I didn't come here as a tourist or even as a concubine." She kissed him and then stood up.

"When you feel like getting decent, look in the camp chest on the right at the end of the bed for some native garb. They're called shalwar chamises. One size fits all." He paused to look back at his wife as he left the room. "Sort of."

Alexander pushed through the bookcase into his office where he found J.D. and Doc. A pot of green tea sat between them on a camp table.

"Hi, boss, welcome back. Looks like you can't take a whole week off from the jihad without getting homesick."

"Thanks, J.D. Let's get moving. Give me an update on everything new since I last talked to you."

Tim Rand came down the spiral ladder from his communications center with a folder of papers.

Alexander gestured to him. "Pull up a cushion, Tim. I'm going to need your advice."

J.D. shuffled through the papers and began his briefing. "Before I bring you up to date on Musawwir, I have something to report on the Algerians. This will touch your soul. The guys who ambushed you belonged to a larger group of Algerians working with Professor Sayyaf. The day you left for Hong Kong, the Mad Mullah went over to their camp on Sayyaf territory. He laid out a great feast, and gave them a spellbinding Friday sermon. He left the goat behind, with two claymores tucked inside it. After he got out of range, he hit the button on a radio. From the way I hear it, you couldn't tell what was goat and what was Algerians. So there's a new weapon in the war: the goat bomb."

Alexander shook his head. "Anything else happen while you were watching the store?"

J.D. shook his head. "Not much. Orlov has been behaving himself, just lying in the sun and reading anything he can get his hands on. He's okay. After we talked to you in Hong Kong, we sent your message to Musawwir and the Boy, and got a handshake confirming they had received it. To summarize, we told them that we were working on getting them out, that they should place the thermal-blanket signal at the top of the ridge at a point where a helicopter could set down—"

Doc broke in. "I've been over every item in the first-aid kit with the Boy. I also told him to give Musawwir the antibiotic injections that are in the kit every four hours until we get to them."

Alexander turned back to J.D. "Did the thermal blanket work?"

"It worked—at least it worked if the guys on that radio are actually Musawwir and the Boy and not some guys named Ivan and Sergei. Here's the imagery from Washington." J.D. spread the fax on the table.

"You can't actually see the blanket in this photograph, but it's at the end of the arrow right there. This picture gives the precise location for a guided approach, using the global positioning satellites. We have all the equipment we need to drop down within ten feet of where the Boy placed the blanket. It looks fine if the winds aren't blowing too hard over that ridge when we go in. Then we sent the question you asked in a second message. 'What is the name of the box that hears helicopters?' We did not close with the usual 'Trust in God'; we just asked the question straight, as you instructed. We got a handshake and ten minutes later got this." J.D. handed another piece of paper across the low table.

Alexander took it and read aloud: "The box is blackout. Trust in God." He reflected for a moment. "If the kid was under control they could probably squeeze him and make him tell them the name of the blackout, but I don't think they'd have the insight to add 'Trust in God,' particularly if we didn't end our message that way. My hunch is that they're not under control."

"I agree," J.D. said. "Next, we sent the Boy a short message telling him to remove the thermal blanket two hours after sunrise this morning and to turn off his radio and save his batteries until sundown tonight—that's an hour and a quarter from now—when we'll transmit new instructions."

"Anything in from the Fort?" Alexander asked.

"The Fort placed the transmitter in the same area we think it is. That may also be a positive; on the other hand, if I were the Soviets and had Musawwir and the Boy under control and was trying to sucker us into making a grab for them, I'd sure as hell do all my business from that mountaintop. So it's a plus, but not a big enough one to rule out hostile control."

"Anything more?"

"You asked about flight activity around Jalālābād. Pakistan radar has followed the whole business from start to finish. There are flights of three to four MI-8s carrying troops and two or three MI-24 gunships escorting them about every three hours from Jalālābād airfield. They're keeping at least four helicopters on station at all times with these rotations."

"How much time do you think he's got left on those batteries, Tim?" Alexander asked.

"It's getting critical. He'll probably be able to receive our message, but

I'm not sure he'll be able to reply. We'll just have to see if we're lucky. He must have moved his radio, because we're getting handshakes now, and he probably is too, since he's not repeating his transmissions like he did before."

"Tim, is there anything about his radio procedure that makes you think the radio might be controlled by the Soviets?"

"Absolutely nothing, but that shouldn't make us feel good."

"What do you think, J.D.?" Alexander asked.

J.D. leaned back and thought for a moment. "We know that the Boy is alive and that he's probably within a few hundred yards of the spot he marked on the ridgeline. We have no evidence that Musawwir is alive since the first transmission saying he was wounded. We don't know if the Soviets have our friends and their radio under control, but I tilt toward thinking they don't—at least not yet. But that's where my instincts start kicking in."

"What instincts?"

"My 'Oh Shit' instincts. A lot of assets on both sides looked very hard at that spot on the ridge. If NSA can pick up the bursts from the Fashioner's radio, it's a good bet the GRU or the KGB have also picked up something. The same goes for the thermal blanket. One of the Soviet aircraft looking for anything in that area probably picked up on that. Finally, I worry that your arrival at Parachinar may have heated up the neighborhood even more. The flight-scheduling smokescreen won't fool the Soviets for long, or even at all."

Alexander nodded in agreement. "The only question is whether the Soviets have someone looking at all this information at the same time, someone who's smart enough to draw the conclusion that we might be planning to drop down on that spot and snatch our guys. If they do, they'll probably figure out that we're going to try something in about twenty-four hours." He stood and paced the room for a moment. "We go in tonight at around midnight. Now, gather around. We'll have to get this right the first time."

KABUL, 1800 HOURS, SEPTEMBER 30

The sun dipped below the roof across the central courtyard of 40th Army Headquarters as Klimenko read through the last of a series of signals and human intelligence reports on curious activities now under way in Pakistan and in bordering Paktia province. Something was about to happen, something that threatened him. Deeply troubled, he reached for his telephone.

Ten minutes later, Krasin noisily barged in. "What's so secret that you can't discuss it on the phones of the 40th Army, my dear colonel?"

Klimenko put his finger to his lips, picked up a pencil, dialed the zero on his desk telephone, and holding it at the top of the dial, stuck the eraser end into the finger hole for the nine. Then he carefully released the dial, which the pencil prevented from returning to its rest position.

Sasha narrowed his eyes. "What in the hell are you doing?"

"This simple trick keeps our friends from turning my phone into a microphone, and my advice to you would be to watch yourself not only on your phone, but anywhere near it. With your beloved General Polyakov smeared all over the Eastern Mountains, I would guess that his order for the Committee to stay off the phones in his headquarters might have been rescinded."

"Okay. Why am I over here?"

Klimenko took a deep breath. "I have independent reports from Peshawar and from Nangarhar province that the big Dukhi you and I have been dealing with in the Orlov trade, the one you were so buddy-buddy with, is the same guy who brought down Polyakov's plane. Everybody in Peshawar is talking about it. He's a modern Afghan hero."

"Let's talk sometime about who's allied with whom, Colonel." Sasha stared at Klimenko.

Klimenko ignored the comment. "A lot of people in Peshawar think that your pal may still be in the area where the plane went down. According to the scuttlebutt from Peshawar he never got back across zero line into Pakistan. Some say he's badly wounded, but about the same number have him dead."

"Who else knows this?" Sasha asked.

Klimenko read the worry in his friend's voice and admitted the question was the right one.

"Probably a large number of people around here know the identity of the Dhuki who fired the Stinger, or at least led the team that got Polyakov. The word was all over Peshawar the same day. Nobody could keep that secret in this kind of war. It's a guy they call Musawwir, which is one of the names of Allah: it means the Fashioner. But the number gets smaller when we talk about who knows the identity of the big Dukhi we've been meeting on the Orlov talks. Some of the people who had all the facts went down on Polyakov's plane. But with the intensity of the search for Polyakov's killer, someone is sure to figure it out. First among the handful who could put it all together is Karm Sergeyevich. He will soon have all the parts of the puzzle, and he will be the first to know that I've had those parts all along. That, I am sure you would agree, is the bad news."

Klimenko continued. "There's more. The 16th Directorate sent over a short report this morning noting that there have been at least three burst broadcasts from the general area of the crash in the last two days. They've picked up an increase in similar broadcasts they think are the other end of the radio link from Peshawar, but they think that's only being relayed from Paktia province, where our CIA friends have their hideout."

Sasha frowned. "Can the 16th Directorate actually decipher the messages?"

"No, they just intercepted short encrypted bursts. They don't even know how long the compressed messages are, just that there's some strange radio activity going on. They send all of these intercepts to me because they're using the same system we've been lucky enough to break in the Alpha broadcasts between our Dukhi friends on the Orlov trade. Any messages intercepted in that system come to me directly and exclusively, but a few others, including Karm Sergeyevich, have access to the intercepted messages that may be related to the Polyakov shootdown." He looked at Sasha. "You still with me?"

Sasha nodded.

"Our communications-intercept people in Islamabad reported this afternoon that there's been a second case of phony cover-flight activity in Parachinar in the last three days. Another CIA flight came in from Karachi, stopped for only a couple of minutes, and went on to Peshawar trying to pass itself off as a Pakistani Air Lines domestic flight. It's on the ground there now. Our Islamabad colleagues think the CIA is planning something special, but they haven't got a clue what."

"Is there more?"

"Yes. I just got a report relayed from an agent in the Peshawar Airport confirming that the CIA's airplane has popped up there. He's put a stakeout on the CIA's hangar on the military side of the runway."

"They've got their own hangar out there?"

"Everybody calls it the CIA hangar. It's been called that for over twenty-five years. It's one they used in the early sixties for their U-2s. They're supposed to have some special equipment in there now— helicopters and maybe a short-takeoff airplane—but it's buttoned up tight. All I've ever been able to do is get a few folks to within half a mile of it, which is what I've got there right now."

"And?"

"And finally, one of the reconnaissance flights standing watch over the crash site reported seeing a reflector of some sort at daybreak this morning high on a ridge near where the Stinger gunners fired. It looked like some sort of a signal and he reported it back through channels. A second aircraft sent a follow-up report two hours later. It went over the area a dozen times. No reflector. It's gone. They're not even sure exactly which ridgeline it was on when the first Antonov spotted it."

"What do you think about all of this?"

Klimenko leaned back in his chair. "First, why don't you tell me what *you* think all of this means—that is, to us personally."

Sasha sat down and put his feet on Klimenko's desk. He looked hard at his friend. "Tolya, I think you are going to tell me what I need to know."

"I will tell you the whole story, Sasha, but only when you're part of it." Krasin snapped forward in his chair.

"For God's sake, this is Sasha, the same Sasha who dragged that worthless Shadrin over that mine back there. I murdered that little pissant. How much deeper can I get? It's too late to keep me in the dark!"

"Okay, Sasha, but no interruptions." He pulled out a bottle of pepper vodka, poured two glasses nearly full, took a sip, and with a sense of relief, began to talk.

By the time Klimenko finished, lights were on in the offices across the courtyard. "Do you want to back out now?"

"I think I may have understated the situation when I said it was too late, Tolya." Sasha rose and paced the room for a moment. "First, you are right about the hunt for Polyakov's killer being the consuming business of the 40th Army for at least the next several days. Nobody really gave a shit that Polyakov got popped, but nobody's going to give up the pursuit of vengeance until it's ordered by General Gromov himself."

Klimenko nodded and added, "And Gromov is off in Moscow explaining what the hell is going on to a pissed-off bunch of folks in the ministry of defense."

Sasha continued. "When they put all the pieces together, they will reach some dangerous conclusions. And they will question why you, Colonel Klimenko, didn't figure it out sooner and alert them in time to do something about it. One possible answer is that you're slow-witted and dumb, but they might not believe that. A second possible answer is that you chose to ignore the signals for your own treasonous reasons, and *that* they might believe."

Klimenko nodded.

Sasha continued, "I think you've already figured out that the CIA is gearing up to rescue its Dukhi friend from that mountain. Am I right?"

"Absolutely right. Go on."

"If that is true, there are four possible outcomes, all of which affect you, and anything that affects you will reflect on me because of Karm Sergeyevich. First, you sit on the information and the CIA pulls off its rescue. After a while Karm and the others start asking you hard questions, and soon after that they will start drawing the correct conclusions. That is not good."

"Go on."

"The next three possibilities are all part of a single set. Let's assume that you have just called me over here to share all of these tantalizing tidbits, and with my invaluable help, have figured that someone is planning to rescue the cold-blooded murderer of Boris Semyonovich Polyakov. You need my help in convincing the Acting First Deputy Commander of the 40th Army that we need to mount a major Spetsnaz effort to interdict the rescue attempt and avenge the death of our leader. You turn to me because people across the courtyard tend to take me seriously in spite of my well-known weakness of character.

"Now come the three possible outcomes of our effort to stop the rescue. First, we give it a heroic try and fail; the bad guys are successful and get away clean. Second, we swoop in and kill all the bad guys. Third, we swoop in and *capture* all the bad guys." Sasha paused and asked, "Did I miss any possibilities?"

"None, though I would have put them in a slightly different order."

"Then going back to your original question, we probably agree that the worst development would be for us to capture these Dukhis and their American CIA friends. The same applies if they are captured by the troops now looking for them. If we do nothing, those troops might get lucky. If the CIA people and the Dukhis are captured, eventually they will talk and we will probably die, assuming they capture someone who knows your dark secrets. I think it's as simple as that."

"Yes, Major. They will take us down into the cellar of the Lubyanka and shoot us. That is guaranteed."

"Then we have to make sure that one of the other two scenarios plays out."

Klimenko looked at his friend and felt a little lonely. "I think the first step is yours." He pushed the telephone across his desk.

Sasha pulled out the pencil and the dial clicked nine times as it returned to its original position. He dialed a four-number extension and cleared his throat. "This is Major Krasin. I must speak to General Titov at once."

Sasha listened. "I understand, Major, but it involves that very issue. I am at this minute with Colonel Klimenko in the Special Action Group, and we have information that has a material bearing on the search for the criminal murderers." He rolled his eyes. "I know you wouldn't want to be viewed as preventing such information from reaching the general. Of course I understand your position. You haven't forgotten that I was the aide of Boris Semyonovich. Yes, thank you." He winked at Klimenko as he waited.

"Yes, General Titov. Krasin, aide to General Boris Semyonovich. Yes, sir, I insisted. I have information I believe must be acted on immediately, and I believe only you can give the orders and the operational guidance that will give us a chance to capture the murderers. Yes, of course I can bring him with me now. We will be with you in ten minutes. Thank you, General."

Sasha turned to Klimenko. "It's showtime over at Titov's office, but believe me, we have a lot more talking to do if we're going to get through this."

Ninety minutes later Klimenko and Krasin had finished their briefing of General Titov and half a dozen of his senior staff officers. Now he looked at Klimenko and Krasin solemnly, drew his hands together under his chin, and tapped his fingertips as he spoke.

"You have presented your facts well and thoughtfully. I agree with you that there is sufficient evidence to conclude that the American special services are possibly planning to mount some sort of a rescue operation into Nangarhar, and that we will have to stop them. I think we must have our plan refined and our resources lined up by noon tomorrow if we are to be in position tomorrow night when, in my judgment, the Americans will move."

Klimenko leaned forward in his chair. "Sir, I agree with you that the evidence points to some action tomorrow night. That would be the best operational choice, but it would also be the most *obvious* choice—by the American special services, I mean. I think they're going to make their move tonight, possibly within the next eight hours and so should we."

Klimenko's suggestion that the general had erred in his conclusion was met by glaring silence. Finally Titov spoke.

"Very well, Colonel, you have a point. None of this is conventional. We move tonight, and then again tomorrow night if necessary. Gentlemen, make the arrangements. Colonel Klimenko, you and Major Krasin will of course take part in the operation. Since you know personally the Dukhi who killed Boris Semyonovich, it will give you some satisfaction to take part in his capture. That is all, gentlemen. You may leave to get on with your planning, except for Colonel Klimenko, with whom I would like to have a few words in private."

Titov's staff cleared out. The general exhaled a blue cloud of smoke before he spoke.

"Colonel, during your otherwise excellent and very convincing presentation, you chose to ignore one very important fact, a fact that no one on my staff dared raise either. You did not point out the possible effects the capture or killing of the man you think was responsible for Boris Semyonovich's death might have on the exchange of Lieutenant Orlov. The man whose rescue you hope to thwart is the same man with whom you have been dealing on the Orlov exchange, is he not?"

"Yes, General Titov, you are correct. He is a man known by the camp name Musawwir, one of the ninety-nine names of Allah. It means the

Fashioner, He Who Fashions All Things." Klimenko paused. Titov watched him closely.

"I chose not to mention this very important fact during my briefing because I did not wish to put the general in the position of having to make a choice between the clear-cut issue of the punishment of those responsible for murdering Boris Semyonovich, and the less clear-cut political matter of Lieutenant Orlov, which has not yet become the general's personal responsibility."

"You are correct, Colonel Klimenko, but I can assure you that if there is a reversal, and Lieutenant Orlov is not handed over in good health, the matter will rapidly become my responsibility."

"Yes, sir, but at this moment it remains a KGB problem, which affords the general a small degree of protection, at least for the next few days. I would have asked to have this conversation in private with the general had he not chosen to initiate it himself."

"Can you keep this operation and the Orlov matter separate, Colonel?"

"General Titov, my best advice is that you remain unbriefed on the Orlov exchange for the time being, and that you let me continue to manage it under the auspices of the Committee. If it goes sour for any reason, the recriminations will be focused on the Committee and not on the general. That is my best judgment, General."

"Colonel, what I'm really asking you is whether the Dushman will still go through with the Orlov exchange if we kill their man."

Klimenko answered carefully. "The rebels chose to broaden the activities of their so-called Fashioner to include the murder of General Polyakov. It is my judgment that they will understand our actions within the context of their own culture. Revenge is not unknown to these people, General. In short, we can kill their Musawwir and still free our lieutenant. If we capture their Musawwir, then we can most assuredly expect them to raise the stakes in the Orlov exchange to include his release, as well as that of the others already agreed upon."

"It would seem to me, then, that the best outcome of tonight's operation would be to kill the Dushman, not capture him. You never heard that from me, however. Is that clear, Colonel Klimenko?"

"Perfectly clear, and perfectly in line with my own conclusions, General."

"Very well, Colonel, you are to proceed. And Colonel, I admire your grasp of the nuances. I will take your counsel for now and will not assume responsibility for the Orlov matter until after we next meet. Of course, if I receive a call from General Orlov in Wünsdorf, I will have to advance my timetable. Thank you. You may go now."

TWENTY-FIVE

Katerina was lying on the bed leafing through the only book she had found in the room, Caroe's *The Pathans,* when Alexander returned. She was wearing one of his white cotton Afghan shirts that came to below her knees.

He took out a dark gray wool shalwar chamise, and as he stripped out of his lighter cotton garment he spoke gravely. "Kat, I'll be leaving you for several hours, maybe for a day or so. There is something that has to be done."

Katerina watched him tie the drawstring of his wide Afghan pants and pull on the long shirt; then he reached into the camp chest for his shoulder holster and Browning, along with a leather pouch for extra clips. The usual playfulness was gone, and for the first time since Alexander had come back to Afghanistan, Katerina was frightened. But her fear somehow reinforced her bond with her husband, one that took into account the risks he was taking now and those they would both take in the future. "I told you I didn't come here as a tourist, but I sure as hell didn't come along to become a widow, either," she said. "Go do what you have to do, and do it well, but you'd better come back here to me."

He sat down on the edge of the bed. "This should all be over before sunrise. I've told Tim to pass along anything important to you." He kissed her lightly on the forehead, squeezed her hand, and then left the room without looking back.

KABUL AIRFIELD, 2000 HOURS

Klimenko and Krasin stepped out of their staff car on the tarmac near a group of ten Spetsnaz troopers waiting to board an Antonov. Their relaxed demeanor might have been mistaken for a sullen attitude or a lack of discipline, but it was neither. They were all seasoned soldiers who had served multiple tours in Afghanistan. They studied Klimenko and Sasha carefully, taking in the salty battle fatigues and the way the two officers slung their stubby AKM assault rifles over their right shoulders, muzzle down.

Sasha walked up to the captain in command of the group. "Lukin! Why haven't you died yet? Maybe tonight you'll get lucky." He punched his shoulder.

"Maybe tonight we'll all get lucky, Sasha. With you along we can guarantee at least somebody a ride home"—Lukin paused and then showed his white, even teeth—"on a Black Tulip!"

Klimenko saw a lieutenant he knew from his early days in Afghanistan. He had gone out on special operations several times with the man, and on one occasion had brought him back from a skirmish in Pakistan badly wounded and slung over the back of a mule. "Rogov! It's your turn to bring me home tonight."

"Better you than me." Vladimir Rogov's smile conveyed absolutely no joy, even to Klimenko, one of the few men in Afghanistan he might call a friend. He felt a rare comradeship with Klimenko, and was able to forget that he was from the KGB, an organization the army despised. But Klimenko was an Alfa guy, he had stuck his neck out for him when he'd caught a bullet. Rogov knew it would have been easier for Klimenko to finish him off with a bullet and head back to Nangarhar, but he brought him back. Rogov wouldn't forget it.

Klimenko slapped Rogov's shoulder where he had been badly wounded. "How's the shoulder now?"

Rogov didn't wince. "No big deal."

PESHAWAR AIRFIELD, 2000 HOURS

With Alexander beside him in the copilot's seat, Fred Underman brought the B-300 down at Peshawar and reversed its props with a jolting blast. As they began to taxi toward the CIA hangar, they saw an assortment of vehicles parked near it.

Alexander tapped the windshield. "With all that activity out here, half of North West Frontier Province will know something is about to happen—the mean and nasty half."

Underman nodded but said nothing as he surveyed the scene. The sun had dropped below the mountains to the west, handing the Eastern Mountains back to darkness. There would be no moon tonight, which would help a little.

Underman shut down the engines as Alexander moved to the rear of the cabin and dropped open the door ladder. The four men walked quickly to the hangar, where Jim Dangerfield was waiting. "Jesus, Alexander, Colonel Faisal picked me up like you said, but he had all these guys out here in case we needed some help. I told him we didn't, but they'd already kicked up a lot of dust."

"I know that. Let's hope we can move faster than the bad guys can figure out what we're up to. How's the bird look?"

"She's fine. Ought to be. I just about built her with my own hands."

Alexander walked across the vast hangar floor to the Puma helicopter modified by the CIA for night operations. Its surface of porous black infrared-absorbing paint gave it an air of menace. There were small, subdued Pakistani roundels on the fuselage, ostensibly marking it as Pakistani Air Force. In every other respect the Puma was unique.

Alexander turned to Dangerfield. "Jim, give us a walk around. J.D. and Doc have never seen this bird."

As he walked over to the black aircraft, the steel wedges in the new heels of his flying boots echoed in the vaulted space, a slightly uneven cadence betraying his wooden leg. "From the outside this bird looks pretty much like a regular Pak Air Force Puma. The black paint job is different, but nobody knows that. About all you can see at a glance is the FLIR pod tucked up under the belly of the aircraft." He bent over and pointed to a small domelike pod attached to the bottom of the helicopter forward of the landing gear. "F-L-I-R. That's forward-looking infrared, which makes a man see in the dark. You all know how important that can be. The bird has pods with Soviet AT-5 and AT-6 rockets and a 23 mm Gatling gun, plus a 12.7 machine gun and, as the pièce de résistance, two reasonably good Soviet AA-8 self-defense missiles in case we wander into anybody up there in the air with us. All the weapons systems have been taken off our growing spare-parts fleet of Soviet aircraft. They work fine, and everything is hooked up to the main control panel where the pilot or copilot can operate the systems. Since I have no real copilot tonight, Alexander is going to fly up front with me, and may God have mercy on your pitiful souls.

"Step up into my office." Dangerfield put his good leg on the step of the Puma and vaulted into the troop-carrying area of the helicopter. The others followed him more awkwardly. "Up here in the cockpit is where you see the old Puma give way to the new high-speed Puma that a lotta guys back at Langley fixed up for me." He slipped into the left seat of the helicopter and motioned Alexander into the right one as he continued his briefing. "This screen on the center panel takes the infrared image intensified by the receiver electronics in the pod under the aircraft and displays the environment all around the bird. This system can look around and can be directed by this little 'coolie-hat' control right here on the panel. Lotta guys got FLIRs that just look straight ahead. With the FLIR system, working with the GPS—that's global-positioning satellites to you—to guide us to within about thirty feet of the three places we want to go tonight, and with our radar altimeter, I can fly us in the dark without running into any rocks."

Dangerfield paused for applause. There was none. "All of us going out tonight will be wearing these goggles." He handed one set to Alexander and held up another for the others to see. "These are ANVIS 6 night-vision goggles. You've all been using the single-tube devices. These have double tubes and give you binocular vision *and* depth perception. That's all you need to know about this bird. I've got pink-light devices, sort of infrared searchlights, but we can't use them if we're going to be around Soviet gunships tonight. They'll be working with infrared and any pink light coming from us will look like a Hollywood opening night. With this dry weather and the Afghan terrain, we'll see just fine, black as it is. There you are, gentlemen; you have been oriented."

Alexander looked at his watch. "It's 2010 hours. In twenty minutes it will be black enough for us to take off. Fred, tell Faisal that we want to move out at 2030 hours, and he'll take care of the rest."

JALĀLĀBĀD AIRFIELD, 2020 HOURS

It was too dark to see the wreckage of the helicopters as the lumbering Antonov touched down at the southeast end of Jalālābād's single runway, but all the men aboard the plane were thinking about the gunners out there. They were relieved to be flying into Jalālābād at night, when, according to their information, the Stinger was ineffective.

After the Antonov pulled to a squealing halt, Sasha asked Captain Lukin to stay aboard while the other troops deplaned for a smoke. Klimenko was forward in the aircraft, standing by the radio console watching a sheet of paper work its way out of the cipher teletype machine. The radio operator pulled the sheet across a cutting blade and handed it to Klimenko, who moved under a dome light to read the message to Sasha and Lukin.

"Here's an update from the operations center. It says that the American special services type C-12 aircraft returned to Parachinar from Peshawar at 1900 hours, stayed on the ground for about five minutes, presumably to pick up passengers, and returned to Peshawar at 1950 hours. It is under standoff observation at this time near the old U-2 hangar. Fortieth Army communications-intercept teams report that Pakistani Air Force communications are forecasting a VIP night flight of two Puma helicopters from Peshawar to the landing pads at Michni Point at the west end of the Khyber Pass at 2030 hours tonight, with a return to Peshawar at 2230 hours. Our intelligence analysts consider this flight highly unusual." Klimenko paused. "There is almost never any nighttime helicopter flight activity in the Khyber. They believe that tonight the Paks will probably fly at an altitude a few hundred feet above the highest peaks of the pass until they spot the lights at Michni, then will drop down. We ought to pick them up on our radar here when they reach altitude above the Khyber."

Sasha read through message. "Then you think the flight to Michni Point is smoke?"

"We have to look at it that way."

Sasha nodded. "What now?"

Klimenko turned to Lukin. "Captain, I think we should get your men aboard the helicopters and take off."

Captain Lukin looked at his watch. "It will take another forty-five minutes to install the communications gear we need."

Klimenko grimaced. "That puts us behind the curve if that flight to Michni Point is a smoke screen. Push the men. Let's see if we can get out of here any sooner."

PESHAWAR AIRFIELD, 2030 HOURS

The two Pakistani Air Force Pumas taxied across the military side of the Peshawar airfield past the old U-2 hangar, but it was too dark for the two Afghans hidden in the brush more than one thousand yards off the end of the runway to see the third blacked-out Puma slip in beside the two aircraft as they took off. They saw only the running lights of the two air force helicopters. They reported via a frequency-hopper radio to an airborne communications platform over eastern Afghanistan that two helicopters had departed Peshawar on a westerly heading at precisely 2030 hours.

JALĀLĀBĀD AIRFIELD, 2035 HOURS

Klimenko, Sasha, and Captain Lukin were in the radar room of the operations center when the watch officer spoke from his console. "There's your Pak Air Force flight!"

As the three men looked over his shoulder at the radar screen, he explained what he had picked up. "See that large blip at three o'clock? That's your flight of helicopters."

"Why do we only see one blip?" Sasha asked, bending over for a closer look.

"They're flying in close formation. It's impossible to differentiate individual helicopters with this type of radar. We might see how many there are when they begin to drop down for their landing, but we'll lose them quickly when they get below the mountains."

"Then you won't be able to tell how many helicopters are out there?"

"No, not with this equipment."

MICHNI POINT, 2055 HOURS

The pilot of the lead helicopter began his descent toward the brightly lit landing pads at Michni Point, leaving his wingman in a tight orbit at ten thousand feet. The landing lights of both aircraft were visible to the reception party on the ground far below.

What was not visible was the third Puma running without lights just above and to the rear of the lead helicopter. As the two helicopters dropped below the ridges of the Khyber Pass the blacked-out one rolled off the back of the lead Puma and veered to the north. After it dropped closer to the earth it would begin to thread its way out of the pass down to the Jalālābād plain. The four Americans in the black Puma had donned their ANVIS 6 goggles and were watching the greenish shades of heat from the terrain as their craft dropped below the gaze of the Jalālābād radar system.

Alexander keyed the intercom button. "We're crossing over into the badlands now. My bet is that they may have figured out what we're up to, but they're going to have to be pretty good to be able to do anything about it."

The Puma flew on for nine minutes at treetop level to a preset destination west of Jalālābād. Alexander tapped Dangerfield on the shoulder and pointed through the windshield. "There they are—ten warm bodies, just like we asked for."

Dangerfield spotted the heat sources near the edge of the Kabul River and set the Puma down on the sandy bank. The GPS computer had guided them to within thirty feet of their rendezvous point with Engineer Youssuf, his cousin Wali Khan, and his fighters. In a minute, five of the fighters had boarded the helicopter, now loaded to capacity with ten men and an assortment of light and heavy weapons. Five of the fighters stayed behind as planned.

JALĀLĀBĀD AIRFIELD, 2100 HOURS

The technicians had shaved five minutes off their forty-five minute estimate as they installed the communications equipment in the four

MI-24s. Lukin went through his check of the secure radio links with the other three aircraft.

"Ilyich One, Ilyich Two, Ilyich Three, this is Ilyich Leader. Do you copy?" One by one, the responses were all positive, so Lukin gave his pilot the signal to take off.

A minute later the four MI-24s were clawing for altitude on a course across the short stretch of the Jalālābād plain and up over the mountains that rose to ten thousand feet on either side of the Kabul River. They followed the contours of the terrain closely, often clearing ridgelines by only a few feet. All pilots and weapons operators were using single-tube night-vision goggles.

After the flight cleared a final ridgeline, dropping off to a sharp north-eastern face, they took a straight line to their destination at Brandy Station at an altitude of eleven thousand feet, three hundred feet above any mountain peak between Jalālābād and Kabul. None of the pilots or crew of the MI-24s had noticed the dark form of the Puma rise up from the slope on their blind side behind them as they cleared the last ridge. It had been hovering on the eastern side of the ridge below the line of sight of any Soviet radar. It waited for the flight of MI-24s, whose position was being tracked from the bunker high above the Hermitage and relayed to the Puma by enciphered transmissions. The dark intruder was now an integral part of their tight formation.

The pilot of the lead helicopter spoke briefly into his throat mike. "Feliks Leader, Ilyich Flight will relieve you on station in nine minutes. Please make your return flight to home base by alternate route green. We wouldn't want to bump into you tonight."

"Thank you, Ilyich Leader. We're heading for home. It's dead quiet up here, no activity at all. Good luck. Feliks Leader out."

BAGHRAM AIRFIELD, 2135 HOURS

Major Ivan Viktorovich Dmitriev had been on duty in the control tower of the large Soviet airfield at Baghram north of Kabul ever since the shoot down of General Polyakov's aircraft four days earlier. Fatigue was beginning to take its toll. Now he stood behind the radar operator and looked over his shoulder at his console.

The radar operator looked up. "Major, we have Ilyich Flight from Jalālābād relieving Feliks Flight at Brandy Station. Ilyich is the large blip at about four o'clock on my screen. You can count the four aircraft in Feliks Flight strung out to their west and south. They'll probably merge into one blip in a couple of minutes, at about the same time Ilyich Flight begins to break its formation and appear as individual blips."

Dmitriev stared at the screen, fighting the exhaustion engulfing him. He watched hypnotized as the separate blips of Feliks Flight began to draw together into a single blip. At the same time, the single large blip of Ilyich Flight began to break up into its constituent aircraft.

The radar officer turned to Dmitriev and smiled. "Now you see it, now you don't. Four little Feliks Bumblebees become one big bird and the big Ilyich bird becomes four little Bumblebees."

Dmitriev counted Ilyich Flight off one by one until he reached five. Five!

"Lieutenant, how many aircraft are there supposed to be in Ilyich?"

"Four, sir. All of the flights over Brandy Station today are four-aircraft flights."

"Count those for me, Lieutenant. Turn around, damn it, and look at your screen!" He massaged his burning eyes and then refocused them on the screen.

"I count four aircraft, Major."

"Count them again. I'm sure I saw five."

"Look here for yourself, sir." The lieutenant adjusted the contrast of the screen. "It looks like the standard four birds to me."

TWENTY-SIX

Alexander stared at the display on the computer and watched its changing calculations of the distance to their next target, a point a thousand feet below the ridgeline of the mountain. Dangerfield was flying the Puma perilously close to the northeastern slope, keeping below the ridge and out of the line of sight of the Soviet radar.

The four MI-24s of Ilyich Flight had taken up patrol stations high above the river, and neither Alexander nor Dangerfield could locate the heat of their engines with their ANVIS 6 flip-ups, but they knew that this could change at any moment on the whim of a curious pilot.

Alexander spoke into the intercom. "We're within fifty feet of the path we're looking for. I'll take a look around with the FLIR."

Dangerfield kept his eyes on the helicopter's rotors; they were close enough to the mountainside to hit it. Manipulating the coolie-hat control of the FLIR, Alexander watched the terrain roll across the six-inch-square screen in the center panel of the cockpit, and within ten seconds spotted their target, a natural footpath that switched back over the summit of the mountain. The spot was just wide enough for the Puma to ease in sideways. Only a few seconds were needed to discharge J.D. and the five *mujāhids*. J.D. would call the chopper in for a pickup if it was safe to do so.

As Dangerfield teased the Puma into position he felt his luck was still holding. No wind buffeted the leeward slope of the mountain, and there were none of the downdrafts that had worried him before the operation began.

"In ten seconds you're out of here, J.D.," Dangerfield said calmly into the intercom. In the rear cabin J.D. took off his headset and gave a thumbs-up to Alexander as he moved to the left door of the helicopter. Dangerfield maneuvered the Puma the last few feet to put the left door directly over the wide spot in the path, his rotors clearing the side of the mountain by less than ten feet. "Go now!" he ordered over the intercom, and J.D. went out the door, quickly followed by Youssuf, Wali Khan, and their three fighters. Seconds later, Dangerfield leaned the Puma away from the cliff face, dropped down another five hundred feet, and then began to work his way along the mountainside toward their third rendezvous point.

Alexander pulled out one earphone of his headset and hooked a smaller earphone to his free ear. He checked its wire connection to a Motorola radio fitted into his vest and pressed the transmit button. Seconds later J.D.'s voice came over the new earplug.

"We're two hundred yards linear distance from the landing zone according to GPS reckoning and about a hundred yards below the ridgeline. The path seems good, but I estimate twenty minutes to rendezvous."

Alexander's response was brief. "I copy. Standing by."

BRANDY STATION, 2202 HOURS

Hunched over the jury-rigged radio rack in the overcrowded cabin of the MI-24, Klimenko scribbled notes on a pad as he listened closely to the message. After another minute he spoke into his intercom.

"The communications-intelligence people in the Antonov are picking up some short, digitally encrypted voice-radio traffic from somewhere very close. They can't read the traffic and can't locate the transmitters precisely—not yet, anyway. But they ran it through an on-board signal analyzer. The signature is Motorola MX-360, system DES." He paused to study his scribbled notes. "They conclude that there are almost certainly American special services people in the neighborhood, because the Americans have never handed over that model to the Afghans."

2209 HOURS

Dangerfield had slipped the chopper along the face of the northeastern side of the mountain to a point about fifteen hundred feet below the landing zone that the Boy had marked on the ridgeline with his thermal blanket two days before. Three GPS satellites confirmed the position to within thirty feet of dead center. Dangerfield had then dropped down the face until he found a sharp outcropping, tucked the Puma under it, and hovered while he waited for a signal from J.D. There was still no wind, he felt reasonably concealed from the MI-24s in their current patrol orbits, and he still had perhaps a thousand yards between his current position and the point to the north where they calculated that Kabul or Baghram radar could get a look at him.

High above the Puma and more than a mile and a half upriver the MI-24s began to illuminate their search areas with infrared light.

Alexander tapped Dangerfield on the shoulder and pointed to the north. "Pink light. They're looking for something, probably us. Maybe they're starting to figure things out."

BAGHRAM AIRFIELD, 2210 HOURS

Major Dmitriev jerked awake in his chair. Realizing that he had dozed off for almost half an hour, he punched a four-digit number into the secure telephone at his desk. "I want to speak to the officer in charge at the Kabul Special Operations Center." As he waited for the connection he looked over at the radar lieutenant and saw him nodding over his screen. They were all too tired, he thought. He pressed another button on his console and spoke loudly into the microphone on the center of his desk. "Lieutenant, stand up if you must in order to stay awake. We cannot have your radar screen untended even for one minute tonight."

The lieutenant lurched out of his chair as Dmitriev's voice exploded in his earphones. "Just stretching my neck muscles, sir. Wasn't asleep."

Another voice came on the secure telephone Dmitriev held to his ear. "Ops Center, Major Shulgin."

"Major Shulgin, this is Major Dmitriev at Baghram Tower. I wish to report a radar anomaly in connection with Ilyich Flight at Brandy Station."

"Go ahead, Major."

Dmitriev mentioned the five blips and his conviction that he had not imagined it. He expected the usual bored lack of interest, but Shulgin asked him several follow-up questions and urged him to call again if he saw anything suspicious. Dmitriev hung up feeling refreshed and alert.

BRANDY STATION, 2218 HOURS

Klimenko had been on the radio to Kabul Ops Center for more than a minute when he turned back to Lukin and Sasha. "There's been a report from the watch officer at Baghram that we may have brought our American friends along with us when we flew up here thirty-nine minutes ago. The Ops Center takes this guy seriously. He's the same major who tried to get Polyakov to abort the Jalālābād flight after the flap on the Kabul Tower radio. I think that our clever friends rode into Brandy Station on our coattails, and that they're somewhere around here right now."

EAST OF BRANDY STATION, 2220 HOURS

J.D. and his five *mujāhids* cleared the crest of the ridge. By now the wind was blowing in from the northwest as he scanned the area with his goggles looking for some sign of heat. Within seconds he detected the Boy huddled behind some boulders ten yards away, and walked over to him, calling out in Dari as he approached. "Young one, where is Musawwir?"

The Boy rose to his feet, relief in his face at the sight of friends. "Musawwir is not far. I helped him most of the way and left him in a safe place to wait for us. He is very weak, but I don't think he is going to die."

J.D. said to Engineer Youssuf, "Go with the young one and bring Musawwir up here as quickly as you can. Take your three *mujāhids* and leave Wali Khan with me." He turned back to the Boy. "How long will it take you to go down and bring Musawwir back up the mountain?"

"Not more than ten minutes, even if we have to carry him all the way."

The four men and the Boy disappeared into the darkness as J.D. pressed his Motorola transmit button. "I have found the Boy and sent Youssuf and three fighters to bring Musawwir to the landing zone. We should be ready for pickup in ten minutes."

J.D. looked out between the two ridges of mountains flanking the river ten thousand feet below and clearly saw the four MI-24s in his night-vision goggles a mile and a half away. As he watched, one of them turned toward him and began casting a long beam of pink light along the ridgeline, closing the distance between them at about five hundred feet a minute. J.D. looked at the glowing dial of his Rolex and calculated that it would take the helicopter ten minutes to reach their position.

BRANDY STATION, 2224 HOURS

Captain Lukin scanned the ridgeline on the northeast side of the river with his night-vision goggles. He was having trouble distinguishing the features of the ridge from the natural hot spots on the rocky crest that radiated confusing signatures. He shook his head and said into the intercom, "We're not accomplishing much like this. Our night-vision equipment is not much good at distances. I'm going to split up the search territory. If any one of us spots something he can get the rest of us back quickly. We're going to have to overwhelm these guys if we're going to take them alive."

Klimenko listened to Lukin, but before he could comment another voice came over his headset from the Antonov orbiting above Ilyich Flight.

"Ilyich Leader, we have that American special services frequency active again. This time we have narrowed down its location to Brandy Station sector eight. This is a rough estimate, but we got lucky and got two separate lines on the transmitters from two points in our orbit. They intersect in sector eight. Those boys are close."

Klimenko saw that Lukin was already checking the chart of Brandy Station that had been secured to the forward bulkhead. Sasha said over the intercom, "Lukin, why don't we call the flight back together and then move in a line across, dropping troops along the way? Sector eight can't be more than half a mile long, and with our boys down on the ground we should be able to make contact."

Lukin looked thoughtful. "Yeah, but we'll also be pretty spread out. You can't move back and forth along the whole ridge in sector eight. If we need to get back together quickly we might lose a lot of time." He paused. "But okay, I think you might be right." Promptly he called up the other three aircraft and ordered them to a rendezvous point 11,500 feet above the river and standing off sector eight by about one thousand yards.

Klimenko understood immediately that Sasha was suggesting a tactic that would necessitate some delays once their targets were located. This could mean either their quarry would make a clean escape, or they would have time to guarantee their deaths. He also sensed that Lukin was going along with Sasha's suggestion reluctantly.

2226 HOURS

J.D. saw the infrared searchlights of the four MI-24s switch off one by one, and through his ANVIS 6 could see the helicopters begin moving toward a line of flight that seemed to converge very close to his position. As the choppers came closer, he could count the lighted windows in the troop-carrying cabins, and he spoke into his radio. "All four of our escorts have changed heading and switched off their pink lights. They seem to be converging on a point offshore my location. ETA about two minutes. Copy?"

Alexander pushed the transmit button of his MX-360. "I copy. Keep us advised real time of their movement. We estimate fifteen seconds to reach your position and pull you out if we have to. You'd better call for help with half a minute to spare. Copy?"

"Copy. Right now we're about three minutes away from being ready for pickup. I'm moving now to see if I can spot the party bringing Musawwir up to the landing zone. Stand by." J.D. looked down over the southwest face of the ridge, Wali Khan crouched beside him. Less than fifty yards away, he could clearly see the greenish images of the group bringing Musawwir up the mountain. He pressed his transmitter button. "Estimate two to three minutes for pickup. Please stand by."

BRANDY STATION, 2227 HOURS

The communications-intercept officer on the Antonov broke the silence in the earphones of the men aboard the helicopters of Ilyich Flight. "We're getting repeated bursts of MX-360 traffic that seem to be related to the maneuvers Ilyich Flight is making. We have you under visual observation, and your last two changes of heading have been followed by short exchanges on the American radios, so they probably do, too. If so, then Ilyich Flight should have a line-of-sight view of the Americans somewhere in sector eight. Do you copy?"

Lukin looked at Klimenko and shrugged; clearly he did not understand the correlation between the American radio bursts and Ilyich Flight. Klimenko put his hand on Lukin's shoulder and pressed the microphone button himself.

"Ilyich Leader copies and understands. We will see if we can provoke a confirmation. Please monitor the target radios closely." His hand still on Lukin's shoulder, he explained, "Here's the situation. When we started forming up and took this new heading, the intercept people up top picked up radio transmissions from the Americans that they think were related to what we were doing. That means they can see us. It also means that we ought to be able to see *them,* and that we're close to each other. We can check the theory by doing two one-eighty-degree turns, one after the other. If they pick up radio traffic upstairs each time we change direction, then we'll know for sure that we're just about on top of our targets and that they are talking about us. Got it?"

"But it eats up more time," Lukin observed, "and I'm not sure what advantage it will give us."

You've got that right, Captain, Klimenko thought, but he continued calmly, "Yes, it eats up a little time, maybe another two minutes or so, but it lets us know for sure that our friends are in sector eight, and once we start dropping troops off there, we're committed."

Lukin nodded reluctantly and quickly ordered his pilot to do two quick 180s.

In Ilyich Four Rogov heard the order. *What the hell is Lukin doing?*

EAST OF BRANDY STATION, 2228 HOURS

When J.D. saw the flight of helicopters bearing down on him veer off in a right turn and begin to head in the opposite direction, an immediate sense of relief swept over him. "Boss, I think we just got lucky. All four of our friends just turned tail and headed back out over the river."

"Watch them closely, J.D. If they turn back on you, they're playing games with us. Call in if they turn back. The radios can't hurt us any more than they already have."

"Boss, they just made another one-eighty and are heading straight back at us!"

"Try to keep your heat profile as low as you can. Get behind a hot rock or you'll guide them right into the landing zone."

"Roger." J.D. and Wali Khan sprinted across the ridge to the rocks where the Boy had been hiding.

Dangerfield leaned the Puma away from the mountain face and began ascending toward its crest, double-checking the switches on the weapons systems as he did so. They were armed.

BRANDY STATION, 2229 HOURS

Klimenko had adjusted his set of night-vision goggles. Lukin noted that they were different from his own. "What have you got there, Colonel?"

"American. PAS 7s, courtesy of the Committee for State Security. They have about twice the light magnification of yours."

"Can I try them?"

Before Klimenko could respond the voice from the Antonov broke in. "Confirm that the MX-360 traffic is tied to your maneuvers. Our last rough direction finding puts the transmitters approximately in the center of sector eight. Good luck!"

Klimenko leaned out the door to get a good look at the sector eight ridgeline. The wind whipped at the straps of his goggles. There they were! He counted four or five human forms moving up the last few yards to the crest. Lukin leaned out. "See anything?" Klimenko asked.

"Nothing yet. How about you?"

"Lot of hot ground clutter, nothing else," Klimenko lied. "My recommendation is that we move into sector eight right now and drop off our troops. We can take the piece of the sector at eleven o'clock and let Ilyich One and Two fan out to our left and Ilyich Three to our right to cover the whole sector. What do you think?"

"Let's just quit fucking around and do it!" Lukin ordered the other choppers to a defined area of the sector. Lukin, Sasha, and Klimenko quickly checked their weapons and body radios. They were less than half a mile from the ridgeline and closing rapidly when Lukin spotted the men.

2230 HOURS

Carrying the Fashioner slung between them, Engineer Youssuf and his three fighters cleared the crest of the mountain just as a burst of red tracer rounds from Ilyich Leader passed over their heads. At the same moment the landing zone burst into artificial daylight as the MI-24's powerful landing and searchlights switched on, temporarily blinding the men on the ground. The helicopter's loudspeaker screamed out a deafening warning message in Dari and Pashto repeatedly. "Stand up! Put up your hands! We see you hiding! Stand up! Put up your hands! We see you hiding!"

Youssuf and his fighters froze in the blinding lights as the lead chopper closed to within twenty yards. J.D. lay pressed behind a large rock with Wali Khan beside him. He knew the surrender demand was a recording, an old ploy designed to provoke them into revealing themselves. "Boss! They're demanding surrender. I'm sending Wali Khan out to surrender the whole crowd until you pop up and take out the helicopter right here on the landing zone. The other choppers are a couple of minutes' reaction time away. But you could even get a shot off at one of them if you're quick when you pop up." He turned to Wali Khan. "Get out there with your hands up and tell Youssuf and his people to do the same. When the Puma clears the ridge, all of you hit the ground. Go!"

As Wali Khan rose from the rocks with his hands raised he yelled at Youssuf. "Do exactly as I do. When the shooting starts, hit the ground. Look at me! Don't look at the lights! Do exactly as I do!"

Lukin shouted into his radio. "Pull in and discharge troops, Ilyich One, Two, and Three! Close in on Ilyich Leader."

As the pilot eased the MI-24 the final ten yards into position over the rugged landing zone Lukin shouted over his radio again. "Colonel! You're first out the door! Then Sasha, then me! You five from the regiment stay aboard!"

Klimenko hit the ground hard. A split second later Sasha was in the air and Lukin was ready to jump when the black Puma popped up above the opposite ridgeline firing. The distance between the two helicopters was less than twenty yards. Instantly, the Soviet officers saw the Puma appear from the blackness. In the next second they were blinded by its powerful searchlights and deafened by its 23 mm Gatling gun and 12.7 mm machine gun.

The cannon rounds stitched along the length of the MI-24, which was turned sideways to discharge its troops. The first burst shattered the Plexiglas bubble of the pilot's cockpit, killing him instantly. The weapons operator forward of the pilot directed his 12.7 mm machine gun to the side of the Puma and squeezed off a long burst before the MI-24 rolled back, pulling his weapon off its target. Half a dozen rounds hit the pilot's compartment, shattering one section of the windshield and setting off sparks in the overhead instrument array.

"You all right, Jim?" Alexander shouted.

"I think they shot my leg off again. Take it for a second." Dangerfield handed the controls over to Alexander. His wooden leg was a mass of splinters, but he was able to keep what was left of his boot and prosthetic foot on the controls.

Alexander continued firing. Lukin had been caught in the chest by one of the large cannon rounds and was blown back into the chopper as it began to fall. In agonizing slow-motion for those still alive on board, it rolled over on its side, its rotors chopping at the rock face and disintegrating into whirling missile fragments. A few hundreds yards later, the fuselage exploded and the burning fragments fell to the river ten thousand feet below.

Dangerfield was back at the controls. Rocking the Puma back as soon as the MI-24 disappeared over the side of the ridge, he fired his two AA-8 missiles at the formation of MI-24s still moving toward their position. For good measure he fired off a pod of antitank missiles in the general direction of the formation to discourage the other helicopters.

Dangerfield stayed lucky. One of the two AA-8s flew straight into the hot turbine of Ilyich Three, which exploded in midair. The remaining two helicopters drew back momentarily before pressing once again toward the ridgeline.

Sasha was hit by machine-gun fire as he jumped to the ground, but before he lost consciousness he fired a burst of his submachine gun into the Afghans crouched a few feet away.

Still blinded by the Puma's searchlights, Klimenko was struggling to regain his vision when J.D. slammed his Kalashnikov into the side of his head, knocking him to the ground. Sasha lay five feet away, a red stain spreading beneath him. J.D. peered into Klimenko's face, then spoke into his radio. "Boss. This is the colonel you brought to the Orlov meeting at the river. Can you believe it?"

"Are you sure, J.D.?"

"Yeah, I'm sure. It's the same guy. The other trooper looks pretty shot up, bleeding badly. I'm going over to check on Musawwir."

Alexander's mind was racing as Dangerfield broke in. "We've got about ninety seconds before we have two MI-24s all over us. I can't outrun those guys. To top it off, I've fired everything I've got that can do anything against them. Tell me what you want to do or I'll start making my own decisions!"

"J.D.! Check to see if the two Soviet officers are carrying radios. They must be."

"Roger, Boss, but we got a bad situation here. Wali Khan and one of the others are dead, and Musawwir caught another round, maybe two. He doesn't look good." J.D. was transmitting on the run. "I'm back at the colonel now. He's got a radio and so does the other guy, who looks to me like he's bleeding to death from a groin shot. There's a lot of wild chatter on both their radios!"

Alexander saw the remaining two MI-24s move into position to make a pass at their landing zone, and shouted to Dangerfield, "Set her down!" He jumped to the ground, racing to where J.D. was standing over Klimenko. He pulled the earphone from the colonel's ear, took the microphone from Klimenko's battle tunic and spoke into it in Russian. "I am speaking to the two Soviet gunships approaching the site of the crash. Do not approach further and do not fire! Do not approach further and do not fire! We have your officers and we will execute them if you approach further or if you fire on us! If you have understood me each of you is to turn on his landing lights and then turn them off immediately. Do as I say now!"

Lieutenant Rogov gave the order. "Flash your lights and hold your positions. What a giant fuckup this is turning out to be!"

Alexander watched the two helicopters flash their landing lights one by one and then stand off. He removed the radio set from the unconscious Klimenko and moved over to where J.D. and Doc were working on the Fashioner before he transmitted again. "Thank you. Now you will stand off from this position one kilometer. One of you may respond on this frequency and stand by for further communications from me. The lives of your officers depend on how you follow these instructions."

Rogov answered, "We are doing as you request for now."

Doc looked up at Alexander. "We got to get him out of here. He's taken at least one more round in the chest. I can't even tell how bad it is because he's so messed up from the older wounds. The other two guys are dead. Nothing we can do for them."

"Get everybody loaded up. J.D., get these two Soviets in the Puma. They're our ticket out of here." He spoke again into Klimenko's radio.

"We are taking your officers with us. You are not to follow. I repeat, you are not to follow. If you do follow we will throw your officers from our aircraft. Please acknowledge."

Rogov pressed his microphone. "We understand." *There's no way to win this one,* he thought as he watched the Puma lift off the ridge and disappear. *Why did Lukin screw this up so badly?*

As Dangerfield brought the critically overloaded Puma down the slope of the mountain Doc worked feverishly on the Fashioner. Klimenko had regained consciousness as they were being loaded aboard the helicopter, and Doc had given him a compress and had told him to apply pressure to Sasha's groin to slow down the blood loss until he could get to him. Watching the blood spread along the corrugated grooves in the steel floor, Klimenko knew his friend was still bleeding heavily. His face was ashen. Klimenko shouted in English, "He's bleeding to death, for God's sake! You've got do something for your prisoner!"

Doc moved away from the Fashioner and bent over to undo Sasha's belt buckle, then turned to Klimenko. "Help me get his pants down. Move quickly."

He and Klimenko saw that a machine-gun round or cannon fragment had struck deep in the groin, at least partially severing both the deep vein and the artery. Putting pressure on the wound with his gloved hand, he told Klimenko to get the trauma kit from the other side of the cabin. Searching it, he thrust three sterile sealed hemostats into Klimenko's hands. "Break them out of the wrapping quickly or your friend is going to die." He turned to Alexander. "Get the torch from the kit and give me some light here."

Seconds later Klimenko watched Doc spread the ragged opening with his fingers until he saw the damaged artery and vein side by side. He reached in with one hemostat and snapped it on the bleeding artery and the blood flow stopped immediately. Then he clamped off the vein with a second hemostat and taped the two instruments to the wounded man's leg to keep them from being knocked loose. He packed the wound with an antibiotic dressing, then gave Sasha a shot of broad-spectrum antibiotic. His pulse was too weak to count in the bouncing helicopter. "This man's got to get to a hospital within a couple of hours or he'll die. At the very least he'll lose the leg if he doesn't get the vein and artery stitched back together."

Klimenko turned to Alexander, blood still welling from the gash above his eye. "Now what?"

"Do you want to go with me to Pakistan?" Alexander mouthed the words in Ukrainian.

Klimenko shook his head.

Rogov listened to the latest demand from the American, then, as instructed, he ordered his pilot to turn on his landing lights and take up a heading of east southeast at a speed of one hundred twenty miles per hour. He ordered the remaining MI-24 at Brandy Station to return to Jalālābād.

After twenty minutes on the east southeast heading, he heard Alexander's voice again. "Take up a heading of due south for five minutes. Remain at one hundred twenty miles per hour. When you see the green flare you may pick up your officers."

Five minutes later Rogov saw the flare and almost immediately picked up Klimenko's form in his landing lights, two hundred yards away. The MI-24 set down. Krasin was wrapped in blankets and zipped into an American body bag.

"Rogov, help me get him aboard. He's running out of time."

PESHAWAR AIRFIELD, 2355 HOURS

As the Puma glided down onto the military side of the airfield, Alexander spotted the lights of the old CIA hangar. A military ambulance was parked on the ramp. He called through the intercom, "Doc, we've got an ambulance. How's your patient holding on?"

J.D. answered. "Doc's been trying CPR on Musawwir for the last five minutes, Boss, but it didn't work. I'm sorry. Musawwir just died."

TWENTY-SEVEN

JALĀLĀBĀD AIRFIELD INFIRMARY, 0900 HOURS, OCTOBER 1, 1986

The next morning Klimenko visited Sasha in the makeshift infirmary at Jalālābād garrison. Clear fluid dripped into Sasha's arm through a jury-rigged IV, as an army doctor inspected his bandages. Pulling the covers back over Sasha's midsection, he spoke stiffly to Klimenko. "Comrade Colonel, the major is, perhaps, more fortunate than many of the young men I see with wounds like his. Whoever preformed the first aid saved his life. He would have bled to death if the vein and the artery hadn't been clamped. And the medicines . . ." The doctor shook his head.

"The Dukhi doctor must have been trained in the Soyuz before betraying socialism and turning against his government, Comrade Doctor," Klimenko said with deadly seriousness, "but the major has always been a lucky man."

Klimenko put his hand on the doctor's shoulder. "Could I have a few moments alone with the major, Comrade Doctor? Sensitive Committee business." The doctor nodded and shuffled out of the room.

Klimenko spoke softly in Sasha's ear. "Can you hear me, my friend?"

Sasha's eyes flickered and he nodded.

"Listen carefully, Sasha. If anybody asks you what happened last night, you are to say that the only tactical involvement either you or I had was to coordinate the efforts of the signals-intercept aircraft with Lukin's attempts to locate the transmitters of the American special services. All other decisions were made by Lukin. Did you understand that, my friend?"

Sasha looked Klimenko in the eye. "Did Lukin catch it?"

"Just as you and I jumped in. He and everybody else on his chopper ended up in a ball of fire down in the river."

"Yeah, I guess he just read the situation wrong."

"That's the story, Sasha. If anybody asks. I mean *anybody*. Lukin called all the shots except for the radio-intercept business. There's nobody alive that can dispute that."

"Did the Dukhis get away?"

"Everybody got away, Sasha. You shot up the crowd as you hit the ground, and I've just heard that you took out the big Dukhi. The 40th Army is already calling you a hero for personally avenging your beloved Boris Semyonovich."

Sasha smiled weakly. "You okay, my dear colonel?"

"I'm okay. We lost another chopper full of boys, but Rogov and his team got out okay and picked us up on the Jalālābād plain last night. I'm leaving you here. I've got a plane waiting to take me to brief Titov. Do you understand completely about last night?"

Sasha nodded and then closed his eyes. "I don't know why, but poor Lukin just fucked it up."

TANK WITH SOLDIERS, 0730 HOURS, OCTOBER 7, 1986

The Fashioner was buried in the small cemetery on the Ponderosa. Green and black battle streamers on wooden poles marked the grave as the shrine of a fallen Soldier of God, Islamic green for the Fashioner's Resistance Party banner, and black for the battle banner of the Prophet.

Word of his death spread immediately through the eastern provinces and amulets containing the Fashioner's Koranic name were sewn into triangles and then into the clothing of the Soldiers of God to bolster the wearer's courage in the face of the enemy. The women tending the shrine were already being asked for small pinches of earth from the grave; these would be eaten by pregnant women in the hope of bearing sons with the courage of the Fashioner. In the six days since his death, over one hundred boys had been born to Afghans in the refugee camps in Pakistan, and more than fifty of them had been named Musawwir.

Alexander had told the Boy that the Antonov he shot down was the one that had directed the attacks against Zhawar Kheli the day his father had been killed, and that Polyakov had been aboard. The Boy understood that he had avenged the death of his father by killing the Soviet general, but said that there were so many dead that every *mujāhid* would grow old and die before their blood debts had been repaid.

Mullah Salang, who had taken the Boy under his protection, announced that it was unbecoming for such a courageous *mujāhid* to be without a jihad name. He thought it appropriate that the Boy be known as Al-Muntaqim, the Avenger.

Alexander had been right about how the rescue effort would be perceived by the jihad, but he was less certain of the 40th Army's response, specifically, Klimenko, who could end up with either another Order of the Red Banner or a reprimand. Now Alexander sat alone at the camp table listening for the Soviet scout car. The note calling for the meeting had been brief.

> Please have your representatives at the place called Tank With Soldiers at 0900 hours on October 7 to conclude the arrangements for the exchange of personnel.
>
> A. Belov
> Major

An expressionless Klimenko took his seat at the table opposite Alexander. There was still a dark bruise and a stitched wound above his left eye where J.D. had clubbed him with his Kalashnikov. He handed a large envelope to Alexander. "Here is our final list. In this envelope are records for each of thirty-seven detainees we have been able to locate, whose names were on your original list. Four of them will probably be delivered to Torkham as corpses, but we will do our best to keep them alive until the exchange. There can be no further adjustment to these numbers. The additional documents in the envelope are the death certificates of those on your original list who have not survived."

"I have no reason to doubt the colonel. As we agreed at our last meeting on this issue, there is no room for deception by either side at this stage of our negotiations."

"Then I may take it that your side accepts this list as final?"

"I will have my colleague take a look at the list, but I think you may conclude that we accept your efforts as complete."

Alexander walked to the Landcruiser where J.D. and Doc sat. "J.D., take a look at these lists. I think this is the end of the game, but give me a quick reading anyway."

He returned to the tent. "I assume the colonel is interested in having one last meeting with Lieutenant Orlov before the exchange here and at Torkham Gate? We have made such arrangements."

Klimenko spoke loud enough for J.D. and Doc to overhear. "The colonel insists on another meeting with Lieutenant Orlov, as do my principals. Today is acceptable for the meeting. Our business here is concluded."

"We will have to travel farther afield today to meet Lieutenant Orlov, Colonel. You should advise your officers that they may have a wait of at least several hours. I will have you back here no later than 2200 hours."

"Then I will change into appropriate attire. I trust that you will take care of the blindfold."

Klimenko walked back to his parked jeep and stripped out of his uniform while he briefed Belov and Panov.

Alexander walked over to J.D. "Does anything jump out at you from their list?"

"It looks like they've kept their word, boss. I don't think you're going to squeeze any more out of these guys."

"Okay, get this material to Engineer Mahmoon at the Ponderosa. He's taken over responsibility for it now. Then get back here and baby-sit this place until we return late tonight."

"Where the hell are you going? Orlov isn't that far away."

"I'm just going to drive him around for a while. With his blindfold he'll never figure it out."

"You can take off the blindfold," Alexander said as soon as Tank With Soldiers was out of sight. "How did Krasin make out?"

"He'll live. The doctor in Jalālābād is still talking about the Dukhi doctor who saved his life and his leg. He's even more vocal about the first-aid kit. He kept Krasin on the antibiotics for two days and beat off a massive infection. Said he didn't have anything like it."

"I'm glad Krasin made it."

"We heard almost immediately about the Fashioner. The word was out on the streets in Peshawar in a matter of hours. In the end, he did me a pretty big favor by dying. He turned our mission into a dramatic success. Vengeance has been extracted for Polyakov. It's our own version of the Pathan law."

"Why the hell did you get yourself involved in something like that?"

Klimenko was incredulous. "Why the hell did *I* get involved! Why the hell did *you* get involved in something as harebrained as trying to rescue your Dukhi pals? And why the hell did you broadcast it so that everyone in Kabul who counts could figure it out sooner or later?"

"But why were you and Krasin along? Isn't that a bit dramatic for a couple of staff guys?"

"We both decided that the 40th Army mission had to fail. Its goal was to capture your Musawwir and his rescuers. You can figure out for yourself why we couldn't let that happen."

"Is that why your helicopters got themselves strung out all over the ridgeline? Did you have something to do with that?"

"Yes, and the only men on the mission who could have reached that conclusion are all dead."

"I guess I should thank you."

"Don't. Once our troops spotted you our option of making sure you got away went out the window. Sasha and I roared in with the intention of hosing down everyone on the ridge. If you were in that crowd, too bad. But your Puma changed all that quickly."

"How did it play in Kabul?"

"Better than it should have. General Titov—who's taking over from Polyakov, at least temporarily—apparently had two choices. Either the operation was a total washout or a brilliant success, and since he ordered the mission, he thought it better to call it a success. Was it your idea to get the word out on the street so quickly that Al-Musawwir was killed?"

"Yes, but now it has a life of its own."

"Yeah, like my brilliant strike against the criminal murderers of Polyakov. By the time I reached Kabul the next day they were already calling the mission a brilliant success. A daring strike to avenge the late lamented leader that took out a rebel commander of stature. Never mind that some fine people got killed in the process."

Alexander nodded. "Yeah, some very fine people."

Klimenko was quiet for a moment. "Anyway, Titov has become Krasin's and my protector. He's moving me over to his staff after the Orlov matter is resolved."

It was dark and cool in Alexander's curtained office. He motioned Klimenko into a chair, and got out two cans of Perrier from the small refrigerator.

Klimenko walked over to the bookcase. "You know, Alexander, this place tells me more about you than you ever will."

"What does it say to you?"

"It tells me that I am dealing with a man who is so hopelessly romantic that he could become dangerous to himself and to others if he doesn't put on some restraints, or have somebody else to restrain him."

"What about you, Anatoly Viktorovich? Are you a romantic?"

"Dreaming was nationalized seventy years ago. I do most of mine very privately."

"Like helping your mother to write fairy tales?"

"You've figured that out, have you?"

Alexander took down the thin, leather-bound volume of "The Maidens of Kiev" from the bookcase and opened it at a bookmark. "Here's where you started telling the story yourself."

Klimenko quietly read the page. "Yes, I wrote most of that part, where the son of the maiden turns against the evil prince in his palace. But my parents and I were talking theoretically. We never got into your gun-slinger fantasies."

"Are you sure? What do you think you were doing on that mountain last week? If you ask me, you and I are already in something up to our necks. But I don't want you to ask me. I want you to ask someone else."

Alexander pushed through the bookcase and spoke to someone in the next room. Klimenko's defenses came alive, and when his host returned a moment later, he was on his feet, glaring.

"Alexander, if you have set me up for something as sleazy as a visit from a CIA recruiter, I have really overestimated you. You can't really be so incredibly stupid!"

Alexander smiled; his guest's discomfort amused him.

TWENTY-EIGHT

The woman's voice was somehow familiar. "Alexander is not stupid at all, Tolya, but he *has,* at least in a small way, set you up." Standing behind Klimenko was a beautiful woman dressed in a white shalwar chamise. Her eyes were the same shade of hazel as his mother's. He felt he was looking at some part of his mother and some part of himself. He knew instantly who she was.

"Katerina Martynova, may I present the excitable Anatoly Viktorovich Klimenko."

Klimenko and Katerina stared at each other for fully ten seconds before she took Klimenko's face in her hands and kissed him on both cheeks. Then she stepped back.

"You look like my mother," she said softly.

"You look like my mother." His voice was barely audible. He held on to her hands.

Klimenko spoke first. "Tell me about Lara, please."

"I will. Then you must tell me about Katerina."

Forty-five minutes later Alexander returned from the communications center to find Katerina and Klimenko still deep in conversation. "Is this a good place for me to break back in?" He didn't expect an answer and didn't get one. He sat down and turned to Klimenko. "First. This is a family affair. There will be nobody else involved. Not now. Not ever."

"I believe that. But you have an off-putting way of turning everything into some dramatic surprise. You're going to have to stop this kind of drama."

"It's the Russian half of him, Tolya. You know how Russians love coarse jokes and surprises."

Klimenko was amused by Katerina's needling of her husband. "I've had to live with Russians all my adult life, and I can see that it's much the same for you."

"Maybe we can save your Ukrainian trashing of the Russians for another time. What I am about to say involves both of you, as well as me and people we all hold dear, so don't mistake my bluntness for an insult."

Klimenko sank a little deeper into his chair.

Alexander continued. "To start with, we should establish where we are in agreement. One. The system we refer to as the U.S.S.R. is irretrievably corrupt. The so-called republics are little better than occupied lands. Two. A tripod props up the Union: the Communist Party, the army, and the KGB. Agreed?"

Klimenko nodded. "A national security elite has been running things at the expense of everybody else since the revolution."

Alexander went on. "Each of the legs of the tripod is getting shaky. The Party is walking into a cyclone with Gorbachev. My guess is that his attempts at reform will spin out of control. He's ignoring the first rule of Russian power politics. Large organs like the Communist Party can only be destroyed."

Klimenko shifted in his seat. "I don't disagree about the rottenness of the system, but I don't think there's any real evidence yet of the Party disintegrating."

Alexander reflected for a moment. "Okay, then let's just agree that Gorbachev is tinkering with a brittle system, that he's starting to let daylight in, and that we don't know what effects this will have. Agreed?"

"Conceded."

"The most dangerous time for a bad government is when it starts to reform itself," Katerina added.

"Who said that? Reagan?" Klimenko asked.

"No, Alexis de Tocqueville, and he was talking about the Bourbons before the French Revolution."

Alexander continued. "Now for the army. Now that it has been out on real deployment for seven years, it's revealing itself for what it is—a fair Third World army with all the problems of its society."

Klimenko interrupted. "You don't have to be quite so dramatic in your definitions. It might force an argument out of me where there really isn't one. The army *is* falling apart to a greater degree than even you probably know. It can't even keep itself clean. In one year alone we have lost fifteen thousand troops to hepatitis. We're using military supplies that were held in reserve for the European war that never came, and don't even fit our needs. I agree with you, but knock off the Third World comparison."

"I'm not looking for an argument. But the Red Army's in trouble. The third leg of the tripod, the KGB, is affected by all the factors sabotaging the army and the Party, but rather than offend you with an outsider's assessment, why don't you tell us where it fits in today."

"The KGB won't easily fall of its own weight. As long as it controls Soviet society through fear, it will be a power to reckon with."

"Yes, but you told me back in September that you could already spot tears in the fabric. You even wondered why we didn't do something to speed up the dissolution. You said that the Russians, to say nothing of the Ukrainians and others, have just about had enough. What I'm talking about is taking a stand and being counted."

"I'm already in so far that I don't see how I could back out now. But I don't know where this is heading. What do you expect of me? For that matter, what do we expect of ourselves?"

Alexander smiled. "It's easy. All we have to do is to work together to get the army out of Afghanistan. That can be done. By going home losers, the army will set in motion all the other forces. Getting the army out of here will also stop at least some of the dying on both sides."

"You flatter me. You make it sound like it will be easy for the two of us to get over a hundred thousand troops across the Oxus."

Alexander leaned forward. "If you make it possible for me to know what exactly is going on in Gromov's planning sessions, precisely what Titov is thinking, what the defense minister is up to and what the Politburo is telling the defense minister, we'll be a lot closer to being able to do something about it."

Klimenko went to the desk and studied the little lacquered Palekh box, the mate to the one his mother had secretly received from Katerina's mother. He saw the IBM Selectric against the wall and examined it. The font was Cyrillic, as he suspected, which made him smile. "Okay, let's do it. The question is how."

"You already have the means to talk to me from Kabul. I gave you a good burst radio a couple of months ago. I'm sure you've been following our traffic about Orlov on it."

"Of course I have. I call it Alpha. And by the way, I knew from the start that your man in Kabul was planting the radio. It was all too pat."

"You didn't tell anyone, did you?"

"Sasha knows that I was bothered by how easy it was, but it's too late to start worrying about him."

"I'll give you another radio just like it, and with your own unique encryption system so that nobody else will be able to read it."

"How can you be sure of that?"

Alexander said, "I know that you're thinking that nobody would give you a system they couldn't read themselves. That's true. But I also know for a fact that the only people copying this traffic over here belong to me. If I ever learned that someone was copying it from anywhere else, I'd shut it down."

Klimenko's face was tense. "Now we're getting into the area of risk management. The radio is probably okay, but we're going to need to meet to pass materials back and forth, and I don't know how we're going to do that after Orlov is handed over and I move to Titov's staff. He told me I'd be spending about a week every month back in Moscow with him."

"A week every month in Moscow?"

"Don't even think about it. I won't agree to meet anyone from Moscow Station!"

"I wasn't thinking that. I told you this isn't a CIA operation. But we have to capitalize on your visits to Moscow."

Katerina said, "It's easier than you think. I'll meet Tolya in Russia. I'll get accredited to Moscow for *Far Eastern Focus*."

Alexander was stunned. "Just like that?!"

"Everything we're talking about goes a bit beyond anything we've ever talked about before."

Klimenko broke in. "It adds to the risk, but I like the idea. We can make it work. But, I have real concerns about the CIA's security before we throw a new maiden of Kiev into deadly battle against the evil prince. We can't have the CIA anywhere near this."

"What concerns?" Alexander arched an eyebrow.

"We . . . the KGB's got one of yours. Someone well-placed."

"A penetration of the agency?"

"Yes. I don't have anything firm, just a string of circumstances, but we have to factor it into the risks we take."

"What kind of circumstances?"

"Well, in the beginning of this year—maybe late January or early February—word worked its way around the Lubyanka that three guys in the KGB had been arrested. Two were from overseas. First Chief Directorate officers. One was from Counterintelligence in the Moscow district."

"Were the overseas officers from Washington?" Alexander's mind raced back to his last meeting with Casey.

"Yes. Both were lieutenant colonels in the Washington Rezidentura. I was back in Moscow when all this was happening, and I had a long talk with Shapkin, my old Rezident from Tehran, and a real old hand. He works with the chairman, Chebrikov, heading up what we call Directorate RI. That's a very tight group that prepares the most sensitive reporting for the Politburo and above, and it is one of the three top political jobs in the First Chief Directorate, if not in the whole KGB. He'll probably take over the First Chief Directorate once Kryuchkov leaves and replaces Chebrikov."

"Kryuchkov is taking over from Chebrikov?"

"That's the word, but who the hell really knows? At any rate, Shapkin treats me well. He probably thinks I helped him get there because of the work we did together in Iran. I told him I had complimented the Second Chief Directorate people on their exemplary service in rooting out the American spies, and Shapkin tells me, his voice full of conspiracy, 'Anatoly Viktorovich, the fools in the Second had nothing to do with catching those traitors. If there was exemplary service it was in the First Chief Directorate, where it always is.' "

"And?"

"Well, to me that means that the foreign-intelligence people have a penetration of the CIA."

"Could it have been someone they recruited from Moscow Station?"

"I don't think so, and I'll tell you why. That would have been a Second Chief Directorate operation from start to finish. They would never turn it over to the First Chief Directorate if they'd picked up the American source themselves, because there's no tradition that says they'd have to and a rivalry that says they don't. If it was a Moscow Station recruitment, my bet is that the Second would still be running it, even if the guy was back home in Washington. They wouldn't even have to tell the First Directorate people. Do you see what I'm getting at?"

"They've picked up a CIA guy outside the U.S.S.R., someone able to betray the crown jewels, and it's a First Chief Directorate operation from start to finish."

"Yes. Shapkin was taking pains to avoid telling me directly, but I'm sure of it."

"What else?"

"In the late spring of this year I was back in Moscow and Shapkin asked me to visit him, but not in his office out at Yasenevo. Instead, he asked me to show up at a posh safe house down by the Moscow River. It's a magnificent prerevolution building that belonged to Beria."

"Beria! That perverted creep!"

"Yeah. Anyway, I showed up just in time to see a very heavy hitter named Stanislav Andreevich Androsov come out and get into a blacked-out Chaika with another guy I didn't recognize. Are you still with me?"

"Stan Androsov? The Androsov from the Washington Rezidentura?"

"None other. It didn't seem like such a big deal to me—at least until I mentioned to Shapkin as a joke that I saw Androsov and another guy stealing out of Beria's old house as if the little pervert had been chasing him with a six-foot dildo himself. Shapkin usually enjoys trashing old Party icons, but this time he didn't enjoy my sense of humor. He put his hand on my shoulder and said, 'Tolya, you are in many ways like a son to me. Take my word on this: you never saw Androsov here today. The American special services doesn't even know he slipped away from them for a quick visit here. I must tell you to forget that you saw him.' "

"So you forgot it, just like he told you to?"

"Exactly. Later on I saw the man who was with Androsov at Beria's. He turned out to be the chief of counterintelligence in the First Chief Directorate, Viktor Bogomolov. He's been in on every American operation that ever came even close to being big—Walker, Barnett, Kampiles, Howard, and all the others. Don't forget, this was right in the middle of Langley's time of trouble. All through the second half of last year and most of this year, your agents were dropping like flies. By this time I think five or six had been rolled up—at least that's how many stories were in circulation."

Alexander looked pained.

Katerina said, "This gives us special burdens, but in a way, I think it will make it easier. We'll know there's a problem in Langley, so at least we can't be blindsided there. None of what Tolya has just told us changes anything."

Alexander saw it was futile to talk Katerina out of the plan they had just put in motion. "Okay. Katerina handles the Moscow connection. I'll get back to Washington now and talk to Casey directly. Tolya, I need you to check the records at the Lubyanka to see what's there on me in my true name, Alexander S. Fannin. And check another name I might use in a pinch. Gromek Jasik, Polish national, born 1950. Do you need to write this down?"

"Gromek Jasik, Polish, 1950," Klimenko repeated the name. "I'll remember that. I can also see what they've got on Katerina, if anything, but you understand, of course, there are special files that I'll never have access to."

"When you check for Kat, you'll have to work with Katerina Martynova, born in Shanghai, Hong Kong British passport holder and Catherine Fannin, born in Hong Kong, U.S. passport holder. That was Bill Casey's wedding gift. Also Catherine Martin, born Shanghai, French passport holder. We'll rely on you to tell us which passport Kat should use."

"And to tell you if there's a problem and that she shouldn't travel to the U.S.S.R. at all. But I doubt I'll find anything like that. We don't have good coverage of Hong Kong, and if there was a problem with the Martynov family, it would probably have led to my own family in the course of any investigation. I don't think that's happened."

Alexander glanced at his watch. "Time's up. We have to see Orlov now. We may still have some time afterward, but we can't chance coming back here."

Katerina rose and took Klimenko's hands. "We had a fine family reunion, Alexander. Anatoly and I will have plenty of time to talk again soon."

Klimenko met Orlov in a small mud-walled compound five miles down the valley from the Ponderosa. Orlov had been blindfolded and driven on a three-hour deception route as an alibi for Klimenko's absence, though Alexander told Engineer Mahmoon it was to protect the location of the Ponderosa.

Orlov was standing in the doorway. "Welcome to Paktia, Colonel. Or are we in Nangarhar?"

"I can see that you're keeping yourself fit, Lieutenant. It's one of a soldier's first duties in captivity."

Alexander interrupted. "The following arrangements will apply. We will walk out of the compound and down the trail for twenty minutes and then return. I will allow you privacy, but I will accompany you from a short distance away. We will not stay here for more than three quarters of an hour. Are these conditions understood?"

"They are," Klimenko said sharply. He and Orlov began walking down the dusty trail. "Lieutenant, your ordeal is coming to an end. I have arranged for an exchange of prisoners to take place in five days, on the morning of October twelfth."

"Colonel Belenko, it would be easy for me to tell you that you will experience the gratitude of others in the Red Army, not simply my own, but I will not. I will say only that I will be in your personal debt."

"Well, if you were able to write that letter to your father that I mentioned last time I would be most grateful. It would help *me* out."

"I did write the letter. The Dukhi in charge here has it."

Klimenko turned back to Alexander. "We have concluded our discussion, and I am prepared to return to my men as soon as we can. I also ask that you retrieve a letter the lieutenant has written from the people here who are holding him."

"The letter is already in the jeep, Colonel, and I didn't even read it."

Alexander and Klimenko made a wide detour on their return. By the time they arrived at the meeting site it was well past 2100 hours, and Alexander was satisfied that all the times reported in the debriefings of Klimenko, Orlov, and Belov would be consistent with their cover story. During the three-hour drive he walked Klimenko through the operation of the burst radio. "You need a danger signal for your radio communications with me, a signal to let me know if you've come under the control of the KGB. At the end of each message you always write END END. If you come under control, use an odd number, either one or three. At all other times use two or four."

They discussed a variety of possibilities for the initial contact with Katerina in Moscow or elsewhere. Klimenko would alert them by radio when he was ready for such a meeting, but they agreed he shouldn't do so for six months. This would give Katerina time to settle in and get a feel for her security situation.

"Katerina should lease a long-term room at the Ukraina Hotel. It's an awful hotel, but freewheeling. It'll give us a number of options. Radio me when she's done that. Tell her she'll receive a call in her room asking her in accented English if she wants 'a pretty young Russian boy to make love.' Remember the exact words: 'a pretty young Russian boy to make love.' That will be me, and she should come down to the lobby within fifteen minutes, after she tells me that I am a sick weirdo who ought to be in the Gulag. Then she should go to the Beriozka, the duty-free store. Make sure you use the exact words I gave you because there may be real calls like that to her room."

Klimenko was silent for a moment, then continued. "I want Katerina to bring in a pill for me. Not on her first trip, because that should be clean. I'll tell you when, but you should have something ready."

"Tolya, don't ask me for a pill. I'll only turn you down."

"What is it that you CIA guys have to do?" Klimenko snapped. "Refuse three times, then say okay? That's it, isn't it? I know the CIA regulations. Go ahead. Tell me no three times. I'll still ask for the pill, not because I want to avoid, shall I say, the personal discomfort of getting caught, but because I don't want to be forced to betray my mother and your wife. Just get me a pill, and let's assume I won't ever have to use it."

THE HERMITAGE, 2330 HOURS, OCTOBER 7

Alexander waited while Tim set up the secure phone call to Casey's office in Langley. True to his word, Casey had provided Alexander with a channel for either voice or cable.

"It's ringing," Rand said, handing the receiver to Alexander, and then disappeared down the spiral ladder.

After four rings someone picked up the telephone at the other end, and after another pause, a voice came over the satellite link, slightly distorted by the encryption, but still recognizable as Bill Casey's. "Hello . . . uh . . . over."

Alexander smiled, imagining the old man struggling with the satellite telephone, then keyed his transmit button. "Bill, this is Alexander. Are you alone right now? Over."

". . . alone . . . I'm alone . . . now . . . over."

"Just listen to me, Bill. I'll make this as plain as I can, but I will not give you full details until I see you in Washington. The last time we spoke you told me that you had some new troubles, something that implied a serious new problem, not the old problem we thought had caused us so much trouble a year ago. Do you know what I'm talking about?"

"Yes . . . know what you're . . . about."

"Bill, I'm coming to see you about that problem. I'll be at your office downtown on October ninth at 1900 hours. I want you to have Middleton there, but don't tell him I'm coming back. If you copy that please repeat it back to me. Over."

Apparently getting the hang of the telephone, Casey's response was clear and firm. "I'll be waiting for you on October ninth at the EOB. I'll have Middleton standing by, but he won't know what's up. Dottie will meet you at the Seventeenth Street entrance and get you in without having to sign in. Is that enough, Alexander?"

"That's perfect, chief. I'll be there day after tomorrow. Hermitage out."

TWENTY-NINE

Katerina returned to Hong Kong the next day by way of Bangkok with Underman, while Alexander caught a ride to Europe from Islamabad on a C-141, finally arriving in Washington at midday on October 9. As darkness fell he left the Hay Adams Hotel on foot for his meeting with Casey. He wandered through the knots of street people clustered in Lafayette Park, their homemade signs crying out against injustice or in advocacy of a noble cause or just announcing impending doom to the White House a few hundred yards away. Crossing Pennsylvania Avenue he walked slowly toward the Seventeenth Street entrance to the Old Executive Office Building where Casey had his downtown office. Soon he spotted Dottie, the DCI's executive assistant, leave the building and step up on the sidewalk near the ornate structure's iron gate.

"Hi, Alexander. The beard's awful," she said as she took him by the hand and led him quickly into the building, stopping before the uniformed Secret Service agent manning the desk. "Mr. Jones for Mr. Casey. No ID required," she said, holding her White House pass up for the officer to see the name and pass number to enter in his computer.

The Secret Service agent looked up at Alexander and then back at his computer screen. "Let's see here," he said, entering the data, " 'Mr. Jones for Mr. Casey, no identification required.' I see you were here two days ago, Mr. Jones, and two days before that, and then . . ." He smiled as he handed over a visitor's pass on a long beaded necklace.

Four minutes later he was sitting across a coffee table from Bill Casey in his high-ceilinged office.

"You're really clobbering them out there, Alexander. Foggy Bottom hates it. Dobrynin's complaining that we've got some guy over there actually killing Russians. Can you believe it?"

"It's always the same, Bill. Someone lays a glove on them, and the Russians cry foul." Alexander was shocked by how tired Casey looked, by how much he had aged in six months. "How are you doing? You look kind of tired."

Casey leaned back in his chair, momentarily distracted by Alexander's question. "Everybody's tired. This is Washington."

Alexander saw something in the old man's eyes that told him to move on. "What's Dobrynin telling Shultz?"

"He says they know the Mujaheddin aren't doing it all—that we've become directly involved."

"And what's State saying?"

"State's saying what the president tells Shultz to say. They're telling the Russians at every level that the pain will stop when they get out of Afghanistan."

"We've had what you'd call the luck of the Irish," Alexander said, smiling.

"Frank told me about your little helicopter chase the other night. Too bad your luck didn't hold."

"Wait until Dobrynin screams about Americans flying helicopter assaults against 40th Army choppers. Then we'll see how tough they are at Foggy Bottom."

"Be your own guy, just like we agreed. But you didn't come here to tell me war stories."

"Bill, my wife's parents have someone in Moscow with access into the heart of the Kremlin. Someone who's in a position to give us a look at their cards before they play them."

"Who is it?"

"I'm not going to tell you."

"Why not?"

"Two reasons, Bill. First because it's my business, not yours. But even more important because you have someone here working for the other side, who's killing all your people in Moscow."

"You got something new on that?" Casey's eyes bored into Alexander's.

"Yes. But I'm only going to give it to you and just enough of it to Middleton to get him on the right trail. I am assuming that neither of you two is the problem."

Casey laughed. "You sure about that?"

"Not really, but I'll take a chance."

Casey pressed the intercom. "Betty, ask Graham to come in now."

Graham Middleton nodded coldly to Alexander, concealing any surprise he may have felt at his presence. He had made his play against Alexander, and he had lost. He had managed to force Alexander's departure from the Agency, but his career had been stalled ever since, and would remain stalled as long as Casey was around.

"Alexander, why don't you tell Graham your story."

"I'll tell him the part I want him to know. Graham, you have been right about one thing all along. There is a penetration of this agency, someone who has been betraying us to the KGB for more than a year now. Whoever it is was working against us at the same time Howard defected and got lost in the noise of the Howard and Yurchenko affairs. You've just been dead wrong about everything else. You were blinded by your need to settle a score with me."

Middleton had spent a career avoiding direct confrontation, making his accusations instead from the insulated maze of the counterintelligence staff. His discomfort was immense. "I don't know where you get that. I've never said anything . . . not officially . . ."

"Forget it, Graham, I'm not here to settle a score, I'm here to tell you there's a mole in Langley."

Middleton leaned forward, eyes narrowing. "Who's your source?"

"I'm not going to tell you. I will only say that the information was passed at a meeting at which my wife was present, and that I believe absolutely in the reliability of the information and the source." Alexander understood the delicate art of saying something that was completely true but not truly complete.

Middleton glanced at Casey, who ignored him.

Now Alexander walked them both through Klimenko's story. He omitted the name of the old Rezident Shapkin, because this might lead Middleton back to Klimenko. As he gave a blow-by-blow description of Klimenko stumbling across Androsov and the American-targets officer Bogomolov speeding away from the Beria safe house by the Moscow River, Middleton straightened in his chair.

"When did your source see Androsov in Moscow?" The counterintelligence chief looked at Casey, still refusing to make eye contact with Alexander.

"Sometime last spring."

Still addressing his comments to the DCI, Middleton said, "That fits with a curious gap that the FBI had on Androsov's whereabouts last June. He just fell off the screen for a while. Nobody thought much about it at the time, but now it seems he might have been smuggled out on an

Aeroflot flight and back to Washington without the bureau picking up on it. If Androsov made a secret visit back to the Lubyanka, it could mean that the topic being discussed was the transfer of their 'asset' now being handled in Washington to their American targets officer, Bogomolov, somewhere else in the world."

"The timing fits with our troubles, doesn't it?" Casey asked.

"Almost exactly," Middleton answered.

"That's the story," Alexander concluded. "There's no smoking gun, but I think it's enough to tell you that in the highest quarters of the KGB the scuttlebutt is that there's an important penetration of CIA. They imply that it is being run by the First Chief Directorate, which probably rules out anybody in Moscow Station having been turned. It's probably someone here in Washington, and their top CIA specialist in the Lubyanka, Bogomolov, will probably pop up in the operation sooner or later. If you can track Bogomolov, you'll probably find their guy."

"I need more. Bogomolov travels under a dozen names, and we don't know them all."

"I'll give Bill what I get when I get it," Alexander said, clearly signaling Middleton that he had said all he was going to say.

"Why is he telling us this?" Middleton asked Casey. "He's outside now."

Alexander was up and leaning into Middleton's face in an instant. "Graham, look me in the eye when you talk to me. Now why don't you get out of here before I pick you up and throw you through the window, you little shit."

Casey seemed to be enjoying the little scene. "Thanks, Graham. I'll get back to you. And don't tell anybody you met Alexander here. If you do, I'll hear about it and I'll really be pissed."

When they were alone again, Casey looked over his glasses at Alexander. "I'd forgotten how much you disliked Middleton."

Alexander shrugged. "Bill, he may be the best you've got in counter-intelligence, but he's a shit."

"I know that, but that doesn't mean he can't handle the job I've carved out for him. By the way, Alexander, you're talking personally to this source in Moscow, aren't you?"

"I've told you all I am going to tell you. Don't make me lie to you on top of everything else."

"Fair enough. I just didn't want you to think I'd forgotten the reason you quit in a huff."

Alexander raised his second issue. "I need two more things from you: a new back-channel cryptographic system to report matters I might think are crucial about the way Washington deals with the Soviet Union, and an L-pill. I may have some information come my way that will make a difference, and my source won't be able to get on with this job unless he's got a little pill tucked away in case the KGB closes in on him."

"You won't report through the other channel we set up?"

"Not until you find the mole that's burrowed in there, and probably not even then. I'll send what I get directly to you at your office here at the White House, bypassing the CIA system entirely."

Casey pressed his intercom again. "Dottie, get one of those communications packages I use for special projects ready for Alexander and tell him what to do with it."

Alexander thought, communications packages for special projects. My God, this guy's running operations against himself and everybody else in town.

"As for the pill, I'll get something out to you. What am I supposed to ask the technical services people to do?" Casey asked.

Alexander took a sealed envelope from his breast pocket. "Give this to Dr. Hanson in Technical Services. It lays it all out. Cyanide for the larger concealment, puffer-fish toxin for the smaller one, and good concealment devices for each of them."

Casey took the envelope. "Both kinds?"

"Just to be flexible. Cyanide works in seconds. But you've got to be able to hide a pretty big pill. Puffer-fish toxin is just as sure, but it takes a lot longer to work. You've got about half an hour to think things over while it takes you out, but you only need a tiny bit. If you want to know more about it, talk to Hanson."

"I'll get your pills, but I don't want to know any more." Casey grinned weakly.

"Bill, that's it. If I leave now, I can pick up a bunk on a plane out at Andrews loaded with your Stingers."

"They're making a difference, aren't they?"

"You bet they are." Alexander rose and shook the old man's hand; it would be the last time, though he didn't know it.

As he left the office, the DCI's executive assistant handed him an envelope with cipher diskettes inside. "Don't lose these, but if you do, let us know," she warned him. "The instructions are all inside. These materials take your normal cipher messages and superimpose another encryption system. Only I can break it out for the DCI. All you have to do is address your messages to the White House for the DCI and we'll get them to the president or the national security adviser. Now get out of here before you miss your plane."

Alexander left Andrews Air Force Base aboard a giant C-5A three hours after his meeting with Casey. He put himself in what the Air Force called "the flow," a transport flight to Europe that had been openly scheduled two weeks before, one that Soviet intelligence analysts tracking U.S. Air Force movements probably carried as routine. He caught another flight to Islamabad, again in "the flow," and arrived back at the Hermitage the morning of October 11, convinced that he had made the round-trip without alerting anyone in Kabul or Moscow. Klimenko's reporting on the Orlov trade scheduled for October 12 had doubtless focused additional KGB interest on the mysterious Alexander of Paktia. If the KGB now noticed his quick trip to Washington, Klimenko himself might attract additional scrutiny. From now on, Alexander knew he'd have to take every precaution to protect Klimenko and Katerina.

TANK WITH SOLDIERS, 0905 HOURS, OCTOBER 12

Alexander stood before Orlov, who was outfitted in starched summer battle fatigues. "It looks like you'll get back to your unit just in time to change over to winter uniforms and go back out on operations."

"It's beginning to get predictable, isn't it?"

"In my experience, Lieutenant, when you get down to cycles as repetitive as the ones in this war, you're in trouble. Winning gets further and further away."

"What's your standard for winning this war?"

"Easy. Not losing. What's yours?"

Orlov looked at Alexander for a long moment before answering. "I have absolutely no idea. At least not anymore. After sitting on a mountaintop for seven weeks with nothing to do but read Solzhenitsyn, newspapers, and newsmagazines and listen to the Voice of America and the BBC every day I've had some time to think about such matters."

"Any conclusions?"

"Yeah. Information flashing around the world without restrictions must scare my father's generation more than all your NATO missiles."

"If your general secretary gets his way with glasnost, you're going to start seeing more of it."

"Well, I think that my generation might know better than Gorbachev's how the country will come unstuck with this thing you like to call freedom. But I'd still take the chance."

Alexander laughed, surprised at how much he had come to like Orlov. "When you get back to Kabul don't forget to tell all the debriefers how many times we waved the blonde with big tits in front of you."

KABUL, 40TH ARMY HEADQUARTERS, 0900 HOURS, OCTOBER 13

The next morning General Gennady Titov called his staff meeting. He outlined the operations that had brought about Orlov's release, never mentioning his pedigree or allowing the men to believe that lesser measures might have been taken for a less prominent lieutenant. He is one of our own, Titov said, and we take care of our own.

He also spoke reverently of the officers and men who had died freeing Orlov and avenging the death of General Polyakov, including the dedicated KGB major who had died in the line of duty at Ali Khel. Finally, he had words of special praise for Colonel Anatoly Viktorovich Klimenko and Major Alexander Petrovich Krasin, who had been seriously wounded during the desperate battle to avenge the death of General Polyakov. Klimenko would be joining his staff as a special adviser on intelligence matters, and Krasin, when released from the hospital, would be his chief ADC. Then, as was his custom, he abruptly dismissed the officers and left the room without further discussion.

During Titov's monologue, Karm Sergeyevich Nikitenko knew he was right about Klimenko. He also knew that he would have to be patient. Only a fool would swim against the tide favoring the Ukrainian colonel right now.

Outside the briefing room Karm waited patiently as senior officers curried favor with Titov's new man. Finally he approached. "Anatoly Viktorovich, may I be the last, but not the least to congratulate you on your bold actions of the last weeks. You are certainly a man to be reckoned with."

"Karm Sergeyevich, I take that as the highest order of compliment from a man of your reputation, but I feel a debt of gratitude is owed those who died in the operations the general mentioned."

"You are too modest, Anatoly Viktorovich, but I couldn't agree more about the debt we owe those who died. Did I tell you that I visited the morgue out at the airfield to pay my respects to Major Shadrin?"

"We haven't had a chance to talk, Karm Sergeyevich. The major and I worked together on some very difficult issues. I shall miss him. He was quite a man."

The major was a shit, and you know it, Nikitenko thought, but he said, "His horrible death still confuses me. Of course I have read all the reports, but why did he wander so far from safety that night?"

"It bothered me as well. Perhaps it was the drink, just another senseless death."

"Yes, I suppose, like all those fine boys up there with you above the Kabul River. There are those here at headquarters who simply cannot understand the tactics of that Spetsnaz captain. How he got so widely dispersed. You and Krasin were with him on his helicopter; maybe you can explain to me what occurred."

Klimenko's mind raced. "Questions have been raised, Karm Sergeyevich, but that happens after any action. Krasin and I were on Captain Lukin's helicopter and we saw the confusion as we closed in on the Dukhis and the American special services officers. We moved in on Lukin's orders. I would be the last to question his judgment in deploying his forces the way he did, particularly since he died bravely in combat and isn't here to explain his actions."

Klimenko realized he would have to watch this man every day. The sheer complexity of his life, as his fortunes shifted between heroism and treason, almost brought a smile of irony to his lips.

FOUR

THIRTY

MOSCOW, 1730 HOURS, FEBRUARY 26, 1988

Katerina's telephone was ringing when she let herself into her room at the Ukraina Hotel.

"Miss Martin Catherine." The English was heavily accented. "How would you like to make love to a pretty Rossiyan boy?"

Katerina responded instantly in Russian. "Listen, you little pervert, I know you're here in the hotel. You call me again and the only lovemaking you'll be doing is with the boys in the Gulag." She slammed down the receiver and stormed out of her room.

Minutes later she was complaining to a bored young man in a shiny tuxedo jacket at the reception desk. "I'm telling you, there is a pervert in this hotel making obscene phone calls to my room and it is your duty to find him and make him stop."

"Miss Martin, that is simply not possible," the desk clerk insisted. "There can be no perverts in the Ukraina because it is practically forbidden strictly. It is not, therefore, possible."

"You tell that to your friends in Dzerzhinsky Square," Katerina snapped and wheeled toward the elevator.

She stepped off at the third-floor shopping area, her pulse racing. Entering the Beriozka she spotted Klimenko in the back studying the political Matryoshkas, the hand-carved stack dolls in the likeness of KGB chairmen going back to Dzerzhinsky. She eased beside him. "This is a cute one," he said glancing over at her. "You might want to buy it." Then he put it down and left.

She found a photocopy of a page from a Moscow walking guide folded inside the third doll. Slipping the paper into her palm, she took the set to the cashier. Back in her room, she opened the note—Please join us for a little walking tour of the St. Prophet Eliah Church at ten o'clock tomorrow. We'll meet at the metro station at Krapotkinskaya. Dress warmly, Helen.

The next morning at ten Katerina started from the Krapotkinskaya metro station on the route she had memorized the night before. She walked first to the Convent of the Conception, and then strolled on to Vtoraya Obydennaya where she turned into a short street to the St. Prophet Eliah Church. After doing an obligatory tourist minute, she walked until she came to Semyonovsky Proyezd. She was studying her guidebook when Klimenko walked up behind her.

"Act surprised to see me and give me a little kiss," he said as he took her elbow.

Katerina spun around and threw her arms around his neck, kissing him on both cheeks. "I can't think of anything to say, Tolya, except, now what?"

"Now we ride around and have a little talk," he said, and led her to a brown Zhiguli parked about two streets away. They didn't speak until they were in the car.

"Katerina, every time we meet I'll have a list of things to go through. You'll have to memorize them as I talk to you. First, have you seen any surveillance today?"

"I don't think so. I don't think they've been watching me for the last three weeks."

"Tell me about every incident in the last month that you thought unusual."

"They started to leave me alone about a month ago. But they had watched me closely for weeks and had taken a few things from my hotel room."

"What things?"

"A pair of panties from my dirty laundry and a panty shield from the wastebasket."

"They do that. It's for the dogs."

"Then everything just stopped."

Klimenko nodded. "I've got a friend in counterintelligence watching West Europeans. He said they're not spending any time on journalists these days. You're looked over routinely during the first few months, and then only spot-checked."

As Klimenko drove, he continued down his list. After half an hour he asked her to repeat the main items.

"You want Alexander to do a name check on Karm Sergeyevich Nikitenko, senior colonel in KGB First Chief Directorate. Prior service in counterintelligence. Served in Beirut 1981 to 1985, Kabul 1985 to 1987; now he's back at Yasenevo working in Directorate RI. Nikitenko was investigating you as late as October 1986, and may still be. He blames you for the humiliation he suffered in Beirut when you came in with a Group Alfa team to free two of his officers taken hostage by Hizbollah. One died in captivity. One of the other two officers was working for the CIA and later defected. Nikitenko took all the blame. Nikitenko's investigation of you was the reason that the major had such bad luck in the minefield at Ali Khel. Alexander will know what you mean."

"That's fine, Kat. What else?"

"You found nothing in the regular indices on Alexander, no reference to other, special indices, and nothing on his Polish alias Gromek Jasik."

After Kat had repeated Klimenko's list back to him almost verbatim, he smiled and said, "Now comes the more complicated part. First, I asked Alexander to send in something they call 'special preparations.' Did he do that?"

"Tolya, if you're talking about your pills, yes, I have them."

From her purse she took out a key chain with a plastic soccer-ball fob and a Soviet-made fountain pen. Handing them over, she explained, "The cyanide pill is in the key-chain fob. Just bite through the soccer ball and immediate effects will follow. The other one is in the cap of the pen. Snap off the part above the pocket clip and you'll find the pill. Pull it apart and let the powder fall into your mouth. It's slower, but it's absolutely effective."

"Thank you, Katerina. I know the rest of it." Klimenko slipped both items into his pocket. He turned to face his cousin. "Now for the punch line. I want you and Alexander to get my mother out of the Soviet Union."

40TH ARMY HEADQUARTERS, 0645 HOURS, MARCH 4, 1988

Krasin's limp was barely noticeable. He felt only an occasional twinge of pain in his groin when he walked over uneven ground. In the commander's wing at 40th Army Headquarters, he nodded to the two paratroopers standing guard outside the conference room and stopped at the horseshoe-shape table behind the chair of the First Deputy Commander, General Gennady Titov.

Sasha laid out a folder containing the briefing notes for this morning's special staff meeting precisely in the center of the blotter at Titov's place and a fresh pack of Marlboros with the front row of cigarettes pressed out of the box in a wedged phalanx. He aligned the general's reading glasses with the top of the blotter and checked that the ashtray had been cleaned. Finally, he made sure the two stainless-steel thermoses of coffee and tea were full. Heavy-tasting mineral water from Tashkent in half-liter bottles, badly scratched from reuse, were set at intervals along the table. He caught the approach of an officer out of the corner of his eye.

"I trust Lieutenant Colonel Krasin is well after his ill-deserved malingering in Mother Russia."

Sasha didn't look up. "Lieutenant Colonel Krasin is extremely well after his much-deserved hero's rest, which didn't end one day too soon. And how is the Committee's most reckless colonel?"

"I'm fine, Sasha. It's good to have you back, though I haven't the foggiest notion why you returned. It could have been over for you. You know that, don't you?"

Sasha turned to Klimenko. "And then what would I do? Don't get me wrong, my friend. I'm eternally grateful for all the special treatment— from Titov, from Orlov's papa, and, best of all, from a wonderful little nurse from Tallinn who proved me wrong when I told her that I feared the Dukhis had ended my fornicating days. But I am back—back because of my devotion to our Socialist Internationalist Duty." The irony in Sasha's voice was heavy.

"Let's get together tonight, maybe get a little drunk and swap some lies after the general's in bed, okay? We need to talk. The war just isn't any fun without my favorite, and now handicapped, lieutenant colonel. I haven't gotten into a good conspiracy since you left."

Sasha arched an eyebrow at his friend, but said nothing.

Klimenko took his seat near the top of the horseshoe. At exactly 0700 hours the officers stood at rigid attention as General Gennady Titov walked briskly to his place. "Seats, please."

He reflexively reached for his cigarettes and lit up, a signal to the others in the room that they could, too.

"Comrades, I have asked you to join me this morning for a special briefing on the state of affairs in Moscow as they affect the fulfillment of our duties here. As you can see from the empty seats this is a highly restricted briefing. Only you were invited. Each of you has been logged on the attendance roster, and each of you will initial that you have attended this meeting and have understood the sensitivity of the topics discussed. I need not stress to you that any discussion outside this room of the substance of this briefing will not be countenanced."

Titov then went straight to the point. "Comrades, the decision to conclude the agreement at Geneva with the Afghan parties, with the Americans, and with the Pakistanis has been reached by our comrade, General Secretary Mikhail Sergeyevich. This decision is, for all practical purposes, irrevocable."

A low murmur went around the room.

"Within the next four to eight weeks the agreement will be concluded, and we will have before us the task of withdrawing our forces from Afghanistan. The timetable may be as short as nine months, or as long as eighteen. Furthermore, we may have to withdraw up to fifty percent of our forces during the first ninety days."

The commanders were stunned. "Yes, comrades, we may have to get halfway out in the first three months. I have made it known to the defense minister that the 40th Army's preference is for a longer withdrawal period and no front-loading. But, in essence, comrades, our internationalist duty in the Democratic Republic of Afghanistan is drawing to a close." Stubbing out his cigarette, he added, "I have spoken personally with the general secretary, on instructions of General Boris Vsevolodovich, of course, and made a number of points."

Klimenko looked at Titov and thought, You bet you talked to Gorbachev on instructions from Gromov. He sends you in every time it looks like there's a political risk. Gromov, the man on horseback, wants to be remembered as the Hero of Afghanistan, so he's setting you up as the man who got run out of Afghanistan.

Titov continued. "I told the general secretary that while the political decision to withdraw from Afghanistan has been made, and while we in the Red Army fully support the Party in all decisions, we were confident that careful thought would be given in Moscow to our important national duty of protecting the Red Army, not only ensuring the safety of its soldiers, but preserving its image as it wades out of this swamp. The general secretary said he understood the position of Boris Vsevolodovich and the commanders of the expeditionary forces, but that he could not imagine any conditions that would cause him to reverse his decision. On the contrary, he said that he would probably have no choice but to go along with the American proposal of a nine-month withdrawal and with the extra demand that we pull half our forces out ninety days after the accords go into effect. He said that it was our responsibility to preserve our honor as we withdraw. I interpret that statement, comrades, as giving us a certain latitude as we prepare for departure. Questions?"

The commander of the 105th Guards Airborne Division spoke first.

"Gennady Ivanovich, now is a hell of a time to start talking of withdrawal. We are experiencing a higher level of rebel attacks than during any winter season we can remember. In a couple of weeks the snow will begin melting in the lower passes and the Dushman will be on the move once again. There is no sign of a letup, and the intelligence reports I have seen tell the same story in all combat sectors. If we are to walk—no, if we are to race out of here with honor—I think we're going to have to teach those people a lesson first. None of us wants to order our troops to fight their way home!"

Titov turned to Klimenko. "Colonel, give us your assessment of the military situation, and a summary of the rebels' supply situation, and what you expect after the snow melts. Please take your time."

The night before Titov had told him to frankly report the realities. Now Klimenko walked to a large pull-down tactical map of Afghanistan.

"Comrades, without exaggeration the last year and a half has brought us an almost unbroken string of setbacks. Since the introduction of new surface-to-air missile systems over a year ago, we have lost our once uncontested control of the air. By the end of 1986 the Dushman were destroying, on average, one of our aircraft a day. They are destroying slightly fewer now, but that is only because we are employing more conservative air tactics in response to the new rebel air-defense systems."

"Tell me about it, Colonel! Tell me about *conservative* air tactics." It was the commander of the 108th Guards Motorized Rifle Division. "I can't get enough air cover to move from one valley to another. The air force can't give us close air support from twelve thousand feet! That's where they fly now! The helicopters don't even drop pickets along the ridges to scout for us when we move into valleys. How can you move anywhere in these mountains without putting out pickets?"

The air force commander at Baghram, a senior colonel, broke in bitterly. "I resent the constant complaints from officers in the ground forces when the officers in the air force have been bearing the brunt of casualties in the last year. Officer casualties, I mean. Comrades, I have several photographs here showing the condition of our pilots who have fallen into the hands of the Dushman. I invite you to take a look. They aren't pretty. I suggest that the only way to change the current status of this war is to attack the supply depots on the other side of zero line. I say we make some strikes inside Pakistan and knock them back on their heels." Titov let the sparks fly for another minute then he broke in. "I understand the problems you all face and the constraints you are under to keep casualties low. I have argued with the defense minister myself and have warned him about excessive caution, so to speak."

There was derisive laughter at the idea of warning Dmitri Yazov against caution. Most of those in the room held the defense minister in contempt, and many were still shocked that Gorbachev had selected him.

"As for strikes into Pakistan by the air force, I'm afraid that's out of the question, regardless of the merit in Aleksandr Ivanovich's suggestion. Although I am in total agreement that a hard blow to their rear-area supply lines might have some effect, Moscow does not have the stomach for a more aggressive posture. Colonel, would you complete your briefing on the supply situation, please."

With a wooden pointer Klimenko showed the scores of forward supply dumps on the Afghanistan-Pakistan border, noting how inefficient it would be to mount air strikes against such scattered targets. Then he selected a spot over seventy miles away in Pakistan's Punjab province.

"Here, gentlemen, is the only place where the Dushman supply line can really be hurt: Ojhri Camp between Rawalpindi and Islamabad. About ten thousand tons of ordnance is stored at Ojhri, the most important of which is over one hundred and fifty Stinger missiles. Another ten thousand tons is on the way there at any given time. In short, the Dushman are well supplied, and we will all see fighting pick up in the coming days and weeks. Thank you, gentlemen."

Titov let the commanders discuss the situation among themselves for a few moments before issuing his orders. "I would like your preliminary thoughts on planning an orderly withdrawal either nine months from the middle of May, or eighteen months from that date. Please do the preliminary work yourselves. No one on your staffs is to be brought into the process until we are ready for the next step. Any questions?"

There were none. Titov turned to Klimenko. "Colonel, please join me in my office in five minutes. You too, Krasin."

Titov motioned Klimenko and Sasha into seats at his office table with a sweep of his hand. "Anatoly Viktorovich, my commanders are right. We need to strike the Dushman at home, but short of a mutiny against central authority, I cannot authorize any such strike using our air forces or regular ground forces. However, that doesn't mean something cannot be done. I am aware that you have some ideas of your own."

Klimenko studied the general for a moment. In the last year and a half he had come to respect the man as much as anyone in the 40th Army command structure. Titov was part of the system, but his underlying honesty made him exceptional. They had more in common than Titov knew.

"General, I have tracked the supply buildup at Ojhri Camp for more than two months. It is clear that the Americans are pouring in supplies in order to have enough on hand in Pakistan if, as part of the Geneva Accords, Washington and Moscow agree to stop supplying the Afghan parties."

Titov nodded. "I didn't mention it at the meeting, but such discussions are under way. It's called 'negative symmetry.' How about that for a tortured diplomatic concept! Nevertheless, General Secretary Gorbachev will probably go along with it. But you haven't answered my question, Anatoly Viktorovich. What can we do about Ojhri?"

"Blow it up."

"Blow it up?" Titov smiled incredulously.

"Yes, General. Just like that. Three ships are now under way for the port of Karachi. They will unload their ordnance beginning late this month, until early April. The normal route for the supplies from Karachi is by special train either to Rawalpindi and Ojhri Camp, or to Quetta in Baluchistan. Our intelligence says that most of the ordnance currently at sea will be delivered to Rawalpindi, where it will be loaded into trucks and hauled the five miles to Ojhri. That's where we would make a switch: the Rawalpindi train station."

"What switch?"

"Switch a wooden crate, or possibly several wooden crates, containing our devices for ones with Egyptian white phosphorous mortar bombs. As soon as the ordnance reaches Ojhri, we press the button. There will be nothing the Pakistanis can do to stop it."

"Can this be done without killing a lot of civilians?"

"Not really. But I don't think we need worry about the civilian casualties. They will be blamed on the people who stacked all the ordnance in the middle of a populated area in the first place, not on whoever blew it up. Besides, it will be ambiguous."

"What can possibly be ambiguous about an ammo dump blowing up?"

Klimenko smiled. "General, you're the one who told me that in this area of the world almost anything can be ambiguous. But I'm talking about the cause of the explosion. The shipments we're targeting will include Egyptian mortar bombs. The Pakistanis have long-standing complaints about the white phosphorous mortar bombs from Egypt. They say they're old and that they leak and spontaneously ignite when the white phosphorous hits the air. They've caused a couple of fires over the years, but no major disasters. People can be made to believe that it was a colossal accident with an Egyptian bogeyman."

"Can you do anything to increase the ambiguity?"

"Yes. The Islamabad Rezidentura has a number of assets in the Pakistani opposition media that will respond to any disaster at Ojhri by raising the cry that the heartless military regime is to blame for endangering civilians. Never mind what caused the explosions; nobody but the Pakistani Army will really care. Another set of press assets, the Islamic fundamentalists, can dredge up the specter of dangerous and shoddy materials being dumped on the jihad by greedy, un-Islamic Egyptians."

"Can you do this by early April? I think we'll probably sign at Geneva late in the month."

"I've already had several of the devices sent to our Rezident in Islamabad. He tells me he has the human assets at the train station to switch the crates. All you will have to do is send me and one 40th Army officer—I suggest Krasin here—with alias identities to Pakistan from Moscow for a few days to push the button."

"Why can't the Islamabad Rezident do it?"

"Because if it succeeds, it should be a 40th Army success. If it fails, then it's another nice try by the KGB."

Titov smiled faintly. "Do whatever it takes to set it off in early April."

Klimenko punched END ENDX into the holes in the subminiature keyboard of the burst radio transmitter and stepped outside his office. The solitary guard was slouched down for the quiet six to midnight shift. Sasha had accompanied Titov to dinner at the general officers mess. Klimenko could safely make his two-second burst transmission, his sixteenth since he had seen Alexander on the day of the Orlov exchange more than seventeen months ago.

Klimenko had monitored the attempts by the signals-intercept unit of the 16th Directorate to locate the new burst transmitter in the Kabul area. Fifteen of his sixteen transmissions had been intercepted and sent routinely to his office with the brief notation UNLOCATED TRANSMITTER, INDECIPHERABLE MESSAGE. He took some comfort in that no less than half a dozen of the same kind of burst transmitters were operating in Kabul with the same negative results. The Alpha system that had been so useful during the negotiations for Orlov had stayed on the air for a couple of months afterward and had then abruptly disappeared after a series of exchanges discussing a dangerous attack against Kabul airfield. The analysts in the 16th wrote off the loss as routine bad luck. Either the agent had been killed in the operation, or had otherwise stopped broadcasting. Perhaps he had a new radio, possibly one of the new ones the 16th Directorate couldn't read. Klimenko was convinced that Alexander had set all this up very carefully to protect their own communications link.

Now he retrieved the other two sections of the radio from his safe. He quickly joined the three sections, and moved over to the table in front of his curtained window. He checked on the guard at the end of the hall one last time, then raised the antenna section and pressed the transmit button. The red light burned for two seconds, followed less than a second later by the green handshake signal from the other end.

Klimenko dismantled the radio quickly, pressed the Message Clear button, and put the radio back in his safe. Two minutes past eight. He felt his pulse racing and sat down.

THE HERMITAGE, 2200 HOURS, MARCH 4

Tim Rand stood back discreetly as Alexander entered the decryption code, read the message on the monitor screen, and printed off a single copy.

"Thanks, Tim. I may have something soon for the special channel to the White House."

Reading Klimenko's account of the Titov briefing, Alexander knew that it heralded a turning point. My God, he thought, they're folding.

THE WHITE HOUSE, 1145 HOURS, MARCH 4

The deputy national security adviser, Jim Taggart, opened the dispatch and saw that it was another of the series on Soviet political and military intentions in Afghanistan. He could tell little about the source of the information, or even where it had been acquired, which was not unusual in sensitive intelligence cases. As he scanned the message's tight language he pressed his intercom. "Get me in to see General Bancroft as soon as you can, please. Tell him it's important."

Five minutes later Taggart sat in front of the tidy desk of retired General Bartlett Bancroft, the president's national security adviser.

"Can we believe this report, Jim? Can we take it to the president? Is this the same guy that's been giving us all the good stuff for the last year?" Bancroft read, " 'The Red Army commanders in the field will interpret a nine-month withdrawal schedule, especially one which calls for a fifty percent withdrawal in the first three months after the accord is signed, as a dangerous humiliation. But Gorbachev has made it clear to the army that protecting the honor of the Red Army is their duty, not his.' My God, Gorby's really got his neck out."

"We can believe it, General, and we can take it in to the president. And yes, it's the same source."

"Let's send this to Rome for Ambassador Armbruster's eyes only. This will give him a look in Vorontsov's briefcase before he meets him for this round of the peace talks. Where do you think this guy is—the Politburo, on Gorbachev's staff, where?"

"That's what it looks like, but they may just want us to conclude that. My guess is he's in Kabul. Wherever he is, he's good and we have to keep him alive."

"Then send it in CIA channels."

THIRTY-ONE

Sasha balanced perilously on the back legs of his chair with his feet on Klimenko's desk. He was on his third vodka.

"So picture this scene, Tolya. I'm six months into rehabilitation down in the Crimea. The head of the place tells me the defense minister himself is interested in my case, but I know it's General Orlov pulling strings for me."

"Yazov, Orlov, Gromov," said Klimenko. "They all wanted you well taken care of. But if we'd screwed up getting Orlov's boy back, they'd have fought for turns at carving us both up." He was matching Sasha glass for glass.

"Don't interrupt. This is important. It's about nine in the evening and this angel-faced night-shift nurse from Tallinn—one of those Baltic blondes—is doing her job real seriously down in my groin with this West German ultrasound wand. Anyhow, she opens her big blue eyes and says in her sweet Baltic accent, 'Major Krasin. I think the doctors were wrong.'

"I'm lying back on starched white linen feeling pretty good. I mean I'm feeling even better than pretty good with this angel and her magic wand working down there right next to my business, so I say, 'Nurse Galina, it's Colonel now. I have been promoted for incredible bravery in action. But how can the comrade doctors have possibly been wrong?'

"She looks out the door to check that no one's wandering around the hall that time of night, and then lifts up my bedsheet and says, 'Colonel, look.' And I see my St. Peter standing right up. Not a diamond cutter, mind you, but a pretty respectable effort for a guy who was led to believe that all his important plumbing had been trashed by a 12.7 round. Then I turn to this angel and say with an absolutely straight face, 'Nurse Galina, Dr. Stepanov said that there was one chance in a thousand, maybe only one in a million that this might happen. My God, it has! But it's too soon. I'm afraid it will all be for nothing.' So little Galina, eyes wide, says, 'What do you mean it will all be for nothing?' "

Sasha took another long pull at his glass. "So I say, 'Dr. Stepanov said that if this ever happened, it was absolutely essential that I make love to a woman at that very moment. He said if I couldn't force myself through a full spontaneous/harmonic sexual regeneration cycle, the opportunity to recover fully would probably be lost forever.' By now Galina is struggling with the enormity of the issue. 'No, Colonel. We can't lose now.' She pops over to the door to make sure the ward is quiet, then says, with a sweetness that can only come from one committed to the highest of vocations, 'Colonel, I will regenerate you myself.' Next thing I know she crosses herself backward, like a Roman Catholic. Then I've got her little head bobbing up and down on my St. Peter and the whole world is looking brighter."

"Soldiers in hospitals have fantasies like that all the time, I hear."

"Tolya, I give you my word of honor, it was no fantasy. Next morning I tell Dr. Stepanov that Minister Yazov will be proud of the exemplary service he provides. I say that there's a particularly kind nurse who puts her duty above all personal considerations. Could he, without mentioning that we have spoken about her, tell Nurse Galina that whatever moral support she is giving the VIP colonel, to keep it up. It's having a miraculous effect. The good doctor is actually moved by my praise of his people, and impressed by my dropping the name of our fat-assed defense minister."

"You have the morals of an alley cat." Klimenko refilled both their glasses.

"Well, my beautiful Galina gives me her special therapy every night until I'm declared whole and kicked out. We even took three vacations to Yalta and Sevastopol. I think I fell in love with her. If I'd had the chance then and there I swear I would have stolen a boat and made for Istanbul and points west, and I bet she'd have gone with me."

"Well, at least you didn't get lonely."

"No, I didn't get lonely. I even had a visitor, a mutual friend."

Klimenko caught the change in Sasha's tone. "A mutual friend? I didn't know you and I had any friends."

"Karm Sergeyevich."

"Oh, shit. What did he want from the wounded hero? I bet you didn't tell him about your bout with spontaneous/harmonic sexual degeneration."

"He said he was visiting some people and thought he would drop in to see how I was doing. He spends about two hours with me, like he really cares about me. He pushes me around the garden in my wheelchair and even gives me his home phone number and address in Moscow in case I ever want to look him up. He clearly has more than a passing interest in everything that happened to you and me in Afghanistan. Did I tell you he visited me in the hospital in Kabul just before I left for the Crimea?"

"He told me himself. Lucky you and I got our story straight while you were in the hospital in Jalālābād and decided you didn't want to die."

"This time it was more of the same. He said he was very proud of what we did, but he also said that some people were still having trouble figuring out just what happened that night up over the river. 'Some people couldn't figure out the tactics that got you boys so shot up. They don't think those tactics sounded anything like what Captain Lukin would have done on an operation. But then poor Captain Lukin is dead, and not in a position to tell his side of the story. Pity.' "

Klimenko nodded. "He ran that by me right after the Orlov exchange. He thinks he smells something, but he doesn't know what. I told him about getting Lukin to do the two one-eighties in a row to smoke out the American radios. I took responsibility for that up front, as you and I agreed in Jalālābād. He probably knew all about that from debriefing the airborne-intercept people who were up there with us, but he sure doesn't want to let it go."

"And he's not likely to ever let it go. He even raised the Shadrin business all over again, sniveling as if Shadrin was a great loss to the nation. 'The poor dear boy. Must have been a terrible sight for you. So hard to believe the major doing something like that. So unlike him. Awful sight at the Kabul morgue.' That kind of crap."

"What do you think?"

"I think that Karm Sergeyevich does not like Colonel Anatoly Viktorovich Klimenko one little bit, so he decided to take a hard look at him at about the same time all kinds of things started happening in your life. But he can't figure it out. He's fascinated by the American called Alexander, but can't seem to make anything out of what he knows. He asked me a million questions about him, but I told him I couldn't really answer most of them. Nothing much but a description of the guy from a distance. I think his problem is that he's so subjective about you that none of the facts fit his prejudices. He wants you, Colonel, but he's nowhere close to knowing what you've been up to. Even in Moscow, he's still coming after you, but he's blinded by his prejudices."

"There's an old saying, Sasha: 'Even the blind pig can find the acorn.' I will not turn my back on Karm Sergeyevich."

After Sasha departed, Klimenko unpacked his burst radio for the second time that day. He had five minutes to receive a message from

Alexander, assuming there was one. The transmission would be repeated on the half hour until it got a handshake from his radio. At exactly 2230 hours he saw the green light on the face of his receiver and he scrolled up the message twice to memorize the points Alexander had made:

> Many thanks for the Titov report. Understand your points that there should be some letup on combat operations by the Mujaheddin, but it is impossible to control, and foolhardy even to try. What do you mean "or there will be a harsh reaction from the 40th Army"? Please clarify. I am moving now to meet with Paul to arrange that he be in position to receive your call within two weeks. He will tell me about your last meeting. I will send one broadcast before you depart for Moscow.

Paul was the agreed-upon cover name for Katerina. Alexander had picked the name himself, probably for Czar Paul I, the son of Catherine the Great. Never mind that Paul I was feckless where Kiev and the Ukraine were concerned, it was a nice touch.

Klimenko cleared the message from the receiver and held the overwrite button on until it blinked. Then he switched the batteries with those in his short-wave radio, tuned it to the Radio Moscow frequency, then turned the volume down. In the morning his staff assistant would find the batteries run down, and would get fresh ones. Klimenko knew that KGB counterintelligence paranoia included watching people more closely if they seemed to be buying too many batteries. To them, batteries meant secret transmitters, and sometimes they were right.

Moscow, 0800 Hours, March 8

Nikitenko had been back at Moscow Center for almost a year. He had shaken the stigma of Beirut and begun to rebuild his career. Serving out his penance in Kabul had propelled him into the middle of the single issue that preoccupied Mikhail Gorbachev in the spring of 1988—getting out of Afghanistan with the semblance of honor.

His valuable new ally at Center, Leonid Vladimirovich Shapkin, the head of Directorate RI of the KGB's First Chief Directorate, recognized his talent for putting together the kind of reporting on Afghanistan the general secretary desperately wanted to hear. Nikitenko understood the process of crafting intelligence to support policy conclusions, and began to deliver a product that bought his chief a coveted seat at Gorbachev's policy table.

But Shapkin was a devoted admirer of Anatoly Klimenko, irrationally so, Nikitenko thought; their service together in Tehran during the Iranian revolution had earned them both decorations, based largely on Klimenko's efforts, and Klimenko had gone on to win a second Order of the Red Banner in Afghanistan. Nikitenko would have to keep his suspicions and his extracurricular research on Klimenko to himself, but he was now convinced he could run his quarry to ground through the American Alexander, the common thread in Nikitenko's investigation of the string of peculiar events that had begun with the death of Major Shadrin at Ali Khel and ended with the release of Lieutenant M. S. Orlov. Nikitenko's pursuit of Alexander fitted neatly with Shapkin's broad tasking to put all possible resources into the investigation of CIA operations in Afghanistan. Shapkin had given him a free hand, and had even agreed to raise the matter of the central CIA figure, Alexander, with a sensitive human source being run by the First Chief Directorate. He didn't identify the source, but Nikitenko assumed the FCD had picked up an American. Why not, Nikitenko had thought. If he could solve the riddle of the mysterious Alexander, the path might lead him to Klimenko.

Now he was about to test his theory that the Russian-speaking CIA man had been in contact with other KGB officers over the years. Nikitenko was going to interview the KGB's most treacherous turncoat, Vitaly Sergeyevich Yurchenko.

When Yurchenko had redefected to the Soviet Embassy in Washington with a bizarre story of being kidnapped, drugged, and tortured by the CIA, KGB Chairman Chebrikov decided to accept his story for the time being. His rationale was that in the short run it was less damaging to the KGB for one of its flag-rank officers to have been drugged, kidnapped, and forced into a debriefing by the Americans than for a flag-rank officer to have defected willingly to the Main Enemy for a million dollars. Chebrikov told those who disagreed that they would eventually have their way with Yurchenko, but in the meantime he would have the outward trappings of a normal life. Most days Yurchenko was locked away in a cramped, one-room crib in the basement of the Lubyanka; his solitude was occasionally broken when he was moved into well-appointed VIP quarters near the Ring Road where, under watchful eyes, he would reassure visiting journalists and their cameras that he was a free man.

Nikitenko waited as the guard opened the grillwork door to the "Yurchenko suite," then opened the inner door and let himself into the stark quarters.

"Karm Sergeyevich, how delightful. I almost never get visits from old friends anymore." Yurchenko stood beside his military-style bunk; the only other furnishings in the twelve-by-twelve-foot room were a straight-backed chair and a standard footlocker with a lamp on it. A naked bulb hung from the ceiling and a five-foot folding partition in the corner of the room partly concealed a sink and a toilet.

Nikitenko took the chair without it being offered. "You look well."

Indeed Yurchenko looked younger than Nikitenko remembered. His translucent blue-gray eyes were clear and alert, and his stringy blond hair showed only a few streaks of gray. Nikitenko wondered if he would look quite as good under similar circumstances, but quickly dismissed such a discomfiting thought.

Yurchenko sat down on the bed. "The doctors have told me that I have almost fully recovered. My short-term memory has returned, the crying jags have stopped, and I'm beginning to feel my old self again. Who knows, they may even let me go back to work soon. You know how I hate all the trouble and expense of this special treatment here in our VIP quarters. You just can't imagine, my old friend, how well I have been treated since I escaped almost three years ago."

Nikitenko felt a strange mixture of disgust and a bizarre, unexplainable sense of camaraderie with this despicable traitor who had been clever enough to buy a temporary reprieve with an inventive story.

"Vitaly Sergeyevich, I have always had the utmost faith in the way the Committee takes care of its own."

"Of course, Karm Sergeyevich. They told me you needed some help. How can I be of assistance?"

Nikitenko unlocked his briefcase on his knees and took out a tape recorder.

"Vitaly Sergeyevich, I need your help in identifying a man I think is doing grave harm not only to the Committee, but to the people of the Soviet Union. I am going to play a tape recording of that man's voice, speaking first in English then in Russian. I want you to listen carefully and tell me if you recognize it. The English part will be first."

Nikitenko pressed Play. *"This is a meeting between Colonel I. V. Belenko of Headquarters, Soviet 40th Army, Kabul, Afghanistan, and Senior Lieutenant M. S. Orlov of the 105th Guards Airborne Division. Today is September thirteenth, 1986. This meeting is taking place in Paktia province, Afghanistan. Will you both please state your name and confirm that the information I have just provided is true and accurate?"*

Nikitenko checked the tape counter. "There's one more segment of English with another voice, Vitaly Sergeyevich. Disregard the voice that belongs to one Lieutenant Orlov. Pay attention only to the other voice."

"Lieutenant Orlov, have you been mistreated while you have been the guest of the people of Afghanistan?"

"I have not been mistreated, but I have been held illegally by Dushman

in violation of international law and of the laws of the government of Afghanistan."

"*Please take off your tunic, Lieutenant Orlov.*"

"Now, Vitaly Sergeyevich. This is the same man speaking Russian."

The second segment was clearly a recording of a radio transmission, only slightly distorted by background noise. "*I am speaking to the two Soviet gunships approaching the site of the crash. Do not approach further and do not fire! Do not approach further and do not fire! We have your officers and we will execute them if you approach further or if you fire on us! If you have understood me each of you is to turn on his landing lights and then turn them off immediately. Do as I say now!*"

"Vitaly Sergeyevich, there is just one more segment. It's also in Russian. Listen carefully."

"*Thank you. Now you will stand off from this position one kilometer. One of you may respond on this frequency and stand by for further communications from me. The lives of your officers depend on how you follow these instructions.*"

"Karm Sergeyevich, you can turn off the recorder. I don't need to hear any more. It is a man I knew as Alexander, a CIA officer. He was born a Russian."

Nikitenko recorded another three hours of conversation with Yurchenko, a rambling defense of himself and a description of the man called Alexander. Despite his failings as a human being, Yurchenko had a good eye for detail and a flawless memory. Nikitenko even had enough on Alexander to run by Shapkin's American source. Maybe something would pop up.

MILAN, 1210 HOURS, MARCH 11

Standing in the taxi queue at Milan's main train station, Aldrich Ames felt a steel band tightening around his head. He pressed his thumb and forefinger against his eyes, as if it might somehow relieve the pressure. He had spent the last four hours in the club car of the Trans-Europe Express from Rome, and the inability of the average Italian to honor an orderly queue was beginning to push his irritation over the edge into rage. He told himself to calm down. It wouldn't do to fly off the handle in a taxi queue on a quiet spring Saturday. He wondered what it would be like to wake up without feeling ravaged by demons. They had been tormenting him since his first steps into treason almost three years before. It was worst when he was alone, or when he was sober. He could see the faces of those his treason had killed; he could feel the depth of his betrayal of Langley, of his colleagues, of his country.

The drinking usually helped. He looked across the square at the

Excelsior Hotel, which had a nice bar, but put the idea out of his mind. After ten minutes his turn for a cab finally came. He told the driver, "Piazza de la Scala."

Near La Scala, Ames began the lazy stroll through a long, preset surveillance-detection route. He wandered through the shopping arcades of La Galleria, reversing his direction several times. He knew there were as many as ten KGB countersurveillants in the area, and also knew there would be a KGB van with a radio team listening to the Italian security service and police frequencies to see if any talk might be linked to the movements of their little rabbit as he hopped around the neighborhood. Vladik had told him that the countersurveillance people thought he was a senior official in the Italian Foreign Ministry, but he didn't know whether he believed this. Certainly he hoped that there weren't a couple of dozen Soviets wandering around Milan who knew who he was and what he was doing.

Ames made what is known in the trade as a "cover stop" along the way at Elvio's, an exclusive shop for men's shoes, where he bought a pair of bench-made ankle-top boots of soft kidskin with the slightly elevated heels he thought made him look Continental, maybe like an Italian diplomat.

After he left the store a Mercedes with darkened windows pulled alongside the curb and the rear door swung open.

Two hours into the meeting in the seedy, underfurnished Milan safe house, Vladik complimented the man on their most productive meeting since his transfer to Rome. Moscow would be pleased with his ability to provide critical counterintelligence information wherever he was, and they would show their appreciation. But before they settled back and switched their mineral water for vodka, Vladik leaned across the table, addressing Ames in his KGB code name. "One more time, Ricardo, please walk me through the Afghanistan report."

Ames read Vladik's face. Clearly he was worried that the memory of the KGB First Chief Directorate's prize agent was fuzzed by alcohol. It wasn't. He could give Vladik the same story a hundred times if necessary.

"It was all straightforward. I was on Saturday duty at Rome Station and received an 'eyes-only' message transmitted by the White House to Ambassador Armbruster in Rome using CIA communications channels. Armbruster was here talking to Afghan exiles, but your people know that. This kind of communication happens all the time, but the information sent this way is usually what the State Department doesn't want to get wide distribution by its own channels. I've never seen what amounts to an intelligence agent's raw report transmitted to an ambassador this way in CIA channels. Your people will take a look at the message in Moscow Center and will know immediately why I asked for this meeting. They'll know there's somebody high in the Kremlin reporting to the CIA. I've told you five times now, Vladik, I think the CIA's gotten to you again!"

Ames smiled and Vladik saw that his teeth had been fixed sometime in the last year. They used to be ugly and discolored. Now they were movie-star's teeth—*American* movie-star's teeth. Vladik wondered why he hadn't noticed this before and who else might have noticed it. Satisfied that he had the story straight, Vladik moved on to his last item.

"I have one off-the-wall request from the highest levels at Yasenevo. Back in 1985, during the Yurchenko affair, an American special services officer, a native speaker of Russian, possibly also a native speaker of Ukrainian, met with Yurchenko. You were working with Yurchenko at the time, and we thought you might know this man, who used the name Alexander. We now believe that this man, still using the alias Alexander, is involved in the war in Afghanistan. It's a long shot, but Center thought you could help."

"It's not an alias."

"What?"

"It's Fannin. His name is Alexander Fannin. Alexander is not an alias."

"Alexander is his true name?"

"Yeah. But he uses different alias identities. I know them because I worked in alias documentation a few years ago. He used very elaborate Polish Central Committee identities to move around in Eastern Europe. It was flashy, and Alexander carried it off well. I still remember the names—Janos Luks and Gromek Jasik. He used the Luks alias with Tokarev, just before you killed him."

Vladik filled the last page of his notepad. "Where is he now?"

"I'd heard he was doing something out in Afghanistan. Casey set him up out there. He left the CIA five or six years ago. He'd married some woman of Russian or Ukrainian background. That caused a giant flap for a while, and he just walked away. Last I heard he was living in Singapore, or maybe it was Hong Kong. He was one of those guys who seemed to turn everything he touched into gold. Casey loved him for all kinds of derring-do he'd done out in Africa, and a lot that he did against you guys."

Vladik pulled out a fresh notebook. "Why didn't you ever tell us about this man before?"

Ames jumped to his feet. "For Crissakes, Vladik! There are probably a million things I haven't told you! How am I supposed to know what you want until you ask?" He calmed himself and flashed his Hollywood smile. "What do I have to do to get a drink around here?"

Vladik walked to a cabinet, took out a bottle of Stolichnaya, and poured two stiff shots. "Now I want you to tell me everything you know about Alexander Fannin. Everything large and small."

THIRTY-TWO

Katerina and Alexander were having breakfast on deck as the junk rode out the morning tide off Wellington Island. They had not seen each other since her return from her third trip to Moscow for *Focus,* and her first secret meeting with Klimenko.

Katerina poured two cups of tea from the antique porcelain pot. "I settled into a routine. I had figured out how most things work in Moscow. I had contacts in the Ministry of Information and in the public-affairs offices of the other ministries I'm covering. It had gotten to the point where I wasn't getting any more of those silly, fumbling harassments from the KGB, just to provoke me or maybe even for fun. They seemed to be looking at other things. I was even getting to feel halfway at home in the Ukraina Hotel, awful as it is. Just as you told me, I lost a couple of pairs of underwear from my dirty laundry and even a used panty shield from the basket in the bathroom."

"How do you know they didn't just empty the basket?"

"Because the other stuff was still in it. Only the panty shield, neatly wrapped in tissue paper, was gone."

"That stuff didn't disappear because of someone's perversion. Your scent is now on file at the Lubyanka in a couple of hermetically sealed jars. If they ever need to turn the dogs on you or sniff out someplace you've been, they've got all they need."

"Tolya told me the same thing. And you don't think that's perverted?"

"Sure, I do, but their tricks don't stop there. When they really want to make sure that dogs can stick on your trail they spray your shoes with the scent they've extracted from a bitch in heat. The dogs don't lose that easily!"

"At any rate, apparently once they've had a look at you for a few months they back off unless you give them reason to stay with you. I'm sure I saw some guys taking more than the usual boy-girl interest in me a couple of times after the first six months, but not often. I also tried hard not to spot them, which only encourages them. I simply lived my life as the *Focus* reporter. When the call from Anatoly finally came, I thought I was ready for it."

"Did he handle it okay?"

"Like a pro. It was about five-thirty when the phone rang in my room. I picked it up knowing it was him, actually expecting it. Then comes the heavily accented parole in English. That's the word for it, isn't it? Parole?"

"Yes."

"Five minutes later I was down at the desk telling a bored desk clerk that I was getting telephone calls from perverts again, and that if they continued I would have every idiot from Dzerzhinsky Square on his case. The guy was totally unimpressed."

"Probably because he was an idiot from Dzerzhinsky Square, and because he'd already heard the pervert call you on the tapped phone."

"Probably. Then I stormed back to the elevator, but I stopped on the third floor for our planned diversion to the Beriozka store. Tolya was there, in the back."

After Katerina described her first meeting with Klimenko, she pulled out a notepad and went down a list.

"You didn't take those notes in the U.S.S.R., did you?"

"Oh, come on, Alexander, of course not. I memorized everything and wrote it out on the way home." Looking back at the list, she continued her report in the clipped phrases of her notes. "Tolya needs help. He wanted you to do a file check on one Karm Sergeyevich Nikitenko. Senior colonel in KGB First Chief Directorate. Prior service in the Counterintelligence Directorate. Served in Beirut 1981 to 1985, during the Hizbollah hostage incident Tolya was involved in. Reassigned in disgrace to Kabul 1985 to 1987. Now back at Yasenevo working in Directorate RI. Career appears back on upswing. He says Nikitenko was investigating him as late as October 1986. He didn't know whether he is still doing so, but thinks he probably is."

Alexander reflected. "Did he give you any more on him, a description?"

"Yes. A soft, almost gentle, sad face. Very intelligent. Speaks nearly flawless English and perfect German. There have been rumors that his bloodlines run to the Volga Germans, but Tolya's not sure of those stories. He thinks they're like the phony stories KGB officers put out about their internal enemies having Jews hidden in the family closet, mostly destructive, malicious rumor. Not many Volga Germans reach his level in the KGB. But suspicions about his perfect German persist." She looked down at her notes. "He's well-read. Likes Elizabeth Barrett Browning, but not Robert Browning. Reads Tennyson. That ought to tell you something about him. Anatoly said he also has a head of striking silver-white hair. And finally, he blames Tolya for his career nearly falling apart when one of the officers Tolya rescued in Beirut defected to the CIA."

"I know about him," Alexander said. "The KGB major we were running in the Beirut Rezidentura, one of the two freed by Tolya, told us Nikitenko was under heavy pressure because of his bungling of the hostage affair. He said there would be even more pressure after his defection and thought we ought to take a close look at Nikitenko. Maybe the pressure would get so great that he would turn to us. I ran a file check on him and got a flag that the Nikitenko dossier was held in a sensitive compartment personally controlled by Middleton in counterintelligence. I put in a request to Middleton for the file, and got a snotty answer from Middleton that I wasn't cleared for it. That was after he had set his dogs after me. I'll ask Frank Andrews to see what he can do, but I doubt he'll get into Middleton's files, at least not on his own."

"Tolya also told me that he had found nothing in the regular indices on Alexander S. Fannin, not even a blind entry referring to other sections. And nothing on your Polish identity, Gromek Jasik. He thinks you've managed to stay out of their records."

"I thought so, but it's good to hear it from him."

Katerina looked again at her list. "Then Anatoly asked me about the pills."

"So you gave them to him?"

"Yes."

"I'm sorry, Kat."

"Alexander, stop trying to protect me."

"Did you ever leave either the pen or the key chain in your room?"

"Never." Katerina handed a thick envelope across to Alexander. "All of the rest of what we talked about is in there—every word of it. What their demands will probably be in Geneva to get an agreement. The length of the withdrawal period, the question of continued supplies to the combatants, stuff like that. How the army is panicking about pulling out. How things are heading for a confrontation with the veterans back home from Afghanistan—the Afghantsis, they call themselves."

Alexander quietly read his wife's notes. After he finished he looked across at Katerina with profound respect. "You know, Kat, these insights are going to be read, in an altered version, by the people in the White House. This stuff on the negotiations in Geneva is like taking a look into their negotiator's briefcase."

"Somehow I was afraid of that."

"This material's no good if we don't use it. With it, we can coax Gorbachev's team into signing the agreement at Geneva and stop the killing."

"I know that. I even see the irony in it all. I spend three hours riding around the Moscow suburbs with a plugged-in guy full of insights into the historical sea change that's under way, and all my editors get—and believe me, they love it—are pieces about the lines being longer at the new McDonald's in Moscow than they are at Lenin's Tomb."

"How is Anatoly doing personally?"

Katerina shifted in her deck chair. "Here's where things get exciting."

"Exciting?"

"Anatoly has decided he wants us to get his mother out of the U.S.S.R."

Alexander straightened. "*He* has decided? Has he talked it over with her?"

"He said that she's made up her mind to spend the rest of her life near her sister."

"Did he give you any ideas on how we can get Katerina out of the Soviet Union so that he can survive and stay there? Or does he want out too?"

"He doesn't want out. He wants to stay and do whatever it takes to make a difference. He told me that you and I could come up with the obvious plan. His exact words were, 'The simplest and most obvious ideas are usually the best in these matters.' "

"You know what he means, don't you, Kat?"

"Yes, and I told him that obvious ideas are obvious even to novices like me. I asked him if he was suggesting that Lara travel to the U.S.S.R. and change identities with Katerina."

"Of course that's the idea."

"Anatoly told me that Katerina had thought through a plan—he called it almost foolproof—to stage her own death. Then she could go underground in Moscow until we were ready to make the switch with Lara."

"What did he mean by 'almost foolproof'?"

"They would have to rely on at least one other person, a Ukrainian physician who is already committed to the 'cause.' They need him to make her death believable and to keep her safe underground while we work out how to get her out."

Alexander paced the deck. "You know the risks involved."

"I know, Alexander, but the twins started this in the first place; we don't have to question their commitment."

"Have you talked to your mother about going into the Soviet Union, handing her passport, clothes, cash, and credit cards to her sister, then turning up at the nearest militia post to report a theft? Or at least some variation of that theme?"

"Yes."

"And?"

"It took her about one second to understand the proposal, then one more second to start making recommendations on how we can make it work."

Alexander sat back down. "Okay, Kat. It can be done, but getting someone out of the Soviet Union—'exfiltration' is the word we use in the trade—is the most difficult thing that can be done operationally. It's even worse in this case because we not only have to pull it off without a hitch, we have to leave no trail. Nobody can ever know that she made it out or it will all blow back on Tolya. Now tell me about how she's supposed to die."

They spent another two hours going over the details Katerina had discussed with Anatoly, until Alexander thought he could deal with all the possibilities. "Kat, once the hard decision has been made, it becomes only a question of timing. If we're going to do this—and I agree we should—let's get it over with. The longer we wait, the greater the chance for the variables to vary, so to speak."

"What are the next steps?"

"I'll go back to Paktia to see if I can send a message to Anatoly by radio before he leaves Kabul for Moscow to advance the schedule for Katerina to stage her fatal illness. You'll have to get Lara down to the Soviet Far East Steamship Lines to book a berth on the MV *Baikal* or her sister ship, the MV *Khabarovsk,* for Nakhodka, plus air connections from Vladivostok to Moscow. She should book one of those promotional transit packages they advertise—the cruise to Nakhodka plus a four-day transit in Moscow and Leningrad."

"Is that going to be enough time? Four days?"

"If we need more than four days, we'll be in trouble, and we'll probably have to abort. Four days in Moscow and Leningrad will have to do. Her transit-visa application will take time because there's no official Soviet representation in the Colony. It will have to be sent to Tokyo. And don't forget, the steamship-line guys downtown are more than likely KGB. Maybe you should let your mother arrange her own travel without tying you into it. Don't try to hide your connection, but don't involve yourself directly. Make someone work to tie you two together on paper."

"She'll travel on a British passport in the name Martynov, so there'll be no direct tie to my French passport in the name of Martin. But anyone could make the link here in Hong Kong if they took a little trouble."

"*Make* them take the trouble. Once she gets to Moscow, you'll obviously have to be mother and daughter, but everything will be in motion by then."

"I'll get her started tomorrow."

"Then you will have to get back to Moscow to meet with our cousin."

Katerina looked out across the South China Sea to Victoria Island in the distance and asked, "When will the switch take place, do you think?"

Alexander calculated for a second. "Fifty days, just after the May Day celebration in Moscow."

MOSCOW, 1300 HOURS, MARCH 16

Nikitenko stood alone in Shapkin's large office at Yasenevo, feeling uncomfortable. But the secretary had insisted he go in; Leonid Vladimirovich would only be a minute. An entire shelf was devoted to books published in the West about the KGB. Another was full of books previously banned: Solzhenitsyn, Medvedev, Daniel and Sinyavsky, even Boris Pasternak, who was once thought so depraved. Nikitenko had read most of these forbidden authors during his postings abroad. There were the obligatory photo of his wife and grown children, a shot of Shapkin with his grandson at a handsome dacha, and a couple of vanity photos of him with Andropov and Kryuchkov. He was admiring the photos when Shapkin walked in.

"Karm Sergeyevich! Good of you to wait. Please take a seat. I have a response for you on the question of your enigmatic Mr. Alexander of the American special services." He handed over a top secret folder with a five-page report inside. "You may take notes, but I cannot let you keep the report. You understand why."

Nikitenko read the report carefully. *It's all here,* he thought, *my Alexander unveiled. Even his aliases.* "Leonid Vladimirovich, I cannot tell you how helpful this information is. I think I'll be able to move much more rapidly ahead in my investigation of the American special services' direct involvement in the war. I hope it may prove useful to the leadership in its negotiations in Geneva."

"Karm Sergeyevich, I may have another important task for you shortly, but I'll have to bring you into a very special security compartment first, and for that I need a higher authority." Shapkin pointed at the ceiling, meaning he would have to clear his idea with the Director of the First Chief Directorate, Vladimir Kryuchkov, upstairs.

"Of course, Leonid Vladimirovich." Nikitenko rose to leave.

Back in his office Nikitenko drafted a detailed priority-trace request for all information on one Alexander Fannin, resident of either Singapore or

Hong Kong, born circa 1947, possibly in Germany but perhaps in the United States, and married to an unidentified woman of Russian/Ukrainian origin who was also a resident of either Singapore or Hong Kong, then took his request to the East Asia office. In explaining the trace request to the department chief, he stressed that it had come directly from the second floor and asked that it be treated with the utmost discretion.

The director of the department told Nikitenko that he might be in luck. There was no Soviet diplomatic presence in the Crown Colony—the Chinese simply wouldn't allow a Soviet listening post nuzzled against their belly. As a result, the KGB had to cover Hong Kong by port calls from Soviet vessels. But as luck would have it, the MV *Baikal* was to pay a call at Hong Kong in two days. It had a floating KGB Rezidentura and they could do at least some of the checks in the three days while the ship was in port. It would be easier in Singapore. One way or the other he would have something for Nikitenko within six weeks.

Nikitenko went next to the commercial-investigation section of the library, showed his special pass to the head of the computer department, and outlined his request. Five minutes later he was sitting beside a young major at a workstation with an IBM computer.

The young man typed in several commands. After about two minutes he turned to Nikitenko. "Okay, we're on-line in East Asia. The easiest thing is to begin with a check of the telephone book. Where do you want to start, Hong Kong or Singapore?"

"Let's try Singapore first."

The young man typed in the search data, with all possible variations. Within another three minutes he had drawn a blank. No Alexander Fannin.

"Do you want me to go into some commercial databases for another look?"

"How easy is it to switch to Hong Kong for a telephone check?"

"As easy as this." The operator typed in a command, and within about a minute Hong Kong was up on the screen. He started the search and sat back to wait.

Two minutes later the answer scrolled onto the screen. "There's your man!" There was a name, an address in a place called Stanley Village, Hong Kong Island, and a telephone number.

"What else can you do with the telephone database?" Nikitenko asked the young man.

"Let's try the reverse directory first and see if there's anyone else at that same number. That's easy enough."

Seconds later there was a highlighted name on the monitor. "Nope. Same name, Alexander Fannin. Must be his private line. But let's try something else." The man keyed in another burst of instructions.

"I typed in the address in Stanley Village to see if there were some more telephone numbers at the same address. Here it comes now."

Nikitenko leaned forward to look at the monitor as the name, K. Martynov, came up highlighted. "Major, what is your name?"

"Bokhan, Comrade Colonel. Sergei Bokhan."

"Sergei, you are nothing less than a modern scientific hero. I believe the Americans would say bingo at this moment. Now please tell me what you can do for me with the name K. Martynov, who, I have reason to believe, is a woman, and who seems to live with Mr. A. Fannin in Stanley Village."

A half hour later Nikitenko reread the printout on Michael Martynov. One of the entries referred him to a photo in the May 1, 1987, issue of *Far Eastern Economic Review*. On page 87 he found the article he was looking for: "Queen's Birthday List Honors Michael Martynov. A knighthood was awarded Michael Martynov for his contributions to the commercial and social integrity of the British Crown Colony of Hong Kong."

He pulled his working files out of the safe. One folder was labeled Alexander. He added the name Fannin; then, almost as an afterthought, he wrote Martynov in parentheses, and put the computer printout on Alexander and the two-dozen pages on the commercial institution called Martin House inside the folder. Now he was getting somewhere.

He pulled out the contents of an envelope, and looked down at the data sheet. A. V. Klimenko. The first sheet contained the standard biographic information. Behind it were summaries of Klimenko's performance over the last ten years, all outstanding in every respect.

A separate, smaller envelope contained a packet of photographs. In one, taken two years ago, Klimenko stood with his mother and father in front of Dzerzhinsky's great bust in the Lubyanka when Klimenko was awarded the Order of the Red Banner for his leadership in the rescue operation in Beirut, heroics that had brought on Nikitenko only humiliation and disgrace.

There was a sidebar on Martin House, and a color photograph of Sir Michael receiving his honors from the feather-hatted governor of Hong Kong. Accompanying him was his wife, Lara.

THIRTY-THREE

PAKTIA, MARCH 26, 1988

Alexander composed his message to Klimenko. He had to balance the usual cool brevity with language that would reinforce the commitment he and Katerina and Klimenko had made eighteen months before.

Paul will be in position and anxious for your call by the time you receive this messagex We have reached our decision on your special requestx It is positive, as you knew it would certainly bex The quote obvious quote solution remains the best and we are prepared to carry it out in early Mayx That will give you very little time for special preparation of the item we are to exchangex That part of the procedure should be completed by the third week of April at the latestx Delays will only provide openings for unexpected and unnecessary complicationsx Let us be bold now that our commitment is madex Please provide Paul with your complete planx As we near our moment of victory our reliance on one another for our very survival shall only increasex

New subjectx I have received from my hqs only standard traces on KSN of Beirut that you requested verbally with Paulx There nothing remarkable in traces, but there is a reference to additional information held in special/sensitive archives controlled by CIx There may be significant data on KSN in those files, but gaining access will be extremely difficultx Sorry not to have been more helpx Trust in Godx

Alexander entered the keyboard command to encrypt it and send it to the electronic broadcast queue for the next opening in Klimenko's broadcast schedule.

KABUL, MARCH 26, 1988

Klimenko was bothered that Alexander had come up dry on Nikitenko. He fired off a two-line response.

> Message received with thanksx Please continue to attempt to develop information on KSNx It is imperativex Finally yesx Let us be boldx End Endx

MOSCOW, APRIL 1, 1988

Katerina was preparing to leave her room at the Ukraina for an early morning interview at the Moscow Central Gynecological Clinic when the telephone rang. She knew who the caller was as she raised the receiver to her ear. "Martin," she answered.

"Cathy. This is Peter. Welcome back to the workers' paradise. I'd heard you were back in town."

"Peter, and how is the messenger to the masses?"

"Just fine. Well, look, Cathy, there will be a bunch of media hacks at Kropotkinskaya 36 at about eight tonight. Dutch treat. If you can break free, join us. A few drinks and some dinner. We can all exchange lies on the Soyuz. Okay?"

"Thanks for the invitation, Peter. I'll try. But don't any of you wait too long for me. I've got one of those days. And if this snow keeps up, I'll probably just call it a night and stay here in the hotel."

Klimenko had told her that the tapes of her phone calls would be reviewed by the West European Department in the KGB's Second Directorate since she was traveling on a French passport, and that her caller, supposedly an American, would have been the responsibility of the U.S. and Canada Department. There was little chance that the KGB telephone monitors could place the accent of the caller. And even less chance that they would try to identify Peter. Anatoly had said that unless there was some good reason, there would be no coordination between the two departments. If it looked boring enough, the transcript would fall into a black hole.

She would go ahead with her appointment at the women's hospital. It would be noticed if she canceled an appointment that had taken her so long to arrange. Anyone following her activities would know she was doing a feature article on the role and status of women in the U.S.S.R. Her nine-thirty appointment would give her just two hours before she had to leave to meet Klimenko at Taganskaya Square at noon.

It was after ten when Klimenko and Sasha met in the basement lounge of the offices of the General Staff near the Arbat in central Moscow. Sasha glanced around at the few officers and decided it was as good a place as any for quiet discussion. They ordered black tea from a sullen matron and settled down at a corner table.

"I was with Titov when he briefed Yazov on the situation with the forces. You will not believe, Tolya, how incredibly stupid our defense minister is. I think he was half drunk. He was blowing about forty percent alcohol content at nine in the morning! I used to hear stories when he was deputy commander of the Vladivostok Region. Yazov's staff was under instructions from the region commander never to let him appear in public for fear that he would get drunk and shit his pants and embarrass the army. Now I know the stories were probably true."

"Did Titov tell him anything about our plans for Pakistan?"

"He tried to. He said that there were some plans under way to teach the Dushman a lesson before the Red Army consolidated its positions and prepared to withdraw. Dumb-ass Dmitri never picked up on it. All he wanted to do was complain about how tough the defense budget problems were, and he wasn't even coherent on that. But his exec did pick up on Titov's briefing, and that's all that counts. I talked to the guy for a minute after the meeting, and told him that Titov was actually saying that there would be an important blow struck for the Expeditionary Forces."

"It's probably better that Titov didn't have to spell things out for Yazov. The less said the better."

"What he did spell out in painful detail was the first ninety days of the bug-out from Afghanistan. I'm telling you, Tolya, after we pull out half our people in the first three months, the other half will be out there hanging by their fingernails." Sasha looked over at the two officers seated across the room. "*Certain people* have to know that it wouldn't help anybody if the Dushman put too much pressure on the boys that are left behind. They had better just let them go."

"Certain people will be put on notice, Sasha. That's the best we can do. We owe it to these boys."

"Tolya, you are surely going to get us killed."

"Talking about that, are you set for our suicide mission into the heart of the American special services? I pick up our phony passports out at Yasenevo this afternoon. I've got an appointment with the head of a special group out there. My old boss from Tehran. I'll give him a briefing on the Ojhri operation. Enough to keep him happy. He put in the fix for the passports and pressured the foreign ministry to get the visas to Pakistan."

Sasha leaned closer to Klimenko.

"I saw Vladimir Rogov last night."

"What's he doing now?"

"Just about whatever he feels like doing."

"What's that supposed to mean?"

"He's working with what he calls a Georgian Enterprise. You can figure that out."

"Oh, Rogov the child of glasnost and perestroika? Rogov the champion of the market economy."

"He says he's making a bundle whichever way it goes. If the hallowed market economy starts kicking in, he rolls it in from the joint ventures. If everything starts going to hell, he turns to the black market and gets just as rich. He told me that if I ever needed anything in the world, just contact him. For you, he would do even more. He said he'd never forget the favor you did him bringing him home slung over a mule. If you ever need anyone to fall into the Moscow River, just let him know."

"He said that?" Klimenko smiled at the image of Rogov the gangster.

"Yeah. And I don't think he was kidding."

Klimenko leaned closer to Sasha. "Let's have a drink with him this evening. Can you set it up?"

"Sure. When?"

"About seven-thirty."

"You want him to shove someone in the river?"

"No. I want to have a drink with him, for Crissakes."

Katerina felt the strain in her legs as she climbed the last fifteen steps from the metro station deep beneath Taganskaya Square. The snow had stopped falling, but its softening blanket still muffled the sound of the city.

She walked across the busy square, past the Skazka Restaurant where Moscow's after-theater crowd gathered, and turned onto Bolshaya Kommunisticheskaya, a quiet, narrow, birch-lined residential street. She felt screamingly obvious to anybody who cared to look in her direction. Here I am! I'm committing crimes against your brutal, corrupt state! She had a rush of mixed feelings, but the growing excitement of her commitment dislodged her fear.

Don't ever get cocky, Alexander had cautioned her. You're never alone. Particularly if you're traveling by the metro. You never see them, but they're there. They might put some microtransponder in your clothing or shoes and track you electronically through the metro system. We just don't know.

She stopped at the two-hundred-year-old Church of St. Martin the Confessor and as she did the obligatory tourist minute, she could see

that the entire street was empty. Then she walked on down to the end of
the street and to Andronevskaya Square. She crossed the square and
walked slowly into Andronevsky Pereulok. Halfway down the narrow
street was the small park she was looking for. She could just see the
whitewashed walls of the Andronikov Monastery through the naked
white birches. Among the trees stood Anatoly. He nodded faintly and
then began walking toward the monastery gates. As he approached the
gate in the outer walls, he slowed until Katerina drew up beside him. "Put
your arms around my neck and give me a kiss. Do it quickly and make it
look furtive."

Katerina played the part of the surreptitious lover.

"How much time do you have?"

"As much as we need."

"Have you had any problems since you came back to Moscow? Have
there been any incidents you need to tell me about?"

"Nothing. Absolutely nothing. But maybe I'm too new at this to see the
things that should worry me." She smiled anxiously.

"You're fine. Your instincts are good. Walk along with me. Hold my
hand like we belong to each other."

"We do . . . sort of . . . belong to each other, don't we."

"I received Alexander's last message. He said we would switch the
twins in the beginning of May. He said, 'Let us be bold.' Your husband
fancies himself a poet."

Katerina saw in her peripheral vision that Klimenko was smiling. "Like
I've told you. It's the Russian side of him that causes all the theatrics. But
in this case, I know he's right. We need to move boldly now. Lara is getting her documentation in order. She's applied to Intourist for her visa, a
four-day transit. But dear Tolya, let us agree not to talk of switching the
twins. That sounds straight out of a cheap spy novel."

Klimenko laughed. "We don't have cheap spy novels here in the
Soyuz. Only heroic ones. But I know what you mean. We will not speak
of switching the twins. But, dear Katerina, *you* will have to prepare my
mother for much of what lies ahead. You will have to go to Kiev within
the week. I'm traveling tomorrow and can't be certain when I will be
back, or even if, for that matter. At least before May. You're going to
have to manage Katerina in Kiev. And then later here in Moscow, after
she has . . ." Klimenko paused. ". . . died."

Katerina didn't betray the shock she felt at being given the responsibility for the escape of Klimenko's mother. "I told you last time that I was
doing a feature on women for my magazine. I've applied for clearance to
travel to Kiev, just like you told me to, to do some interviews. The travel
clearance was waiting for me when I got back. Approved."

"Then you'll have to get down there in the next few days."

"I can call your mother's clinic and get an appointment. Set up an interview. Should I do that?"

Klimenko shook his head as he handed Katerina a folded piece of paper, which she slipped into her coat pocket. "No. I've arranged for you and my mother to meet without you making any official contact with her in the clinic. She expects your call. Speak Ukrainian and tell her that you are Raisa Lysenkova and that you are having a tough time with cramps. Couldn't she do anything? She'll tell you to keep taking your medicine. It will take some weeks to take effect. Do you understand?"

"Yes. Do I call her from here?"

"No. Wait until you're in Kiev. Call from a public telephone. After you have spoken to her, you will meet at the Babi Yar memorial at ten o'clock the next morning. You can take the trolley bus from the center of the city. Number sixteen or eighteen. Either one will get you to Babi Yar."

"Is her telephone number on the paper you just gave me?"

"The telephone number and the address of the clinic are there. Plus her address and home telephone number if you absolutely need them. Do like we agreed. Memorize some of the information and bury some of it in harmless-looking notes. *Don't* make any notes on your map of Kiev. Then flush my note down the toilet. Use the one in the rest room on the third floor at the Ukraina."

"I understand. When do we meet again? How do we proceed once I've met with Katerina?"

"I don't know. It's best that you and Alexander take over the planning entirely independent of our contact here in Moscow. I don't want a situation to develop where if something happens to me the whole exfiltration falls apart."

"That's the word Alexander uses."

Klimenko laughed at the irony. "Maybe because it's a practice used exclusively by Western intelligence services, usually English-speaking ones. There isn't much of a need for the KGB to exfiltrate agents from America or Britain to the U.S.S.R. It's always the other way around."

"Anatoly, I must also ask you once more if you want to be exfiltrated yourself. Alexander said I must ask you that."

Klimenko turned toward Katerina. "You know my answer. I told you back in Paktia about a hundred years ago that I wasn't anybody's spy. That I wasn't working for anyone but the people of my Ukraine, and possibly for the Russian people as well. No, Katerina. I do not want to be exfiltrated."

"Then this is it, as far as getting Katerina out. It's up to us. Alexander and me. Just like that?"

"Just like that. My mother is ready. She's tough and determined. What she needs only you and Alexander can provide."

Katerina nodded. "I think I understand. But if you do get back here before we . . . exfiltrate Katerina, you will contact me, won't you?"

"Of course I will. I just don't want the operation to be dependent on me from this point on." Klimenko paused. "There might be one last loose end. Something I need to get to my mother. You can do that for me. If it turns out to be the case, you'll get a call from me tonight. From Peter again. If it's too late, and the Beriozka is closed for the night, go down to the lobby. Wander around down there until you see me and then follow my lead. If you don't hear from me tonight, don't worry. Just get on down to Kiev."

Katerina looked down at the soot-covered snow on the path. "Is that it?"

"Yes. But one final instruction. When we next set up a meeting over the telephone, it will be at the café on the ground floor of the House of Artists, across the street from the entrance to Gorky Park. It's crowded, but we can pass a message there. You know the place?"

"Yes."

Klimenko squeezed her hand. "I'll leave first. Then you follow." She pulled him to her and raised her face to his, then gently kissed him on both cheeks. "Let us be bold, Tolya. Let us be bold."

He smiled sadly. "Yes, let us be bold. But let us be right!"

He walked with surprising ease out the gate. To any casual observer it might have looked like a quick meeting between clandestine lovers.

Katerina retraced her steps to the metro. The street still looked deserted, but she didn't feel cocky anymore.

KGB, First Chief Directorate, Yasenevo, April 2, 1988

"Anatoly Viktorovich, when are you going to give up on your little war and join me here in Yasenevo? Everybody else has."

"Everybody else has joined you here, Leonid Vladimirovich?" Klimenko set his trap for Shapkin.

"What? No. Of course not. I meant everybody else has given up on your war. That's what I meant, and I think you knew that." Shapkin really did like Klimenko, one of the few First Directorate officers below general officer rank who dared joke with him.

"In all seriousness, Anatoly Viktorovich. The war is done for. Take it from me, the decision to get out has been made. Our side will agree to whatever they are offering in Geneva and be happy with it. And then God help the Soyuz. Now what is this desperate mission you're running off to Pakistan on?"

"Leonid Vladimirovich, our army might even have to shoot its way out of Afghanistan. I am just trying to do something in Pakistan that will give us some relief on the way out."

"Why are *you* doing it? Why can't our Rezidentura in Islamabad do it?"

"Army politics. The 40th Army will take credit for a success, if there is one. You'll take the heat if there's a failure. You and Chairman Chebrikov, and Kryuchkov upstairs."

Shapkin looked closely at his protégé. "With your luck, Anatoly Viktorovich, you'll make it work. I only hope you remember what I told you so often in Tehran."

"I know exactly what you told me in Tehran." Klimenko continued with a very serviceable imitation of Shapkin's deep, resonant voice and dramatic, gesticulating manner. "You said, 'Anatoly Viktorovich, luck is an important thing. You must recognize when it is running in your favor. And exploit it to the fullest. More important you must recognize when your luck is getting tired. Never, Anatoly Viktorovich, become addicted to your own luck. Like all addictions, it will eventually kill you.' "

Shapkin enjoyed Klimenko's little impersonation immensely. "Precisely, Anatoly Viktorovich." He pointed to the ceiling. "The illustrious one calls. Anatoly Viktorovich, I want you to have an explosive success in Pakistan. But be careful. And just in case you're not, before you leave here today I want you to spend a few minutes with our mutual friend, Karm Sergeyevich. He's with me now, and he speaks most highly of you from your service in Kabul. He's working on the Afghan project for me and for the chairman. Almost indispensable. Help him if you can."

Klimenko felt no warning signals. Neither Shapkin's voice nor his manner bore a trace of guile. "Of course, Leonid Vladimirovich. I'll help wherever I can."

Nikitenko welcomed Klimenko with a warmth that was overdone, even considering they were brought together under Shapkin's discerning eye. But Nikitenko continued his charade of comradeship after Shapkin departed.

"Anatoly Viktorovich, you are looking very well, as usual. Director Shapkin tells me that you are off on another of your dangerous missions, this time into Pakistan. One day you must give this up, you know."

"I got the same lecture about pressing my luck from the director. But I do appreciate your concern, Karm Sergeyevich."

Nikitenko eyed him closely. "Anatoly Viktorovich. Perhaps you could give me your absolutely unvarnished opinion of the endgame of ten years of doing our internationalist duty in the Democratic Republic of Afghanistan. How will all of this play out?"

Klimenko heard the warning bells go off.

"Karm Sergeyevich, it is no secret in the Kremlin, or in Kabul, or in Directorate RI, that the Soviet Union will agree to the proposals on the table at Geneva. That decision, I believe, is irrevocable."

"You are absolutely right." Nikitenko smiled with his face, but not with his eyes. "But I am working right now on a position paper for the director and have to make some assessment on how the army will, how shall I put this, adjust to these realities. You could certainly give me some fresh insight."

Klimenko wasn't taken in.

"Karm Sergeyevich, our army is responsive to the political leadership of the Party. It always has been and it always will be. It will follow orders and do its duty."

"Of course. But surely there must be some things you would like to see taken into consideration as we move down the road chosen by the competent authorities? Surely you would like to see your own well-conceived thoughts factored in as we help our leaders through these difficult times. Director Shapkin had high hopes that you could help us with this difficult task. He said you probably had a better idea of what was right and what was silly than anyone else in Kabul. I will be frank, Anatoly Viktorovich, it is for his briefing of the general secretary."

Klimenko would have to give Karm Sergeyevich something he could use. He couldn't dodge it now that Nikitenko had characterized it as a personal request from Shapkin.

"Karm Sergeyevich. This has been a difficult year. There have been many setbacks. You know that from your own time in Kabul."

"Yes, things were already difficult at the end of 1986."

"Yes, and it has continued. The commanders are very concerned that they may have to fight their way out of Afghanistan if they are forced to withdraw their troops too fast."

Nikitenko took notes. But as always, he was also recording the conversation on a cassette recorder concealed in his desk drawer. He knew the note taking gave assurances to the contrary.

"May have to fight their way out. Yes. Yes. That would be bad. Very bad." Nikitenko finished scribbling and smiled with his sad eyes, expectant.

"Karm Sergeyevich, the Red Army commanders in the field will interpret a nine-month withdrawal schedule, especially one which calls for a fifty percent withdrawal in the first three months after the accord is signed, as a dangerous humiliation. General Titov will report that finding to the defense minister and, perhaps, the general secretary himself this week. All in the name of General Gromov. But I have heard that the competent authorities have made it clear to the generals that protecting the honor of the Red Army is their duty, not the duty of the Party."

Nikitenko scribbled down everything Klimenko had said. Christ, what a plodder this guy is, Klimenko thought. He never lets go.

"Surely you are not suggesting that there might be trouble with the army?"

"Of course not, Karm Sergeyevich. I am only trying to be as frank as I can. You asked me what I thought would be helpful to Director Shapkin. All I am saying is that the true needs of the army must be considered when the party makes its decisions. Is that mutiny?" It was Klimenko's turn to smile blankly.

"Of course not. And of course I understand the spirit in which you have spoken. You know I no longer have the unpleasant task of listening to others complain, or recording their words of complaint. That was a temporary sidetrack for me in Kabul. I am now making what I sincerely hope is a significant and positive contribution. And it is frank exchanges like the one we have just had that will allow me to do my duty."

"Well, I tried to be frank. I know the difficult position of Director Shapkin."

Nikitenko seemed distracted, eager to end the session.

"Anatoly Viktorovich, I mustn't keep you any longer. You have been most helpful. I wish you only the best in your endeavors."

Klimenko rose, slightly taken aback by Nikitenko's abruptness. He would normally have gone on for an hour or more. Well, maybe he's actually busy now that he's got a real job, Klimenko told himself.

"Karm Sergeyevich, if what I have said will help you and Director Shapkin I will be pleased. These times call for great courage on the part of our leaders."

"Yes, let us hope there is true courage to match the difficulties."

Nikitenko escorted Klimenko back through the Directorate RI Secretariat and through the controlled-access entrance. Before they parted he shared one of his small confidences with Klimenko.

"Too bad our visit is so short today. Perhaps next time. I have been working on the case of the mystery American special services officer in Paktia. I think I am finally on his trail, and it seems to be leading in the most unlikely direction. But that's for next time." Nikitenko shook his hand and turned back through the controlled entrance, leaving a rattled Klimenko staring after him.

Klimenko and Sasha were ushered through the crowded dining area to a private alcove in the back of the Tblisi Restaurant where former Lieutenant Vladimir Ivanovich Rogov waited. His salty military appearance, seasoned by three combat tours in Afghanistan, had been replaced by the exaggerated trappings of the new class of Moscow entrepreneur who worked around and outside of what used to pass for law and order. His hair was stylishly longer now, with a pampered, well-tended look. He wore an expensive Turkish suede jacket over an Italian silk shirt, open at the neck to reveal a heavy, double gold chain that matched his even heavier bracelet. Rogov took a cigarette from a pack of Marlboros and lit it with a gold Dupont lighter. Without a word of greeting he poured three glasses of Georgian red wine, and raised his in a toast.

"To the colonel, the one man who tried harder than all others to get me a ride on a Black Tulip."

Klimenko drank half his glass and then raised it. "To the Black Tulip and all the fine boys she brought home to their mothers."

Krasin offered another obligatory toast. "To glasnost, perestroika, and whatever else it is that turns hired Afghantsi guns like Rogov here into the new Moscow Mafia."

"Sasha, when you're finished playing soldier, come to me. I'll make you a millionaire. Just like I'm going to be.

"Tolya, things are happening here in Moscow and all over the Soyuz that they aren't telling you about. All of the creeps in the Party are screaming about organized crime. What they're really howling about is that someone else is taking it over. The organized crime. After seventy years of running the syndicates in the name of the Party, it's our turn. You will see it all when you get back here."

"I think I'm seeing it now, Volodya. But can it last?"

"It's almost at the point of no return. You hear about grumbling among the old guard. But if a bunch of vodka-soaked old farts think they can stop this, let them try."

Klimenko took another sip of his wine. "Volodya, I may need your help on something very important to me in the next month or so."

"Tell me what you need." Rogov snapped his fingers at the young waiter. He held up the empty bottle and the man disappeared behind the bar.

"If I had a friend who wanted to disappear completely here in Moscow, I mean literally cease to exist, could you handle it?"

"I can do that. There is an underground in Moscow numbering in the tens of thousands. People are here that don't exist as far as your 'competent organs' are concerned." Rogov smiled when he used the euphemism for the KGB. "I take it that you mean concealing someone's presence from your own illustrious organization."

"That is precisely what I mean."

"I can do that. Moving someone farther afield, out of the country, is more difficult. But just disappearing someone here is no problem."

Klimenko chose his next words carefully. "How does someone initiate such a discussion with you?"

Rogov flashed his white smile and wrote a telephone number on a paper napkin. "For you, Tolya, someone should just call this number any evening and tell whoever answers that Volodya is expecting the important call from friends in Tbilisi. Then when I come on the phone, that someone should say that he . . . or she is a refugee from a Black Tulip. I'll take care of everything after that. Okay?"

Klimenko nodded and folded the napkin into his shirt pocket.

Sasha took the second bottle of Georgian red wine from the waiter. "I offer the toast, comrades. To the new Soviet man."

THIRTY-FOUR

BABI YAR, 1000 HOURS, APRIL 3, 1988

When the old electric trolley bus finally came to a tilting halt Katerina could hardly have been more relieved. The constant screech of the tires rubbing against the wheel wells had frayed her nerves. She quickly set out on the pathway to the Babi Yar memorial where a hundred thousand people were murdered during the Great Patriotic War. Even before the monument came into view, she felt the oppressive terror that still swamped the place. Below the statue of the young mother about to die was an understated description:

> MONUMENT TO SOVIET CITIZENS, SOLDIERS, AND OFFICERS,
> PRISONERS OF WAR, WHO WERE TORTURED AND KILLED BY THE
> NAZI INVADERS, 1941–1943

Katerina took stock of her surroundings. She had gotten off alone, but she took no comfort in that. Anyone following her would have seen her take the trolley and could easily have had someone waiting for her, but as she looked around at the half-dozen people milling about in the warm spring sun, she sensed no threat from any of them.

Anatoly had told her that his mother would approach her at the Babi Yar monument at ten. It was a few minutes past when she felt the woman come up behind her.

"Are you still troubled by the cramps, my dear?"

Katerina turned around and looked into the face of her namesake. The face, the eyes, the mouth, everything was the same. But this one had a gray and drawn look she had never seen in her mother's face, in Lara's face. The woman before her was dressed in a plain gray wool coat with a matching gray woolen scarf tied under her chin. She was bent over slightly, and seemed to be supported by a sturdy oak walking stick.

"Don't draw any quick conclusions, beautiful daughter of my sister. Your auntie looks a mess just now, but I've had to work hard at it."

"Auntie, you'll have to excuse me if I'm too stunned to speak. It's just that after waiting all these years, nothing seems appropriate. Except for, now what do we do?"

"Now, my dear, let's go over by the awful ravine. Then we'll walk down to my car, and then we'll take a drive. Here, let this old woman take your arm."

MOSCOW, 1130 HOURS, APRIL 3

Shapkin rose when Nikitenko appeared at his door. "Karm Sergeyevich, please come in and close the door behind you."

They took seats across from each other at the narrow table. "Karm Sergeyevich, the chairman himself has approved my request that you be brought into one of the smallest and most secret compartments we now have in the First Chief Directorate. Before you is a carefully selected series of reports from a penetration of American special services. I am not speaking about another low-level army intelligence sergeant in Berlin. I am talking about a penetration of Langley itself. And finally a good one. I have cleared you for the compartment because I need your help."

Nikitenko felt no need to make any gratuitous comment. He simply said, "How can I help?"

"You're going to help me find a spy in the Kremlin. A very dangerous spy."

Nikitenko hoped he looked calm.

"You will remember the spate of spies we rooted out a couple of years ago? Some out of the First Directorate, a couple out of the design bureaus of the defense industries, even one out of the Second Directorate. Quite a handful when it was all over. You have surely heard all of the speculation about the disgruntled CIA officer, Howard, being our prime source. We called him Mr. Robert. He's still drinking himself silly out in his dacha almost every day. Then there was the fiasco in their embassy with those marines. That planted seeds of doubts that their communications were no longer secure. We helped keep those nagging little doubts alive and growing in Langley."

"Of course I am aware, at least in general, of these successes."

"I'm also certain that you heard the usual speculation on what was behind the disasters that befell the Main Enemy in 1985 and 1986?"

"Everybody has his own pet theory, Director Shapkin."

"Karm Sergeyevich. Please call me Leonid."

Nikitenko shifted in his seat. "Leonid Valdimirovich. We all had our theories, but idle speculation can be dangerous when sensitive sources are involved." He felt a little silly sounding like the student of KGB dialectics trying to win points with his teacher.

"Precisely. There is always the problem of those who speculate being right for all the wrong reasons. But let me continue. During the last few years we put a number of subtle, but false clues out on the street for the Americans to pick up. Clues that played to their natural optimism. After watching matters closely, I think the trail has gone cold at Langley. It appears that they may have lost interest in solving the riddle of their catastrophic losses of 1985. The '1985 problem,' they called it. That may be particularly true since they have compelling evidence now that whatever problem they may have had has somehow, shall we say, gone away."

"How do you mean?"

"Karm Sergeyevich, I have asked you here to read through this file. Take all the time you need. You will see that Langley has recovered its equilibrium. Its optimism. Langley has once again penetrated into the inner circle of our leadership councils. You will see that someone very close to the general secretary is reporting, in painful detail, the deliberations on our, . . . uh, disengagement from Afghanistan."

"I see, Leonid Vladimirovich." Nikitenko felt light-headed.

"Please do not take notes or remove any paper from the file. First, break the seal and sign the acknowledgment of my briefing of you on the Ricardo Compartment, our code name for this valuable agent. Then sign the standard secrecy agreement. Those two documents are the first papers in the file. I have an appointment for half an hour. We can talk later. I will have to ask you to stay here with the materials until I return and reseal the file. Even my secretary is not cleared to handle Ricardo."

"May I ask who in the First Directorate is cleared for Ricardo?"

"It doesn't really matter. You won't have occasion to discuss the operation with anyone else in the Committee, with the obvious exception of the chairman himself or Comrade Kryuchkov, unless I am present. But I can assure you that the list is not much longer than those names. Plus a very few of Ricardo's handlers who know the full story."

Nikitenko broke a red wax seal and took out the two briefing documents. Then he signed both, committing himself to secrecy, and turned to the first page of the file. Instinctively, he knew what he would find there.

KIEV, 1040 HOURS, APRIL 3

In the half-hour drive to the Klimenko hideout on the Dnieper, they had spoken only of family and of the enduring love of the twin sisters.

Katerina Klimenkova turned off the rough road parallel to the river and drove along a narrower dirt track, mushy from the early spring thaw, and came to a stop within view of the river. She parked and led Katerina to a small, nondescript dacha of rough-hewn planks and red shutters, one of several nestled among the birches.

Katerina Klimenkova moved quickly, still carrying the walking stick but no longer using it for support or otherwise betraying the infirmity that appeared so obvious at Babi Yar. She opened the door of the dacha and led Katerina in. The cabin was musty and sparsely furnished but decorated with taste and loving care.

"We will be completely alone today. The people won't come out here until after the middle of April. It's a little escape from the Soyuz. I haven't been here since Viktor died. I don't think I could bear to be out here alone."

"How much time do we have, Aunt Katerina?"

"Not much. An hour at most, and then I must be back at the clinic."

"Tell me, Auntie, what are we to do?"

"It's all quite simple, my dear. I'm going off to Moscow next week to die. Then I'm going to wait until my sister comes to give me a new life. That's all there is to it." Her eyes sparkled and color came into her cheeks as she spoke.

"It all sounds very straightforward. But there is a saying in English, Auntie. The devil is in the details."

Klimenkova laughed. "Yes, my dear, he *is*. Well, here are some of the details for you. First, what probably shocked you when you first saw me at Babi Yar was my studied version of the symptoms and appearance of profound anemia."

Klimenkova settled back in a brightly covered rocking chair and began to speak with professional confidence.

"I have been working on this dreadful physical appearance of mine for almost three weeks. Ever since Anatoly and I reached the decision that I must join Lara."

"And to which my mother and I have unhesitatingly agreed, Auntie. But, then you are not actually ill?"

"No, my dear, I am as fit as you. But my colleagues in the clinic are deeply convinced that I am quite seriously ill. I am not happy in such a deception, but their belief that I am gravely ill is crucial to our success."

"Please go on. I won't interrupt anymore."

"Interrupt all you like. But here is the exact situation. I have been using the case history and laboratory results of a gynecological patient of mine who recently and quite suddenly died of acute myelogenous leukemia. She fell ill and died within six weeks. Acute myelogenous leukemia is sometimes that quick and that destructive. I have been mimicking her symptoms and using her lab results for the last twenty days."

"How can you make certain that they will believe you? Please, Auntie, I am sorry I have to ask this, but my Alexander and your Anatoly will ask me these same questions when I see them."

"I know how Anatoly can bore in on an issue. Just like Viktor. But on this you can trust me. They will believe me. You cannot begin to imagine the medical horrors in the Ukraine just now, almost exactly two years after the disaster at Chernobyl."

"Are you making a link between your leukemia and Chernobyl?"

"There is very little evidence linking myelogenous leukemia to radiation exposure, but we're still writing the book on such disasters. Yesterday, I discussed my case with the clinic director. I used the subterfuge many of us doctors use when discussing our own medical problems. I told him I wanted to consult with him about a patient who had come down with the flu, but couldn't shake the infection. She was constantly fatigued, but didn't think much of it until the nosebleeds and the bruising started, and then bright red blood showed up in her urine. Her white-cell count was about sixty thousand. Very high."

Katerina committed the symptoms to memory, while Klimenkova went on.

"After I told my colleague about the symptoms, I showed him the lab work and some radiological evidence I had in the file to back it all up. He took my hands, looked me straight in the face and asked me if, in fact, I was my patient. It was easy for me to cry at that moment with all the sadness in my life. Even my deception of this fine man made me want to cry. I said that yes, I was the patient."

"He believed you?"

"Yes. But he said he wanted to examine me himself to confirm what he suspected. That's where I need your help, my sweet namesake. I hope you are as tough and strong as your mother and I."

"I hope I am, Auntie."

"I'm afraid, my dear, that I will need some bruises if I am going to be convincing tomorrow when my colleague looks me over. If I am not, he will probably insist on a bone marrow test. But if I look as sick as he thinks I am, he will not ask for the new tests. He knows that the fatality rate for this leukemia, at least here in the U.S.S.R., is very high in persons over fifty. When he sees me tomorrow, he won't need any tests. I will make certain of that."

"Bruises? You want me to help you get bruises?"

"Precisely. If all my symptoms—the nosebleeds, the blood in the urine, the white-cell count, the obvious fatigue—are backed up by some black-and-blue on my thighs and hips tomorrow my dear colleague will know that the only hope is the cancer clinic in Moscow. I'll . . . how shall I put this . . . die the next week, or the week after."

"How does the Moscow end work?"

"I have . . . your uncle, Viktor, and I had . . . a very good friend in the Moscow Oncology Clinic. He is a Ukrainian nationalist who has been working with us over the last twenty years. He will report back to my colleagues at the clinic here that I died after a total collapse shortly after I arrived in Moscow. That would be perfectly consistent with the diagnosis my colleague will confirm tomorrow. He will say that he arranged for a speedy cremation, as I had directed. My colleagues here will ask the authorities to notify Anatoly that I have suddenly died. The dying part is all very simple. But my dear, I will need those bruises."

Klimenkova retrieved the walking stick from the hand-carved birch umbrella stand and handed it to Katerina.

"Hold it by the thin end, my dear. Then just give me two or three good solid hits here," she pointed to her right hip, "and a good one lower down on the thigh. I'll say I keep bumping myself just getting into my car. Then we'll try one on the other side for good measure. Don't hit too high or you might hit a kidney, now."

"Auntie, I don't know . . ."

"Please just do this, Katerina. It's no time to be weak, for God's sake!"

Gripping the walking stick like a cricket bat, Katerina brought it around sharply against her aunt's right hip. Klimenkova held on to the edge of the table for support as she was struck.

"You'll have to do better than that, I'm afraid. I'm like your mother. We don't bruise easily. Please now. Just do it!"

Katerina felt tears welling in her eyes as she brought the stick back for a second swing. This time she put her weight into it. The older woman gasped. Katerina hit her two more times on the hip and once on the upper thigh.

"That's the spirit, Katerina," Klimenkova said through the pain. "Now just give me one good one on the other side, just like that last one, and we'll be done with this."

Katerina adjusted her stance and laid one more heavy blow on the other hip. Tears were streaming down her face when she set the walking stick back down on the floor and leaned against it. The older woman took her niece in her arms.

After a while, Katerina told her aunt everything she had discussed with Anatoly, beginning with their talk at the Hermitage, ending with their last meeting in the Ukraina Hotel two nights before. The older woman copied down the telephone number in Moscow and memorized the words she was to use when she contacted Volodya with an important call from Tbilisi, as a refugee from a Black Tulip.

She and Katerina worked out a plan for contact between them in Moscow. She would simply call Katerina at the Ukraina Hotel, identify herself as a physician willing to be interviewed for Katerina's story on women in the Soviet Union. They would agree to arrange a meeting at the hotel in the next two days. They would meet two hours later, but not later than nine o'clock in the evening at Moscow's indoor swimming pool. It was the world's largest and probably most crowded year-round pool, and they could easily meet there without detection. If the call came after seven in the evening, the meeting would take place the next morning. Katerina had even bought a lifeless Polish swimsuit at the Gum department store.

Before they left the dacha Katerina Klimenkova hiked up her dress for a look. The bruises were already beginning to show.

Klimenkova dropped her off at a deserted bus stop on line 18 near Babi Yar. Both women knew they would have only another brief moment together in Moscow before Katerina Klimenkova departed the Soviet Union as Lara Martynov.

Moscow, April 3, 1250 Hours

After studying the Ricardo file for over an hour, Nikitenko returned to his own small work space. One sentence in the English language report the Americans had cabled to Rome on Gorbachev's discussion with General Titov screamed out the identity of the source and the traitor he was seeking. He purposely avoided using the official Russian translation as it would have almost surely contained the usual errors. And errors contaminate the mind.

Nikitenko translated the sentence into Russian, then opened his safe and retrieved the tape recording of his conversation with Klimenko the day before. Halfway through the tape he calmly pushed the stop button. There it was! He listened to Klimenko's precise language on Gennady Titov's position.

". . . the Red Army commanders in the field will interpret a nine-month withdrawal schedule, especially one which calls for a fifty percent withdrawal in the first three months after the accord is signed, as a dangerous humiliation. But I have heard that the competent authorities have made it clear to the generals that protecting the honor of the Red Army is their duty, not the duty of the Party."

Nikitenko felt the rush of vindication.

Nikitenko retrieved from his safe all of the materials he had collected on Klimenko and Alexander Fannin. As he reviewed the Klimenko family history, he found an innocuous notation he had missed before that Klimenko's mother had been a twin and that her sister had disappeared in 1943, and was presumed dead. That small fact was not unusual; everybody lost close relatives during the Great Patriotic War, including himself. But his instincts sent him shuffling through the files until he fished out the photograph of Klimenko with his parents at the Lubyanka award ceremony, and studied their faces for the first time. With a calmness that surprised him, he pulled out the issue of *Far Eastern Economic Review* from the Alexander Fannin/K. Martynov folder and flipped to a paper-clipped page. Holding the photograph of Sir Michael Martynov and his wife, Lara, at the Queen's Birthday reception in Hong Kong and the Klimenko family portrait side by side, Nikitenko knew he had linked Klimenko to the American CIA man, Alexander Fannin. All he needed to do now was to drop the portrait of treason on Shapkin's desk. The moment to do so, he sensed, was rapidly approaching.

ISLAMABAD, 2100 HOURS, APRIL 3

Everything had gone like clockwork. Two hours after sunset, in five-minute intervals, the Islamabad Rezident and then the Deputy Rezident followed by the KGB security officer left the walled embassy compound in separate cars. The first car containing the Rezident and a driver drew off the lone Pakistani surveillance vehicle, a white Toyota Corolla with darkened windows, conspicuously parked five hundred yards away in front of the Chinese Embassy. Inside the compound, Klimenko and Sasha and two officers from the Rezidentura had loaded the three green wooden crates into the Nissan van and driven out the gate.

After about a mile, the KGB driver received a coded message from his colleague in his embassy. All clear. Pakistani surveillance had not picked up their van.

Five minutes later a small Suzuki van pulled alongside the Nissan and the green wooden boxes were transferred. Klimenko gave the driver his instructions in English. Get the boxes onto the trucks at the Rawalpindi train station during the transfer of the ammunition shipment the next morning. Then he should forget about the matter altogether.

RAWALPINDI, APRIL 4, 0800 HOURS

Since he had volunteered his services to the Russians over a year ago, Mohammed Qureshi had been doing very well. As dispatch agent at the Rawalpindi train station he realized he had access to information that would be of value to the Russians, and one day he got his courage up and passed a letter to the driver of the Soviet Embassy truck that picked up diplomatic cargo. In it he stated that he was willing to provide information on certain deliveries to Rawalpindi. He would do this for money and would meet with an intelligencer at the time and date and place indicated. Qureshi slipped his envelope into the paperwork that he handed over to the driver. The driver asked no questions; he had been well briefed by the KGB to expect such approaches from volunteers. Two nights later Qureshi was in business. He noted the size and any markings on the boxes off-loaded in Rawalpindi and shifted to the fleet of trucks operated by Pakistani Interservices Intelligence and reported the information, along with anything he picked up from the Pakistani drivers, to his contact, Igor. In return, Igor would give him an envelope with $150 each time he reported on an ammunition shipment. It had been a great year so far. Deliveries were up and there seemed to be no end in sight.

But a few weeks ago Igor announced that the arrangement would end if he didn't accept an upcoming job. He also made it clear that if he was successful Qureshi would be paid ten times his normal fee, $1,500.

Qureshi arrived at the Rawalpindi Station late the night of April 3. It had been easy enough to put the three wooden crates on a baggage cart near the rail spur the ordnance train would use in the morning and where he could see it from the dispatcher's window.

Rawalpindi Train Station, 0800 Hours, April 4

As a boxcar full of crates of mortar bombs was being loaded onto trucks, Qureshi, clipboard in hand, wearing his Pakistani Railways official's hat, stopped two bearers and instructed them to add the three crates to the load. Minutes later the trucks sat in the lengthening convoy loaded with nearly two thousand tons of explosive ordnance. Returning to his office, Qureshi collapsed into his chair, perspiration dripping from his brow, struggling to regain his self-control.

Islamabad, 0850 Hours, April 4

Klimenko and Sasha rode in the back of the Nissan van with the transmitting equipment, as it made its way from the pastoral, planned national capital of Islamabad along Murree Road to the bustling provincial capital of Rawalpindi. The Pakistanis had been very accommodating to let Ojhri Camp, smack in the middle of a commercial zone between the two cities, become the primary ammunition dump for the Afghans.

Past the main entrance to the camp, Klimenko saw the Bedfords and Hinos with garish scenes painted on their high sides moving through the gate. The trucks all flew small black banners from the side mirrors on the driver's right side. The banner of the Prophet. Five minutes later the van made a cover stop at a small market area known as Round Market.

Rawalpindi Train Station, 1100 Hours, April 4

Qureshi was beginning to feel exceedingly proud of himself when the door of the dispatch office flew open and three Pakistani Interservices Intelligence officers entered with drawn pistols.

"Gentlemen. You have forgotten something?"

The senior officer pointed his pistol directly at Qureshi's forehead, which was once again beading with sweat.

"You will tell me now who gave you that box and what your instructions were. You will tell me this immediately or I will shoot you right here!"

Qureshi's mind raced. *That box. He said that box. They've found only one of them!* "What box? What box?" he stammered.

The officer grabbed Qureshi by the collar and jerked him out of his chair. "Bring him," he snapped to the two others.

Moments later Qureshi was in the back of a Toyota Crown with blacked-out windows racing through Rawalpindi in a convoy with siren blaring and blue lights flashing. He wondered if things might have gone better if he had just thrown the boxes in the river.

Klimenko heard the sirens approaching on the Murree Road before Sasha did. He tapped the driver on the shoulder.

"Tell me what you see."

"Three cars and a motorcycle. Interservices cars. They're slowing down. It looks like they'll turn into Ojhri Camp."

Klimenko looked at his watch. Eleven twenty-five. "Go into the store and signal your colleague. We may have trouble and I want to get moving."

OJHRI CAMP, 1130 HOURS, APRIL 4

Mohammed Qureshi stood in the middle of a large storage area two stories high stacked with mountains of rockets, mortars, explosives, and small-arms ammunition. A green box sat at his feet. Its lid had been pried off, revealing the incendiary sticks taped together and attached to a radio receiver. No attempts had yet been made to disarm it.

"Who gave this to you and what were your instructions?" The senior officer again pointed his pistol at Qureshi's head. Qureshi tried to think of something that would ease his situation, but the only image in his mind was of the three boxes floating down the river. He decided his best option was to cry, and as he began sobbing the box exploded, throwing burning white phosphorous over everyone. At precisely that moment, the other two boxes with incendiary devices exploded among the ammunition stacks. Within minutes the world was filled with fire. The rockets were still going off the next day when the first of many accusing fingers began pointing in Pakistan.

THIRTY-FIVE

The day after the sabotage of Ojhri Camp, Nikitenko accompanied Leonid Shapkin to KGB Headquarters to brief Chairman Chebrikov on the brilliant operation. Kryuchkov, Shapkin confided to Nikitenko, intended to recommend to the chairman that Klimenko be awarded the Order of Lenin. It was a race with Yazov to see who could claim the credit. Yazov was already moving forward on a decoration for Krasin.

As Shapkin's car sped down the "Chaika lane" reserved for Moscow's ruling elites, Nikitenko considered how ironic it was that Shapkin's mission was to make Klimenko a Hero of the Soviet Union while Nikitenko was only a few steps away from exposing him as one of its betrayers.

The Chaika pulled to a squealing halt in front of the Lubyanka and Shapkin strode toward the main entrance. He was partial to the Lubyanka's parade entrance, especially when the mission was as dramatic and pleasant as today's. Vladimir Kryuchkov met them in Chebrikov's outer office. "The chairman asked us to give him a couple of minutes before we join him," he said. "I think he's on the line to Mikhail Sergeyevich's office."

Shapkin spoke expansively. "I hope the chairman will be as pleased as the defense minister apparently is at the turn of events in Rawalpindi. From the way I hear it over at the Defense Ministry, the operation was entirely an army job. Not a word about the Committee's role."

Kryuchkov was about to speak when Chebrikov waved the visitors into his large office. Nikitenko took a seat next to Shapkin.

Kryuchkov moved quickly to the point. "Viktor Mikhailovich, we have some exceedingly good news to report at a time when there has been very little good news associated with our efforts in Afghanistan. One of your officers from the Kabul Forces carried out an act of sabotage against the main Dushman supply depot in Pakistan. The operation was a brilliant success and will surely be a major setback for the rebel forces. This will give the general secretary the breather he so badly needs to withdraw his forces safely."

The KGB chairman looked over his glasses at Kryuchkov, his distrust and contempt barely concealed. "Leonid Vladimirovich, surely you don't think this is the first I have heard of this operation. Everybody in town is talking about it. *And* taking credit for it. If the operation was a success for the KGB, why is it that the defense minister is crowing so loudly that it was a 40th Army operation? I have already heard that the general secretary has been briefed by General Yazov himself to the effect that the entire operation was his superb idea. I have just a moment ago tried to speak with the general secretary, but he is, understandably, far too pressed by events."

Nikitenko saw Kryuchkov stiffen slightly as he replied. "Comrade Chairman, I was called by the general secretary's office just before I left Yasenevo. I have been asked to brief Mikhail Sergeyevich on the Rawalpindi operation early this afternoon. I assumed you would be there."

Chebrikov's ears reddened. Gorbachev had bypassed him to go directly to the head of the First Chief Directorate.

"You may be certain, Viktor Aleksandrovich, that Mikhail Sergeyevich will understand the truth about Rawalpindi after I have spoken to him. You may also be certain that he will understand the role the FCD . . . the uh . . . Committee . . . played in this brilliant operation."

Nikitenko couldn't bring himself to look at Chebrikov's face at his moment of discomfort, but he could feel the chairman's sheer hatred for the man who was shoving him aside.

Moscow, 1130 Hours, April 5

Rogov walked behind the bar of the Tbilisi Restaurant and took the telephone from the waiter.

"Rogov."

"Volodya, my dear young man. This is another of your warm refugee girls from the Black Tulip. I hope you still have time for me."

Rogov didn't hesitate. "Can you come to me right this minute? I will show you how I treat my little refugees from the Black Tulip."

"I'm in the neighborhood, my dear Volodya. I'll be there in minutes."

"I'll see you at the door, my little one."

Rogov was eager to see what kind of refugee girl Tolya had sent to him to disappear. He thought that the girl sounded a touch older than the usual lady callers, but he doubted anyone who might be listening to his phone would pick up on that. He paid good money to the boys in the Committee to make sure no one was eavesdropping.

KABUL, 40TH ARMY HEADQUARTERS, APRIL 12

Klimenko and Krasin got a heroes' reception at the briefing the morning after the sabotage. But in his first message from the Hermitage, Alexander was less than enthusiastic, tersely telling Klimenko to disregard his earlier request for clarification of the statement that the reaction from the 40th Army would be harsh if the resistance persisted. Events at Ojhri had been clarification enough.

Klimenko responded by outlining his meeting with Katerina in Moscow. All parts of the exchange were now in motion. There was no return to safety now. He also reminded Alexander to continue to press for more information on Colonel KSN, who was not only investigating him, but attempting to identify Alexander, possibly with some success.

MOSCOW, APRIL 24

The report Nikitenko had finally received from the floating Rezidentura aboard the MV *Baikal* confirmed what he and the young man in the computer library had already unearthed. Among the few details it added was the anglicized version of K. Martynova's name, one Catherine Martin.

A few days later Nikitenko sat beside Sergei Bokhan, the computer whiz, to take an electronic look at what the plodders aboard the MV *Baikal* had brought him.

"Let's take a look at Katerina Martynova, aka Catherine Martin, born 1949 Shanghai," the young man suggested. "Hong Kong British passport, French passport, U.S. passport, Sorbonne doctorate. Let's see if she ever visited the Soyuz." Seconds later the answer rolled onto the screen.

"Your girl is right here, Comrade Nikitenko. Right across the Moscow River."

"What do you mean, my girl is right across the Moscow River?"

"It says right here that one Catherine Martin, French passport holder born in 1949, is the accredited Moscow correspondent for the *Far Eastern Focus*. Her last entry at Sheremetyevo Airport was on March 28. She has a leased room at the Ukraina Hotel. She applied for and was given permission to travel to Kiev in early April."

Nikitenko scribbled on a piece of paper for a moment and then pushed it in front of Bokhan. "Is there a means of monitoring the movements of these persons on a worldwide basis?"

Bokhan thought for a moment. "It's odd you should ask, Comrade . . . uh . . . Karm, but I have suggested to the competent authorities that just such a watch-list search method was possible."

Nikitenko nodded his head in anticipation. "And?"

"And they said that computer resources were too precious, particularly since the Committee has sufficient manpower to conduct such investigation in the old way."

Nikitenko placed his hand on Bokhan's arm. "Could you place these names on a watch list as a little test and report the results only to me?"

Bokhan looked at the list again. "It would be an interesting operational test of my theory. Yes, I can do it. Actually, since you only have a few names we can try it now." Bokhan typed the names on Nikitenko's list: Martin, Catherine; Martynova, Katerina; Martynova, Lara; Martynov, Michael; Fannin, Alexander; Jasik, Gromek. He waited another minute and then the information began scrolling onto his screen.

"Here's the confirmation on your girl," Bokhan said as Catherine Martin's flight information came up. "It confirms her arrival at Sheremetyevo on the twenty-eighth and has her booked for a departure from Leningrad on Finnair flight 4976 on May fourth."

Nikitenko could only shake his head as he read the information.

"Wait a minute!" Bokhan said, leaning forward. "Here comes another one!"

An instant later Nikitenko was reading the flight arrival information on one Lara Martynova, born on April 4, 1926, Hong Kong British passport. The woman was departing Hong Kong today aboard the MV *Khabarovsk,* with a four-day transit itinerary that would bring her from Nakhodka/Vladivostok to Moscow by Aeroflot flight number 534. She would leave aboard Finnair flight 4976 from Leningrad for Helsinki on May 4.

"That's the same flight the Martin woman is taking, Comrade Colonel."

As Nikitenko returned to Directorate RI, Shapkin called out to him through the open door of his office. "Karm Sergeyevich, I have some very sad news that I am sure will disturb you as it has me. I have just received word that Anatoly Viktorovich's mother has died suddenly here in Moscow, and I have the unhappy task of notifying Klimenko. I just wanted you to know that so that you could share in his grief."

Nikitenko struggled to show proper concern. The confluence of events was making him feel light-headed again. "Are there funeral arrangements, Leonid Vladimirovich? Perhaps I could assist."

"Thoughtful of you, Karm Sergeyevich. But I already inquired. Katerina Klimenkova was cremated yesterday. It was her wish that it be done immediately after her death. There is no other family. Only Anatoly Viktorovich. His father died just two years ago, you may remember."

"Yes. A great pity. A great pity. But perhaps I could at least talk to the people at the hospital to see if there is absolutely anything we can do for Anatoly Viktorovich. Surely his mother's belongings need to be looked after."

HONG KONG, 1745 HOURS, APRIL 24

Alexander briefed them the evening of Lara's scheduled departure.

"The days on the *Khabarovsk* will be routine. You know about the floating KGB Station on board, a full-fledged Rezidentura, but they won't pay special attention to you unless they have been asked."

Michael felt helpless. He was not used to dealing with situations he couldn't control or influence. "All you need to do is get a good rest while you're at sea, my dear."

"Yes, Misha." Lara used the diminutive of her husband's name. "The real fun starts in Nakhodka. Right, Alexander?"

"Actually, Nakhodka will probably be pretty routine as well. There will be the transfer at the port, a long bus ride to the airport near Vladivostok, and then the flight to Moscow. The Nakhodka KGB won't be paying much attention to the transit crowd passing through on the way to Moscow."

"I suppose I should prepare myself for the shock of seeing Nakhodka after all these years. The last time I saw either place was in 1944. It should bring back some pretty awful memories."

Alexander went on. "You and Michael know most of what I'm going to say, but we'll go over it anyway. When you arrive at Sheremetyevo Airport in Moscow, you will be treated like an international arrival. It's almost always the same. The KGB border guard in the booth will look barely old enough to be away from his mother. But your rosy-cheeked boy will look you over very closely. He'll hold your passport in front of him while he works a foot pedal to photograph each page. He might ask how long you're staying, but otherwise he'll say nothing to you. Then he'll make one, possibly two telephone calls. You won't be able to hear him from inside his booth. But you need to know that this is all routine. The honest visitor, and that's most travelers, gets exasperated, maybe even blows off some steam. Anybody with anything to hide stays very quiet. Maybe even begins to sweat. You might want to try limited exasperation."

Lara laughed. "Very limited exasperation."

For another hour Alexander walked Lara through every detail of her time in Moscow and Leningrad. She was a quick study. Finally, Alexander said he and Michael would pick her sister Katerina out of the crowd when she cleared customs at Helsinki Airport on May 4. The three of them would wait in Helsinki until Lara and Kat arrived a day or two later, after the tempest over Lara's "lost" passport subsided. With the British Consulate General pressuring the Leningrad authorities, he told Lara, it shouldn't take more than two days for them to be on their way.

KABUL, 2345 HOURS, APRIL 24

It was nearly midnight when Krasin called Klimenko to General Titov's secure communications room. A grave Sasha met him at the entrance to the secure area.

"Tolya, there's a call coming in for you from the Committee."

"Why so serious, Colonel? What's up?"

"I'm sorry, Tolya. I'm sorry. It's your mother. Shapkin's coming on the line." Sasha handed Klimenko the secure radio telephone.

The voice on the other end was distorted by the process of encryption. Klimenko could not understand every word.

"Anatoly Viktorovich. This is Leonid. . . . terribly sorry . . . mother . . . gravely ill . . . very short . . . passed away."

"Leonid Vladimirovich, I can hardly hear you. Are you saying that my mother has died?"

"Yes . . . don't have . . . details . . . Karm Sergeyevich to check . . . at the clinic. . . . You are coming to Moscow, aren't you?"

"Yes. Of course. But it had always been my mother's wish to be cremated. Do you know if that has happened?"

". . . understand . . . Karm Sergeyevich . . . looking into . . . as well."

"Leonid Vladimirovich, thank you for your sensitivity in this very personal matter. You need not have Karm Sergeyevich bother himself with this. I'll catch a flight home as soon as possible and take care of everything myself."

"Don't worry, Anatoly Viktorovich . . . Karm Sergeyevich . . . true friend . . . as you know."

"Yes of course, Leonid Vladimirovich. I know what kind of friend Karm Sergeyevich is. And thank you. Thank you for the call."

"Wait . . . Karm Sergeyevich. . . ."

An instant later Nikitenko's voice, barely recognizable, came on the line. "Colonel . . . sorry to . . . to you on such an occasion . . . do what I can . . . tragic moment."

"Really, Karm. You mustn't bother. I insist."

". . . little consolation . . . mother is finally rejoining her long-lost loved ones. . . . important that is to you . . . now . . ."

Shapkin came back on the line. "You will come here to me as soon as you can, Anatoly Viktorovich. I hate to bother you with this right now, but Chairman Kryuchkov has asked to see you. He would like for you to meet with the general secretary to tell him personally how the operation in Rawalpindi has supported his momentous policy decisions. The Geneva Accords are now just waiting for signature. The general secretary has told Comrade Kryuchkov that he can now instruct Vorontsov to sign with dignity. That is much your doing, Tolya."

Klimenko was immensely distracted. He barely heard Shapkin's last words. "Yes. Yes, Leonid Vladimirovich. I will check in with you as soon as I can. And thank you again."

Klimenko and Sasha sat alone in Titov's office. "What do you make of that Chekist bag of shit poking around in your mother's phony ashes, my dear colonel?"

Klimenko barely heard him. "He said that my mother was finally rejoining her long-lost loved ones. He said that he knew how important that was to me. I don't know what to make of that. It is so incredibly coincidental that it must be just that."

Sasha's face was a mask. "I'm going with you back to Moscow. I'll get Titov to recommend it himself. I want to be handy in case you try something else that will end up getting us both shot. Something even crazier than staging your mother's phony death."

HONG KONG, 0140 HOURS, APRIL 25

The ring of Alexander's bedside telephone brought him out of a light sleep. "Fannin," he answered.

"Alexander, please set up your other telephone for a special message." He recognized the voice immediately as Rand's.

"Give me five minutes." Minutes later he was on the verandah, the small fan-shaped antenna locked on the communications satellite deep in geosynchronous orbit.

"Hermitage, Hermitage, this is Hong Kong. Do you copy?"

"I copy, boss. I have an urgent message to relay to you."

Alexander listened as Rand read the message from Kabul. "You must abort the departure of your traveler. Repeat, abort the departure of your traveler. There is a strong possibility the Moscow operation has been compromised and your traveler may be walking into a trap. KSN is behind what I believe is a serious threat to the Maidens and probably to

Paul. He must be neutralized. Your assistance in this is urgently needed. I am departing in thirty-six hours for Moscow where I will attempt to get a firm reading on the nature and depth of the compromise and make plans to deal with KSN. I will stand by for your response until 0500 hours local April 26. Trust in God. End End."

Alexander knew that the MV *Khabarovsk,* with Lara aboard, had sailed from Hong Kong five hours and forty minutes ago and there was no way to intercept her before she landed at Vladivostok.

WASHINGTON, D.C., 1530 HOURS, APRIL 24

Frank Andrews had remained "downtown," as he called it, after Bill Casey's death at the request of Jim Taggart, the deputy national security adviser. Some activities Casey had set in motion continued to be run out of the NSC, and Andrews's involvement in the final stages of the Afghan war was one of them. He answered his satellite telephone in his cramped basement office at the Old Executive Office Building. "Let me guess, it's A calling from Hong Kong. What time is it out there, my friend?"

"Frank, it's early tomorrow morning to you, but there's no time for horsing around. I need a couple of very big favors from you and I need them now. Okay?"

"Christ, Alexander, here we go again."

"Item one. You've got to get into the special/sensitive archives on the KGB colonel I asked you to trace for me, Karm Sergeyevich Nikitenko. I don't care about the boilerplate information in the other indices. I only want whatever it was that put him in the special/sensitive archives. And I don't care how you get it."

"I don't know if I can get in there unless I pull every string between Pennsylvania Avenue and Langley."

"Pull the strings, Frank. It involves protecting the source that's been giving us everything the Soviets are bringing to the table in Geneva. Item two. I want you to meet me in West Berlin at 1900 hours three days from now, that's the twenty-seventh. Meet me in the lobby of the Kempinski Hotel. We'll both stay there. Book a suite. I want you to bring my Polish alias identity package in the name Gromek Jasik. There are travel documents and some clothing from Eastern Europe. Technical Services is holding it for me. You'll have to make sure that all the necessary travel authorizations and border crossing stamps and visas are entered in the passport and in the Warsaw Pact travel documents. I'll need pocket litter to back up Jasik's travel this month to Prague, Berlin, Warsaw, Budapest, and everything Jasik might need to go from Berlin to Moscow."

Andrews scribbled furiously. "Is there more?"

"Yeah, I want you to prepare to stay around for a few days, maybe a week. I'll need an escape in East Berlin and a pickup three or four days later."

"Why not?" Andrews turned sarcastic. "I told you a long time ago, Alexander, you're going to get me killed or fired."

"Frank, I might just get us all killed. And on that cheery note, my friend, I'm signing off. See you in Berlin."

Alexander saw that it was too early to call Michael. He would reach him in a couple of hours and just tell him something had come up and that he might not make their rendezvous in Helsinki. Michael didn't need to know more than that.

KABUL, 2100 HOURS, APRIL 25

As he read Alexander's response rolling across the liquid crystal display, events seemed to be racing out of Klimenko's control. Alexander acknowledged receipt of Klimenko's request to abort Lara's travel but stated it was too late. He would redouble his efforts to develop information to neutralize Nikitenko. Klimenko should take whatever action necessary to protect the Maidens and Paul. He would try to be of further assistance, and Klimenko should be prepared for emergency contact from any quarter at any time after he arrived in Moscow.

KABUL, 1430 HOURS, APRIL 26

Klimenko met Sasha at Kabul Airport a day and a half after the telephone conversation with Shapkin and Nikitenko.

"Tolya! Look out the window there! There is our transport back to our beloved capital. Isn't that just what you've always wanted?"

Across the tarmac an IL-76 was loading its cargo for the flight to Moscow. About two-dozen zinc boxes, each neatly welded shut with a dead boy inside, were lined up on the ramp behind the plane.

"Well, Sasha, it looks like we're finally getting our ride on a Black Tulip."

THIRTY-SIX

Nikitenko looked across the tidy desk of the director of the Moscow Oncology Clinic. Arkady Shevchenko was fastidiously turned out, his starched white smock spotless, his nails manicured, his hair perfectly trimmed. He carefully cultivated the appearance, and his reputation, as the attending physician of the nomenklatura. But why, then, is this distinguished and protected physician so nervous? "Dr. Shevchenko, it is truly tragic that Dr. Klimenkova died so suddenly, and so shortly after her husband's death. My dear colleague, her son, has now lost both parents while doing his internationalist duty."

"Yes, it is mournful. But there was nothing that could be done for her. Acute myelogenous leukemia is vicious and cruel and is almost impossible to treat successfully, particularly at her age. But her death was swift and reasonably painless. We were able to keep her comfortable until the end." Shevchenko looked at Nikitenko's face intently. He knew the man was from the KGB. He had even anticipated such a visit after he had agreed to help Katerina Klimenkova disappear. But this man with the gentle face and the cold, sad eyes frightened him. He knew his own fear showed and that terrified him.

"I can see, somehow, that these things are often rapid and irreversible. But why didn't she let her son know before she died that she was gravely ill? Surely she knew what was happening to her. She was a physician herself."

Shevchenko chose his words carefully. "Of course she knew what was happening to her. She told me when she arrived here that she doubted there was anything we at the clinic could do for her leukemia, but she wanted to make one last attempt."

"Then you knew Klimenkova before all this."

"I've known the family for years. We were together at the university in Kiev after the war. I came on to Moscow to specialize in oncology and Katerina stayed in Kiev in obstetrics."

"Her son, Anatoly, will arrive in Moscow from Afghanistan in the next few days and I'm afraid I'll have to explain to him why his mother was cremated before he could pay his last respects. He will think that a bit . . . unusual. Actually, I am myself a little confused. Cremation never caught on after the Revolution, despite the perfect logic of it. Particularly odd for a believer like Klimenkova." Nikitenko took a chance, a slight one, he thought, that Katerina Klimenkova was a Catholic. The payoff was in Shevchenko's face.

"Klimenkova was a beautiful woman. And understandably, even a little vain. She was sorrowfully wasted by the disease in the last weeks, and she wished to be cremated immediately after her death. She told me she couldn't bear the thought of people, even her son, seeing her in a coffin wasted and ugly. I told her that was nonsense, but she made me promise. I had no choice but to follow her wishes. As for being a believer, I'm not sure what that might have to do with it, Comrade Nikitenko."

Nikitenko had what he wanted. "Of course you had no choice, Doctor Shevchenko. We all have our vanities. Perhaps I could take charge of Klimenkova's things. It is a task I sadly know too well from my days in Afghanistan. Taking charge of the effects of the dead."

"Of course." Shevchenko got up. "I imagined that you would want to make that part easier for Anatoly. I have her small traveling bag. Come with me."

Karm Sergeyevich followed Shevchenko into a small storeroom. "Here is the list of the contents of the bag. You'll have to sign for the articles. It's regulations." Shevchenko handed over a single sheet of paper with less than ten neatly typed lines on it.

"Klimenkova certainly didn't come to Moscow with a very positive outlook."

"What's that?" Shevchenko was on guard again.

"I said Klimenkova didn't have a positive outlook. It looks like she brought only one change of underthings. And I'm assuming she had one set on when she was cremated. That seems strange for a woman as vain as you describe Klimenkova. I mean that in the most positive sense, mind you."

Shevchenko felt his face flush. "I hadn't really noticed what she left behind. But these things have a way of disappearing around here; there are those who think Klimenkova's personal effects could be put to good use. I'm sure you know what I mean, Comrade."

"Of course, but there's not even a toothbrush here, or any toiletries. How could anyone take the toothbrush of a dead woman? Well, Comrade Doctor, life never ceases to amaze me. But now, I shall leave you to your patients and their suffering. I only hope that you understand that I know the full meaning of what you have done for Klimenkova." Nikitenko smiled gently.

Shevchenko felt the clammy moisture in his palms. He furtively wiped his right hand on his smock before he offered it to Nikitenko.

MOSCOW, 0430 HOURS, APRIL 27

Klimenko and Sasha had changed planes in Tashkent, happily leaving the IL-76 with its cargo of dead Russian soldiers. They had caught a ride on a giant, overcrowded Aeroflot Antonov arriving at Moscow's Domodedevo Airport well past midnight. As they cleared the baggage area, Karm Sergeyevich Nikitenko called out to them from the crowd crushed behind the iron barriers.

"Anatoly Viktorovich, Colonel Krasin!" Nikitenko hailed.

"Oh, shit! Can you believe this, Tolya?"

"Careful, Sasha." Klimenko spoke under his breath and then waved, smiling just enough to show appreciation but not so much to detract from his somber mission. "Karm Sergeyevich. You are too kind. It is no joy to travel all the way out here to Domodedevo and sit around for hours on some vague promise of the arrival of the flight from Tashkent."

"Nonsense, Anatoly Viktorovich. Director Shapkin, by the way, sends his personal greetings and deepest sympathies."

"I am comforted by your concern, Karm Sergeyevich, and by that of Leonid Vladimirovich. Your thoughts mean a lot to me."

Nikitenko turned to Sasha. "Colonel Krasin! It is proof of your friendship that you have come with Anatoly Viktorovich at this time. You are a true friend."

"General Titov insisted, Comrade Nikitenko. It is the least we could do."

Nikitenko smiled sadly. "Anatoly Viktorovich, I want you to know that I met with the director of the clinic. You must know him, a Dr. Shevchenko. He told me your mother's passing was peaceful. He was with her until the end. I have also retrieved her effects. Some things were obviously missing, but we can look into that later if you like."

"Some things missing?"

"So it appeared. Your mother, in my opinion, would not have traveled to Moscow with so few things. No woman would have, in my opinion. But now, let's get both of you into town."

Nikitenko led Klimenko and Sasha out of the rundown terminal to two white Volga sedans, their drivers sound asleep behind the wheel. He took Klimenko's hand and moved close to his face. "You and Colonel Krasin will be taken to the guest house on the Moscow River. You know the place, Moscow River One. Director Shapkin insisted on it. You will stay there for as long as you remain in Moscow. The driver will be with you for any of your transport needs. And finally, Director Shapkin has arranged for a plane to take you to Kiev today. He was sure you would need to look into your mother's affairs there. He asked you to call him whenever you're back from Kiev. Any time, day or night, he said." Nikitenko handed Klimenko a sheet of paper. "These are his private numbers. Only he will pick up."

"Karm Sergeyevich, this is all too much trouble for you and for Leonid Vladimirovich. Please tell him I am grateful and tell him I'll call as soon as I'm back in Moscow."

"Say no more about this, Anatoly Viktorovich. I will see you at Yasenevo May second at around eleven. It's the Monday after May Day, and almost all the comrades will still be on holiday. I myself would take a few days off, except for your visit . . ."

"Of course, Karm Sergeyevich."

Nikitenko paused for a moment then gently changed course. "And by the way, Anatoly Viktorovich, you asked by radio telephone from Kabul if your mother had been cremated, as was her wish. I can confirm that it was done. It seemed odd to me, though. Dr. Shevchenko insisted that it was her last-minute decision, so I was a little confused that you knew of her plan."

Klimenko weighed Nikitenko's every word and decided not to rise to the bait. He cursed himself silently for having asked about the cremation.

"Karm Sergeyevich, you are a true friend in need. Thank you for your thoughtful concern and assistance. I will see you at the director's office after the May Day holiday. We can talk then." Klimenko shook Nikitenko's hand while he looked into the cold, sad face.

FRANKFURT/MAIN INTERNATIONAL AIRPORT, 1330 HOURS, APRIL 27

Alexander studied his face in the men's room mirror at the departure terminal. After half an hour in a barber's chair his beard was gone; only a bushy mustache remained, and his fresh haircut looked as close to socialist realist styling as he could coax the reluctant barber to produce. Alarmed at the sharp contrast of his cleanly shaven, but pasty complexion compared with the rest of his deeply tanned face, he decided to spend a few minutes in the airport tanning salon.

MOSCOW, 1430 HOURS, APRIL 27

Sergei Bokhan eagerly stuffed the printouts in his pocket and raced for the second-floor offices of Directorate RI. Nikitenko was waiting for him at the access control point.

Nikitenko was in an expansive mood. "Welcome to RI, Sergei. Without the vigilance of Directorate RI, the Party would be without eyes and ears." Things were going so well that giddiness kept encroaching on his sense of decorum.

"Comrade Karm, I have something, possibly something important for you on the test you asked me to conduct. One of your watch-listed people is traveling." He handed one of the printouts to Nikitenko.

Nikitenko saw the name Bokhan had underlined. "My, my. It seems that Mr. A. Fannin has suddenly flown from Hong Kong to Frankfurt."

"He just booked it yesterday. He's connecting to Berlin. It's on the next page," Bokhan said.

"Sergei, you will change forever the way we do our business. I promise you, young man, you will receive recognition beyond all your expectations."

"Just making the leadership of the Committee aware of the investigative possibilities of electronic information management is enough, Comrade. . . . And by the way, you may have noticed that there is no indication anywhere in A. Fannin's booking record of a return reservation. It looks like he might be going to Germany without plans for onward travel."

"I wouldn't be too certain of that, Sergei. But please keep an eye on Mr. A. Fannin."

"There's another hit on the watch list, Comrade Karm. I found it when I was looking for A. Fannin's return booking, and at the same time discovered a flaw in the way I'd programmed the watch list. I had it programmed only for travel actually under way. I reprogrammed it for all bookings, current travel and future, and that's when the second hit turned up."

"Second hit?"

"Yes. Michael Martynov has booked a complicated itinerary beginning tomorrow. He's flying to New York, then London, then Helsinki, arriving there the day before Lara Martynov arrives from Leningrad. I guess they're linking up. You remember, as well, that Catherine Martin will be arriving on the same flight as her mother from Leningrad."

All my little chickens are coming home to roost, Nikitenko thought.

Back in his office he called Bokhan.

"Sergei, this is Karm again. I know I needn't ask you to pay particular attention to A. Fannin and G. Jasik, but please be sure to check those names, particularly the Polish name, against any databases on travel in the fraternal socialist countries or from those countries to the Soviet Union."

"Yes, Comrade Karm. I can put your people on watch there, too. And I'll report to you immediately if I learn of any movement."

"If anything comes up over the weekend, call me at home. The duty officer at RI has my home number."

Nikitenko struggled to contain himself. We're going to have a family reunion right here in Moscow, he thought.

WEST BERLIN, 1900 HOURS, APRIL 27

Alexander dropped in behind Andrews as the big man strolled through the ornate lobby of the Bristol Kempinski on the Kurfürstendam. He followed him into an elevator just as the doors were closing. "You're on time," he said with a smile.

"Of course I'm on time. And look at you, for Crissakes, you look like the young Joe Stalin with that mustache and the Bolshevik haircut."

On the fourth floor, the two men walked quickly together to Andrews's corner suite. Andrews hung out the DO NOT DISTURB sign and chain-locked the door. "My friend, before we go any further, why don't you tell me what's going on. I've done what you've asked. At some personal risk, I might add."

"This will take a little time." For the next hour, Alexander told his friend the story that began eighteen months earlier, and that ended in the defection of Klimenko's mother. When he finished, he smiled. "There it is, Frank. You've got it all."

"Alexander, at this moment I am more convinced than ever that you are going to get us killed." Shaking his head, Andrews fished a manila envelope from his flight bag and handed it over. "First, let's go over the documentation."

As Alexander laid out the half-inch stack of documents, Andrews briefed him from a typed set of notes. "Your Polish passport in the name of Gromek Jasik is completely up to date. You've got service visas valid for Warsaw Pact travel, and we've added entry and exit chops for the last eighteen months to establish a travel pattern like the one you're going to use now."

Alexander studied each page of his passport, concocting in his mind the travel history to back up the exit and entry stamps. Then he picked up a smaller envelope containing an assortment of papers and receipts.

"Those are your hotel receipts, travel vouchers, and currency-exchange certificates for the last three months. There's a small pocket diary with daily expense notations in Polish, including some spicy entries on a woman you spent some time with in Prague. They were written by Helga, the 'wicked witch' in graphic analysis using your handwriting samples. None of it's backstopped, nor are any of your Warsaw addresses."

Alexander smiled. Helga was the CIA's ancient graphologist, who, according to legend, copied the final draft of the Gettysburg address in Lincoln's own hand.

"The next set of documents is your Polish Communist Party Central Committee identity booklet and a thirty-day priority travel order covering the Warsaw Pact area. With it is your pay booklet showing you've taken travel advances in Prague, and again in Wünsdorf at Western Group headquarters. You have separate packets of East German marks, Polish zlotys, and rubles. The amounts match your currency declarations and the receipts for expenditures. There is a hard-currency declaration approved by the Polish Interior Ministry. You can fill in the amounts of dollars or DM. Keep the amounts low, or you'll attract attention. Don't use U.S. hundreds. Everybody's worried about them these days. DM are okay in any denomination. Okay so far?"

Alexander nodded as he made mental notes.

"There are notations in your pay booklet that you were provided quarters along the way, the most recent being the next couple of nights when you're supposed to be staying at transient quarters at Western Group of Forces headquarters in Wünsdorf. Then, there is a WGF priority travel order for your trip to Moscow and points within the Soviet Union. This will get you a seat on a flight from East Germany to Moscow. It might be a hassle, but a hundred marks will turn the trick at Schoenefeld. We've given you the option of scheduling your trip to Tula outside of Moscow to visit the airborne garrison, or to Leningrad to visit naval headquarters, or even to Vladivostok to visit the Far Eastern regional headquarters. None of it's backstopped for the ultimate destinations, but I'm assured it's absolutely valid for getting you to Moscow by air and for official transient quarters in and around Moscow."

"I'll be arriving the day before May Day. The place will be a madhouse. Accommodations will be a nightmare, just the way I want it. When there are no vacancies, they only check your money."

"Finally, there's your Party cadre booklet, an All Union Sports Member's booklet, a Warsaw Pact ration card, half used, and a special security pass for the Magdalenka compound outside Warsaw. Is your Polish still good enough for this story?"

"It's good, but I'd rather not be interrogated by the Poles anywhere along the way. I'm skipping Poland, as you can see, and going straight to Moscow from East Germany."

Andrews rose and retrieved a sports bag from the closet. "And then there's all this."

Looking inside Alexander found one neatly folded man's suit with Hungarian labels, two dress shirts, a couple of handkerchiefs, one belt, and two neckties, all from Czechoslovakia, and two changes of underwear from East Germany. At the bottom of the bag he found a pair of shoes, also made in Hungary. "I'll need some toiletries and possibly some prescription and over-the-counter medicines and a couple of other things, but you can get those on the other side of the wall for me tomorrow," he said as he stuffed Gromek Jasik's wardrobe back into the bag and zipped it up.

"And that's it. My people said that their documents are as good as they come and the clothes are stuff you picked out yourself. But everything has a built-in potential for failure. You're going to have to stay lucky."

"This is all fine, Frank. But now tell me what you were able to do about my problem in Moscow, my friend Karm Sergeyevich Nikitenko."

Andrews set up his laptop computer. He entered a password and a command that brought a document classified "secret/sensitive" to the screen. "Read this, Alexander. Take your time."

As Alexander began to read the electronic file code-named Dakota, Andrews mixed two strong drinks at the minibar and sat down, rubbing his eyes with exhaustion.

Two hours later, Alexander awakened Andrews, who had fallen asleep in his chair. "What did you have to do to get this and who else knows you've got it?"

"I just marched into the DCI's office in the Old Executive Office Building and told him there was a file in sensitive archives that had a material bearing on the survival of the source on Soviet planning in Afghanistan that he and the president valued so highly. The director asked if it was for you; he knows those special reports come from you. I told him yes, and he told me that Graham Middleton hardly let a month pass without denouncing you to him as the mole they've never caught. He told me what you told Middleton and Casey before Casey died, what you'd learned about the KGB penetration of CIA. But he also told me Middleton suspected you gave him the information to throw him off the track of the real mole—you."

"He hasn't gotten anywhere with what I gave them?" Alexander asked.

"Dead end. He thinks you put him there intentionally."

"What's the DCI think?"

Andrews shrugged. "I'm not sure. You know how the director is—thoughtful, deliberate. He struggled with my request for about a minute before he decided the Agency had nothing to lose by giving you a look at the entry on Nikitenko. Then he let me sit down at his White House computer and make the query using his password and access level."

"Middleton will see he logged into the archives," Alexander said.

"Yes, but he probably won't ask the DCI about it anytime soon. He'll stew for a while before he figures out a way to snivel into the DCI's office and ask his questions. This director doesn't like him any more than Casey did, but for different reasons. He'll hold him off until I get back and tell him what the hell is going on."

"Middleton will figure it all out sooner or later. But by then I'll have done what I have to do."

"You know he's really after you, don't you, Alexander?"

"I know, but we'll worry about that later. I'm taking two copies of this with me to Moscow, one for our friend Nikitenko and one as my travel-insurance policy. And you, my friend, will make another floppy and hold it until you pick me up in East Berlin. If I don't show, then drop it off at the nearest KGB Rezidentura. When Middleton finds out about that he'll just about choke."

MOSCOW, 2240 HOURS, APRIL 27

Vladimir Rogov filled two shot glasses with Hungarian schnapps and handed one to Sasha. They were seated in the cozy, dark-paneled, private dining room of the Tbilisi Restaurant.

"Where's my favorite Committee colonel?"

"He's off to Kiev, to see about his poor mother's affairs." Sasha spoke cautiously, glancing up at the ceiling.

"It's okay to talk here. I make a monthly payment to certain quarters, the same guys who would put in the bugs if I didn't pay them. We're okay."

"Tolya will be back tomorrow. He had to make the quick trip to Kiev or things would have started looking odd, and at the worst possible time. We'll meet him tomorrow."

"Tell me what's got you so worked up, Sasha. You need someone killed?"

"I might, Volodya. Now I want you to listen carefully to my story, because it involves all of us."

Sasha recounted Nikitenko's tightening noose on Klimenko and Katerina Klimenkova. When he was finished, Rogov's smile had faded. "Why don't we just go ahead and have Comrade Red Army Nikitenko killed? Right now. Tonight."

"That's an option, Volodya. But then we'll never know what he really knows and who else knows."

"Tell me how all this got started," Rogov said, filling both their glasses.

After another hour and half a bottle of schnapps, Rogov and Sasha had the beginnings of a plan.

MOSCOW, 1000 HOURS, APRIL 28

Arkady Shevchenko's handshake was clammy. Klimenko could almost smell the fear. "Dear Anatoly Viktorovich, I am so very saddened about your mother, but you must know that her passing was merciful." Shevchenko pointed knowingly to the ceiling fixture, and then continued. "Walk with me to the storeroom where we have your mother's ashes. Your colleague has already picked up her effects. I'm afraid he's convinced some items are missing, but we come to accept such sad losses these days."

When they were out of Shevchenko's office, Klimenko spoke in a hushed voice. "I know about Nikitenko's visit and I know he suspects something. I just don't know how much he knows or if he's shared his suspicions with anyone else. I'll try to find out how badly we're compromised. And please understand how much we value the risks you have taken for our family. I simply cannot say more about the dangers until I know more."

Arkady Shevchenko's smile was weak, but sincere. "Anatoly Viktorovich, I have been involved in these things for a long time. I thought I knew the risks I was taking, and I thought I was courageous enough to accept them, but to you I must admit that the deep fear in the pit of my stomach is almost overwhelming. I am a little shocked and quite a little disappointed in myself. But intellectually, at least, I have no regrets about what I have done to help your wonderful mother. Please do what you must, and don't spend too much time worrying about me."

Shevchenko led Klimenko into a small storeroom and handed him a sealed zinc box from a shelf. The initials KCK were scratched into the surface.

Klimenko stared the man in the face. "Arkady, I will do whatever I can to resolve this problem. Please bear with me for a few more days. Can we return to your office now? I need to make a telephone call, and those who might be watching us should have the opportunity to listen in."

"Of course." Shevchenko led the way.

Leonid Shapkin picked up his private line on the second ring. "Shapkin."

"Leonid Vladimirovich, it's Anatoly. I have just returned from Kiev, and thanks to your help and the good work by Karm Sergeyevich, everything has gone very smoothly. I am calling from the clinic where my mother died . . . I have her ashes."

"Anatoly, please accept again my deepest condolences. We all know we must lose our parents some day, but none of us are ever prepared for it. If there is anything I or Karm Sergeyevich can do that would make your loss more bearable, name it."

"I'll be certain to see you on Monday at eleven as Karm mentioned."

"Anatoly, we can speak more when I see you, but the chairman wants to see you later in the week, perhaps on Friday, May fifth. He wants you to brief him personally on, how shall I put it, certain events in Pakistan; and we should be prepared to go with him to see Comrade Mikhail Sergeyevich. You are much in demand, my dear young friend."

"Thank you, Leonid Viktorovich. I was only doing my duty, as you well know."

"Nonsense, Anatoly. We'll save it until Monday. Now go take care of your family tragedy and call me if you need anything. I mean anything."

"I will, Leonid Vladimirovich. I will"

Outside the clinic Klimenko spoke softly. "Doctor, right now all my instincts tell me that Colonel Nikitenko has not shared his suspicions with anyone. I don't believe he's told his story to the man I just spoke with, his superior, Leonid Shapkin. And I doubt he'd dare reveal it to anyone else, because he knows that the first person he tells will race to Shapkin with the information, if only to protect himself. If I'm right, and I think I am, Nikitenko is keeping what he knows to himself for now."

By the time they reached the parking lot Shevchenko had regained some composure. "You'll have to excuse me, Tolya. Memories of the times of great terror in this country run deep, and fear has its way with all of us, doesn't it?"

Klimenko took the man's hand in his own and spoke gently. "Yes, Arkady. Fear has its way with us, if we let it. Stay by your telephone for the next few days. I'll be in touch."

THIRTY-SEVEN

Katerina Klimenkova and her son were on the metro, and Klimenko was to get off at the next stop. She would pass three more stations before she would get off for a bus ride and a long walk to the block of workers' flats where Rogov had kept her hidden in a safe house.

"Tolya, I know when I see worry in your face. Are you going to tell me what's wrong?"

Klimenko had decided not to share the depth of his concerns with her. "Mother, this affair is enough to make anyone nervous. Of course I'm concerned. Surely you'll allow me that."

Klimenko's weak smile didn't reassure his mother, but she decided not to probe further. "I'm meeting Lara's Katerina tomorrow morning at the pool. It will be our final meeting. I'll tell her you're back in Moscow. That should give her spirits a lift. When she visited me in Kiev she said that you might not make it back to Moscow in time for the celebration. That bothered her."

Distracted, Klimenko asked, "Celebration? You mean May Day?"

"Of course not, Tolya, I mean the celebration of the reunion of what's left of our family. But then you haven't been listening to a word I've been saying, have you?"

"Of course I have. Tell Katerina tomorrow that I am, indeed, back for the celebration, and that if she needs to contact me for anything whatsoever, she should call Volodya. He will set it up. And tell her that I am proud of her."

The train slowed. "This is your stop, my darling son. I don't even know when I'm going to see you again. You know I love you, don't you?"

"And I love you, Mother. Be strong, as always." Klimenko kissed his mother lightly on both cheeks and stepped out of the train just before the doors closed. He didn't look back.

East Berlin, 2227 Hours, April 29

The three East German *Volkspolizei* whispered into the microphones concealed in their collars as the Americans struggled with the largest of the three crates they were unloading at the steps of the American Embassy. The burlapped diplomatic cargo was clearly important, otherwise the Americans would have had their local East German staff manhandle it. None of them heard the faint scraping of metal as Alexander lifted the secret hatch in the blue van parked in the embassy lot across the street and dropped down under it. In less than a minute he had crawled silently under the line of parked cars and into the darkness. He slipped out of his jumpsuit, stuffed it in his small bag, and began to walk northeast to the Alexanderplatz U-bahn station.

Moscow, 1000 Hours, April 30

Katerina swam a slow breaststroke into the tunnel between the pool and the dressing area of the massive Moscow swimming pool. She felt awkward and self-conscious, even in her shapeless Polish swimsuit. Several women in the changing room had looked her over carefully, their eyes taking in the outlines of her bikini tan from her days on the *Hoping Jiang* with Alexander. She decided they must have written her off as a nomenklatura doxy, as Alexander would have put it, who had spent her spring vacation on the beach in Havana and her nights on her back underneath some fat Party hack. The thought made her smile. After a while she began to feel a comforting anonymity among the bobbing crowd of Muscovites. As she swam by a woman in a black rubber swimming cap, she heard a soft voice.

"Stop for a moment, daughter of my sister. We can talk here."

Katerina faced the wall of the tunnel and treaded water in what she hoped would pass for some form of aquatic exercise.

"Auntie, I cannot tell you how glad I am to see you. Have you already . . ."

"Died? Yes, I have died, and now I am ready to go to heaven."

"Lara will arrive this afternoon. She is flying from Vladivostok. Are you ready?"

"I am more ready than ever. Anatoly is in Moscow. I met him

yesterday, but only for minutes. He said he may not see me before I leave. Security, he said. But for the time being I am very safe with Anatoly's friend, Volodya. Do you still remember the telephone number?"

"Yes, Auntie. I remember it." Katerina repeated Rogov's number softly as she treaded water.

"Anatoly insisted that if you need to contact him for any reason, call the number you have just repeated to me, ask for Volodya, and tell him you have some fresh flowers for him from Tbilisi. Repeat that to me, my dear."

Katerina repeated the verbal parole word for word. "Auntie, in three days you will have to be at Leningrad Railway Station to switch the bags. You or someone who is helping you. You will first have to go to a Beriozka and buy a blue Three Dragons brand suitcase with the dollars Anatoly gave you. Make certain it is blue, not black. They sell both colors. All of the Beriozkas are full of the Three Dragons brand suitcases now. You must buy what they call the two-suiter. Can you remember that? A blue Three Dragons brand two-suiter." Klimenkova repeated the instructions word for word.

"Then you will call Volodya for the time of the meeting in Leningrad Station. But you must be certain that it is he on the telephone. Only Volodya."

"How will I know that?"

"When you tell him you have brought him fresh flowers from Tbilisi, he will tell you that the cornflowers are his favorites. Georgia is full of them in the spring. Volodya may be the one who comes to Leningrad Station to change the bags. Swim away now."

Katerina swam the rest of the way back through the tunnel without ever making eye contact with the woman in the black rubber swim cap.

SCHOENEFELD, EAST GERMANY, 0930 HOURS, APRIL 30

"Comrade, you must be joking. You walk up and ask for a seat on the next flight to Moscow, just like that? No reservation. Do you know what tomorrow is in Moscow?" The clerk at the Aeroflot military charter counter at Schoenefeld was a Russian, but he had clearly been serving in the "workers' paradise" of East Germany long enough to be wearing a gold-plated Seiko watch, and Alexander caught a glimpse of a thin gold chain inside his collar. He didn't buy things like that on his ruble salary, Alexander thought, as he leaned closer to the man.

He spoke with an exaggerated Russian socialist argot. "Comrade, I know precisely what tomorrow is in Moscow. As you can see I have a priority travel requisition for a flight today with a return late on May third.

Urgent Party business. But the much-vaunted German efficiency at Wüns-dorf broke down, and that, Comrade, is why your computer has no record of my reservation."

The clerk eyed the tall man before him. This one's papers say he's a Central Committee hack, but from the snotty sound of him my bet is that he's Polish Intelligence, probably one of those three hundred percenters who's been a toady at the Lubyanka for most of his worthless life.

"Comrade, just look down the hall there. All those people are waiting for a seat on the flight to Moscow. There are a hundred fifty on the waiting list. I'm sure I could put you on the list, maybe even near the top, but I must be honest with you, Comrade, your chances are very poor. The return flight on May third looks easier. I can get you a seat on Aeroflot from Sheremetyevo to Schoenefeld at 2030 hours. But that's not much good if we can't get you to Moscow, is it?"

At a carpet bazaar in Peshawar or a ticket counter at Schoenefeld, the rules were about the same. "Comrade, did I fail to mention that I am authorized by my sponsoring office to pay the usual surcharge for a pri-ority, no-reservation seat? I believe this is the correct sum." Alexander slid an envelope across the counter.

The clerk raised the flap of the envelope to see two West German fifty mark notes and slipped it in his pocket. "I'm not too sure that even with the priority, no-reservation surcharge, I'll be able to make this work, Comrade. I'm efficient, but not a magician."

A couple of minutes later the clerk announced, "Comrade, you must live a blessed life. I've just found a seat held in reserve for priority Cen-tral Committee business, but of course with the usual no-reservation sur-charge. The flight leaves at 1712 hours."

Alexander smiled broadly, and then with a wink said, "Comrade, I must tell you what a joy it is to work with the efficient men of Mother Russia. These Germans have a way of ruining just about everything they touch. Have you noticed?"

The clerk returned Alexander's conspiratorial smile.

Moscow, 1450 Hours, April 30

Sergei Bokhan had been at his terminal since noon. He had just screened the Polish and Czech databases for any hits on Nikitenko's watch list, and was now logging on to the East German database. He keyed in his request and straightened his back for a moment to stretch his cramped muscles while the computer did its search. When he turned back to his screen the information was just scrolling on. Seconds later, Bokhan had the Directorate RI duty officer on the telephone. "Yes, Comrade,

Colonel Nikitenko asked specifically that I advise him on a specific matter at his home." Bokhan wrote down the number, hung up, and then dialed again.

MOSCOW, 2045 HOURS, APRIL 30

Alexander handed his passport through the slot in the border guard's booth at Sheremetyevo Airport and began counting slowly to himself. The KGB guard flipped through the pages, shifting his weight slightly each time he pumped the foot pedal activating the overhead camera. When he had finished photographing the passport, he reached for his telephone. Alexander had reached eighty when the guard hung up and looked at him.

In a small second-floor room with a view through a one-way mirror looking over the entry hall, Nikitenko watched the passengers from the flight from Schoenefeld lined up to clear customs and immigration. Three KGB officers sat in front of a bank of telephones. Each one answered the calls that came in continually as the guards in the booths below phoned in names and passport information from the flight arrivals. They checked these names against large binders of watch-listed names, a tedious, manual process.

One of the men turned to Nikitenko. "Colonel. What was the name of the man you're expecting?"

Nikitenko kept his eyes on the one-way mirror. "I'm afraid I'm not absolutely sure, Comrade Major. I think the name is Jirousek, but it came to me a bit garbled."

"There's a man in front of booth number three named Jasik, Gromek Jasik, a Polish Party official. I thought maybe he was your man."

Nikitenko stared through the window at Alexander, a sense of discovery and accomplishment washing over him. "Oh no, Comrade. This is not the man I'm looking for. Perhaps he didn't even come on this flight. With the May Day celebration, I'm sure he's been delayed. Maybe I'll just walk down around the hall and take a look, and then go home. Coming up here was a long shot. But thank you, Comrades. You can't know how much your vigilance serves the motherland."

Nikitenko walked down the narrow stairs from the KGB observation post and fell into step behind the tall man in the black suit just as he cleared immigration.

MOSCOW, 1400 HOURS, MAY 1

Lara held Katerina's arm as they walked across the parking lot at the entrance to the Park of Culture, known by most Muscovites as Gorky

Park. Lined buses stood waiting for their passengers to return from the traditional May Day celebration. They felt safe, lost in the crowd.

"Look, Katerina!" Lara pointed at the giant Ferris wheel swinging up with squealing passengers. "My sister and I rode on that when we were just eight years old. In 1934, our father brought us here for the Spring Festival. We thought it the most awe-inspiring sight of our lives. This is the first time I've been back to the Park of Culture since that day."

Lara went on, old memories flooding to the surface. "The people are almost the same, except that I think now they have no souls. There's no optimism in their faces. I think I must have seen what I thought was optimism. Or maybe it was the hopefulness of a very young girl in 1934. Times were difficult then, but there was a brief respite in the long suffering of Russia. I couldn't have known what was to follow even by the end of that year. The purges began in December and then continued until the beginning of the war. There has been nothing but sadness since."

"Mother, we need to talk. Tell me anything you think is important. Anything that happened to you on the ship, or in Nakhodka, or at the airport. I might be hearing from Anatoly in the next day, or I can contact him through the man protecting Katerina. I want to understand everything that is happening."

"The cruise to Nakhodka was absolutely routine. The food was awful and the service was worse. But it was exactly as Alexander had said. I talked to almost no one. No one, to be sure, seemed to take interest in me. Nakhodka was routine, too. A ride to the airport near Vladivostok. No landmarks were familiar to me. And the routine at Sheremetyevo was just like Alexander said it would be, down to the rosy-cheeked border guard and his photographing my passport and making two short phone calls."

Kat still held on to Lara's arm. "I met with Katerina yesterday. At the swimming pool. We're ready to make the exchange of the suitcases on May third. Two days from now at Leningrad Station. Katerina will have an exact copy of the bag I brought back with me to Hong Kong last time. After the bags are switched, we just go on to Leningrad and let the plan unfold. Three more days and Katerina will be on her way to freedom."

"Alexander and Michael will meet her in Helsinki. They decided to do that just before I set sail from Hong Kong. Then the three of them will wait for us to arrive a few days later."

"Is there anything else?"

"Nothing we need to worry about now. Let's just play tourist for a while."

They strolled through Gorky Park for another half hour, wandering down by Happy Garden near the Moscow River, past the piers with their packed excursion boats, and back around toward the main entrance. When they were about a hundred yards from it, Katerina gripped her mother's arm tightly. She had spotted Alexander casually strolling toward them.

"Mother, don't be shocked, but the man walking toward us eating ice cream is Alexander."

"My God, Katerina, it is. Now what is this supposed to mean?"

As Alexander walked past Katerina he spoke quickly. "Turn and follow me back down toward Happy Garden. I'll be close enough to speak to you, but don't try to make eye contact with me."

After meandering through the throngs for five minutes, Alexander had positioned himself near the two women. "I have to see Anatoly," he said, seemingly more interested in his ice cream than in Katerina and Lara a few feet away. His voice was calm, but Kat heard the underlying tightness.

"I have a number to call . . . but what . . ."

Alexander cut her off. "You've got to set something up now."

"We're supposed to meet Anatoly at the House of Artists tomorrow at three. But that's not even certain."

"That's too late. I need to see him now."

"I'll call Rogov now. He'll know what to do."

Alexander finished his ice cream bar and turned to walk away, issuing clipped instructions as he did. "Kat, call Rogov and ask him to meet you as soon as possible. Take public transport or walk wherever you go. I'll follow you until you've met up with him. Then look around for me; I'll make myself visible and you can send Rogov to me. When Rogov and I have met, go back to the hotel and wait with Lara. Lara, please stay in your room until Kat gets back to you."

Lara smiled weakly, looking off in the distance at the Ferris wheel as she spoke. "It seems there are some complications in our plan."

Alexander began to walk away. "Yes, Lara, but it's going to be all right."

As Katerina turned and began walking toward the main entrance of the Park of Culture, Alexander dropped about a hundred yards back. His instincts told him they were not being followed. At least not yet.

MOSCOW, 1445 HOURS, MAY 1

Katerina's hand trembled as she dropped her tokens into one of the public telephones in Kiev Station. She heard her own fear as she asked for Volodya.

"Hello." The man's voice was neutral, guarded.

"Volodya, my dear man. You told me to call you if I ever came into some fresh flowers from Tbilisi. I have some beautiful ones here now."

"Just bring them to me, my little flower lady, and I will buy you a wonderful lunch. Maybe I'll even serenade you with Georgian songs. You know where I am."

"Volodya, my sweet. I cannot come to you. I simply haven't enough time. Can you meet me somewhere near Taganskaya?"

Rogov hesitated for a moment and then responded. "Yes, my pretty one. I will meet you in front of the Taganka Theater. Let's make it right away since you're so short of time. Can you be there in half an hour?"

"Yes, Volodya. But first I want to be sure I brought your favorite flowers. I would just die if I made a mistake."

"How could you ever forget how much I love the wild Georgian cornflower? Can you forget the time you wore one in your hair for me? And nothing else?"

"I didn't forget, my dear. I couldn't. See you soon."

MOSCOW, 1610 HOURS, MAY 1

Katerina was short of breath as she cleared the last of the steps up from the metro under Taganskaya Square and moved into the pedestrian flow. She crossed the square and had stood near the main entrance of the popular comedy theater for two or three minutes when a man in his mid-thirties crossed the square and made eye contact with her. He was wearing a suede jacket. Two heavy gold chains were visible through the open neck of his silk shirt. As he stopped before her, Katerina looked into the handsome, bitter face. He spoke in a charming, even cultured, voice.

"So this is the beautiful flower lady. I had no idea I was dealing with such class. I am at your service."

"Thank you for coming. I must see the son of your other flower lady. Do you know whom I mean?" Katerina felt awkward talking around Anatoly's name, but she wanted to be sure she was really talking to Vladimir Rogov.

Rogov looked into Katerina's face and saw Anatoly Klimenko's features. He smiled and began to speak as if reciting a schoolboy's lessons. "Cornflowers are my favorite flowers. I know Katerina Klimenkova. I know Tolya. He is my friend. And he is in Moscow now. Now are you satisfied that you're not talking to some creep from the Committee?"

"Thank you for that, Volodya. You've made things easier for me." She touched his arm and looked across the square. "Now I want you to do something for me and for Tolya. Don't look, but there is a man over by the ice cream kiosk. He is wearing a dark suit and has a heavy mustache." Rogov's eyes flashed with distrust. "It's all right, Volodya. Please go and talk to him. He will explain everything. You've got to trust me."

"All right, my beautiful flower lady, I'll go meet the man, but this little affair of ours is becoming more and more complicated, and, I fear, more and more dangerous." Then he quickly leaned over and kissed Katerina on the cheek and turned to walk across the square.

Rogov walked briskly toward the stairs to the metro, pacing himself so that Alexander could keep up. Minutes later both men were on a train heading for the eastern Boulevard Ring. Rogov didn't speak until after they had left the metro at Kirovskaya station.

"Tell me now who you are and, please, don't play games with me. If your answers aren't the right ones, I can kill you here and now." He pulled open his suede jacket to revel the butt of a Tokarev semiautomatic pistol.

"I am a friend of Tolya's. It involves his safety. And yours."

Rogov's eyes narrowed. "Come with me."

MOSCOW, 2230 HOURS, MAY 1

For the last hour and a half Rogov and Sasha had been quietly drinking Georgian wine in the back room of the Tbilisi, listening first to Klimenko and then to Alexander, who finished telling the story of Karm Sergeyevich Nikitenko.

"And there it is, the tale of Red Army Nikitenko, Tolya. It's all here on this diskette, your insurance policy, if it's not too late." Alexander pushed the floppy with the Dakota file across the rough pine table. "I have another copy here." Alexander patted his breast pocket.

Klimenko picked up the diskette. "Our insurance policy. And I believe it's not too late." Turning to Sasha and Rogov, he said, "Let me explain where we stand. First, I'm convinced that Nikitenko knows what we are trying to do with my mother and her twin sister. Second, I think he's chosen not to share his information with anyone else for two reasons. He needs to have more facts before he goes to Shapkin since he'll be swimming against the tide when he denounces me. But more important, I believe he wants to see my face when he springs his trap and pays me back for his humiliation in Beirut. Volodya, are we still clean? Have we picked up anybody?"

Rogov nodded. "This place is still clean. My people have picked up no surveillance."

"Can you believe them?" Sasha asked.

"I pay them more than the Committee does. And they know the cost of betrayal." Rogov's smile was cold.

Rogov considered the three conspirators. "If you're right, Tolya. If he hasn't told anyone else, why don't I just have some boys drop by Nikitenko's apartment tonight and put him to sleep. It would be easy. Things like that happen all the time here in Moscow."

"We can't do that. Because I'm convinced that after you've put him to sleep, as you put it, someone will go through his office and find enough to hang us all. I'm going to give him a little present." Klimenko held up the floppy disk. "He'll be able to look at it before we meet him. At the very least he'll know that there are more of these floating around and that if anything happens to us, he goes down too."

THIRTY-EIGHT

Klimenko arrived at Yasenevo with half an hour to spare, but he expected Nikitenko to be waiting for him and as soon as he entered the outer offices of Directorate R, he knew he'd been right.

"Anatoly Viktorovich! You're early. I somehow thought you would be. Good! We can have a nice talk while we wait for the director to return from the chairman's office." Klimenko followed Nikitenko back into his office. He had confidence now that he was facing the threat head-on and had a weapon of his own.

"Karm Sergeyevich. I must thank you again for your thoughtfulness at this difficult time. I can't tell you how much I appreciate what you've done."

Nikitenko drew two cups of black tea from a stainless steel electric samovar. "It was little enough, Anatoly Viktorovich. I won't be divulging a state secret when I tell you that you are a very important person here at Yasenevo. It is not only down at the Lubyanka that they are speaking of your name and your deeds. Mikhail Sergeyevich himself has noted your actions. There is an Order of Lenin in the works, but you didn't hear that from me."

"I am humbled, Karm Sergeyevich." *He's enjoying himself,* Klimenko told himself. *He's got this all scripted.*

Nikitenko shuffled through a small stack of papers. "Now for some unpleasantness. This is the inventory the clinic provided with your mother's effects. You can see for yourself why I was concerned that perhaps some of her things had been taken by the hospital staff. This is hardly what one would expect to find in the effects of a woman traveling from Kiev to Moscow for a . . . lengthy visit. Wouldn't you agree?"

Klimenko decided to let Nikitenko play out his hand. Looking at the list he immediately saw what bothered Nikitenko. His mother had barely left behind enough items for an overnight stay. She must have taken most of her things with her after she and Arkady Shevchenko staged her death.

"My mother was a very practical woman, Karm Sergeyevich. I wouldn't have expected her to have brought along too much baggage for a trip to Moscow under these sad circumstances, particularly since the diagnosis in Kiev was so pessimistic. Her colleague in Kiev confirmed that there was almost no hope for her when he sent her to the Shevchenko Clinic. But even then, it is clear that there may have been some pilferage."

"Fine. That settles it. You can leave the rest to me. Some people must learn that there are limits to what we can all endure. Stealing from the dead is one of them. I will personally organize an investigation at the clinic."

"No, Karm Sergeyevich." The firmness in Klimenko's voice startled Nikitenko. "There will be no need for that. My heart would not be in it. And it would ultimately cause some harm to Dr. Shevchenko, who has been a good friend of the Klimenko family since I was a child. For all we know my mother simply gave away her things to the hospital staff when she knew the end was near. She was that kind of woman. Thank you, but I couldn't allow an investigation. I must insist."

Nikitenko shook his head in righteous exasperation. "It's entirely your choice, Anatoly. Perhaps I have overreacted. I had the same reaction at your mother being cremated so quickly after her passing. If you yourself had not told me later of her wishes to be cremated, I would have considered it some sort of a subterfuge. For what, I couldn't say. Death is still a mystery to many of us. It is to me." Nikitenko paused. "But somehow I believe that your mother is now with her loved ones. Perhaps even with her sister. But cremation is so unusual, particularly for Ukrainians, and for a believer." Nikitenko took a sip of his strong tea.

Not very smooth, Karm, Klimenko thought. "My mother was a believer as was yours to the very moment of her tragic death. Yes, death is mysterious, particularly the death of a mother, wouldn't you say, Karm Sergeyevich?"

Nikitenko felt the sea change.

"Karm, you brew an excellent tea. Do you mind if I freshen my cup? How about yours?"

Nikitenko smiled and nodded. "Please, Anatoly Viktorovich, help yourself. I am fine."

After he had refilled his cup, Klimenko handed Nikitenko an envelope.

"Karm Sergeyevich, in that envelope is a computer diskette that contains a story that is no less than heartbreaking. It is a story of devotion and betrayal and death, a great Russian tragedy. A man's search for the truth. I hope you have a chance to look at it before I come visit you tonight. Tonight will be fine, won't it? Perhaps I'll bring a friend with me. You wouldn't mind that, would you? Say, around nine o'clock? And don't worry about that floppy disk, Karm Sergeyevich. If you have any problems with it, I can get you another copy. There are many."

MOSCOW, 1455 HOURS, MAY 2

Katerina and Lara had spent more than half an hour walking around the House of Artists. Katerina didn't think they were being followed, but that hardly calmed her. She felt that the risks she was taking with her mother's life were escalating out of her control.

"I'm going down to the café now. Maybe I'll bring Anatoly or Alexander here to you. Or maybe I'll come back alone. I just don't know what's to happen next."

Lara smiled gently and touched Katerina's arm. "Do whatever you must. But stop trying to worry about everything by yourself. I'm no fool, dear. I know precisely what risks we're taking. Everything will be just fine. Now go."

On the first-floor landing Alexander startled her when he reached out for her arm as she hurried past him. "Let's go back up the stairs. We can talk on the landing above. The café is too crowded now."

"Alexander! Did you meet Tolya?"

"Yes. I've met him. I brought him some information on Nikitenko. I think we can neutralize him."

"But what about Lara and Katerina? What do we do?"

Alexander held her arm gently. "Tolya and I have agreed that you and Lara must proceed with your scheduled departure. Go to the Leningrad train station tomorrow as planned. If Rogov shows up to switch your bags, it will mean that everything is still all right. If he doesn't change your bags, both of you just go on to Leningrad and depart for Helsinki as scheduled. If anything happens along the way, anything at all, stick to your plan and stick to your cover story. Your mother came to visit for a few days and you're leaving together."

"What about Tolya's mother?"

"She's okay for now. If Rogov doesn't switch the bags tomorrow, it will mean that she's not going. Now get Lara and get out of here, Kat. It's going to be all right."

MOSCOW, 2130 HOURS, MAY 2

Nikitenko had settled down to listen to some music at the end of a day that had brought an old truth crashing down on him. Truth! He smiled when he thought of the word, its cynical uses and clever mutations. He closed his eyes and waited for the knock at his door, knowing it would drive away the soothing picture of Schubert's carefree trout in the crystal brook. He didn't have to wait long.

"Anatoly Viktorovich, how nice of you to visit." Turning to Alexander, Nikitenko said, "And what shall it be, Mr. Fannin or Comrade Jasik? Come. Both of you, please come in. We can drink tea and speak of many things. Isn't that what the Persians say?"

Nikitenko brought out three porcelain cups and a teapot with a coarse red and green Uzbek design. He poured the tea with slightly exaggerated ceremony and set the steaming cups in front of his guests.

"You drink your green tea without sugar. Just like me, Anatoly Viktorovich. I remember that. But Mr. Fannin, many of your tastes are, shall we say, a small mystery to me."

Alexander smiled at the white-haired man, seeing him diminished, even vulnerable surrounded by his modest possessions. "Without sugar, just like you, Karm Sergeyevich. My compliments on your knowledge of Alexander Fannin *and* Comrade Gromek Jasik. But for tonight, at least, please call me Alexander."

"I have you to thank for bringing me the Dakota file. I did read it through. My admiration to those who compiled it."

Klimenko put down his cup. "Why don't you tell us the story the way you lived it, Karm Sergeyevich."

Nikitenko held Klimenko's eyes for a long moment, then leaned back in his chair and began to speak.

"Your Dakota file is correct, but only as a practical record. My mother was what we to this day call a Volga German, but she was as Russian in her heart as I am now. Her great-great-grandfather came in the wave of German settlers drawn to Russia in the early nineteenth century under the edict of Alexander the First. My mother's forebears established a Lutheran village along the Volga, named it Oberwinter, and set out to farm the rich soil. After four or five generations they even thought they were good Russians. Of course, many still spoke German at the hearth, but they were Russian in their souls. I've always believed that." He paused.

"She was a student in St. Petersburg in 1917, and was captured body and soul by the rebellion. From that moment on she and my father never turned back, not from each other and not from the revolution. When I was born my parents named me Karm as living proof of their devotion to the dream. Think of going through life with a name like 'Red Army' Nikitenko.

"The Germans in Russia suffered in the early years, but my mother accepted the hardship as the cost of the dream. After Germany attacked Russia, everything changed. My father was convinced that Hitler would push straight for Moscow, and decided to send my mother and me and my sister, Natasha, to safety in my mother's village near Stalingrad. It was a huge miscalculation and the consequences were calamitous. Hitler did the unthinkable and decided to throw his army away at Stalingrad. In the end it destroyed him. And in the end it killed my mother."

"But Hitler didn't really kill your mother or her dream, did he, Karm Sergeyevich?" Alexander asked.

"No, it wasn't Hitler. At least not directly. At the time there was great fear, almost panic, in Stalin's circle that the Volga Germans would rise up in murderous rebellion as the German Army approached. That was one of the interpretations of why he veered off toward Stalingrad in the first place. Lavrenty Beria devised a plan to prove the point and save the day. It was simple and evil, like Beria himself. In early 1942 he parachuted German-speaking NKVD troops into the Volga region to pass themselves off as German spies sent to organize an underground resistance from among the 'sympathetic' Volga German population. The plan fizzled, and most of the parachutists were turned over to the Soviet authorities, though a few were killed. It was over quickly and proved nothing. But that wasn't enough for Beria. He decided that regardless of the truth, there would be a Volga German rebellion, and ordered a massive roundup of 'partisans.' My mother was arrested, literally at random, taken from our little house, marched off with a group of about two hundred confused men and women and summarily shot. Along with the old and the young of the village, I was forced to watch.

"I have never forgotten the look on my mother's face the moment before they shot her. It was not fear. It was sheer disbelief that the revolution she had so deeply believed in could do this to her.

"But one survives. The war took my sister's life, but in that case the Germans were unambiguously responsible. I was eventually reunited with my father, and watched him live out his remaining years in lifeless service to the Motherland in the Moscow State Bureau of Statistics and Records. His only comment on my mother's death was that it all had been a 'mistake.' Then he erased that part of his life and, he thought, mine from all official records. Nowhere in my official personal history is there evidence that I was the son of a so-called Volga German.

"The single object I had that belonged to my mother was her family Bible, a fragile book dating back to the founding of the Volga German settlement of Oberwinter more than a century before. I never fulfilled my duty; the record stopped with the entries in my mother's hand. But it was in that Bible that I found the names of my mother's forebears who had left Oberwinter at the middle of the last century to join German relatives who had fled Germany's time of turbulence to America, to the lands called the Dakotas. I built the names of the Oberwinter family and their imagined stories into a mosaic of fantasy until I, too, became part of building socialism. Then I tucked the Bible away and cleared my mind of such things." The Schubert record had ended; Nikitenko turned it over and continued.

"But it was in Beirut that the past confronted me, and quite by chance. I met the pastor of the small Lutheran church in East Beirut, an American, as it turned out. Soon we discovered that we both spoke German. I began to visit him often, and one day I showed him my Bible, my mother's Bible, but I told him I had bought it in a flea market. He only smiled at me and with his wise eyes told me that he knew it was mine. I asked if he thought any of the names in the Dakota branch of the family tree could be traced. He said he would try to help me, and within a month, I had met a man I believe to this day was a distant relative, a cousin."

Alexander nodded. "You were right, Karm. The man the pastor found was, indeed, your distant cousin, a farmer named Peter Graber. The pastor made the introduction, but he never knew the rest. He didn't want to."

Karm was silent for a moment. "Mr. Fannin, why don't you fill in the next part. I think you might understand the nuances of the American special services file better than I."

"What followed was predictable. As your dialogue with Graber deepened, you began to explore the proposition of walking away from your life, from the hypocrisy, you told Graber, and set down new roots. But you knew that you'd need help if you were to do it right. Graber understood, and he set up your first meeting with the man from the CIA. Right so far?"

Nikitenko nodded and picked up the story again. "Right so far. Your man began meeting me at the Jouneiyeh Yacht Club in East Beirut. I liked him because he was patient. He never spoke of price, what I would have to pay for his help. We devised a simple, believable plan, one that almost certainly would have worked. I was to be kidnapped by Hizbollah, and after failed negotiations, I would be 'killed.' To make the disappearance work, the CIA had to be involved. A boat was needed to take us from the yacht club to an American Navy ship twenty miles out at sea; arrangements had to be set in place for a bold daylight 'kidnapping'; and the cast had to be broadened to include very convincing kidnappers who would make impossible demands, and ultimately kill me off. Intelligence 'sources' would have to be fed to my colleagues in the Beirut Rezidentura, all confirming the dreadful story. Only a special service like the

CIA would have the capabilities to deliver all those necessary elements. There would have been a brief diplomatic uproar, but soon enough it would have been forgotten and I would have just disappeared. Everything was in place and a date was set."

It was Alexander who asked the question. "Why didn't you show up that Sunday morning, as you had agreed, Karm?"

"I am still here, I suppose, for at least some of the same reasons that Anatoly Viktorovich is still here. He could have disappeared when you met him in Afghanistan. Certainly you and he had ample opportunity to stage a credible disappearance. But you didn't. Anatoly must have decided, as I finally did, that he belonged here, in Russia." Karm turned to Klimenko. "But please make no mistake, Anatoly. There are very few similarities in what we have done, you and I. Yes, I may have planned to leave, but I stopped short of that, and I did not, for example, betray my government."

Alexander leaned toward Nikitenko. "Karm, do you think that Anatoly, by helping the Soviet Union to sign the Geneva Accords and end the killing, really betrayed the Russian people? And do you really believe that you could have gone off to your dreams in the Dakotas without eventually doing the same?"

"I accepted the reality that I would have ultimately been asked to pay a high price—betrayal of the Motherland."

"Do you believe you accepted that reality then because you had courage, or because you lacked courage, Karm Sergeyevich?" Klimenko asked.

Nikitenko hesitated. "I don't know, Anatoly. But what I do know is that you carried out your decision to betray. I didn't. Others can decide if it was your courage or your cowardice. Maybe it was both."

"If deciding it was my duty to destroy a system that has itself destroyed so many countless millions—your mother and my father included—is betrayal, then yes, Karm Sergeyevich, I took that final step. And I have no regrets."

Nikitenko studied Klimenko's face. "I knew you were convinced that you were right and just. I knew that as soon as I read your agent report to Alexander." Turning to Alexander, Nikitenko smiled and shook his head with irony. "It seems that you Americans always get the better of the bargain in the espionage game. Those of us from the Committee who work for your side are always the committed ones, the idealists like Anatoly here. The rare ones we get from your side are always the shallow, troubled, venal ones. That bothers us greatly, you know, though we won't admit it."

"Including the one who has betrayed us now? Is he another of them driven by greed?"

Nikitenko hesitated. "Yes, Alexander, most assuredly the one who has betrayed you and Anatoly is driven only by greed."

Alexander picked up a new note of caution in Nikitenko's voice. "Don't worry, Karm, I'm not going to try to squeeze the identity of your man in Langley. He'll be found."

Nikitenko sighed. "And soon. With what you already know, providing you get back safely to your people, you'll find him soon enough. It's always that way, isn't it? We always use them up."

"They use themselves up. That's why you pay them. So you feel less guilt when they self-destruct," Alexander said.

"So where does our talk tonight leave us, Karm Sergeyevich? You and I are the central figures in this standoff. But there are others involved who have done nothing that you yourself have not considered."

"Let them go, Karm." It was Alexander who spoke.

"If I do that, then I will almost be forced to ignore Anatoly's betrayal, for were I later to reveal his crimes it would become clear to some that I may have allowed his mother to escape."

"Then don't reveal what you know about Anatoly."

"That is what it comes down to, isn't it?"

"Yes, Karm."

Turning to Klimenko, Nikitenko asked, "Why didn't you arrange for one of Krasin's Afghantsi friends to eliminate me? I doubt there'd be any shortage of volunteers."

Klimenko paused. "That thought has occurred to others. I've only been able to keep them from carrying out what seems an eminently logical act of self-preservation because I've convinced them that you've left detailed evidence behind that would incriminate most of those helping us."

"Yes, Anatoly, I have, but I'm sure that there are some who will not be discovered."

"Yes, Karm, and it is they who will finally kill you if you move against any of us."

"Then you have come here to tell me that this standoff you and I find ourselves in should continue without, shall I say, resolution. Am I right, Anatoly?"

"You're right, Karm."

"I suppose I will have to sleep on that, Anatoly. I have told Director Shapkin that I needed a few days' rest."

"When will I have your answer, Karm?" Klimenko asked.

"It will begin to be evident to you and to the others tomorrow evening when Comrade Jasik's flight from Sheremetyevo lands in Schoenefeld, and it will be even more evident when the Finnair flight leaves Leningrad on the morning of May fourth. Not before then. And when will I know that you have convinced the others that they accomplish nothing by killing me?"

"I suppose that, too, will be evident, Karm Sergeyevich. Within the next forty-eight hours. But why the delay, Karm? Surely you can reach a decision, the right one, without the dramatics."

"Possibly, Anatoly. But tonight I am going to read my mother's Bible. Tomorrow is soon enough."

THIRTY-NINE

Katerina and Lara sat crowded onto one of the hard wooden benches of the waiting room at Leningrad Station. They had almost an hour before their train departed. Their two suitcases stood among a pile of luggage near the door.

Katerina first saw the man's Three Dragon brand two-suiter. He looked like many other Muscovites, overdressed on a May afternoon in a heavy coat and woolen hat. He set the suitcase down next to Lara's identical one, and when he finally turned in her direction, she saw the hard-set features of the handsome man she had met the day before at the Taganka Theater.

A half hour later Katerina watched Rogov walk over to the luggage and depart carrying a blue suitcase. Fifteen minutes later Katerina and Lara retrieved their own bags and boarded the Leningrad train. It left precisely on time, as usual, and soon the Russian landscape was racing by the window and Lara saw how little things had changed in fifty years.

LENINGRAD, 0030 HOURS, MAY 4

Katerina had dialed the number of the British Consulate in Leningrad a dozen times before she got through to the officer on duty. It was well past midnight.

"British Consulate."

"Oh thank God. There is somebody there. My name is Martin,

Catherine Martin. Moscow correspondent for the *Far Eastern Focus*. I'm traveling with my mother, Lady Lara Martynov from Hong Kong, and I'm afraid she's fallen ill. I'm quite concerned, and don't know what to do."

"Of course, Miss Martin. I'm an avid reader of your articles from Moscow. It's right that you called. Where are you now?"

"We're staying at the Leningrad Hotel. And I'm not afraid to admit that we would much rather not use the clinic the hotel recommends. I'm sure you'll understand why."

"You are absolutely right. I can send a car for you if your mother can travel."

"She can travel, but she is in some distress."

"The car will be there in less than half an hour. I'll send a colleague along, a Miss Davies. She'll bring you to the consulate straightaway while I try to get a doctor over here. What's your mother's condition?"

"It's chest pain. Shortness of breath and chest pain."

Katerina sat down on the bed where her mother lay with a damp cloth on her forehead.

"Are you feeling any better, Mother? The British Consulate is sending a car for us. And they're getting a doctor. God, what a time for you to fall ill! I feel absolutely helpless and completely responsible."

Lara Martynova's voice was weak and thready. "Stop blaming yourself. This trip was my idea, not yours. Now just let me rest here for a moment until the car comes for me. I'm certain I'll be fine."

Neither Katerina nor her mother deviated from their careful script as they talked to the microphones they knew were there.

LENINGRAD, 0200 HOURS, MAY 4

Ian Bland was the consummate diplomat, particularly when dealing with a British subject involving both the media and the Queen's honors list.

"Miss Martin, I'm really very pleased that Dr. Allen is convinced that your mother will be fine in a day or so. She should stay right here in our guest quarters, and so should you. I'll have my staff call the airport and cancel your flight first thing in the morning. No sense in trying now. By the way, you do have your passports and tickets with you, don't you?"

"I'm afraid Mother's passport and ticket are in her bag at the hotel. She said she had been told that suitcases were safer than purses."

"I'm afraid I would disagree. I'll send someone over to the hotel right now to bring both your bags back here."

Katerina's mind raced. She couldn't have this very helpful civil servant canceling flights and fetching bags.

"Thank you, Mr. Bland. I'm most grateful for all your help, but please don't bother with canceling the airline bookings. I'll handle that first thing in the morning."

"It's really no bother at all, Miss Martin. My staff will rebook you and your mother in about two days. Dr. Allen said she should be fine by then."

Katerina touched Bland's arm. "Mr. Bland, I insist that you not bother your staff with my airlines bookings," she said.

Bland wondered why all the fuss over some canceled flights. "Fine, Miss Martin. But do let me know if we can do anything else."

They had reached the safety of the British Consulate, but Katerina knew that their worries were far from over.

EAST BERLIN, 0420 HOURS, MAY 4

The three Vopos were halfway through their eight-hour tour at the American Embassy and had written off the night as uneventful. None of them saw the dark form crawling slowly under the line of cars until it reached the blue van parked in its accustomed place in the lot, nor did they hear the faint metallic grating a moment later.

The cellular phone on the desk in front of Frank Andrews on the embassy's fifth floor began blinking. "Yes."

"I'm in," said the voice on the other end, then hung up.

Five minutes later Andrews and two men came out, all three dressed in the casual work clothing of the Seabee team that had been working in the secure area of the embassy for the last four nights. They climbed into the blue panel van and headed out the lot toward Checkpoint Charlie.

LENINGRAD, PULKHOVO AIRPORT, 0530 HOURS, MAY 4

Katerina Klimenkova arrived exactly two hours before her Finnair flight. She had spent the night at the apartment of a Rogov associate, who had driven her to Leningrad from Moscow the afternoon before.

She slept fitfully and got up at three. She dressed in Lara's clothes, beautiful things that she had found neatly folded in the suitcase that Volodya had switched at Kiev Station. Going through the articles, she had nearly cried when she found a single sheet of paper folded between two silk slips. She read the two lines of beautiful Cyrillic script:

> *For the maidens were marked by the love of their*
> *God who had laid His hand on their shoulders,*
> *and leaving His mark He fused their hearts, and*
> *promised them never to part.*

For the next hour Katerina reviewed all aspects of her new persona, Lara Martynova of Hong Kong. She quizzed herself on her life history in Shanghai and Hong Kong, concentrating on the last ten days since Lara boarded the MV *Khabarovsk* at the Ocean Terminal in Hong Kong, a detailed account of which Lara had left in a small diary in the suitcase. She memorized the details of her Soviet Far East Steamship Lines ticket, her Aeroflot flight from Vladivostok to Moscow. The weather on the sailing from Hong Kong to Nakhodka and Vladivostok. Everything that Katerina Klimenkova as Lara Martynova would need to know, and much more, she hoped, that she would never be asked.

MOSCOW, 0530 HOURS, MAY 4

Klimenko and Sasha rose before five to make the meeting at the Tbilisi Restaurant. Rogov quickly filled them in.

"Okay. Here's the situation. Fannin's gone. At least he was seen boarding Aeroflot to East Berlin. If he made it out of East Germany, he'll get word to whoever's meeting the flower lady. I have a man watching the Finnair flight who will call me when it takes off. That's when we begin our countdown. Before I sent her on her way, I told the flower lady to call me when she arrives in Helsinki."

"She'll make the call if she gets on that plane." Klimenko had no doubts his mother would do exactly as Rogov had requested.

Rogov nodded and continued. "I have two men watching Nikitenko's apartment. It's his day off."

PULKHOVO AIRPORT, 0705 HOURS, MAY 4

"Excuse me, young man. Would you repeat yourself, please?" Katerina Klimenkova looked at the boy in the immigration booth. He looked barely old enough to be away from his mother, much less be a KGB border guard. He had looked over her documents, checked her currency-exchange document stapled inside her passport, and even thumbed through her receipts. Now he was trying to ask her a question in English, and Katerina wasn't sure what he had said. He repeated his question, but it was still unintelligible. She decided to swallow her fear. She spoke in the bitchiest exile-Russian she could muster, imitating the voices on the Voice of America broadcasts, a Russian devoid of socialist jargon.

"Young man, you speak beautiful English, but why don't we just speak Russian."

The border guard grudgingly did so. "You have no receipt from a Leningrad hotel. Where is your receipt from a Leningrad hotel?"

"I didn't stay at a hotel, young man. I spent the night at the British

Consul's home as a guest. As you surely know, they do not give receipts to their guests."

The KGB border guard looked again at the passport, looked again at the documents before him, and then picked up the telephone.

Katerina couldn't hear him, but she thought she could make out the name Lara Martynova on his lips. She kept smiling and held her breath. A moment later the guard handed her papers through the window and waved her through. It was a while before Klimenkova was breathing normally again.

The border guard continued to study her. Then he picked up his telephone.

Leningrad, 0800 Hours, May 4

Ian Bland was beginning to understand that his houseguests at the British Consulate were very special indeed. "Please let me try to sum this up. First, when you got your bags back late last night, you did not notice that Lady Martynova's bag was not actually her bag, but someone else's bag that had been put in its place somewhere between Moscow and Leningrad. Switched name tag and all. Is that correct?"

"That is exactly right. My mother was sound asleep after Dr. Allen gave her the sedative, so there was no reason to open her bag. When she woke up she found she couldn't open the bag with her combination. She woke me, and I finally opened it myself."

"How?"

"I thought that maybe she had not set it right, so I tried putting the combination on all zeroes. It worked."

"Very resourceful, Miss Martin. Then you tried to cancel your flights, but you couldn't get a telephone connection. That happens all the time around here. Sometimes I think we're still using the telephone system Peter the Great installed." Bland laughed at his little joke.

"Miss Martin, I'm certain you'll be very surprised to know that I've just been rung back by the diplomatic office of the local authorities— that's shorthand for the KGB, you know—with the most unlikely story. They said that not only had your flights not been canceled, but that your mother actually made her Finnair flight this morning. She's presumably in Helsinki at this very moment. They did note that Catherine Martin missed her flight, but they didn't tie the two travelers together. But the KGB man here in town has most assuredly tied Martin and Martynova together. Now what do we make of that, Miss Martin?"

"It would appear that whoever stole my mother's bag stole it for the purpose of using her passport and her ticket."

Ian Bland leaned back in his chair. "Just so, Miss Martin. That is precisely what I told the gentleman from the KGB with whom I have been having such an unpleasant dialogue. I also told him that it is my belief that he should look very closely at his own people for the culprit, since the only possible way someone could have stolen your mother's passport and tickets yesterday, and then used them this morning, was if that very someone was also aware of your mother's sudden illness last night. I told our friend from the Committee for State Security that only someone from his organization could have done all that."

"And what did he say?"

"He, of course, denied that was possible. In fact, he thought my very suggestion a provocation. Then he told me I should draw my own conclusions. That perhaps only the lady who fell ill could tell us what really happened."

"That is to be expected, isn't it?"

"Yes, of course it's to be expected."

"Do you think they will hold up our departure while they investigate this? That would be such a terrible bore."

"Unless they find someone missing, someone who they know for certain traveled out this morning on Lady Martynova's passport, they'll have a very difficult time doing anything at all. You don't think they'll find anyone missing, do you, Miss Martin?" Bland smiled cordially, but his eyes bored in on Katerina's.

"Please call me Catherine."

"Catherine, do you think they'll turn up someone missing?"

"I would say that they will never find anyone missing. But that's only my opinion."

"So it would appear. I think we'll hear some bluster for another day or so, and then you'll simply get on a flight out of here. Shall I have our people book you and your mother out, say, day after tomorrow? I've already issued her a new passport for the travel home."

"Of course. Finnair to Helsinki. I'll take care of things after Helsinki."

Ian Bland looked at Katerina, wondering what kind of intrigue this beautiful woman was capable of. "I'm sure you will, Catherine. I would only add that it seems to me that you and your mother have managed this whole affair, uh, marvelously."

HELSINKI AIRPORT, 0850 HOURS, MAY 4

Michael Martynov watched the word LANDED replace ON TIME beside the notation for the Finnair flight. Fifteen minutes later, he saw her come through the sliding doors of the customs hall.

As soon as she cleared the barrier with her baggage cart, Michael made his way to her. "Welcome to Helsinki, my beautiful maiden of Kiev. I'm Michael."

Katerina Klimenkova felt no shame as the tears welled up in her eyes.

MOSCOW, 0855 HOURS, MAY 4

Rogov's telephone rang, startling the three men.

"Volodya. I have very good news for you. For us. I have got all the financing tied down. Marko has just called from Berlin. He says everything is in order. We can move ahead. When shall I come to see you?"

"Riitva! Great news! Come anytime, the sooner the better. But first, let me put one of my partners on the line."

Rogov handed the receiver to Klimenko.

"Riitva, this is Tolya. You have succeeded once again. But there is still much to do. There are still problems to be worked out. But my compliments to you. And please give my best to your family."

"Tolya, my dear man. Of course there are still problems ahead. But with what we have already accomplished, the rest will have to be easy. Now let us get off the telephone, my dear friend. I will be in touch with you soon."

"Riitva. We'll soon be in touch."

The phone rang again almost immediately. Rogov picked it up on the first ring.

"No. You don't do anything special now. He's out walking? Yes, go to him, but don't do anything special. Just give him the thing in the box."

Rogov turned to Sasha and Klimenko, smiling his million-dollar smile.

"It's over. Nobody dies. At least not today."

MOSCOW, 1030 HOURS, MAY 4

It was warm enough for Karm Sergeyevich Nikitenko to take a walk in Gorky Park without his woolen topcoat. He stopped in front of the news building to read the latest news from *Novosti* in the glass display case. As he scanned the pages he saw the reflection of the two men who had been following him. As he neared the park, they fell into step about a hundred yards behind him.

After half an hour he took a seat on a sunny bench. He waited for the men to come to him. One man approached him with purposeful strides and drew a rolled newspaper from his raincoat pocket. "This is for you, Comrade. You might have earned it under different circumstances."

Nikitenko took the paper and was surprised at his welling sense of relief as the man walked briskly away. He let the sun warm his face before he unrolled the newspaper. A silk flower. A Black Tulip.

EPILOGUE

FEBRUARY 15, 1989, FRIENDSHIP BRIDGE, SOVIET/AFGHAN BORDER

Gromov wanted arrangements to be just right. The body of a hapless minesweeper had been quietly carried across the bridge before the press had time to reason that his blanket-wrapped form was the last Russian soldier killed in the ten-year war.

In the center of the bridge, a lone Soviet tank had pulled to a halt. The diminutive figure of General Boris Gromov jumped nimbly from the turret and strode purposely over the last hundred yards toward the Soviet side of the Oxus. Near the end of the bridge, his son Maksim, a slim, awkward fourteen-year-old, greeted his father with a stiff embrace and presented him with a bouquet of red carnations.

Sasha and Klimenko watched the drama from beside the press pavilion. Sasha couldn't resist sharing one last commentary.

"Tolya, I would probably cry were I not so strong. Everything is just perfect for our Hero of Afghanistan, except somehow they screwed up on the flowers. It shouldn't have been a dozen red carnations. A single black tulip would have been just right for our hero."

Before Klimenko could respond, they heard a woman's voice coming from the throng of foreign journalists. Her Russian was flawless.

"Colonel, Catherine Martin. *Far Eastern Focus.* Can I quote you on the flowers, Colonel?"

MILT BEARDEN retired from the Central Intelligence Agency in 1994, after thirty years in its Clandestine Services. In a career that took him from the diplomatic world of German-speaking Europe to Hong Kong and through Africa, Milt Bearden spent over two decades locked in a deadly contest with the Soviet Union and the KGB. He directed the final years of the Agency's secret war against the Red Army in Afghanistan, and capped his career as the CIA's chief of station in Germany, where he witnessed the retreat of the Soviet occupation forces in Berlin. He now lives with his French-born wife, Marie-Catherine, in New Hampshire, where he is working on his second novel.

ABOUT THE TYPE

This book was set in Times Roman, designed by Stanley Morison specifically for *The Times* of London. The typeface was introduced in the newspaper in 1932. Times Roman had its greatest success in the United States as a book and commercial typeface, rather than one used in newspapers.